Praise for

"A vivid creation.… This story burns w[...]" [...]es

"A tremendously involving, extravagantly sensuous, and imaginatively detailed and interpretative portrait of a fascinating and influential artist."
—*Booklist*

"The best kind of fictionalized biography: rich, vibrant, and psychologically acute."
—*Kirkus Reviews*

"A delicious blend of fiction and biography.… A captivating introduction to the life—and death—of Frida Kahlo."
—*Grand Rapids Press*

Praise for *Sister Teresa*

"Bárbara Mujica's well-researched novel reimagines famed 16th-century Teresa of Ávila as a vibrant and fully fleshed woman."
—*Entertainment Weekly*

"[A] richly entertaining historical novel from Mujica."
—*Kirkus Reviews* (starred review)

"This brilliant fictional biography of Saint Teresa of Ávila breathes new life into a sacred subject."
—*Booklist*

"This engaging novel depicts Teresa of Ávila as an extraordinary woman… Surprisingly light and entertaining."
—*Publishers Weekly*

Praise for *I Am Venus*

"Mujica's prose is vigorous and intense, and the story is paradoxically both dark and illuminating."
—*Kirkus Reviews*

"A well-plotted read with engaging characters and rich detail. Fans of Tracy Chevalier and Elizabeth Kostova as well as art history buffs will enjoy Mujica's interpretation."
—*Library Journal*

MISS DEL RÍO

A Novel

BÁRBARA MUJICA

GRAYDON
HOUSE

GRAYDON
HOUSE®

Recycling programs
for this product may
not exist in your area.

ISBN-13: 978-1-525-89993-5

Miss del Río

Graydon House
22 Adelaide St. West, 41st Floor
Toronto, Ontario M5H 4E3, Canada
www.GraydonHouseBooks.com
www.BookClubbish.com

Printed in U.S.A.

To my husband, Mauro, and my children, Lily, Mariana, and Mauro III

MISS
DEL
RÍO

PROLOGUE

Los Angeles, April 11, 1988

I can hardly believe she's gone. She died on April 11, 1983, exactly five years ago. I lit a candle and said a prayer, but I wasn't able to lay a bouquet on her grave. She's buried in the Panteón de Dolores, in the Rotonda de las Personas Ilustres, in Mexico City, and I can no longer travel. I'm too old. Arthritis has stiffened my legs and fingers, and I just can't handle the hustle and bustle of the airport.

To the world, she was Dolores del Río, Hollywood star and first lady of the Golden Age of Mexican Cinema. She was Mexico's first international female film personality, a celebrity on three continents. She was the embodiment of beauty, glamour, and elegance. To me, she was Lola, my best friend.

It seems like yesterday we were little girls exchanging secrets under the ahuehuete tree in Don Francisco's garden. And then, unexpectedly, we both found ourselves in Los Angeles, where Lola was launching her career in the movies, and I was twisting ladies' hair into Marcel curls at Marie's Beauty Salon. Lola was the daughter of a wealthy banker, and I was the daughter of a maid, but we were like sisters.

After Lola died, a customer at Marie's suggested I write

down her story. "You knew her better than anyone," she said. "You're the one who should do it."

I tried. I was good at English in school, so I didn't think it would be that hard. But I'm a hairdresser, not a writer. I struggled to find the right words, and gripping a pen for hours on end made my fingers ache.

Now, though, I see that I don't have much time left. I'm approaching the end. Maybe, before long, Lola and I will be exchanging secrets in heaven—if you believe in that sort of thing. Anyhow, if I'm ever going to finish this memoir, or chronicle, or whatever you want to call it, I have to get to work, even if it hurts my fingers. After all, working through the pain is something I learned from Lola.

PART I

1

Lola crouched beside the armoire the way her mother had told her. Something was going on, something awful. Everyone looked terrified. Even Mamá, usually so regal and poised in her bustled skirts and lacy, tight-sleeved blouses, was tense and angry. Nearly all the maids had disappeared. Where were they? Only Juana—loyal Juana—had stayed behind to care for her, but now there was so much work to do that Juana couldn't spend the whole day in the nursery. She had to take over the kitchen and do the jobs of the laundress and the parlormaid and the chambermaid, too. There was no one around to sweep Mamá's hair up into a bird's nest, and the strange thing was that Mamá didn't seem to care. She pinned up her thick brown mane herself without fussing when a whole lock came loose and fell defiantly over her shoulder.

Lola began to whimper.

"Chatita!" hissed Doña Antonia. "I told you to be quiet. Don't make a sound! It's dangerous!"

She tiptoed across the bedroom where they were hiding and squatted beside Lola.

"Maman, I have to pee."

"You can't pee now. You have to be very, very still. They

can't know we're here. And don't call me *maman*! You're going to get us killed!"

"But, Mami, I have to pee!"

Doña Antonia crawled toward the bed, grabbed the chamber pot from underneath, and dragged it back behind the armoire. "There, go ahead."

Six-year-old Lola picked up her dress and pulled down her bloomers. When she was done, Doña Antonia pushed the pot away. "I can't empty it now," she whispered. "Just leave it there."

Lola bit her lip. She knew better than to ask again what was going on. The tightness of her mother's jaw, the way she rubbed her hands against her long black silk skirt, her hushed voice and edgy gaze—all these things told Lola that from now on she would have to sniff back her tears and not ask questions.

Things had begun to change months ago. Now she could no longer tear through the patio with Juana, screeching with laughter, while her dog, Siroco, yapped happily. She was no longer free to dance for hours to the music of the Victrola. She could not ride out to the country house in the landau with Mamá and Papá, or trot around the orchard on her milk-white pony. She had to stay where she was, be very still, and creep around on all fours like a baby so that nobody would know they were hiding in their own house.

"How long do we have to stay here?" whispered Lola. She was tired of crouching by the armoire. The air reeked of piss, and the heat was stifling.

"I think they've gone. I'll send Juana out to the patio to check."

"Who's gone, Mami?"

"I thought I heard a noise…but…let's see what Juana says. If she says it's clear, you can play, but stay indoors and away from the windows. Holy Virgin, this is a nightmare."

A moment later, Juana entered the bedroom and assured them that no one was in the patio or the stables, and the doors were all secure. Lola sprang up, but Doña Antonia held on to her ankle.

"Wait," she whispered. She still looked worried.

Lola squirmed. "Why? Juana says it's alright!"

Doña Antonia sighed. She looked wistful, but after a moment, she said, "Alright. Go play."

Lola had noticed that lately the grown-ups had been speaking in muffled voices. Her parents thought that Lola wasn't listening, but she was. They tried to shield her from the truth, but they couldn't. There had been stories about people just like them, the Ansúnsolo López Negrete family. Decent people who shared their idyllic existence in beautiful Durango, a city filled with elegant, colonial-style homes and wide streets upon which stylish carriages rolled day and night, a city that boasted a seventeenth-century baroque cathedral considered the jewel of northern Mexico. Decent people who came to her mother's soirees, the men in top hats and tails, white boutonnieres in their lapels, the women in frilly, high-collared blouses. People whose children were learning French and believed Porfirio Díaz had saved Mexico from barbarism and superstition. Stories, for example, like what had happened the month before to the Pérez Lorenzo baby.

She had pieced it together from scraps of speech and muffled sobs behind closed doors. Pablito had been playing in his room, attended by his *niñera*. Lola had seen the child often—a roly-poly two-year-old with soft brown curls and rosy cheeks, the spitting image of his father. His mother, Doña Mercedes, gave him a kiss and told the nursemaid to put him down for a nap. The weather was lovely, temperate and dry, and she had instructed the servants to set up tables outside on the veranda for her weekly card game. But the tables weren't there, the potted dahlias she had ordered the kitchen girls to place on each one still sitting in rows in the patio, fuchsia, crimson, orange, and yellow blooms opening to the sunlight like tiny origami forms. Doña Mercedes glanced at her watch. The ladies would arrive soon. She breathed deeply and listened. Silence. Suddenly she felt her blood turn to ice. She spun around, darted up the stairs, and ran to the nursery. A scream of terror froze in her throat. The nursemaid had vanished. A ladder rested against the unbolted window. Pablito was propped up in his little chair, his head thrown back, his mouth and eyes wide-open. Someone had arranged the scene to produce maximum horror when his mother found him sitting there, his throat slit from ear to ear.

Lola understood what had happened, but why did it happen? Could it happen to her?

After the tragedy at the Pérez Lorenzo estate, her mother became increasingly anxious and angry. She stopped being meticulous about her dress and hair. She sent Siroco to the country to be cared for by a farm family. Often she and Lola's father, Don Jesús Leonardo, locked themselves in the study for hours, leaving Lola to fend for herself or hang on to Juana's skirts while the maid ironed in the laundry room. Lola was bored and she missed her dog, but after a week or so, she began to lose her fear. She had heard of no other murders of children. Besides, she knew that Juana would never abandon her the way Pablito's *niñera* had abandoned him. Juana had come to work for the Ansúnsolos as a ten-year-old and had lived with the family her whole life. She'd been taking care of Lola since she was born. She wouldn't just disappear through an open window. Anyway, her parents were dead. Where would she go?

Sometimes Lola snuck away from the nursemaid and pressed her ear against the study door. She heard words like *cash, accounts, liquidate*, but she knew that her father had a high position at the Bank of Durango, so these were the kinds of words he always used. Then one day there were new words, words she hadn't heard before: Pancho Villa. Lola didn't dare ask her mother what these words meant, so she ran to Juana.

"Oh, Pancho Villa is a very famous man," explained the maid nonchalantly. "His real name is Doroteo Arango. He shot a man to protect his sister's honor. Right there in rancho El Gorgojito, one of your father's properties. Your father is a very rich man, you know, señorita. Anyhow, now Pancho Villa has become a protector of the people."

"Protector of the people? What does that mean?"

"Nothing you need to know about, little one. Now go and play. Do you want me to turn on the Victrola so you can dance? Only don't dance near the window. It's too danger-ous." Juana stroked Lola's cheek and dug into the pocket of her apron. She pulled out a brightly colored candy and handed it to her. "Don't tell your Mami," she whispered with a wink.

Lola took the sweet and giggled. She felt safe with Juana.

One evening, a few days after that conversation, Doña An-tonia instructed Juana to give Lola her supper and put her to bed early. Lola fell asleep almost immediately, but suddenly awakened in the middle of the night. She looked around. Something was off. A luminescent moon cast a diffused glow over the room. Why wasn't the window shuttered beneath the gauzy curtains? Shadows flickered on the dimly lit wall. The silhouette of a person seemed to form and then dissolve. Lola trembled. Her eyes darted around the room. She saw the armoire, the dresser, the shelf for her dolls and toys. She saw the crucifix above her bed, a small table and chairs where she often took her meals, and the cabinet where the Victrola sat. Everything was in place. The statue of the Virgin stood white and ethereal on the nightstand. But where was Juana? She wasn't on the cot by Lola's bed, where she usually slept. Lola began to whimper.

"Juana!"

"Shh!" Juana stepped out from the alcove, fully dressed, a frayed rebozo thrown over her shoulders. She was carrying a candle. Its glimmer made the shadows on the wall dance and twist like rag dolls.

"Juana, I'm scared," whispered Lola. "I think I heard a noise."

"No, you didn't. Go back to sleep."

Another shadow appeared on the wall. Lola squinted hard. It wasn't on the wall at all! It was a man standing in front of the wall! Lola couldn't see his features, but she was sure this form was solid. The man took a step toward her. Lola screamed.

Juana raised her hand and slapped the child across the face. "Shut up!" she snapped.

Lola couldn't believe the sting on her cheek. And she couldn't believe the hatred in Juana's voice or the cruelty in her eyes. Lola opened her mouth to say something, but Juana raised her hand again and the words stuck in her throat. A warm, sticky wetness oozed out of her body, covering her thighs and bottom, and then trickled down her leg. She had to scream. She had to call Papá. But she was paralyzed.

Juana said something to the man in a language that wasn't Spanish. Lola didn't understand it, but she knew it was a dialect of Nahuatl. Juana sometimes spoke it with the other maids or at the marketplace. Lola knew what was going to happen next. The man was going to grab her by the hair and Juana was going to hold her down. Then they would slit her throat. They would place her head on the pillow soaked with blood, and Mami would find her dead in the morning, just as Pablito's mother had found him. Once again, Lola opened her mouth to scream, but before she could hurl a bloodcurdling shriek to wake up her parents, she felt something warm and gooey and disgusting on her face. The man wiped his lips and Lola grabbed a sheet to wipe the spit out of her eye. *"¡Viva Pancho Villa!"* he hissed.

The man grabbed the porcelain Virgin from the nightstand and smashed it against the edge. Then he snatched some silver knickknacks from the dresser. In a heartbeat, they were gone. They didn't go out the window but ran down the stairs. Lola hardly heard them open the front door. They were careful. They didn't slam the door. They didn't want to wake up Papá, because Juana knew he had a gun and would use it. In her mind's eye, Lola could see them seize the key to the front gate—Juana knew where it was hidden—and then cross the yard and exit.

As soon as she could move her legs, Lola ran to her parents' room. Doña Antonia took one look at her little girl and began wailing and shaking like a branch in a storm. She held Lola to her. "Oh my God," she cried. "Oh, my dear God!"

Lola's father leaped out of bed and grabbed his hunting rifle. He lit a torch and surveyed the perimeters of the property, then came back inside, bolted the doors and windows, and went into the bedroom. He sat on the bed behind his wife and rubbed her shoulders. Doña Antonia was sobbing violently, but struggling to contain herself. When at last she'd steadied her hands, she rose and poured water into a basin. She washed Lola from head to toe, put a fresh nightgown on her, and rocked her like an infant until the child fell asleep. She placed her in her own bed and lay down beside her.

"They've invaded our home," she said to her husband. "We have no choice now. We have to leave."

An instant later—at least, that's how it seemed to Lola—her mother was grasping her arm and shaking it hard.

"Wake up! We're leaving!"

"What?" Lola yawned. She was dizzy and nauseous. She looked around and realized she was in her parents' room. She vaguely remembered a man creeping along her wall and speaking a strange language, then lunging at her. Was it a dream?

"Get out of bed, Chatita! We've got to get out of here."

"Where's Juana? Why am I in here?"

Doña Antonia didn't answer. It was still dark, so Lola pulled on the clothes her mother had laid out for her by the light of an oil lamp. Don Jesús Leonardo was already up and dressed. He had paid a driver an exorbitant sum to help him place five heavy wooden trunks in a lorry and transport them to Mexico, DF. It was hard to find that kind of help. Workers and peasants were leaving towns and fields in droves to join Pancho Villa. Besides, the roads weren't safe. Everywhere bandits and rebels lay in waiting.

Lola crossed the corridor to her room. Antonia had started ransacking Lola's drawers, throwing clothes into suitcases and linens into a large, strong wicker basket.

"Hurry up!" she snapped. "Help me! Take out your best clothes and put them in that suitcase! Don't worry if something gets unfolded. But don't make it too heavy. I'll have to carry it myself, along with the basket."

When the suitcase was full, Doña Antonia ran to the maids' quarters and rummaged through her servants' belongings. "Not this, it's too new," she murmured. "Not that, it's too fine—an old skirt of mine I gave to Cintia for her saint's day." She rummaged some more. "Not this, it's too bright." Finally, she found a discolored homespun blouse, a dingy black skirt, a ragged rebozo, and well-worn sandals. She put on the clothes and then went to get Lola.

The child gawked at her mother. "Maman? You're going out like *that*?"

Don Jesús Leonardo was on the front patio. There was no time for farewells. He kissed his wife and daughter, and then he was off. A carriage would take him to the station, where he would catch the 6 a.m. train for El Paso. Then it would return for Doña Antonia.

Doña Antonia salvaged what she could. A carved ivory comb. A lace hanky. The silver crucifix that hung in Lola's room. A rag doll. A wedding photograph. By the time the carriage returned, she was ready. The suitcase stood by the door alongside the basket.

"Get in," Antonia ordered Lola.

"In the basket?"

"Make yourself into a little ball. Cover yourself with the linen and don't make a sound."

Lola looked at her mother in disbelief.

"Don't you know what they do to the children of the rich? Get in!"

Doña Antonia lifted up her daughter and positioned her gently in the basket. She covered her with sheets and pillowcases. Then she drew the tattered rebozo over her own head and around her mouth, almost completely covering her face.

From her third-class seat on the train to Mexico City, Doña Antonia looked out the window and gave thanks to God that Lola, safe in her basket, couldn't see what she could see. The war was only starting, and already cadavers dotted the strip of barren land along the tracks. Bodies hung from trees, their heads drooping like rotting melons. On the ground lay sprawling campesinos with holes where their eyeballs should be, ribbons of rust-colored blood streaming from their blackened mouths and noses. No one claimed them. No one buried them. It was dangerous to venture out to retrieve a fallen rebel. The hacienda owners had placed paid snipers everywhere. When they brought down an insurgent, they threw him in an open field or by the tracks. If family members tried to recover him, the thugs brought them down, too. Men, women, and children lay in the dust, their flesh rotting in the sweltering sun or gnawed away by dogs.

Doña Antonia looked away and closed her eyes.

At last they arrived in the capital. She pulled Lola out of the basket where she had fallen asleep, and together they made their way to the nearest public lodging they could find.

Of course, I didn't witness any of these things myself. Doña Antonia told me this story many years later, when we were all living in the North. My own escape from Durango was different. Much different.

2

I didn't ride to Mexico City in a wash basket. I walked...or maybe I didn't. I don't really remember. I was only about four, little more than a toddler. I do remember Tía Emi dragging me along by the wrist. "Don't fall behind," she snapped. "If you get lost, I won't go looking for you."

Tía Emi was a seamstress. Her job was to make sheets and curtains and to repair tears in the children's clothes. A tailor came from the city to make shirts for Don Adalberto and the boys. Doña Verónica chose dresses from magazines for herself and her daughters and had her own private dressmaker sew them. I remember Tía Emi running her fingers over the soft muslin of a petticoat. It had a tear in the hem, and Tía Emi was fixing it.

"Soft as a nun's tit," she whispered, in some sort of momentary stupor.

I had no idea what she was talking about. I didn't know what a nun was and couldn't think why her tit would be softer than anyone else's. Maybe a nun was some sort of animal with smooth, cream-colored tits? My job was to pick scraps of cloth and thread off the ground and place them in a basket so that the older girls could sort them by color. Later, when my fingers were steady enough to hold a needle, I learned to make simple stitches. Before I knew the rosary, I could make flowers on cloth. You stick in the needle and make a loop with the thread, then you bring the needle back up through the loop and tack down one end. That makes a petal. Those petals were the only beautiful things in my life.

Tía Emi said she wasn't really my aunt, although *tía* means "aunt." She said she just took care of me because my mother was dead and in the big house where we lived, it was the custom for one of the servants to raise the child of another servant who had died. According to Tía Emi, my mother named me María Amparo because she knew she was going to heaven and I was going to have to depend on the Virgin to help me. *Amparo* means "help" in Spanish. They called me Mara because María Amparo was too long. I had no idea who my father was. Maybe some peasant on his way to an uprising or maybe a passing fabric salesman, Tía Emi said. Nobody worried about such things at the estate. As far as I knew, none of the children who scampered around the sewing room had a father.

I was content scavenging for snippets of thread and fabric, but what I liked best was hiding under the table and listening to the women sing as they worked. I especially loved the dark ballad of Miguela Ruiz, who murdered the son of the hacienda owner.

> *Don Pedro amaba a Miguela*
> (Don Pedro loved Miguela)
> *La persiguió noche y día*
> (He pursued her night and day)
> *La agarró sola en la cuadra*
> (When he saw her alone in the stables)

La tumbó y dejó con cría
(He knocked her down and left her expecting)

Un puñal entre las faldas
(A dagger hidden in her skirts)
Se coló en sus aposentos
(She snuck into his rooms)
Lo encontró besando a otra
(She found him kissing another girl)
Y el vil pagó sus tormentos
(And the bastard paid for her suffering)

"*Puta madre!*" Tía Emi would exclaim, a cigarette dangling from her fingers. He got what he deserved! The fucker had it coming!

"*¡Se lo merecía!*" echoed the other women. "He had it coming!"

I was an orphan, that's true. I had nothing, but I don't remember feeling neglected. I just didn't think about it. Up at five in the morning, prayers at five fifteen, in the workroom by five thirty. At eight, a breakfast of tortillas and beans. I didn't crave anything else. I didn't know there *was* anything else. Day after day, gathering up snippets, handing Tía Emi the right needle, and then, when I was about four, hemming rags so that I could edge towels and sheets when I got older. Before supper, the women would sit on the floor smoking and singing, and I would breathe in the scent of sweet, cheap, black tobacco and doze. "Life, liberty, and the pursuit of happiness" were not things anyone thought about. It never occurred to us that we were supposed to be *happy*. We were just supposed to *be*. To sew. "The pursuit of happiness" was something I learned about years later, in the North.

I didn't question my routine, but I did notice things.

For example, when Tía Emi placed her strong, chunky hand over my tiny fingers to guide the needle, I noticed that her skin was the shade of rich dark chocolate, while mine was the color of honey.

I noticed that when the women sang "The Ballad of Miguela Ruiz," they looked sideways at me out of squinty eyes and sometimes whispered to each other in Nahuatl.

I also noticed that Tía Emi sometimes snitched things from Don Adalberto and Doña Verónica—small things, like thimbles and leftover skeins of thread, fabric fragments, ribbon, and trimmings, or a tape measure. She even stole a pair of gloves that Doña Verónica had left in a pocket. Later, she started taking foodstuffs: beans, tortillas, a small container of dried fruit. There were some tins of condensed milk in the pantry.

"What about those?" I suggested.

She considered it and even picked one up and bounced it around in her hand.

"Too heavy," she concluded. "Anyhow, that's the sort of thing that would be missed. Preserved food is a luxury. Doña Verónica keeps track of the cans on her shelves."

Instead, she took a mamey from a bowl on the kitchen counter.

"That's as heavy as a couple of cans of milk," I said.

"But we'll eat it," she said. "It's not to sell."

She hid her loot in a burlap bag she kept in a wooden box in the corner of the maids' dormitory. Nobody said anything. Why would they? They were all doing the same.

Every once in a while, Tía Emi would take the sack out of the box and jerk it up and down as though weighing it. Then she would sling it over her shoulder.

One night, everyone went to bed earlier than usual. Ordinarily, Tía Emi fell asleep before me. I'd doze off lying next to her on the petate, listening to her soft, uneven breathing. I'd stare at her high, hard cheekbones in the moonlight that crept through the slats of the window. She reminded me of Chalchiuhtlicue, the water goddess, whose statue stood in the corner. She had Chalchiuhtlicue's heavy nose, square jaw, thick lips, and perpetually open mouth, her low eyebrows and broad forehead, her surprisingly long and graceful fingers. That night, though, Tía Emi never seemed to fall asleep. I could hear her squirming on the petate, whispering into the darkness, scratching on the floor, coughing a kind of artificial cough.

Suddenly, someone was shrieking. Women were running around, baying at each other in muffled voices. Sometimes they spoke Nahuatl, but mostly they spoke Spanish. I strained my ears. In the distance, I could hear screams. "*¡Fuego! ¡Fuego!* Fire!"

Tía Emi and the other women were already dressed and pulling the children out of bed.

"Let's go," Tía Emi said calmly, but firmly. "It has started."

She grabbed me by the wrist and shoved a bundle into my arms. She'd tied some of the smaller items she'd stolen into a neat parcel small enough for me to carry.

"Don't lose this," she snapped. She was pushing me out of the room.

Before I knew what was happening to me, I was out on the road, swept forward in a crowd of what seemed like hundreds of people.

"Stay by my side," ordered Tía Emi. "Don't fall behind. If you do, I can't be responsible for you."

The burlap sack was fastened to her back. It must have been heavy, yet she moved at an astounding pace. I looked around. Other seamstresses walked with us, sometimes three or four abreast, each with a sack on her back.

I heard what sounded like an explosion. "Look!" someone yelled. Everyone turned toward the estate. The manor house was ablaze.

"Keep moving!" ordered Tía Emi.

The blaze engulfed the house, the stables, even the nearby fields. The flames seemed to lap at the sky, an iridescent groundswell of fire so bright that it dimmed the moon and stars.

"Stop gawking and walk!" barked Tía Emi. "I don't have to watch over you, you know. If you get lost, I don't give a pig's pussy."

It's true, I thought. She's not my mother. If I get lost, she won't care. If I get trampled or die by the side of the road, no one will give…well…a pig's pussy.

I scampered beside her for what felt like hours. We trudged and trudged along the road. My legs felt like sticks ready to snap. My ankles were swollen and filthy. My feet burned as though fire ants were gnawing my soles and under my toenails. I was hungry and sleepy and had to pee, but I tightened my crotch and pursed my lips. I couldn't have asked to stop even if I'd dared to. My throat was too scorched to produce sound. I stumbled, righted myself, then stumbled again.

"Walk!" commanded Tía Emi. She was dragging me now.

I'm going to fall, I thought. I'm going to be left behind, and no one will come looking for me. I was… I know the word now, but then, I only knew the feeling… I was expendable. I'm going to die, I kept thinking. I didn't know exactly what that meant, "to die." Tía Emi had told me that my mother was dead, so maybe it wasn't so bad. Maybe if I were dead, too, I'd get to see her.

I felt like I was sinking into the earth, and then, I was flying, flying as though invisible arms were carrying me through the air.

3

Mexico City, 1910–1911
Play

The next thing I remember is being flung on the ground like a sack of dirty laundry.

"Get down," said Tía Emi. "We're here."

"Where?"

I saw elegant carriages and electric motor cars, but also pack mules, horses and braying burros, carts, wheelbarrows, and cycles. Human piss and horse dung ran in the gutters, and flies swarmed franticly around the turds. Cigarette butts were scattered everywhere.

"Mexico City," she said. "We've walked all the way from Durango."

By "we," she meant she and the other women. I didn't know how I'd gotten there, but I knew I hadn't walked much. What's more, I didn't know what Durango was. I'd never thought about the name of the place where we'd been living. After all, I was only about four. I say "about four" because I wasn't actually sure when I was born.

Tía Emi and the other women found an alley where they could squat and pee, and then looked for a church portal to sleep in. Tía Emi pulled some crusts and fruit out of her sack for me, then lay down, tucking her rebozo under her head to protect it from the hard stone. In an instant she was snoring.

We spent a couple of days loitering near the cathedral and occasionally begging for work. It was just after Epiphany—what they call Three Kings Day, January 6—which means that people weren't feeling as generous as before Christmas, when they still had religion in their hearts. We ate the fruit first because it would go bad. Then we ate the tortillas and cheese. The food wouldn't last long, we knew, so Tía Emi began offering fabric remnants, ribbons, and scraps of lace to passersby. Finally, she sold the gloves. With the few centavos she earned she bought fresh tortillas. After a week or so, we began venturing into the fancier neighborhoods—Colonia Roma, Condesa. Tía Emi would knock at the servants' door and try to look self-assured. "Any work?" she'd ask. "I'm an experienced seamstress." It wasn't easy. We had no references, and besides, servants usually found positions through the gossip chain. One lady would tell another, "My maid Luisa has a niece who just came in from Oaxaca." Or else, "Ludovica Barrada's maid is looking for work on the sly because Ludovica is as bad-tempered as a puma with a thorn in its paw."

In most houses, no one even bothered to open the door. In a few, the *ama de llaves*—the head maid—would look at me and shake her head.

"A kid? No, we're not taking anyone with a kid."

When the money ran out, Tía Emi learned to steal from street vendors and beg on church steps. Sometimes she'd snitch a cigarette from an urchin selling chewing gum and butts on a corner. She taught me to steal and beg as well. "Wait until he's haggling with a customer, then nab an avocado," she said. We were desperate. "*Puta madre,* I have to find work," she moaned, "and you, you're a burden."

Don Francisco's mansion looked pretty much like the other

grand houses in the neighborhood—two stories, wrought iron over the windows, a locked gate. Tía Emi had heard from a woman in the marketplace that Doña Sara, Don Francisco's wife, needed a housemaid.

We knocked on the door, but the *ama de llaves* said they didn't need a seamstress.

"I can do other things," said Tía Emi. "I could work in the kitchen or clean the house."

"What about the girl?"

"I'm taking care of her," said Tía Emi. "But I'm not her mother. I can get rid of her."

Get rid of her? What did she mean? Was she going to slit my throat?

"She's fair-complected," explained Tía Emi. "I could probably get a good price for her from some white couple that can't have a child."

The *ama* stared at me. "That's true," she said finally. "What is your name?" she asked Tía Emi.

"Emilia Rojas-Moreno. They call me Emi. The child's name is María Amparo, but we call her Mara."

The *ama* placed her hand gently on my head. I shuddered. "Pretty little thing," she murmured. I held my breath, wondering if she planned to sell me.

Her eyes were kind, but I was afraid. I wasn't used to displays of affection. Neither Tía Emi nor the other servants in Durango cooed over children. Children were just there, like furniture. You put them where you wanted them and then forgot about them.

"You can keep her," said the *ama*. "We have other girls with children in this house. We could give you a try...in the kitchen."

"Yes, ma'am," said Tía Emi, taking me by the hand.

"Another thing," said the *ama*. "Don Francisco Madero believes that all children should learn to read and write."

"What for?" asked Tía Emi.

"He believes it will make them responsible citizens. Mara
will go to school in the morning with other servant girls."

"Sounds like a waste of time," said Tía Emi.

The *ama* shrugged. "Don Francisco has ideas about education. He believes that if people are literate, they will be able
to govern themselves responsibly."

The *ama*'s name was Marcela. She gave Tía Emi a uniform—
a loose gray dress with an apron—and showed us where we
would stay. Instead of on a petate, we would sleep on a cot in
a room we would share with another kitchen maid, Rosario,
and her daughter, Anita.

"Maybe if Doña Sara could see how well I sew…" ventured Tía Emi.

Marcela turned to her, her eyes in their sockets like two
stones in dry earth. "Doña Sara has no children," she said,
"and she dresses simply. She doesn't need a seamstress. If you're
set on sewing, then you should have gone elsewhere and not
wasted my time."

"Yes, ma'am," said Tía Emi, trying to sound meek. "I'm
very happy to peel potatoes."

Anita and I attended class in an open room that looked like
an abandoned workshop, but was freshly painted and had pictures of animals on the wall. The littlest girls sat in one sec-
tion, the six- and seven-year-olds in another, the eight- and
nine-year-olds in another. The boys were in a different room.
We wore white blouses and blue skirts. Marcela gave Tía Emi
some cloth, and she whipped up a uniform—the first new

clothes I'd had in a long time. We carried little slates to write
the letters of the alphabet on.

On the first day, we learned "*a* is for *asno*, *b* is for *burro*," and
the numbers from zero to ten. After two hours, the teacher
said, "It's time for *recreo*. Please form a straight line and follow
me to the plaza at the end of the street, where you can play
for fifteen minutes."

I wasn't sure what I was supposed to do. I didn't know what
"play" meant. Anita seemed to understand, so I followed her.

In the plaza, the younger girls divided themselves into two
groups, five on each side, and kicked a rag ball from one side to
the other. The teacher gave the older girls a long rope, which
two of them whirled around while a third jumped up and
down over it, trying not to get her feet caught. I grimaced.
Was this "playing"? It didn't look like fun.

"Go ahead, María Amparo," urged the teacher, a squat,
dark woman who reminded me of a ripe eggplant. "Go stand
next to Anita."

I cringed. "I don't want to," I whimpered.

My own words astonished me. I was used to obeying com-
mands, not giving opinions, but chasing after the cloth ball
seemed terrifying.

"Don Francisco says exercise is healthy for children."

I didn't answer. I took the wide stance of a mule, head
down, eyes half-closed. The other girls were running and
kicking and shrieking with laughter.

"I… I…don't know how…"

I felt a sharp pain on the side of my skull. Tía Emi had
cuffed me on the ear before, but never so hard. "Children
don't make the rules," snapped the teacher, grabbing me by
the arm and shoving me into the group.

I stood next to Anita and prayed the ball wouldn't come

to me, but a moment later, it rolled in my direction. "Kick!" shouted Anita. "Kick!"

I lifted my foot, booted the ball with all my strength, and watched it roll toward the opposite side. No one jeered. The girls on the other team kicked it back, this time toward Anita, and we continued playing. I had done it right.

We'd been working at the Madero house for a couple of months. I was in the kitchen helping Tía Emi pluck stones out of lentils when I heard the crack of the heavy knocker against the brass plate of the front door. Blanca, the parlormaid, went to answer, and two people I'd never seen before stepped inside. Marcela recognized one of them: Doña Antonia López Negrete de Asúnsolo. She was a distant cousin of Don Francisco's, and she had visited once or twice before, long ago.

"The little one must be her daughter, Dolores," said Marcela.

They said she was six, but she was smaller than me. She wasn't particularly pretty. She was white, that's true, but olive-complected. (You have to understand that in Mexico, "white" was not just a skin color, but a whole way of being—a culture, a class, a bank account.) She wore a frilly organdy dress with bows and edgings, patent leather shoes, and white stockings. I was fascinated.

Blanca showed the visitors into the parlor. Doña Sara called for coffee and little cakes, which Blanca brought in on a tray. I went back into the kitchen to help Tía Emi prepare broccoli and asparagus for French-style soufflés. At Don Francisco's house, I saw foods I'd never seen before and even tasted some of them. Don Francisco had lived abroad, and he liked dishes with French names and lots of butter. Even the servants ate

well at Don Francisco's. At Don Adalberto's, it had been tortillas, rice, and beans for breakfast, *comida*, and supper.

Marcela said the visitors would be staying awhile. For the
moment, they had no place to go, but they were relatives,
so Doña Sara took them in. In Mexico, you can't depend on
the weather or the government, but you can always depend
on your relatives. People called Doña Antonia a cat, Marcela
said, because she always landed on her feet. Even when fate
knocked her from her comfortable perch on the windowsill
into a cold, filthy alley, she licked her paws, stretched her legs,
and sauntered off in a new direction. "How many times do cats
crawl out of the rubble after an explosion or an earthquake,
sometimes carrying a kitten by the scruff of the neck?" said
Marcela. "Cats are clever."

Later that evening, Doña Antonia and Doña Sara sat on the
patio in the shade of a massive ahuehuete tree. Colorful pots
with cacti, Mexican heather, and herbs bordered the flagstone.
While Doña Antonia recounted to Doña Sara how she had
escaped from Durango with Lola hidden in a laundry basket,
I flitted around inconspicuously, watering the cilantro and
basil and pretending not to listen. I wondered where the girl
was. I wanted to get a better look at her.

In the slums near the train station, Doña Antonia encoun-
tered squalor like she'd never seen before, she told Doña Sara.
Squat, defeated men whose eyes never left the ground. Tattered
women, with babies on their backs and outstretched hands.
Old women—actually, not much older than Doña Antonia
herself, but prematurely gray, with bleary eyes and decaying
gums. In her plain black skirt and shabby rebozo, Doña Antonia looked as poor as they did. She could have gotten away
without opening her purse, but once, in a flash of compas-
sion, she thrust her hand into the mass of rags where she'd

stashed some money, pulled out a few coins, and gave them to an abscess-ridden hag.

"*Toma, madre,*" she murmured. "Take this." Immediately scores of beggar children surrounded her, squawking like starving chickens before a mound of grain.

On the walls, the graffiti screamed *¡Viva Madero! ¡Viva la democracia!*

"I can't help but wonder," Doña Antonia said as they sipped coffee from Limoges cups, "How much longer before these downtrodden creatures rise up and demand the morsel of tortilla they are now begging for?"

"Francisco wants it to happen *now!*" said Doña Sara. "He says that without a total transformation, this country will rot."

I could see that Doña Antonia was listening closely. She must have realized that even though her circle argued that Porfirio Díaz had brought growth to Mexico, the masses were weary of begging and eating slop. Don Francisco Madero was from one of the richest families in Mexico, but he'd been attracting crowds with his democratic ideas, crowds so large that Díaz saw him as a threat and had him imprisoned. What Díaz hadn't realized was how much clout Madero's family had. Before the dictator knew what hit him, Madero was out on bond and had hightailed it across the border. In San Antonio, November 1910, he called for a revolution, declaring himself provisional president. Then he lay low and prepared for the attack against Díaz. After some delay, he finally crossed the border into the Mexican state of Chihuahua on February 14. In the meantime, Revolutionary forces were organizing against Díaz elsewhere under Emiliano Zapata and Pancho Villa. I didn't grasp any of this back then, of course. I was just a child. All I knew was that after Tía Emi and I moved into the Madero house, Don Francisco came and went. Sometimes he lived at home, but sometimes we didn't see him for weeks at a time.

As Marcela had said, Doña Antonia was a cat, and she possessed a cat's fine timing. She knew how to make the necessary adjustments in the air to land with all four paws solidly on the ground. She arched her feline back, raised her feline nose, and sensed which way the wind was blowing. Then she made a decision. It was clear that it was only a matter of time before Madero took over, and when he did, the great landed families would lose everything. But Doña Antonia's family would be alright, as long as they made a few alterations to their political affiliation. And it would be easy enough, because Antonia was Francisco I. Madero's cousin.

"I'm sure Paco is right," she said, using her cousin's nickname.

The nice thing about being a servant's child is that nobody notices you. You're invisible. People say all sorts of things, and they don't worry that you might hear them.

Marcela came out to the patio with Lola, who looked as though she were just waking up from her siesta. Lola crawled into her mother's lap and snuggled against her like a baby. Doña Antonia ran her fingers over Lola's hair and coaxed a strand off her damp cheek. I felt a surge of disgust. Tía Emi never fawned over me like that.

The ladies got up and Marcela followed them into the house, holding Lola by the hand. I went back into the kitchen, where Tía Emi was husking corn, pulling the leaves off the ears with one swift yank, as though she were ripping cloth.

"I've already cleaned off the silk. Now you put the husks on a plate for tamales," she ordered me.

Marcela came in, shoulders back, chin thrust out. She obviously had an important message to convey.

"Emi," she said. "Doña Sara would like you to attend to Señorita Dolores. Get her dressed in the morning, bring her meals, stay with her while she eats… She's too little to sit at the table with the adults. You'll start tomorrow. They'll only be here a few weeks, so it's not a permanent arrangement."

Tía Emi nodded. *"Puta madre!"* she said, when Marcela was out of earshot. "This could be a lucky break!"

"Why can't she dress herself?" I retorted. "And why does someone need to stay with her when she eats? No one sits with *me* when *I* eat."

Tía Emi looked as me as though I were a bug. "She's not the same breed as us," she said.

In the morning, while I was getting ready for school, I asked Tía Emi, "Did you take her breakfast?"

"She isn't up yet."

"Doesn't she have to go to school?"

"I suppose she will eventually, some special school for rich people."

I burst into tears. "This isn't fair!"

"Listen, Mara, if Doña Antonia likes me, maybe she'll hire me as a *niñera*...or a seamstress. I don't want to spend my life pounding corn into cornmeal. A seamstress earns more than a kitchen maid."

She was just using the girl to get a better-paying job. I calmed down.

For a while, I forgot about the girl. In the mornings I went to school with Anita. I was already starting to read and could do sums up to ten. Every day we also learned a few words in English—*dog, cat, How are you?* During the *recreo* I played ball or tag with the other girls. After the midday meal, I helped the maids clean up in the kitchen. They sang "Adelita" and the "Corrido de Pancho Villa" while they worked—they didn't even have to hide their singing from the *patrones*—but never "The Ballad of Miguela Ruiz."

One day, when I came home, I found Tía Emi in the kitchen

with her needles and thread on her lap. The girl had snagged the hem of her frock, and Tía Emi was going to mend it.

"Take off your dress," she ordered.

The girl caught my eye and raised her eyebrows. I shrugged. She shrugged, too, and threw the dress over her head. She stood there a moment in her camisole and petticoat. Then she smiled.

"Hola," she said. "I'm Lola." She held out her hand.

I didn't respond. A white girl had never greeted me like that before. I was confused.

"My real name is Dolores," she went on, "but they call me Lola. What's your name?"

I blinked and looked down at my sandals, so shabby alongside her smart white boots.

"Tell her," snapped Tía Emi.

"My name is María Amparo," I said, "but they call me Mara."

She was still in her underclothes, hand outstretched.

"Shake her hand," directed Tía Emi, looking irritated.

How was I supposed to know? I thought. What do I know about hand shaking? I reached out and took her hand.

"Let's be friends, Mara!" said Lola. Her smile was warm and engaging. I thought it might be a trick. I stared at her blankly. Was she really asking me to be her friend?

"Come with your aunt when she brings me my supper!" she said. "That way, we can play awhile."

"Play?" Were we going to kick a ball across her room?

"Are you sure your mother won't mind?" said Tía Emi.

"Oh no. Mami doesn't like me to be alone all the time." She paused and bit her lip. "I don't have any brothers or sisters, you see. Mami can't..."

"I'll bring your tray up later," interrupted Tía Emi.

When we entered the room with her supper, Lola was sitting on the bed in a frilly white nightgown, holding a rag doll. Doña Antonia had draped Lola's dress over a chair.

"Look," Lola said, handing me the doll. "Her name is Beti. She's my favorite. I have others, though. Our trunks haven't arrived yet."

"Are you going to a party?"

Lola burst out laughing. "No, silly. I'm going to have supper and then we can play a little. Then I'll go to bed."

"Dressed like *that*?" I'd never seen such a fancy dress for sleeping. I slept in my underpants like the other servant girls, and Tía Emi slept in her drawers and a slip.

Lola sat down at a small table. "Here," she said, "share my supper."

Tía Emi had prepared a light evening meal of *sopa de fideos*—noodle soup—and rolls. Lola gave me a roll, crisp and fragrant, and I gnawed on the crust. Afterward, we ate mangos and dragon fruit cut like flowers, almost too beautiful to bite into.

I kept waiting to see if Lola would bring out a ball or a jump rope, but instead, we pretended to feed the doll and looked at one of her picture books. When Marcela came in and turned on the Victrola for her, she started to dance around the room.

"I love to dance!" she squealed. "What about you?"

"Me, too," I said, although I had no idea how to dance.

"Can you come again tomorrow?" said Lola, once it was time to leave. "I know we're going to be good friends."

"Yes!" I said excitedly. "We'll be good friends."

I was thrilled. "Tomorrow I'm going to go play with my new friend Lola," I told Anita before bed.

"She's not your friend," Anita murmured.

"Yes, she is," I insisted. "She said—"

"Listen, Lola," interrupted Tía Emi. "You can't be her friend." Her tone was matter-of-fact. She wasn't trying to be unkind. "You can play with her, but you can't be her friend."

"Why not?" My chest was throbbing.

"Because," she said. "That's just the way things are."

Within a couple of weeks, Doña Antonia had found an elegant two-floor apartment at 8 Calle de Berlín, in Colonia Juárez, one of the toniest neighborhoods in the city, right down the street from her cousin Francisco.

"She's going to need a staff," said Tía Emi. "She didn't bring any servants from Durango. She's going to want curtains and linens for the new house. She's an elegant lady who wears tasteful, high-quality clothes, not like these city women who go around with no corsets and their bloomers showing. They look like *putas en vacaciones*. Besides, she has a child, and with a child there's always mending. She'll need someone who can sew, and she saw how nicely I repaired the señorita's dress when she tore it."

Putas en vacaciones? What did a *puta* on vacation wear? I had an idea what a *puta* was—I'd seen whores in the alleys by the cathedral—but what was a vacation?

Doña Antonia didn't offer Tía Emi a job, but she did ask Doña Sara for permission to borrow her for a few days so she could make window hangings for Lola's bedroom. We'd go over there after school, and I'd play with Lola while Tía Lola measured and sewed.

Before long, I realized that Lola was as fascinated with me as I was with her. At first, I assumed it was because I was light-skinned and didn't look like the other servants' children. But then I understood it was because she thought I was smart. I could already read as many words as she could, and do other things as well, like sew. I made a pinafore with tiny embroidered pink flowers around the hem for her doll Beti. A pinafore is easier to make than a dress because it has no sleeves or armholes.

"It's beautiful," she gasped. "Could you make one for my other doll, too? For Lisi."

I wanted to please. "Of course," I said.

"Just like the rich," muttered Tía Emi, when I asked her for another scrap of cloth. "You give them your hand and they take your whole arm."

About a month after they'd moved into the new apartment, Lola's father arrived back from El Paso. Jesús Leonardo Asúnsolo was a distinguished-looking man who always wore a stiff white collar, a tie, a dark, double-breasted Edwardian vest, and a tight-fitting jacket. He had a rectangular face made severe by slicked-down hair parted perfectly in the middle—you would have thought he measured his forehead with a tape every morning—and a meticulously trimmed moustache that extended just to the corners of his lips. Thanks to his banking connections and Doña Antonia's powerful friends and family, the Asúnsolo-López Negretes were once again living in style. Don Jesús Leonardo had deposited his fortune in a US bank and made investments. He had rescued not only their money, but also—and much more important—their social position. After all, eventually Lola would need a husband, Doña Antonia reminded him frequently, and given that she was a little on the dark side, they were going to need plenty of cash and social pull to make up for it.

Don Jesús Leonardo didn't like me. That is, he didn't like that Lola was hanging around with a servant girl. It was time for her to start mingling with her own set, so he and Doña Antonia began looking for the right school in earnest.

They decided on the Colegio Francés, a French convent school run by the Sisters of Saint Joseph, on the Rivera de San Cosme. At the Colegio Francés, Lola would receive a solid education in French language and culture, and she would mix with the right people. Besides, all those sweet little disciples of the Sisters of Saint Joseph had brothers.

Lola was a quick study. She learned to say, *Oui, ma soeur* and *Non, ma soeur* with bowed head and lowered eyes. She read the Bible and learned on which side of the plate to place the dessertspoon. She learned when to wear black leather Mary Janes and when to wear button-down boots. And she learned that she must not give up her virginity until she was married. "A woman's body is sacred," said the nuns. "You must never defile your body by allowing a man who isn't your husband to touch you."

"Who's going to want to touch *me*?" she giggled. "With you, it will be different. You're very pretty."

I began to fidget. People had called me pretty before because I had light skin and wavy hair, and it made me uneasy.

On Sunday afternoons, the Asúnsolos would come for the *comida*, the midday meal, and I'd get to see Lola. We'd hide behind the ahuehuete tree, where we'd play with dolls and share secrets. Lola liked to imitate the nuns, with their pinched noses and French accents. Sometimes I'd brush her hair and tie bits of brightly colored ribbon or yarn into fanciful braids or twists.

"You see," I hissed at Tía Emi one Sunday after Lola had left, "we *are* friends."

Tía Emi grimaced and gathered up potato peels to throw to the chickens Doña Sara kept in the backyard. "Child," she finally said, "you have a wild imagination."

Even though I was living in his house, I didn't know that Francisco I. Madero was the most important man in Mexico. Lola called him Tío Paco (even though he was actually her cousin), as though he were like any other grown-up. However, in November 1911, Don Francisco became president of

Mexico. Then, everyone treated him with great respect and called him *Señor Presidente.*

Now, on Sundays, the dining room filled with important men who smoked and decided the future of the nation. Tío Gustavo, who was Don Francisco's brother and adviser, would become agitated and use words like "national reconciliation," "freedom of the press," "bipartisan cabinet." He would jump up and thrust his fist into the air demanding justice for the peasants. Of the two brothers, I liked Tío Gustavo more. He had a soft look about him, as though he'd like to forget about all this political nonsense and take a long nap. His face was fleshy and round, like a peach with bifocals, and he wore his hair combed back in a spectacular pompadour. His moustache formed an inverted *V* above his upper lip, giving him a perpetually surprised look. Even though he was very rich, his clothes never quite fit. His jacket was too tight and stretched unbecomingly over his chest, and his tie was always askew.

One evening, the men were in the smoking room arguing, puffing on cigars, and drinking liqueurs from decanters on the serving cart by the door. A new cousin was visiting that day, Mariano Samaniego. I'd never seen him before, but I knew from the way he dressed and spoke that he was part of the *crema y nata* of Mexican society. Lola told me that he had studied in the States, but then moved to Durango, where his family owned a large estate. He and his wife had twelve children, and he wasn't willing to risk a hair on the head of a single one of them, and so, when the violence started a year before, like Lola's father, he left Durango and set up house in Mexico City. But Lola wasn't interested in all that. What interested Lola was Ramón, Don Mariano's handsome and lively twelve-year-old son.

I expected that Sunday to be like any other. I expected Lola to meet me behind the ahuehuete tree, where we would play

with dolls and giggle about the French nuns. But instead, she
disappeared with her cousin, and I didn't see her all day. Tía
Emi was right, I thought. We're not really friends. She only
wants to be with me when there's no one else to play with.

I was in the kitchen drying dishes when I heard a commotion in the smoking room. I ran to the door. Lola and Ramón
had burst in while the men were arguing about politics, Lola
wearing a wide, garish pink and purple skirt, her eyes lined
with kohl and her lips painted red, and Ramón dressed all in
black, holding a guitar.

Ramón pushed away the rug in the center of the room,
took his position, and bowed.

"Ladies and gentlemen," he began.

Lola giggled. "There are no ladies!"

"Call the ladies!" commanded Ramón.

"Ramón!" bellowed Don Mariano. "What is the meaning
of this? Leave this room immediately and go play outside!"

"Please call the ladies," insisted Ramón. "We have prepared
a marvelous spectacle for you. I will play the guitar while Lola
dances a famous dance from Andalusia."

"Ramón!" exploded Don Mariano. "We are talking about
important things here. This is no place for children!"

"Oh," murmured Don Francisco tiredly, "let them do their
show. We could use a break." He rang for a servant and instructed him to fetch the ladies, who were smoking cigarettes
from long gilt holders in one of the parlors.

Doña Antonia entered the room and caught her breath.
Lola stood by the decanters, one leg raised in an arabesque,
one arm extended toward the audience. In her hands, she held
castanets. Doña Antonia looked as though she didn't know
whether to haul her out and spank her or burst out laughing.
Lola shifted her weight and brought down her leg, then raised

her arms above her head and looked over her shoulder with Andalusian arrogance. She clicked her castanets.

"A *copla* from Sevilla," announced Ramón.

"From Sevilla!" Tío Gustavo jumped up and growled with mock indignation. "We are Mexicans here. We don't need Spanish music. Play a *corrido* or a *ranchera!*"

"Today's program features music from Andalusia," Ramón continued calmly. "Please be seated and enjoy our performance."

With a flourish and a sweep of his fingers, he made the guitar sing. Lola moved to the center of the room and clacked her heels, as she had once seen Spanish dancers do in a show.

"*Ole!*" cried Tío Gustavo.

"Brava! Brava!" shouted Don Francisco.

"She's usually such a quiet little thing," said Lola's father with a sigh. "It's only when she dances that she lights up like an electric bulb."

Tío Gustavo started to clap in time to the music and soon everyone joined in. Doña Antonia, caught between mirth and mortification, pursed her lips. Lola clicked and clacked, moving her hips like a pro, turning this way and that, twirling and twirling.

"Watch out!" shouted one of the men.

Lola was spinning like a top. I could see she was going to lose her balance.

Ramón played faster and faster, his fingers flying over the strings. Suddenly, the tail of Lola's skirt caught on something. She whipped around and extended her hand to yank it free from the cart with the liqueurs. The crystal decanters wobbled, teetered, and crashed to the floor with an earsplitting clatter. Splinters of expensive lead crystal cascaded over the floor, the ladies' gowns, and the carpet Ramón had pushed to the side. Port, sherry, and French liqueurs flowed in abandon over the wood, joining together in crevices and cracks, then finding their way into the fibers of the carpet. Antonia hid her face in her hands.

The guests sat stunned, immobile, silent. Meanwhile, the liqueurs continued to ooze through the floorboards.

Doña Antonia seemed to be searching for something to say. But she was speechless with embarrassment.

Without warning, Lola moved toward the center of the room and stood before her uncles. With consummate poise, she took a wide step, bent her front knee, brought her opposite foot behind her, and curtseyed.

Francisco I. Madero, the president of the Republic, bit his lip and bowed his head. Don Gustavo stared into space, his eyes bulging. His moustache twitched. His fleshy face convulsed into a snarl. He opened his mouth to say something. Then, he burst out laughing.

"I'm so… I'm so sorry," stammered Doña Antonia.

"Of course, we'll take care of…" spluttered Don Jesús Leonardo.

Don Gustavo wasn't listening. He was quaking with laughter. "Brava, Lola!" he shouted. "Brava, *hijita*! You are a real performer!" He shook his head. "Hard to believe she's only seven."

Don Francisco started to chuckle, and then, one by one, the guests began to roar with laughter. Lola took one bow after the other.

"I bet she'll be a movie star!" thundered Tío Gustavo.

"Over my dead body," mumbled Doña Antonia.

After the Samaniegos had left, I found Lola in the garden. She was singing to herself, clicking her heels to the rhythm of a flamenco number.

"Oh, we had so much fun tonight," she cooed. "My cousin Ramón brought costumes and his guitar from home, and we put on a show." She giggled. "Only the most awful thing happened…"

I cut her off. She'd ignored me all day, and I was furious. "Yes," I snapped. "You made a big mess in the smoking room. I was watching from the doorway. You can go ahead and laugh about it, but somebody had to clean up after you, you know. Tía Emi and I have been picking the glass splinters out of our knees for hours." I raised my skirt and showed her my bloody kneecaps. Snot was dripping from my nose, and tears were rolling down my cheeks.

Lola looked mortified. "I'm… I'm sorry… I didn't think…"

"No, you don't think. You just have fun and forget that the maids have to scrub the floors afterward. And by the way, that skirt you were dancing around in was horrible. You looked like a *puta en vacaciones*!"

She stood there staring at me. Ha! I thought. For once she had nothing to say.

I wasn't resentful because I had to clean the floor. I was jealous. I'd thought that Lola was *my* friend. Yet she'd spent the whole day with Ramón without thinking of me even once, I was sure. And there was something else, too. *Him*. Ramón. He was handsome and spirited, and he had the most beautiful smile. Why couldn't *I* be his friend, too? Why couldn't *I* be his cousin, instead of her? I knew these were silly thoughts. Tía Emi had said that these people were not "the same breed" as us. Even so, I could feel the green-eyed snake gnawing at my heart.

4

Mexico City, February 1913
Something Terrible Has Happened

Things were going from bad to worse. I could see that Don Francisco and Don Gustavo were worried. They were always grumpy now, and Don Francisco hardly touched the delicious *enchiladas de pollo* and *carne guisada* we made for him. So much the better, I thought. More for me. In Durango we ate worse than the dogs, but here in Mexico City, Doña Sara let us cook extra and eat whatever was left in the pot after she and Don Francisco had their midday meal.

I didn't like it when the men locked themselves in Don Francisco's office and howled. I could hear them through the door, and I guessed it had something to do with the newspapers.

"Now that they can publish whatever they goddamn please, they're attacking us right and left. They're biting the very hand that freed them," Don Gustavo growled. "You wanted freedom of the press, Paco, and this is how they thank you."

I listened and scrubbed and wished it were Sunday. Lola and I hadn't been mad at each other for a long time—over a year. Rage between little girls never lasts long, especially when there's no one else to play with. Whenever she came over, we'd find our old spot by the ahuehuete tree and tell secrets like before. The Samaniegos no longer visited. They'd moved to

California. The situation in Mexico was too dangerous, said
Don Mariano. He spoke English and could make it in Los
Angeles. People always needed a good dentist.

One day, Lola asked me, "What do you want to be when
you grow up? I want to be a ballerina!"

"Me, too!" I giggled. It was a stupid answer. I didn't even
know what a ballerina was.

"You're pretty enough to be a movie star, Mara," said Lola,
without a trace of mockery. I shrugged. I'd never seen a movie.

We laughed and played, but the grown-ups' worry had infested the air, and both Lola and I suspected that terrible things
were going on around us. What we didn't—and couldn't—
understand was that the tide had turned. The peasants had
flocked to Madero, spurred on by his promises of agrarian
reform, but now that he was in office, his base was cracking.
The followers of Villa and Zapata, once supporters of Madero,
now found him weak, and the conservatives resented his ea-
gerness to seek national reconciliation. All I knew was that the
streets were throbbing with rock-throwing protesters. Sometimes we weren't even allowed to go to school.

All the while, I could see that Lola was changing. She was
almost nine and becoming a señorita. Gone were the pudgy
cheeks and fingers. Her features had sharpened. Her forehead had grown broad and smooth, her eyes wide-set and
intelligent, her nose well defined, and her lips full. She'd become more self-confident and poised. She still conjugated her
French verbs and practiced her spins and leaps to the music of
the Victrola, and with her hair in ringlets fastened by wide
white bows and her dancer's slender body, she looked like a
princess-in-training.

I was changing, too. I could read and do simple arithmetic.
I knew enough English to ask about the weather and tell time.
In the evenings, Tía Emi taught me more advanced stitches,

and I could hem a skirt. Using scraps of thread, I embroidered my clothes with flowers and birds.

"You're going to be a good seamstress," Tía Emi told me. She'd become a little more expansive, a little less harsh. "You won't be shelling peas for a roof over your head when you're my age." She started to hum "The Ballad of Miguela Ruiz."

"If you hate shelling peas so much, why did you even come to this house?"

"A falta de pan, tortillas," she said. "You take what you can get."

She reached out and squeezed my wrist, and for a moment, I almost thought she liked me.

"Remember when we first came here?" I said, feeling brave. "You told Marcela you could get rid of me. What were you going to do with me? Were you going to kill me?"

Tía Emi burst out laughing. *"Puta madre,* child! You've got shit where your brain should be. Of course not!"

I imagined my skull full of dog excrement.

"I knew if they took me, they'd take you, too. How could you think I would kill you, you mouse-brain? I carried you all the way from Durango, didn't I?"

"Did you? I don't remember anything."

"Of course. Did you think you flew?"

"You didn't have to..." I hesitated.

She looked at me long and hard.

"Of course I had to," she said softly, and I think I actually heard tenderness in her voice.

After that, I didn't see Lola for a couple of weeks. The streets were wild with screaming workers and students—*Zapata! Zapata! Zapata!* Better not to venture out, warned Doña Sara.

Then something awful happened. The next time Lola and her parents came to see Don Francisco and Doña Sara, it was for a wake. A few days before... Well, this is what happened:

It was still light out, even though it was nearly five, and Lola was standing in the courtyard waiting for her nanny, Rosa, to pick her up from school. It had been a beautiful day, sunny and dry. February was the perfect month to jump rope in the school patio. The rains hadn't started yet, and every day was warm and pleasant. Happily, the nuns were nice about letting the children be children during the recreation. "After all," said Lola, imitating Sister Madeleine, *"on n'est enfant qu'une fois."* "You're only a child once." Now the girls weren't playing, though. They were lined up to go home. But where was Rosa? Lola watched as one girl after the other left the courtyard with her nanny.

She turned to Sister Madeleine. "Rosa is always on time. I wonder where she is."

"Don't worry. She'll be here," said the nun reassuringly in French.

It was growing dark. It was time for vespers. Lola was sure Sister Madeleine wouldn't leave her alone in the yard, but still…she wanted to go home. Where was the *niñera*?

Sister Françoise came out to get Sister Madeleine for the evening prayer. *"Viens,"* she said, signaling to Lola, *"toi aussi."* Lola followed the nuns into the convent chapel adjacent to the school. She knelt beside them and sang: *Deus, in adiutorium meum intende. Domine, ad adiuvandum me festina…* "O God, come to my assistance. O Lord, make haste to help me…"

After vespers, she listened as Sister Madeleine read from Saint Teresa's *Camino de perfección* in French. An hour later, they all sat down in the refectory for a light supper. Lola forced her lips not to tremble. She tightened her jaw and ate the meager meal. What could have happened? Had her family forgotten her? Had they abandoned her? Several girls lived at the convent. Was she going to be a boarder, too?

"Can you send a messenger to my house?" Lola was fighting back tears. She loved the nuns and knew she was safe with them, but she had never spent a night away from her mother.

"Of course," said Sister Madeleine, this time in Spanish. "We will find someone to go."

The bell clanged at the entrance to the convent. Maybe it was Rosa. Maybe she had been delayed by a commotion in the street or maybe...maybe something had happened to Mami or Papi. Lola held her breath. At last the *tornera*—the door-keeper—appeared at the entrance to the refectory accompanied by a woman.

But it wasn't Rosa. It was Doña Antonia. She was disheveled and unsteady on her feet. Her blue shawl was thrown around her shoulders as a protection against the evening air, but she had carelessly forgotten to fasten it with a brooch. Her hair had worked its way loose from her bun and flew out in all directions. Her eyes were red and swollen.

Lola knew she should curtsey and say, *Bon soir, Maman*, but instead, she ran to her mother wailing. "I was afraid something had happened to you!"

"Nothing has happened to me," said Doña Antonia calmly. "And nothing has happened to Papá. But something has happened." She was forcing her voice to be steady.

Doña Antonia disappeared into a small parlor with Sister Madeleine. When she reappeared, both women were pallid.

Doña Antonia took her daughter by the hand and left the convent. When they arrived home, Papá was sitting at his secretary writing a letter.

"What's wrong?" Lola blurted out. "What happened? Why won't anyone tell me?"

Don Jesús Leonardo put down his pen and went into the parlor. "Come here," he said gently. "Mami and I have to explain something."

Doña Antonia was standing in the arched doorway, a look of resignation on her face. She reminded Lola of the Virgin of Guadalupe in her niche.

Don Jesús Leonardo pulled Lola to him and sat her on his knee. "Tío Gustavo has been killed," he said simply.

"Killed?" Lola felt her hands tremble. Tears burned her cheeks.

A long, piercing pause. A halting sigh.

"Some very bad men who don't want democracy to triumph in Mexico..."

That's all he said. How could he tell her the whole story? Could he explain that Victoriano Huerta, now commander of the armed forces, had conspired with Porfirio Díaz's nephew against Madero, and that Huerta had had Gustavo kidnapped off the street, locked up inside the Gambrinus restaurant, and then tortured and murdered? Could he tell her that Doña Antonia, upon hearing of her cousin's death, collapsed on the floor unconscious? Could he tell her that while she was waiting for Rosa in the courtyard of the Colegio Francés, her mother was lying in the hospital in a state of shock?

As Lola recounted the story, I could see it all unfolding in my mind—Tío Gustavo sprawled on the ground, a bullet hole in his head, his spectacular pompadour steeped in blood and mud. Lola sobbing. Jesús Leonardo cradling his little girl in his arms and soothing her, carrying her to her bedroom and tucking her in.

What none of us knew at the time, or could possibly suspect, was that three days later, we would be going through it all again. On February 18, Huerta staged a coup d'état and took over the presidency of Mexico. Then, a few days later, he had Lola's Tío Paco taken out and shot.

"*Puta madre!*" moaned Tía Emi. "Next they'll come after everyone in the household."

She grabbed a pillowcase from Doña Sara's linen closet and stuffed her few possessions into it. "Get your stuff together," she barked. "We can't stay here!"

Before I knew it, we were out on the road again, this time headed north.

PART II

5

Los Angeles, 1913–1920
Learning to Breathe

It's funny how you have such a clear picture of certain things in your mind—even things that didn't actually happen to you, like the scene at the Colegio Francés the day that Don Gustavo died—while other things just disappear from memory. It's like they never even happened, even though you know they did, they must have, because afterward, everything is different. Take, for example, the trek from Mexico City to Los Angeles. I don't remember much, only a few gruesome scenes: a man with his eyes gouged out hanging from a tree, a dog with a human foot in its mouth. At the edge of a village a pretty little girl, probably a landowner's daughter, all dressed up in a lacy dress with a pink sash and shiny black shoes. She could have been on her way to a party...except that she had no head. They'd cut it off and placed it on her lap, propped her up on a rock, probably as some kind of warning. I didn't scream. I didn't vomit. I just stared at her—a little girl like me, like Lola, like Anita or any of the girls in my class. But dead. Headless. After that, I kept my eyes to the ground. I took one step after the other without looking up. I forced myself to go numb. Yet even now, after all these years, the image of that child returns to me when I least expect it. It makes me shud-

der. I think of my own children, my grandchildren, and...
and...the tears just come...

The ground was so hot, it burned through our sandals as
we fled. It smelled like scorched tortillas. At some point, Tía
Emi gave a man a few coins to let us ride his donkey. He had
two. One he rode, and the other he led with a rope. Tía Emi
and I crawled up on the second one, she in front, me behind
her with my arms wrapped around her waist. I rested my head
on her back, and I guess I fell asleep because the rest is pretty
much a blur until we got to the Río Bravo—what Americans
call the Rio Grande, but that doesn't make any sense at all
because it's not *grande*. In fact, it's so narrow and shallow that
we waded across it in the moonlight with no trouble at all.

Once we made it to El Paso, Tía Emi spent another couple
of coins, this time for a ride on a rickety train to Los Angeles.
I was worried because I knew she didn't have many pieces of
copper, even though she'd saved every *centavo* that Doña Sara
paid her. I'd never been on a train before, and I stared out the
window at the wide, dry landscape, afraid we were going to
hit a rut in the track, and I was going to land on the floor.

The ride took more than a day. At last we were in Los Angeles, a sprawling mass of nothing. Tía Emi pressed the pillowcase containing everything she owned to her chest, and
we ventured out into the street. The sounds were recogniz-
able, yet different. The clip-clop of horses' hooves against
cobblestone, the clang of a streetcar, the scream of a policeman's whistle, the beep of a claxon—all that was familiar, but
not the clipped syllables and lazy vowels of English. Words I
might have recognized in a schoolbook were unintelligible
when they gushed from people's mouths. Floods of words that
all ran together—heybuddygedoudamyway! And then I'd hear
a familiar syllable or two—*¿quiubo, mano?*—that dangled in
the air like a priceless ornament, only to dissolve into the din.

As we stopped to take it in, I became aware of my own breathing, my chest expanding and contracting unevenly. My inhalation felt shallow, as though I was afraid to draw in this new, unfamiliar air. The sky was blue, but as though seen through a faintly smoky glass. The odor of horse dung mingled with cumin and chili, just like at home, but there were strange aromas as well—aromas I would eventually learn were of sauerkraut and frankfurters, corn fritters and roasted peanuts, collards and fried catfish—the wares of street vendors and eateries in this bustling corner of Los Angeles. I'd never seen so many snow-white arms, so many straw-colored heads, all in one place. And I'd never seen so many Black faces. Los Angeles was a relatively small city, with less than six hundred thousand inhabitants, while Mexico City had over a million. But there, most people were different shades of coffee, while here, the variety of hues, from vanilla to espresso, was astounding.

"*¡Hola, mana!*" The woman who stood before us looked Mexican and spoke Spanish, but the way Tía Emi peered at her through the slits of her half-closed Chalchiuhtlicue eyes made it clear she didn't trust her.

She had a boardinghouse, she said. Were we looking for a place to stay?

"*¿Cuánto?*"

"One dollar a week. That includes meals."

"I don't have that kind of money."

"You will. Besides, there's two of you."

I waited for Tía Emi to say she could get rid of me, but instead she said, "She doesn't eat much. She's a little thing."

"She can work. She'll help pay for the room."

What Tía Emi said next left me dumbstruck. "She's not going to work. She's going to go to school. She already knows how to read."

"Well, fuck," said the potential landlady. "Been here ten minutes and already putting on airs!"

Tía Emi held her ground. "I'll give you eighty cents, and even that is a lot for us."

"No puedo," said the women, but in the end, she gave in.

We followed her to a ramshackle, one-story house in a seedy-looking neighborhood. She shoved us into a room not much bigger than an outhouse, but at least, she said, we wouldn't have to share it with anyone. Her name was Nuria.

"I get paid in advance, the first Sunday of the month. You can pay me now."

Tía Emi took out her coins.

"What's that crap?" said Nuria, scowling. "That's not real money. José the money changer will take care of you. He takes his cut, of course, but it's not too much."

Tía Emi picked up her pillowcase. "I don't think so," she said. She took my hand and we walked back to the train station. On the way, she didn't say a word.

Well, I wanted to ask. What now? But it was clear she was in no mood for talking.

The station was full of people running in every direction. I eyed a stand where a man was selling what looked like twisted bits of bread. They smelled good.

"I can't buy anything," Tía Emi said. "All I have is Mexican coins, and they won't take them." She pulled a dry tortilla from her pillowcase and handed it to me.

We wandered around the station looking for a bench to sleep on, but we wound up settling against a wall in a little corridor where brooms and buckets were kept.

"You sleep," said Tía Emi. "If I close my eyes, someone will steal the pillowcase."

"We can take turns," I offered.

"You think you're going to fight off some motherfucking

thug for me? You really do have shit where your brain should be." But she laughed gently and squeezed my wrist.

She must have dozed off anyway, because the next thing I remember was screams.

"You bastard! You son of a bitch! I shit on the mother who gave birth to you!"

I opened my eyes in time to see a boy in a shabby sombrero disappearing behind a corner, the pillowcase dangling from his fist. The sun was just coming up. Dusty rays were creeping through the huge station doors.

I started to cry. Tía Emi bopped me on the head.

"*¡Puta madre!*" she said. "What's the point of sniveling?" She was laughing.

"What's the point of laughing?" I rubbed the back of my skull. "He just ran off with everything we own."

"Yeah, but imagine the surprise of the *pendejo* when he opens the sack and finds there's nothing in it but a couple of ragged shifts and the used bloomers I stole from Doña Sara."

I imagined the boy holding up the bloomers, sniffing them, and vomiting into a trash bin.

"What about the money?"

"It's in my blouse. You got your stuff?"

I'd wrapped a change of clothes into a little bundle, which I used as a pillow. We stumbled out into the street. Nuria was there again, offering her squalid room to newly arrived Mexicans. Apparently, she had no takers, because a few minutes later she caught sight of us and came ambling over.

"Listen," she said. "You look like an honest person, and in my business, I have to be careful. I'll take your Mexican money, and I'll help you find a job." She smiled broadly. Her teeth were yellow, crooked, and tinged with black, like the kernels of a rotting ear of corn.

Tía Emi thought about it a moment, but we didn't have many options.

"Está bien," she said finally, "but I won't give you a *centavo* until you find me work, and they pay me."

Nuria looked Tía Emi up and down. "I don't think you'll get much for that sack of bones. You look like you've got cobwebs in your cunt." Then she looked at me. "But maybe the baby…"

"We're not whoring her out. *Me cago en la leche.*" Whenever Tía Emi didn't like something, she'd say, *"Me cago en la leche,"* "I shit in the milk." What sense did that make? I didn't ask. Nuria shrugged, and we followed her back to the house.

Breakfast, *comida,* and supper at Nuria's were rice and beans, just like in Durango, but at least we had a roof over our heads. Within a few days, Nuria found us a job cleaning floors and toilets in a beauty shop—in those days, we said "beauty parlor"—about three miles away, an easy walk. For the moment, there was no more talk of school, and I began to think that Tía Emi had mentioned it just to get Nuria to lower the price of the room.

The owners of the shop told the customers they were from Paris because it seemed more elegant. I guess they thought that to Americans, all foreign accents sounded the same. But I knew they were lying, because I'd hear them arguing in the back room, and the language they were speaking wasn't French. I'd heard Lola speak French, and it sounded different. They called themselves Mr. Edmond and Miss Kathy, although I don't think those were their real names. I once asked Mr. Edmond where they were from.

"We have to pretend we're French," he said. "Women aren't going to pay to have their hair cut by a Romanian." He winked and patted me on the head.

Mr. Edmond spoke some Spanish, which, he said, wasn't

that different from his native language. "You say *casa,*" he said.
"We say *casă.* It's almost the same."

They paid us seven cents an hour, and we worked from
seven in the morning until seven at night. We thought it was
a good deal. Tía Emi was able to pay Nuria on time and buy
us both something we had never had before: hairbrushes.

I couldn't believe the things ladies did to their hair. Some
of them had it rolled up into ringlets or twisted into elaborate
updos, with braids coiled into neat buns on either side. Most
ladies had their hair arranged at home by servants, but Mr.
Edmond bought advertisements in newspapers to expand business, and it had worked. "The latest styles, right from Paris!"
he advertised. "The most advanced techniques in hair styling!" Usually customers—in those days, we called them "patrons"—had their hair washed at home, before they came to
the beauty parlor. (Back then, people only washed their hair
about once a month.) Sometimes they brought in copies of
Photoplay, the new film magazine, to show the hairdressers—
we called them "beauty operators"—the hairdos they wanted.
Mr. Edmond didn't believe in cutting ladies' hair. For a bob, a
lady would have to go to a barbershop. But he could dye hair
with the exotic new German coloring products he ordered.
Only Mr. Edmond was allowed to apply color, and he did it
very carefully, like a seamstress embroidering a delicate gown.

Soon we started hearing rumors that Mr. Edmond was
going to open another shop, this one in Hollywood, on Las
Palmas Avenue, and that he would be offering a new hair
treatment called a "permanent." It would take all day and cost
nearly a hundred dollars!

"I hear he's going to transfer his most accomplished girls
over there," whispered Miss Marie, breathless. "He's going to
have a trainer come in to teach us to apply permanent wave

lotion. Everything will be different at the new place. Modern and glamorous!"

I noticed she said "teach *us* to apply permanent wave lotion." Miss Marie had studied at the Marinello School of Beauty in Chicago and clearly thought she would be chosen.

"He'll definitely take Elaine," whispered Miss Marie to one of the other operators. "He's got his eye on her, if you know what I mean. Someday I'll have my own shop and won't have to put up with pigs like him."

To our amazement, when Mr. Edmond finally made the official announcement, the first ones chosen for the new shop were Tía Emi and me.

"The place has to be spotless," he said. "You're good workers, and I can depend on you." He turned to Tía Emi. "Maybe you could even learn to brush out the wigs." In those days, women used hairpieces to fill out their hairstyles.

"Yo no quiero ser peluquera," said Tía Emi, a little too imperiously for a toilet cleaner. "I don't want to be a hairdresser."

Brushing out hairpieces is better than cleaning toilets, I thought. Tía Emi should be happy. I remembered when I used to comb Lola's hair and tie it into fancy plaits.

"I could brush out the wigs," I whispered. But no one was paying attention.

Apparently, Mr. Edmond hadn't consulted Miss Kathy about his decision, because she jumped into the conversation and asked Tía Emi if she knew how to cook.

"Claro que sí," said Tía Emi. "I was the cook for the president of Mexico."

That wasn't exactly true. She was a kitchen maid who helped prepare meals, peeling potatoes and shucking corn.

"I need a housemaid," said Miss Kathy, "to cook and clean and take the dog for walks."

"How much?"

"Four dollars a week, plus room and board. A half day off on Sunday. Mara can keep on working at the shop."

"Mara has to go to school."

I flinched. How did Tía Emi have the gall to make demands? And when did she suddenly remember that I had to go to school? School seemed to come up only when she was trying to negotiate a better deal for us.

"You're right," said Miss Kathy, to my amazement. "There's a grammar school near the house. She can go there, and after school, she can work in the new salon. It's walking distance."

I didn't realize at the time that elementary school had become mandatory in California.

"I'd like to learn to brush out the wigs," I piped in.

Mr. Edmond smiled. "You'd make a wonderful operator, Mara," he said. "You're very beautiful yourself. You could even be a model."

"Actually, I'm a *costurera*," said Tía Emi dryly. "A seamstress."

"Really? Do you know how to make a dress with a pattern?"

"I don't need a pattern."

Miss Kathy looked skeptical. "If I bring you a piece of cloth, could you make me something?"

At the end of the week, Tía Emi paid Nuria what she owed her and told her we were leaving. Nuria spat in the sink and shrugged.

"Too good for this place now that you've made a few bucks at the beauty shop *I* found for you, right?" she hissed.

"Right," said Tía Emi.

We traipsed the three miles to Mr. Edmond's beauty shop, the old one, not the new one. He told us to get our things together and climb into his automobile, a Dodge Touring with soft black leather seats and a top that you could open or close, depending on the weather. Miss Marie and Miss Elaine

were already in the car that would take us to the new shop…
I mean *salon*. We were supposed to say *beauty salon,* not shop.
I'd never been in an automobile before, and I was terrified.
There wasn't much traffic, but as the car wove its way through
boulevards filled with horse-drawn carriages and other motorcars, hitting runnels and bumps, swerving this way and that
to avoid pedestrians, peddlers, cyclists, and animals, I held my
breath. I'd never seen such a world—roads lined with crimson oleanders or towering palm trees that looked too slender
to withstand a gust of wind. Bright green lawns, manicured
and endlessly hosed. Lovely Spanish-style villas, with stucco
walls and wrought iron fences. Lush gardens, with orange trees
bulging with fruit. On the horizon, low-lying hills dotted here
and there with graceful mansions. It all seemed unreal. The
salon was at the end of a residential street that abutted a new
and burgeoning business district with elegant dress boutiques
and an Italian shoe shop called Ferragamo's.

That evening, Tía Emi and I went home with Mr. Edmond
and Miss Kathy in the Dodge Touring. They lived in a yellow
stucco duplex with an orange tree in the front yard. It was
not a grandiose house, but they'd converted the garage into
a bedroom, which was to be ours. It was the largest room I'd
ever slept in, and it had a window. In the morning, the sun's
rays danced along the windowsill and nestled in the folds of
the curtains, then scattered among the floor tiles, illuminating the clay inlays. I was in paradise.

Miss Kathy's dog was a poodle named Yap. Tía Emi refused to go near it, so it was my job to walk it in the morning. I didn't like the idea. I had never lived in a house with a
dog, and I didn't know what it might do to me. It was a little
thing, and it had curly white hair with poofs on the top of its
head, the tip of its tail, and its ankles—a ridiculous-looking
animal. In Durango I'd seen farm dogs, stately and serious,

dogs with a job. You didn't play with those dogs. You stayed out of their way. In the city, I'd seen guard dogs, dogs that meant business, dogs that protected homes or shops. But this dog was different. Miss Kathy picked it up and cooed over it as though it were a baby. She had no children, so I guess that's why.

The school was nothing like my school in Mexico. Boys and girls sat together in the same classroom, and no one wore a uniform. There were all kinds of kids—rich, poor, and in-between. In Mexico, girls like Lola went to fancy private *colegios*, but in those days, there were no private *colegios* in Los Angeles, aside from parish schools. Bells told you what to do—when to come in, when to have lunch, when to leave. I was always hungry because instead of a big midday meal, we ate *lunch*, a snack you brought in a cloth bag and ate out in the patio instead of going home and taking a siesta. Worst of all, you had to speak English all day.

One day a girl named Clara asked me for a pencil. *"Psst, ¿me prestas un lápiz?"*

Pum! My skull smarted as though someone had lit a fire-cracker in my hair. My eyes filled with tears. I turned quickly enough to catch sight of my teacher, Miss Grunwald, a ruler with an edge as sharp as a blade in her hand.

"No Spanish," she snarled.

"Yes, ma'am," I whispered.

Clara and I were told to leave the room and stand in the hall. I was only a kid, but I already understood that Mexican was not a good thing to be.

After that, I was careful. I stayed away from Clara. I remembered how Lola had practiced French pronunciation when she was with the Sisters of Saint Joseph, sitting in front of a mirror for hours at a time, shaping her lips just so, placing her tongue just so. I began to get up earlier than usual so I'd have time to practice my English. "Yes, not jes," I told myself. "Sheet, sheeeet, sheeeeet, not shit." I'd grown to like Yap. He was playful. He jumped up and down when he saw me take the leash off the hook for his walk. I began to speak to him in English. "Come here, Jap… I mean Yap. Seeet dow'." He was generous. He never made fun of my pronunciation. That's the nice thing about dogs. They're forgiving.

At the shop, I sometimes helped Miss Marie when she was giving a permanent, passing her end papers and rollers, and I asked her to correct my English when I made a mistake. When I had a free moment, I'd go into the back room, where they had a couch and copies of *Photoplay* and *Modern Priscilla*, and I'd read them aloud to myself. Learning English felt like learning to fly! At first, I flapped my wings and nothing happened, and then, suddenly, I could feel myself lifting off—making sentences, paragraphs even! I was soaring!

At school, I could answer questions in class. The popular girls let me jump rope with them. It helped that they thought I was pretty. I still stayed away from Clara. She was a poor little brown-skinned thing, with pigtails and ragged clothes. Now I feel ashamed, but back then, all I wanted was to fit in.

At first, things didn't go so well for Tía Emi. Miss Kathy was not impressed with her cooking. Mr. Edmond's favorite dish was *sărmăluțe în foi de viță*, vine leaves stuffed with ground pork and topped with a cream sauce, but Tía Emi couldn't make it. She resorted to serving *enchiladas de pollo* whether they liked it or not, and Mr. Edmond started eating out more and more.

It went a little better with the sewing. Tía Emi made Miss Kathy a few serviceable skirts and blouses, and Miss Kathy thanked her and paid her extra. Eventually, Tía Emi learned to make uniforms for the operators and chemises and petticoats for Miss Kathy.

We settled into an easy routine, with Tía Emi cleaning, sewing, and preparing Mexican delicacies in the kitchen, and me going to school and working in the salon.

Before I knew it, I was in sixth grade. I was taller than Tía Emi, and I'd begun to fill out. Boys had begun to notice me, especially Nick Wasserman, the cutest boy in the class. Sometimes he walked me home. "Stay away from him," hissed Tía Emi when she caught sight of him. "I already raised one kid who isn't my own. I'm not going to raise another one."

"What are you talking about? All he did was carry my books."

"That's how it starts. You must be about eleven already. Going on twelve. You have to be careful."

Suddenly, Tía Emi looked ugly to me. I hate her! I thought. She's stupid. She can't even speak English.

"How come *you* don't have a boyfriend?" I snapped. "You're not *that* old."

Tía Emi just stood there staring at me with her stone-hard Chalchiuhtlicue eyes. "I know about boyfriends." Then she turned and went into the kitchen.

"Why don't you come with me?" Mr. Edmond said one night when he was leaving the shop… I mean *salon*. "I'll teach you how to drink wine." I figured he was teasing and ignored it.

The customers at Mr. Edmond's new salon were stylish. The most daring had ditched their corsets and wore loose-fitting tunics that draped gracefully over the body. Some were movie actresses or the wives of rich businessmen. I wanted to be like them. I didn't want to wear the simple jumpers and skirts Tía Emi made me. The shop was full of mirrors, and I began to study my own image. What I saw was a ridiculous-looking kid with braids and a cheap peasant skirt. The girls at school—

at least the popular ones—wore store-bought, drop-waisted sailor frocks or frilly blouses with puffed sleeves.

"It seems frivolous to be thinking about clothes when a war's going on," Miss Kathy said when she noticed me reading a fashion magazine.

"What war?" I asked. I'd heard people whisper about the possibility of war, but I hadn't heard any shots or seen corpses lying in the road, so I didn't pay much attention. I didn't read newspapers. I didn't go to the movies and see the newsreels. I had no brothers who were going to be shipped off somewhere. Besides, I was eleven, and when you're eleven, what interests you most is your own life, not what's happening to other people.

"Not here," said Miss Kathy. "In Europe. Germany against France and England. But now the Americans are probably going to get involved, too, fighting against the Germans."

I didn't see what that had to do with me. But then I thought, what if the Germans barge into the beauty shop and grab Mr. Edmond, the way the Huertistas went after Don Gustavo and Don Francisco?

I must have looked worried because Miss Kathy said, "It's far, far away, Mara, but eventually, Americans will have to tighten their belts to support the war effort."

I imagined the ladies who came into the shop tightening their belts until their faces turned blue and their eyes bulged like frogs'. It was scary.

"I know about war," I said. "We had a war in Mexico. That's why we left."

I'd already decided that I didn't want to be a seamstress like Tía Emi. I wanted to be a beauty operator like Miss Marie. I wanted people to call me Miss Mara, and I wanted to have a job, earn money, feel important.

Mr. Edmond liked to watch me work. "You'll be a wonderful operator someday, Mara," he said. "And you're so pretty. That's important. Your own looks are your best advertisement. Why don't you let Miss Marie do your hair?"

That evening, I went home with a glamorous updo. Miss Marie had pinned a form around the back of my head and swept my hair into a soft roll that went from one side to the other. I felt very grown-up.

Tía Emi took one glance at me and exploded in laughter.

"¡Puta madre! You look like a monkey with a turd on its head!"

I froze. "You're just jealous!" I screamed. "I hate you!"

"I think she looks lovely," said Mr. Edmond from behind me. "She's a beautiful girl. Anyhow, I'm the one who told Marie to put up her hair."

Miss Kathy and Tía Emi exchanged glances.

I went to the room I shared with Tía Emi and brushed it all out.

By the time I turned fourteen, in 1920, the war had been over for two years, and Marcel curls were the rage. I figured that as soon as I finished eighth grade, I'd work full-time for Mr. Edmond. He'd promised to let me apprentice with Miss Marie.

"You'll have to learn to marcel the hair," he said, running his fingers through my waves and twisting strands around his thumb as though it were a curling iron. His touch felt like a feather flicking across my skin. He smiled and winked, and I felt giddy.

A couple of days after that, Miss Kathy and Tía Emi were sitting at the kitchen table when I came home from school, drinking coffee and smoking. It struck me as odd. What was Miss Kathy doing home so early? And when did she become so cozy with Tía Emi? Doña Verónica and Doña Sara never sat in the kitchen schmoozing with servants.

"¡Puta madre! If he ever lays one finger on her," Tía Emi

was saying, "I'll string him up by the balls, then hang him on some cactus so the vultures can peck out his eyes."

"I'll help you," said Miss Kathy.

I imagined Mr. Edmond naked, strung up by the balls on a big desert cactus with thick prickly green arms. I felt sorry for him.

Then, out of the blue, Miss Kathy announced that she'd found Tía Emi a position with an acquaintance of hers, a lady who came into the salon once in a while, a *couturière*—"That means dress designer," she explained—who needed an assistant. "It's a wonderful opportunity for both of you," she concluded.

"But I can keep on working at the salon, can't I?" Her words had thrown me off-balance.

"No. You and Emi will live with Madame Isabelle. There's a high school nearby."

High school? "I thought I was going to apprentice with Miss Marie."

"You can apprentice with Madame Isabelle. You can learn to sew her designs and create elegant dresses! Besides, you'll meet actresses… She makes costumes for films. And at the same time, you can go to high school."

"No!" I screamed. I threw down my books and ran into the garage.

But by the following fall, I was registered for classes at Gilmore Secondary School.

6

It had been twelve years since I'd seen Lola, and to be honest, I'd pretty much forgotten all about her. That's why, when she tapped me on the shoulder as I was leaving the studio canteen, I had to do a double take.

"Mara!" she gasped. "Is it really you? I thought so! I'd recognize that beautiful brown hair anywhere!"

We hugged and kissed each other on the cheek.

"I'm so happy to see you, Mara!"

"Me, too," I murmured. And I was. Of course I was. It's just that it had been such a long time. I'd thought I'd never see her again. I was taken aback. She seemed so…how can I say it?…so different, and yet, not really. She was all dressed up, very stylish, but I knew enough about fabric to realize that her clothes were not expensive. Still, her hair and makeup were perfect. She talked and moved…not exactly like a movie star… but like she seemed to think a movie star ought to talk and move. She's still playing the diva, I thought, just like when we were little.

Before I knew it, she'd dragged me into the green room and launched into a long, breathless story:

"With a sweeping movement, she stretches her arms to the

heavens as though preparing for flight." She closed her eyes as if she were reliving the scene. "Fingers fluttering like feathers, she circles the stage *en pointe*. But then, with an elevation of the elbows, her powerful wings wilt into fragile plumes. She bows her head and folds her wrists across her breast as she turns and rotates in the tiny, close steps of a pas de bourrée. She seems to be sinking into her own soul, detaching herself from all that is earthly. Her legs and arms quiver. Her shoulders hunch slightly, as she continues her descent into darkness. She is a cloud of feathers, as ethereal as a seraph. Gracefully, she extends her right leg and bends her left knee. Then, slowly, she crumples over her outstretched limb. The quivering ceases. The strains of Saint-Saëns's *Le Cygne* fade to silence. The swan is dead. I caught my breath. Tears were trickling down my cheeks. The other spectators leaped to their feet applauding wildly, even though the figure on the screen couldn't hear their accolades. 'Brava, Pavlova!' they screamed. 'Brava, Anna Pavlova!'"

Lola stopped talking and stared at me. What was I supposed to say? Did she expect me to be impressed?

"Ah," I muttered finally. "So that's what you were doing while I was sweeping floors and scrubbing toilets all these years. Watching pretty girls flit across the screen in tutus." I *had* been happy to see her, but now I felt irritated. You'd think she would ask me what *I'd* been doing all this time. But no, blah blah blah about this damn Russian ballerina.

"She was so beautiful, Mara," Lola murmured. "I wanted to dance just like her, to be in a movie just like her! I wanted to *be her*! Anna Pavlova is the greatest ballerina in the world, and imagine, we were able to see her right there in Mexico at the cinema!

"Once we got out in the street, I floated along as though in a trance. I started to chant, 'I want to be a ballerina! I want to be a ballerina!' It had rained while we were in the movie theater, and the air smelled so clean and crisp. The buildings sparkled in the artificial light of the streetlamps. Horses trotted by, splashing muddy water onto the passersby who were maneuvering this way and that to skirt puddles. I struggled loose from Mami's hand and twirled like a dervish. 'Lola!' Mami snapped. 'Stop it! You can't prance around in the street like that!'"

"How adorable," I said sarcastically. But she was too absorbed in her story to notice.

"I said to Mami, 'If Papá says I can study ballet, will you let me?' Then I said, 'Papá, would you let me study ballet? If I study Mexican dance as well, will you say yes? If I don't play the Victrola too loud… If I if I ifIifIifI…'"

Lola started to giggle. "Fortunately, Papá took my side. He said that dance is good for girls, that it teaches them grace and poise. Mami argued that a señorita from a good family should never perform in public, but Papá said that God had blessed them with only one daughter, and he wasn't going to deprive her of anything. 'Find the best dance teacher around,' he said. 'If she's going to study dance, let her learn it right.'"

"I finished high school," I said dryly. "Did you?"

Lola stopped talking and opened her eyes wide, as though she'd just realized I was there.

"With honors. Straight As in English. The teacher said I had a marvelous imagination."

Lola looked wounded. "I'm sorry, Mara. I didn't mean to go on and on…"

"But you *are* going on and on."

I really didn't want to hurt her. "So what happened?" I said after an awkward pause. "You took dancing lessons and then?" I hoped she'd make it short.

"Yes, with Felipita López, a very famous teacher. Ballet,

flamenco, traditional Mexican folk dance. I was good at it. They said my extensions were the highest, my pliés were the deepest...but you probably don't care."

She was right. I didn't care, but I didn't want to sound nasty, so I said, "So how did you get to be Dolores Del Rio instead of Dolores Asúnsolo? How did you get to Hollywood?"

She bit the knuckle of her index finger and looked down. "Are you sure you want to know?" I'd deflated her balloon.

"Go ahead," I said, not sounding too enthusiastic.

It had all started, she explained, when the ladies from the Hospital Auxiliary asked Doña Antonia to give permission for Lola to dance at their fundraiser. Of course Doña Antonia refused. "It's not for some cheap cabaret," the ladies assured her. "It's for a worthy cause, and only the best people will be there."

Lola turned the story into a performance, mimicking her mother, stone-faced and stubborn, and the snooty Hospital Auxiliary ladies with their noses in the air. She's good at what she does, I thought. She really is an actress.

Well, Doña Antonia was in a bind. She didn't want to anger these ladies, but on the other hand, she didn't want her daughter performing for an audience, even an upper-crust audience. Finally, she agreed to put it to the nuns at the *colegio*.

"To Mamá's horror, my teachers were delighted," Lola twittered. "'A hospital benefit? God's work!' said Sister Madeleine." She did the nun's voice with a thick French accent.

Still, Doña Antonia resisted. She put off calling the dressmaker to design Lola's costume. She forgot to buy new castanets. Finally, Lola threatened to do it all herself.

"Mami was perplexed," said Lola, laughing. "Where was her obedient little girl? Although, secretly, I think she was happy to see me so determined."

The outfits were another issue. Lola wanted a tight, ruffled, Andalusian dress for the flamenco number, but Doña Antonia insisted on something more discreet. But then, halfway through rehearsals, she changed her mind. Lola would need a sleek, formfitting dress after all, she decided, one that showed off her tiny waist and blossoming curves. She would need a gentle décolletage and short sleeves that revealed her graceful arms. She would need a flattering, curved heel that highlighted her beautiful calves. Why? With her sharp feline senses, Doña Antonia had noticed that the event organizer, Jaime Martínez del Río y Viñent, one of the richest men in Mexico, attended every rehearsal and couldn't take his eyes off her daughter.

"Ah…del Río," I said. "You married him!"

"Wait!" Lola tittered. "I'll tell you *everything!*"

She plunged back into her story. She made Don Jaime sound like the *príncipe azul*, Prince Charming. At thirty-four, he was a jet-setter and a smooth talker. His family had hung on to their cotton plantations during the Revolution, and now the money was rolling in. Men were back from the war, and everybody needed clothes. The Americans weren't producing enough cloth to fill orders, which put the Martínez del Río y Viñent family in an excellent position. Jaime played the part of rich landholder to the hilt. His father looked on indulgingly when Jaime showed off his English suits and Italian ties. He never demanded that his son sit by his side and learn the hard lessons of running a business. "Let him have fun," he said. "The kid has no head for numbers, anyway."

Jaime smoked black cigarillos in long, jewel-encrusted cigarette holders and had never been married. People said he was "puffy"—back then, we didn't use the word *gay*—but Lola brushed it off. "He's artistic," she said, whenever people made insinuations. "He wants to be a scriptwriter."

She lowered her voice as if confiding a secret. "When I rehearsed, I felt his gaze on my body, caressing my neck like the quivering wing of a butterfly. I began to dance only for him. I imagined him touching my earlobes, my elbows. These are things I can tell only you, Mara."

Jaime exuded a charisma that Lola found irresistible. A man of dazzling arrogance who moved with the self-confidence of a bullfighter. He wasn't handsome. He was balding, and his elegance verged on ostentatiousness, but Lola didn't seem to mind.

Neither did Doña Antonia. For her, Jaime was a catch because class and wealth were everything. He had inherited a fortune—vast land holdings and cash—and for a man like that, you could overlook certain things. You could choose not to hear certain rumors.

Lola didn't need her mother's encouragement to flash her huge brown eyes at Don Jaime del Río. She didn't need Doña Antonia to show her how to thrust her shoulder forward and tilt her head provocatively. At almost sixteen, she was already a sensuous creature.

"One day during a break, he said to me, 'What a lovely bolero. You know, the bolero is a dance of seduction.' 'I'm—I'm not trying to seduce anybody,' I stammered. 'No?' he said. 'How disappointing. I was hoping you were trying to seduce me!' 'Well,' I said, 'you certainly think you're the last bean in the chili pot!' 'And *you* certainly know how to make a man feel like yesterday's tortillas!' he responded."

I knew I was supposed to laugh, but I didn't. "Do you know how to make a Marcel curl?" I said suddenly. "It's quite a demanding process. First, you have to heat the curling iron. Next, you slide it down a strand of hair to warm it. Then, you roll the hair around the iron... You know, you haven't stopped talking about yourself all afternoon. You're putting on a show where you're not only the leading lady but all the bit players besides."

She pursed her lips. "You asked me about my marriage," she whispered. She looked contrite. "I was so happy to see a friend from home that I…"

She'd called me a *friend*. Suddenly, I felt sorry. During those early years in Los Angeles, my mind was on school, work, learning to marcel hair. Kids live in the moment, not in the past. But then, the memories came tumbling back to me— those hours under the ahuehuete tree, the confidences, the giggles. Memories I cherished. Lola was the first real friend I'd ever had, and I still loved her. She hasn't changed, I thought. She still thinks she's the center of the universe…but she's the one who taught me the meaning of friendship. I have to accept her as she is.

"I'm just exhausted," I said. "I work at a beauty salon called Marie's. I used to work at Edmond's, but when Mr. Edmond started paying too much attention to me, Tía Emi yanked me out of there. Miss Marie was one of Edmond's operators, and she hired me when she bought her own shop. I like her. She's flexible. Tía Emi is assistant to a costume designer named Madame Isabelle, and Marie lets me take a day off once in a while to help Tía Emi when there's a crunch. I was at the studio today because they're doing costumes for a movie called *The Panther's Rage*."

"Sounds like your Tía Emi has done well for herself."

"Her lot improved when she finally learned how to say more than 'fuck you' in English."

Lola burst out laughing and threw her arms around me. "Oh, Mara, here we are giggling and sharing secrets, just like when we were kids. Tell me how you got to California."

"We walked from Mexico City to Los Angeles," I said, exaggerating. "Tell me about Jaime."

"Well, he asked me to have a cup of coffee with him. We sat down at a table at one end of the room, where they served coffee and sweets, in full view of the ladies of the Hospital Auxiliary. 'All the angels in heaven are crying today,' he whispered. 'I know,' I said. 'Because the most beautiful angel flew back down to earth. I've heard that line before!'

"That evening, he took me home in his automobile. His chauffeur drove, and we sat in the back seat. I was nervous, Mara. I couldn't believe Mami had allowed it. He kept looking at my necklace, a gold filigree cross hanging from a chain. 'It's twisted,' he whispered. I raised my hand to adjust it. 'No,' he said softly. He brought his lips close to my ear. 'I'll do it.' His breath was sweet, like spiced oranges. The clasp had worked its way to the front, and he took the chain between his fingers and ran the hook around my neck to position it. I could feel his knuckles moving subtly over my skin. I wanted to gasp, but I was afraid he would laugh. Then he kissed me, and I felt something between a tickle and an electric shock. Do you remember your first kiss, Mara?" Her eyes closed. She was reliving the scene.

"It was wonderful being with Jaime," she went on. "We talked about art and music. He liked cubism and jazz, but also opera and ballet. He especially loved film. He called it the art form of the future. It was the first time anyone had ever shared ideas with me like that. I began to daydream about him. Instead of doing homework, I wrote my name over and over in my notebook—*Señora Dolores Asúnsolo de del Río. Dolores Asúnsolo del Río. Dolores del Río.*

"I memorized his love letters. *'My Darling, You are a coffer of treasures that I yearn to possess. Your lips are rubies gleaming with passion; your teeth, precious pearls; your skin, lustrous alabaster...'* I was sure that with a pen like that, he would write spectacularly successful movie scripts—if only, someday, we could go to Hollywood. *'My darling Lola, My day begins when you appear. You are the rising sun that brings the dawn.'*

"One morning, I overheard Mami and Papá talking in the dining room. 'Well?' said Mami. 'His holdings in Durango must be worth millions,' said Papi. 'The cotton operation alone generates more than the national reserve. Of course, he's nearly twenty years older than she is.' 'Bah, what difference does that make?' said Mami. 'She'll live like a queen, with plenty of servants to take care of the babies.'

"Before I knew it, the marriage was settled and preparations began. The guest list! The flowers! The food! The music! And the dress, Jaime himself designed it!"

"Your husband designed your wedding dress?" I was incredulous.

"It was a marvel—long and white, with simple, uncluttered lines, slightly puffed elbow-length sleeves, and a train from here to Oaxaca."

An extended European honeymoon followed. London, Paris, Madrid. I imagined Lola at the opera and at the theater or sipping champagne with Jaime on the terrace of an elegant hotel by the sea, gentle waves rippling like thick, wavy ribbons of blue and green crepe.

"You're so lucky, Lola!" I breathed. "You married your *príncipe azul* and had a fairy-tale honeymoon. Your life is perfect!"

"No," she said, suddenly sullen. "It's not."

"But your rich, powerful husband brought you to Hollywood so he could write scripts and you could act!"

"It wasn't like that." The color had gone out of her cheeks.

It took a moment for me to realize the truth: she'd fleetingly lost herself in the role of romantic heroine, but then, inevitably, the lights came on and the screen went dark.

7

Martínez del Río Estate, 1925
Dangerous Times

Lola continued her story one afternoon as we sipped lemonade in the kitchen of her tiny bungalow. As kitchens go, it was a simple affair, modern and efficient: a worktable, a freestanding cabinet, a wall-mounted sink with running water, and an icebox. I was living with Tía Emi at Madame Isabelle's, and, to be honest, my living quarters were nicer than hers. Anyhow, this is what she told me:

She knew he was keeping something from her. The frenzied way he chattered on about Picasso's Blue Period or the production of *L'Avare* they'd seen in Paris. The way he held his fork in midair, then brought it back to his plate without eating a morsel. The way he caressed her hand à propos of nothing or stood staring at her as she applied lipstick. She couldn't quite put her finger on it, but something was wrong. He was feverishly attentive and distracted at the same time.

Jaime was spending more and more time away from the estate, sometimes coming home in the wee hours of the morning or not at all. Lola looked for face powder on his collar and sniffed for telltale scents. Was he bored with her already? she wondered. He didn't seem interested in other women, but...

Strange people started showing up at the door—men with

high-collared shirts and serious-looking suits, men who reminded her of her father when he went to his office. Jaime
would escort them into his study and close the door. When
they emerged, Jaime's face would be pasty and his hands trembling. Félix, the chauffeur, disappeared. Then the Daimler
disappeared.

In some ways, life went on as usual. On Saturday evenings,
they took the Ford to the Mendoza plantation, some fifty ki-
lometers down the road. Jaime drove. They ate quail on fine
china and éclairs prepared by the Mendozas' French chef. Silver spoons clinked on porcelain teacups. Gossip and laughter
filled the air, just as before. But there were worried sighs, too.
The drought had been awful, Mendoza said. He had lost a lot
of crop. Jaime looked forlorn.

"Is everything okay?" Lola ventured one evening on the
way home.

"Better than okay, *mi amor.* I'm married to the most beautiful girl in the world!"

Lola let it go. She had her mind on other things. She hadn't
felt well lately, and she missed her mother. She read and knit-
ted or danced to fill the time, or else she wandered around the
house as if she were still trying to figure out the floor plan.
There was no one to talk to. Jaime was always busy. Instead of
riding his horses or sipping rum by the pool, he spent the hours
poring over account books. One day oozed into the next. It's
not so bad, she told herself. Everything will change after...

Lola was reading in the patio, stretched out on a chaise
longue, when a farmhand burst through the gate. "Señora!
Señora!"

"What is it, Lucio?"

"Something terrible, señora. They've shot the patrón! Come
quick!"

Lola darted out of the patio behind the man. Jaime had

taught her how to drive the Ford, but did she remember? What was that? The clutch! And that? The brake!

The farmhands had carried Jaime to a shed to get him out of the sun. He lay on a pile of straw, blood trickling from a wound in his shoulder, but he appeared more dazed than hurt.

"Get on your horse and go for Dr. Gracián!" Lola commanded Lucio. The sky glimmered like tin. Lucio disappeared into the whiteness.

After the doctor assured her that the bullet had only grazed Don Jaime's flesh, Lola had her husband carried back to the house. She put him to bed and sat by his side while he slept. Then she contacted the family lawyer and demanded an explanation—but Don Filoberto was not about to share confidential information with a child.

Lola went to her husband's study and rattled the knob, but the door was locked. She sat down and wrote a note to her father.

"Take this to the city," she told Lucio, shoving an envelope in his hand. "Make sure you give it to Don Jesús Leonardo personally. And wait for a response."

When Lucio returned, he handed the unopened letter back to her.

"Don Jesús Leonardo left for Texas yesterday morning," he said forlornly, as if the whole thing were his fault.

"And Doña Antonia?"

"I don't know, señora. You didn't say anything about finding Doña Antonia."

Lola knew it would be counterproductive to badger Jaime for information now. He would just clam up or start babbling about the Paris opera. She had to bide her time.

After about a week, he felt well enough to get out of bed and come to the table.

"I'm sorry, darling," he whispered. She could see the anguish in his eyes. "I've been keeping something from you."

Instead of hurling an acerbic remark—*No kidding! You just took a bullet in the shoulder! You mean something's going on?*—she smiled kittenishly. "Well," she purred, "I've been keeping a secret from you, too."

Jaime looked alarmed.

"You tell me yours, and I'll tell you mine," she said, winking.

"Mine is serious." His face was pallid.

"So is mine." She was still smiling, but her voice had taken on a hard edge.

"Please, Lola, I'm not up to playing games. Just tell me."

"Okay, I'm going to have a baby. I'd been feeling a bit odd for weeks, so I called for Dr. Gracián. He came to the house just before you got shot and confirmed it. That's my secret. Now, what's yours?"

"A baby! Lola, darling! That's wonderful!" He brought her hand to his lips.

"What's yours?" She was no longer smiling.

As Lola suspected, Jaime had badly mismanaged the estate. They'd spent a fortune in Europe, nearly all Jaime's liquid assets. The drought had ruined last year's crop, and no money was coming in. Creditors were calling in their loans, and Jaime was having trouble coming up with the cash. He had had to sell things, to bargain, to stall. But the creditors were growing impatient. What's more, the peasants were still resentful. The Revolution hadn't solved their problems. It was easy for the creditors to rile them up, to get them to give the patrón a good scare. This bullet had been a warning, they threatened. The next time...

"I think we should go back to the city," Jaime said finally. "You're not happy here, and to be stuck out in this no-man's-land with a baby… I'll have to sell property, but we'll still have enough to live comfortably. My brother can manage what's left of the estate. I've never been cut out for this kind of life. I hate cotton. I hate dirt!"

Lola sobbed softly. Tears of joy, she told herself. After all, her prayers had been answered. In the capital, she would be near her parents. She would have places to go, friends to visit. Her baby would have a grandmother and everything it needed. But would it really be like that? Her family had survived the terrible losses of the Revolution because her father had known how to shelter his assets and invest, and her mother had known how to use family contacts to build social capital. But would Jaime be so smart?

"Could you take me to Durango to send a telegram to Mami, Jaime?" she asked softly.

"Yes, I guess you have to tell her the truth. But I wouldn't send a telegram. Those telegraph operators are such gossips."

"I'm going to tell her about the baby…that I want her with me when it's born."

Lola forced herself to concentrate on the task at hand. They had to decide what to sell and what to keep, what to take and what to leave with the Mendozas until things were settled.

"I'm taking all my clothes! I just had three new dresses with accordion pleats made. At least I'll be stylish in the city. And I have lots of cloches."

"Don't forget, you'll be losing that pretty figure very soon, Lolita."

Lola giggled and set about organizing her wardrobe. Once in a while she noticed a twinge in her side.

"It's nothing, señora," said Luz, her maid. "It's just the body getting ready."

"Isn't it too early for that?"

"Some women have light cramps all the way through."

Jaime was carving up his estate, but Lola was not concerned with property prices and contracts. She piled her dresses on the bed, then placed them in trunks—summer frocks here, party frocks here, winter frocks there. The twinges became stronger.

Nice things happened that muted the sting of her husband's financial plummet. Jaime brought her a pearl necklace, "for my favorite *mamacita*." Félix returned. The Daimler returned.

One afternoon, as she was organizing her jewelry—brooches, necklaces, and earrings spread out like a terrain of gold with knolls and valleys—a twinge became a spasm, and then a debilitating pain. Lola dropped the emerald ring she held in her hand and teetered. "Oh my God!" she cried. She touched her belly and struggled for breath. She felt as though a vise were tightening on her uterus.

"Luz!" she screamed. "Luz!" She crumpled onto the floor. Hot tears poured onto her cheeks and chin. "Luz! I need you! Please!"

The maid came running, sized up the situation, and threw her arms around her mistress. She tried to pull Lola upright, but her body was locked into a slump. "Oh, holy Virgin!" Lola wailed. "The pain! The pain!"

Underneath her, a pool of thick blood was swelling and seeping into the carpet.

Jaime burst into the room. He struggled to speak, but the words withered in his throat. He took a step toward Lola, but then balked, unable to move. He looked as though he might faint.

"Señor, get Dr. Gracián right away!" commanded Luz.

A maid was giving him orders. He might have reprimanded her, if he'd had his wits about him, but he didn't even hear her. Trembling, he turned and grabbed a basin to throw up.

Luz ran to find Félix and ordered him to bring the doctor back in the Daimler.

By nightfall it was over. Lola had lost her baby after massive hemorrhaging. Now she lay in a morphine-induced sleep.

"But she can have another one, can't she?" Jaime asked Dr. Gracián anxiously.

"I'm sorry, Don Jaime… Another pregnancy would kill her."

Jaime stood there, staring at Gracián as though he were some sort of monstrous animal. As soon as he'd closed the door behind the doctor, Jaime collapsed into a chair and sobbed.

Once Lola was back on her feet, they wasted no time moving back to the capital. Jaime looked for distractions—plays, concerts, receptions, charity events—to lift Lola's spirits. Fortunately, in the city, something was always going on.

"Adolfo Best Maugard is giving a party! We simply must go, darling!" he told her. Three months had passed since the miscarriage, and Lola was eager to socialize.

"Of course, we'll go, *mi amor*," she said.

Best Maugard was considered one of Mexico's most innovative artists. In the heady days following the Revolution, he created a new style of painting that combined the motifs of Mexico's great archaeological treasures and those of early European masters. But for Jaime, what really mattered was that Best was connected with the new artistic élite—Diego Rivera and his wife, Frida Kahlo, Rufino Tamayo, Miguel Covarrubias. What's more, Best was friends with the leaders of the US film industry, people who might connect him with Hollywood producers.

"He wants you to dance," Jaime told Lola, "but it might be too soon…"

"If he wants me to dance, I will dance!" she insisted. "I've been experimenting with interpretive movement. Dr. Gracián says the exercise is good for me! You can play the piano."

"Albéniz and Manuel de Falla! That's what you've been practicing to."

The night of the party, Lola draped herself in a delicate tunic like the ones she'd seen Isadora Duncan wear in photos and danced to Jaime's playing. She stretched and twirled, leaped and skipped. Best Maugard was breaking the old restrictions in art, doing away with perspective and shading, and Lola was eager to do the same in dance.

One of the guests couldn't take his eyes off her. He was wearing a double-breasted suit and sitting between the host and a glamorous blonde. Lola was used to the attention of men who weren't her husband, but this man wasn't even discreet. His gaze was intense, even aggressive. When her performance was over, he applauded frenetically. Lola went to stand by Jaime. The man left his stunning companion and strode up to them.

"*Yo soy Edwin Carewe,*" he said in passable Spanish.

Best appeared suddenly by her side, assuming the air of a gallant caballero come to rescue her. But why? Her husband Jaime was standing right there. She didn't need rescuing.

"I want to introduce you to Edwin Carewe, a dear friend and renowned Hollywood director," said Best. He signaled to the blonde woman to join them. "And," he added pointedly, "his bride, Mary Akin. They're on their honeymoon."

Carewe's gaze fluttered over Lola like a butterfly over a blossom. "You, my dear, are lovely," he said. "And your dancing is divine."

"Actually," quipped Lola, "it's quite human. If it were divine, my leaps would be higher."

Mary stood there smiling like a wax doll. She didn't understand a word of Spanish.

Lola welcomed Carewe's attention. If he befriended her, she thought, maybe she could convince him to give Jaime a chance as a screenwriter. She had failed Jaime in a big way. She had lost their child. Now, she thought, perhaps she could redeem herself.

They were relaxing after breakfast when Lola heard a knock. She got up to open the door, and a messenger handed her an enormous bouquet of flowers with a card that read, *"Con cariño y admiración"*—"with affection and admiration"— Edwin and Mary.

"He wants us to have dinner with them tomorrow at the Rosa de Seda," said Lola. "You'll be able to tell him your story ideas. This could be your big chance!" She kissed Jaime gently on the cheek. "I love you," she whispered. "All I want is to make you happy."

"I know," he murmured. He took her hand in his and ran his lips softly over her fingers. But somehow, he didn't seem as delighted about the prospect of having dinner with Edwin Carewe as she thought he would be.

The Rosa de Seda was a posh little restaurant that featured a violin quartet, crystal chandeliers, and succulent dishes from every region of Mexico. Lola ordered *pollo al carbón* and Jaime *mole poblano*. Carewe wanted "plain old tacos, like the ones we have back home," and ordered the same for Mary.

"I was thinking," he said, after the waiter brought the appetizers, "Lola should join us in Hollywood. With her looks and talent, she could be a star. I already have an idea…"

Jaime stared at Carewe in disbelief. *"Lola?"* he said. "Just *Lola*?"

"No, of course not," stammered Carewe, realizing his blunder. "You would go with her, of course. You could, well…"

"I could write," interrupted Jaime, furious. "I could write screenplays."

Carewe turned to Lola. "You don't have to know English," he coaxed, "since there's no sound. There are lots of foreign actors in Hollywood—Ramón Novarro, Pola Negri. Say, isn't Novarro a cousin of yours? He was a huge hit last year in *Scaramouche*!"

Lola glared at Carewe. "Jaime has a real gift with words," she said coolly. "He belongs in Hollywood more than I do."

Carewe pursed his lips, then angled toward the violins and pretended to listen. Lola smiled at Mary and tried to say a few words in English. "Hon-ey-moon… Con-gratu-lations!"

"We'll think about it," Jaime interrupted.

But in the end, he had to say yes. There were simply no possibilities for him at home.

Lola closed her eyes. She was done with her story. I sat there in silence, peering into my glass of lemonade. The afternoon sunlight poured through Lola's kitchen window.

"Not as glamorous as you thought, right, Mara?" Lola said finally.

Jaime was making forty dollars a week filing scripts. There were no screenwriting jobs available for him at the moment, Carewe explained, but anyway, it would be better for him to start at the bottom. That way, he'd get a feel for the business.

On the other hand, Carewe had cast Lola in his new film *Joanna* right away. She was to play Carlotta de Silva, a wily seductress from some unidentified Latin country. She had that sensuous sway, that amazing control of her hips that came from being a dancer. First one buttock tightened and veered to the right and then the other tightened and veered to the left.

The studio gave her a contract for $250 a week, and with the forty dollars a week Jaime made as a script clerk, the couple had rented a house and bought a secondhand car.

"Ed says he's sure I'll be a hit," she told me. "He's directing the film himself. Harry Wilson, the publicist, insisted I shorten my name. Asúnsolo López Martínez del Río is far too long. From now on, I'll be Dolores Del Rio. Del with a capital *D*, and no accent on the *i*. That way, it'll look exotic, but not *too* exotic. Ed says he'll make Dolores Del Rio a household name!"

Lola squeezed my shoulders and kissed me on the cheek. "You've been such a good friend, Mara. You listen to me as I ramble on and on. I want to do something for you!" She paused. "What if I asked Ed to give you a screen test? You're pretty and smart. I bet you'd be good at acting."

"I don't know…" I stalled. "I've never thought about it."

"Of course, I may regret this," she teased, "when you're my rival for top billing!"

When I got home, I said to Tía Emi, "You know who I ran into at the studio the other day? My old friend Dolores Asúnsolo."

Tía Emi was stitching the sleeve of a flouncy blue blouse. Needle perched between thumb and forefinger, she pricked the fabric and pulled the thread with such dexterity that her hands seemed to float over the cloth.

"Ah," she said, without looking up. "The Asúnsolo girl. She's not your friend, Mara. You're nineteen years old, old enough to understand how things are."

"She *is* my friend," I said quietly.

"She'll spend time with you now, while she's lonely. You'll be her rainy-day playmate, just like back then."

I could feel my face growing hotter, the old rage numbing my tongue like a toxin.

"That's not true!" I snapped. "She wants to help me! She even said she'd get me a screen test at her studio! Only a true friend would do something like that!"

I don't know how I expected Tía Emi to react, but her sudden, stone-cold Chalchiuhtlicue glower threw me off balance. *"¿Estás loca?"* She threw her sewing into the basket and balled her hands into fists. "After all these years of protecting you, of hiding you, now you're going to go and fuck everything all up."

I was stunned. "What do you mean, *hiding* me? You're talking nonsense."

"If you pass that test and appear in a film, someone might see you. And if they see you, they might come after you! They might *kill* you!"

"Kill me? What are you talking about?" She's old, I thought, and she's lost it. Looking back, I realize she wasn't old. She couldn't have been more than forty. "Nobody's going to kill me," I said, trying to make my voice sound soft and composed. "I'm just an obscure hairdresser, not important enough to kill."

I don't think I'd ever seen Tía Emi cry, but her jaw slackened, and tears trickled from her water-goddess eyes. I took her hand in mine and caressed it. My rage had passed.

"Promise me you won't do it! Stay away from that Asúnsolo girl, Mara."

"Okay," I whispered, "okay." The truth is, I didn't want to take a screen test anyway. The movie life didn't seduce me at all. But Lola's desire to help me, that meant something. Let *her* be the movie star, I thought. Let her set the world on fire in Carewe's *Joanna*. Just having her as a friend is enough for me.

8

Joanna had just been released, and newspapers were talking about Edwin Carewe's "sensational discovery." They gushed over Lola's breathtaking beauty and described her as a "wealthy aristocrat" with a jewelry collection valuable enough to finance ten films. Her full-length photo appeared in the *Los Angeles Times*, and, along with Joan Crawford and Mary Astor, she was named one of the "Baby Stars" to be presented at a ball sponsored by the Western Association of Motion Picture Advertisers—WAMPA. Reporters called her a "mysterious black orchid" whose carriage, elegance, and coloring were remarkable. She should have been on the top of the world. Instead, she looked like a bird had flown by and pooped on her new hat.

"*Joanna* was a disaster," she said simply. We were back in her kitchen, this time sipping coffee.

"The critics loved it," I said.

"The critics don't know, or care, that in the original version, I was featured in nearly every scene. Ed cut all my best shots. They even wrote my name wrong in the credits! Dorothy instead of Dolores!"

"And Jaime? What does he say about it?"

"Jaime doesn't care. Ed still won't even listen to his ideas about screenplays, so he's in a perpetual funk. I do understand how he feels, Mara. He was supposed to be the one with a brilliant Hollywood career, and…well, at least I've got my foot in the door, but Jaime is still filing scripts. He…" She bit her lip.

"What?"

"He…well, maybe I'm wrong, but I think he resents me. Ever since we got here, he won't even…you know…"

I didn't know. I was so young and naive that I had no idea what she was talking about.

"I'm sure he still loves you," was all I could think of to say.

"But he doesn't show it, not the way he used to. After I lost the baby, he had an excuse not to touch me. I was delicate. He didn't want to hurt me. He was tender, but we didn't make love. But now, he won't even come near me. It's as though he finds me… I don't know…repulsive." She burst into tears.

It took me a while to calm her down.

"The loss of your baby… I know it was devastating for you, Lola, but it must have been shattering for Jaime as well. Every Mexican man dreams of a son, but for a man of his social position…an heir is…" I didn't want to say "essential." I didn't want to make her feel like more of a failure than she already did. "An heir is important," I said finally, "but of course, so is work. As soon as Jaime gets one of his scripts produced, things will change. I'm sure of it." I went to the cupboard and got out some bread to make sandwiches. All she had was fluffy white American bread that tasted like hair perm wraps.

"We live like paupers, I know," sniffed Lola, struggling to regain her composure. "I'll ask Papá for money. Mami is going to send my clothes from Mexico, and she can bring my jewelry when she comes to visit." She sighed and went on. "Another man would balk at the idea of his wife appealing to her father for living expenses, but Jaime just shrugs. Papá, on the other hand, is indignant. He thinks Jaime has turned out to be useless, and he hates that I'm up on the screen where, as he says, 'every whore's son' can see me. He was fine with my taking dancing lessons, but dancing in the movies, he thinks that's an outrage."

"And your mother?"

"Mami has pretty much accepted the situation. She never wanted me to perform in public, but she understands how things are. Jaime's parents, that's another story. You have to understand that in Mexico, Martínez del Río stands for something, Mara—moral values, daily mass, white gloves. For them, it's a tragedy that their daughter-in-law associates with divorcées like Mary Pickford and drunks like Clara Bow."

They might forgive her if she were on her way to stardom, mused Lola, or if Jaime were churning out one successful script after the other, but as things stood, it looked like she and Jaime might have to drag themselves back to Mexico, their tails between their legs.

"Maybe it's because I'm too dark," she moaned sullenly. "When I first arrived on the lot for my screen test, the makeup lady said, 'You're a little swarthy, honey, but I'm gonna fix you up just fine.' So she powdered my face and rouged my cheeks. But maybe I just don't have the right look. I'm the fish they threw back into the water because it was too ugly."

I thought she was being melodramatic. I got up to leave.

"Listen, Mara," she said, jumping up. "I have an idea! How would you like to be my personal hairdresser? All the actresses have their own stylist. What do you say?"

I looked around the shabby little apartment. Who knew if her second film—if there was one—would make her any richer than the first? And who knew if Jaime would ever sell a script?

"I don't know," I said. "Do you make enough to pay me?"

She thought about it. "What if I could convince Ed to make

you the hairdresser for the whole cast of the next production? Then, the studio would pay you, not me."

I shrugged. I knew better than to get my hopes up.

When I got home that evening, Tía Emi was in a funk.

"You're late," she said. "We already ate. There's food in the oven."

"Lola asked me to be her personal hairdresser," I said by way of greeting. "What do you think of that?"

"Eres tan tonta que haces llorar a las cebollas."

"Really? I'm so dumb I make even the onions cry? What's so dumb about working for an actress? I'd get to be on a movie set all day instead of in a smelly beauty shop."

"Me cago en la leche."

"Well, it's not sure yet, but I'm going to think about it."

Obviously, she didn't think much of Lola's suggestion. She was still shitting in the milk, the stew, the bathwater, and Madame Isabelle's best perfume when I went to bed.

9

Sam Edelstein, the assistant publicist, Max McClelland, the advance man, and Edwin Carewe were sipping bourbon in the projection room. On the screen, Lola flirted with the camera, winking, puckering, giggling, and looking altogether seductive.

"Isn't she lovely?"

"I don't know, Ed," murmured Sam.

"You don't know? The girl is gorgeous! I'm going to star her in *High Steppers*."

"She has possibilities, Ed," piped in Max. "I have to admit she has possibilities."

"Listen," said Ed, incredulous. "She's going to be the next 'It' girl. Look at those cheeks, that hair. Look at that figure!"

"Yeah, just like every other broad who comes out here looking to be a star," mused Sam, sucking on his cigarette. "Does she fuck?"

"She's married."

"That's not what I asked you, Ed. You fucking her?"

Ed Carewe mashed his cigarette into an ashtray and lit another. He looked at Sam Edelstein in disgust.

"Not yet, huh?" said Sam with a smirk. "But you want to. And you will, if she's serious about her career."

I was gathering up some hats and falls that had been left in the corner of the room, but they didn't notice me. Lola was paying me fifteen dollars a week to work for her part-time. With that and what I made at Marie's, I got along. Lola was still promising to talk to Carewe about hiring me for the studio, but, she said, he was a busy man.

"The thing is," Sam was saying, "who's going to go to the movies to see a Mexican? You got Mexicans cleaning your house, doing your laundry, mowing your lawn. You want to see Mexicans, all you have to do is look out the window... We're not going to be able to sell her."

"Oh, we can sell her," interrupted Max. "If it's true she went to a fancy French school, we can reinvent her."

I felt like vomiting. These men were talking about Lola as though she were a lawn mower or a dishmop—a product to be marketed. I knew this sort of thing went on in Hollywood all the time, but still, I found it disgusting.

"Reinvent her as what?" Ed was interested.

"As some mysterious European aristocrat," said Max.

"Aristocratic family. Fluent in the old parlez-vous." Ed was beaming.

"Here's the story—she's a Spanish aristocrat," said Max. "She might *play* a Mexican dance hall girl, but she's *really* European nobility. Enigmatic. Glamorous. Dress her in white to highlight her coloring. Don't overdo it—just enough to accentuate her foreignness. Get the makeup girl to emphasize her cheekbones. She's the daughter of dons, of conquistadors. Dress her in gauzy frocks that will flow around her body as though they were caressing it. Sensual. Sexy. Cover the kid in diamonds and emeralds, Ed, and while you're at it, get her a nose job."

"Plastic surgery? You really think she needs it, Max?"

"Absolutely. Her nose is too wide. It has to be reshaped."

"Is it safe?"

"Sure it is. The boys who came back from the war with burns and wounds…the doctors sewed them up just like new. And while you're at it, get her bigger tits."

I slipped out the door. I don't know whether they saw me, but if they did? They'd just think I was one of those Mexican cleaning ladies, too ignorant to understand their conversation.

According to studio gossip, at the get-together to celebrate the New York release of *Joanna,* Ed had toasted Lola as the next new Hollywood knockout. Everyone seemed happy except Jaime. He smiled in his forced way, rubbing his hand over his bald head and staring into the champagne bubbles as though he were reading tea leaves. But you didn't need to be clairvoyant to know what was in store for Jaime. He was going to lose her. Lola was too much woman for him—too energetic, too sassy, and too ambitious.

Carewe was still beaming over the New York reviews when Lola stomped into his office at First National, threw him her most seductive look, and arched her back. I could hear them from the hallway.

"How are the English lessons going?" he asked jauntily.

"We have to talk. *Joanna* was a calamity!"

"Darling," cooed Carewe smoothly, "the reception in New York has been magnificent! *Joanna* is a big success!"

"I was practically edited out of it," she hissed.

"Well, I can't control…"

"You most certainly can," Lola shot back, but without raising her voice. "You're the director. You're the one who took out my scenes!"

"I cut the scenes in which you didn't look your best, darling." He pinched her cheek teasingly. "My beautiful tiger with lacquered nails and magenta lips. So adorable!"

But Lola's exquisitely ovaled nails were poised to scratch.

"Maybe I should go back to Mexico," she said, pouting. "Maybe I have no talent. Maybe I'm too ugly."

Carewe must have seen this act before: the self-deprecation, the sniffing. I peeked through the door crack.

"This time it will be different," he murmured, pulling her close to him. She wriggled away, but he caught her and kissed her gently on the mouth, then stroked her hair. She laid her head on his chest.

This couldn't be happening, I thought. They were both married!

"Take your hair down, Lolita," whispered Ed.

She looked up at him and giggled. "What? Why?"

"I want to run my fingers through your hair. Undo your chignon."

"Promise that next time you won't kill my scenes?"

"Promise!"

She reached behind her neck and began to pull out hairpins.

After that, I could hardly look at her. Poor Jaime, I thought. But then I put the whole thing out of my mind because something...someone else was occupying my thoughts.

Ever since Tía Emi had a fit because Nick Wasserman had walked me home from elementary school, I'd shied away from boys. I wasn't afraid of them. I was afraid of her. She didn't care much for men. She didn't trust them and didn't want them around me, so I kept my nose to the books while I was at school and my eyes on the curling iron while I was at work. I didn't flirt. Sometimes I wanted to because they said I was pretty, and I knew the boys liked me, but I didn't want to tangle with Tía Emi.

But now, this boy, this carpenter I'd seen working on the sets, his muscles bulging under his cheap cotton shirt, his taut skin the color of dark molasses, his angular jaw, high cheekbones, and spectacular smile, this boy was grinning at me. I didn't know how to react. Should I grin back, or should I keep my eyes glued to the ground? Should I pretend not to notice?

It took him a while to say hello, but one day, as I was unpacking hairbrushes, he came and stood beside me. He was so gentle looking, so earnest and unaffected. I had the impression he was mustering courage to say something.

"*Está usted...está usted muy linda hoy,*" he finally whispered. "You look very pretty today." He said *usted*, formal usage. He's courteous, I thought. Respectful. I like that. I looked down and smiled. I think I may have blushed.

"*¿Cómo se llama usted?*"

"Mara. María Amparo, really, but they call me Mara."

"Hey, Gabe! Stop fooling around and get back to work!" shouted one of the other men.

"Sure thing, boss!" He laughed nervously.

It didn't sound like he had an accent in English. I asked him if he was from Mexico.

"I was born here," he said. He glanced over at the other men. "I've got to go," he murmured.

I watched him heave a board the size of a locomotive onto his shoulder, then carry it off. Inexplicably, I started to giggle.

"What's the matter with you?" barked Tía Emi when I got home. "You look like a kitten in a bowl of catnip."

I considered what to tell her. "I met a boy," I said simply.

"Well, *estás en la edad del pavo.* You're expected to do stupid things."

Estar en la edad del pavo literally means "to be in the age of the turkey," but it actually means to be young. "I haven't done anything," I said. "I just met him."

"White?"

"No."

"Good. Rich?"

"No."

"Good. Don't get pregnant like your mother."

I was furious. Tía Emi was not only ignorant, she was cruel. Why had she never told me anything about my mother? "What do you mean?" I snapped. "What happened to my mother?" But she just clammed up and left the room.

My anger didn't last. I was, in fact, in the age of the turkey, and I had no time for Tía Emi's absurd reactions. I went into the kitchen and started peeling carrots. They'd called him Gabe, I remembered. Was it Gabriel? Gabor? Gabrián?

In the morning, I looked for him at the studio, but didn't see him. I felt irritable. I barked at the costume assistant and jabbed Lola with a hairpin.

"Ouch! Please, Mara, be more careful!" she complained.

In the afternoon, he finally appeared, lugging in furniture for the English estate scenes in *High Steppers*. He smiled at me and winked. His smile was so broad, his dimples so adorable, his teeth so perfect. What could I do but smile back?

During the break, he invited me to have a soda with him. He bought two Coca-Colas at the canteen, and we sat on a little bench on the studio grounds. He lit a cigarette and offered me one. I shook my head.

"I don't smoke," I said.

"Of course not. Anyone can see you're a nice girl."

In those days, nice girls didn't smoke.

"You don't drink either, I bet."

I shook my head. "No," I whispered.

"Because of Prohibition?"

"No," I said. "I just don't." That wasn't exactly true, but I liked him, and I knew what he expected of me.

He told me that his father was a traditionalist from an old-style Spanish family, and his mother was from Oaxaca. He'd been born in Los Angeles, but they spoke Spanish at home.

His name was Gabriel Estrada, and he wanted to be a master carpenter.

"What about your family?" he asked me.

What was I going to say? I'm a bastard, and I have no family? "I'm an orphan," I said. "I live with my aunt Emilia in the home of Madame Isabelle, who is a *couturière*." I said *couturière* very distinctly, with a French *r*. "My aunt is Madame Isabelle's assistant."

"Ah," he said, "I know who she is. She makes costumes for movies."

"Yes," I said. "She makes costumes for movies." My use of the word *couturière* obviously hadn't impressed him.

"Could I take you out this Saturday night?" he asked after we'd met a couple of times during breaks. "There's a dance at my church."

I hesitated. "I… I don't know…"

"I promise never to get fresh with you, Mara. I can see you're a nice girl."

He thought I was afraid he'd touch me. Actually, I was afraid of how Tía Emi might react. What if he came to pick me up, and she accused him of being a murderer?

"Let me ask my aunt," I said. But of course I said yes. I was already in love with him.

That Saturday, I begged Tía Emi to put on a nice dress and comb her hair. She wasn't unattractive. Her ebony mane was turning salt-and-pepper, and her jaw had grown a bit slack, but she still had her high cheekbones and her fire-and-ice sea-goddess eyes. A bit of lipstick and a pretty updo, and she would look presentable.

Gabe was supposed to pick me up at six o'clock. At five thirty, Tía Emi went into our room and closed the door. She's getting dressed, I thought. She wants to make a good impression.

At about 6:10, the doorbell rang. "He's here!" I called.

Gabriel was dressed in what must have been his Sunday best—a gray double-breasted suit (probably a hand-me-down from his older brother), a white shirt, and a wide burgundy tie. He held two bouquets of flowers. "One is for your aunt," he said, handing me the smaller one.

"I'll put these in water and go get her," I said. I showed him into Madame Isabelle's living room.

"Hurry up!" I called softly through Tía Emi's door.

"¡Me cago en la leche!" she called back.

I went into the living room to join Gabe. In a few minutes, Tía Emi came ambling in. She looked as though she'd just gotten up from her siesta. A frayed, flowered housedress sagged loosely over her body. A dirty slip hung out from under the hem. On her feet, she wore old huaraches I hadn't seen in years. She'd worked her hair into straggly braids, like a *campesina*. A cigarette drooped from her lips. Gabe stood up and handed her the bouquet. She looked at it as though it were a basket of toads.

"What's this?" she said finally.

"I brought you flowers," he said.

"What for?"

"A gift."

She started to scratch her arm violently, all the time staring at the flowers as if she had no idea what to do with them. Finally, she gave them back to him.

I must have turned magenta. "I'm sorry..." I began. But Gabe didn't look perturbed at all. He handed the bouquet to me. "Lovely flowers for a lovely girl," he said, as though that had been his plan all along. "You can put them together with the others."

Soon we were spending every single break together. Of course, Lola noticed.

"So," she teased, as I combed out her hair, "you've got a beau!"

So do you, I wanted to say, but I didn't. Ed Carewe had been clinging to her like a moth to a wool coat, and I was afraid the result would be just as destructive. Were they really having an affair? Or was she just flirting and having fun?

Lola and I had just had lunch and were listening to music on the Victrola. As I remember, Ben Bernie's "Sweet Georgia Brown" was popular that year. A car pulled up in front of the bungalow, a brand-new 1925 Lincoln touring car, midnight blue with a white canvas hood. Through the window, I watched Edward Carewe scurry up the walkway to the front door.

"*Hola*, Eddie." Lola smiled self-consciously as she turned the knob. Carewe pushed into the house and gripped her around the waist. She knew I was watching and pulled away. He looked at her as though she were a huge chocolate candy he was about to bite into.

"I have news," he whispered mysteriously. "Where's Jaime, by the way?"

Lola looked down. "He's at the studio. They gave him some scripts to read...well, to file...by genre."

"That's good. Your luck is about to change, Lola." He kissed her on the cheek. A frisson shot through me. Obviously, he hadn't noticed I was watching from the kitchen. He took her in his arms and pressed her against him. "The great Hollywood director Carl Laemmle has invited you to appear as guest artist in his new movie, *The Whole Town's Talking*. And after that, you'll star in my latest venture, *Pals First*. You're a bona fide celebrity, kid. Never doubt me."

He kissed her firmly on the lips. His cologne was musky, masculine—not that sweet-smelling cinnamon-vanilla stuff that Jaime wore.

I cleared my throat. Lola caught my gaze and tried to pull away, but Ed was engrossed in his seduction. "Ed!" she whispered. "Stop!"

Instead of stopping, he pressed against the small of her back until she was locked against his pelvis. "Ed!" She squirmed free. "Darling, we're not alone!"

Ed reeled around, saw me, and stepped away from her, teetering. His hair was disheveled, his cheeks beet-colored, feverish. Lola's warning had clearly interrupted an oncoming erection. I bit the insides of my cheeks to keep from laughing as he stood there, flummoxed. You idiot! I thought.

"Ed," murmured Lola. "You remember Mara, my hairdresser."

Ed opened his eyes wide, grasping that I'd been there the whole time.

"I was just leaving," he stammered. "I just came to tell Lola about the new film, but I can't stay." If I hadn't been present, they'd have made love right there in the living room.

When I saw Lola again, I avoided the topic of Ed Carewe. I was in love, I wanted to get married, and I thought her behavior was disgusting. She was the one who brought it up.

"You know what I was thinking about while Ed was coming on to me?"

"I can't imagine," I said dryly.

"My school in Mexico. The lilting prayers, the sweet incense, the weeping Virgin. *Notre Père, qui es aux cieux*… I can't do this with Ed, I kept thinking. I just can't."

"But you did."

"Yes," she whispered softly. "Not then, but I did."

10

Lola's cousin Ramón Novarro was the new Rudolph Valentino.

Ramón had come to Los Angeles with his brother Mariano right after the Revolution. The war had swept away everything—the family estate, their father's cash, their mother's jewels—and so Ramón did odd jobs, worked in community theater, waited on tables, and modeled for artists to survive. But what he wanted was to be in the movies. Mariano might pump gas or sweep floors. Ramón looked for work that would advance his career. He hung around the studios, auditioned for parts, and lingered outside the doors of directors.

In the end, it paid off. The director Rex Ingram liked his face and decided to give him a break. He played up Ramón's sultry good looks, his athleticism, and his youth. He played down his height—about five feet ten inches—and his emergent belly. He starred him in hit after hit. The most recent was *Ben-Hur*, for which, according to the newspapers, Ramón was getting ten thousand dollars a week. Even though it wasn't true, the report made for good publicity.

Lola hadn't seen him since she'd danced to his flamenco guitar at her Tío Francisco's house, about fifteen years before. He was five years her senior and knew English, which made her think of him as superior, even though her father said it was shameful that the boy had his heart set on being a ballet dancer. Lola never saw anything wrong with his desire to dance. He was funny, and he could sing American songs. He knew all the numbers from *Sally* and taught her to sing "Look for a Silver Lining." As for me, I remembered him as my first crush, the boy I wanted to notice me, but never did.

Now he'd invited Lola and Jaime to lunch, but something was strange. Why, she wondered, hadn't he invited her to his home on Gramercy Street, where he lived with his parents and siblings? Why were they meeting at the home of a friend?

"Mara," she said. "I want you to come with me. Jaime refuses to go."

I didn't want to go with her. For one thing, I was revolted by her carrying on with Carewe. For another, I was miffed that she still hadn't asked Ed to hire me as a regular employee of First National. "Jaime should accompany you," I said smugly. "After all, he's your husband."

But in the end, I said yes. She was paying me to be her hairdresser, and I needed the money. I wanted to keep her happy.

Lola was becoming used to the company of celebrities. Carewe made sure she was included in every Hollywood bash he could wriggle an invitation to. But now she was a bit nervous. She remembered Ramón as a fun-loving boy who pirouetted around Tío Paco's patio, but here he had the reputation of being something of a recluse, a star who shunned Hollywood parties altogether or attended for a few moments, then discreetly disappeared.

A valet answered the door. He wore blue trousers and a tight blue-and-white-striped shirt instead of a uniform.

"They're in the sitting room," he said with a wink. "Come on, follow me." No "good afternoon, ma'am." No "may I take your jacket, ma'am?"

"They?"

"Ramón and Lou."

"And you are…?" ventured Lola.

"Ray, the valet," chirped the young man. "Ray, the valet, from Mandalay! Whore by night, whore by day!" he chanted in a singsong.

"Stop that, Ray!" called a voice from inside.

A young man appeared in the vestibule. He had the same perfectly sculpted face that I remembered, but a higher forehead, a more pointed chin, broader shoulders, and a pudgier build. He wore his hair slicked back Valentino-style. He sported a silk foulard and an Arrow shirt.

"Lola, darling!" Ramón took her jacket and led her to the drawing room. "This is Lou Samuel, my secretary," he said, nodding at a handsome young man in a golf shirt. "This is his house. And *that* mischievous boy is Ray Albrecht, Lou's manservant."

"Manservant!" snorted Ray. "I'm Lou's assistant, Ramón, not his servant!"

"Isn't he impossible? Come, Lola, sit down. Aunt Antonia wrote to my mother, and suddenly it occurred to me that you've been here for months, and I haven't even invited you for lunch. It's just that I was abroad in Italy filming *Ben-Hur*, and then, well, my schedule has been just atrocious, Lola. My next movie project is *The Student Prince in Old Heidelberg*. Aunt Antonia says you're almost fluent in English already. Is that true?"

"I've been studying very hard. Ramón, I'd like to introduce you to my friend María Amparo Rojas."

"They call me Mara," I said shyly, holding out my hand.

"That's wonderful, darling. You have a gift for languages. I still have an accent after all these years. Welcome, Mara."

"Ray, bring us some drinks and hors d'oeuvres, please,"

ordered Lou amiably. He slapped Ray gently on the behind. "Come on, lazy boy, get moving."

"I rarely drink," murmured Lola.

No, but she cheats on her husband, I thought. Once he sat down with a gin in hand, the old Ramón began to surface—animated and affable and full of news. He'd just engaged the famous psychotherapist Sylvia of Hollywood to help him screw his head back on, he said, and no, it wasn't true what people said about him, that he slept in a coffin. *Ben-Hur* was a huge success, and no, he wasn't embarrassed by the revealing costumes he had to wear. After all, during his hungry days he'd posed nude for artists.

"Ramón has a beautiful body," murmured Lou, "and he doesn't mind showing it."

I looked from one to the other, trying to figure out exactly what was going on.

"What do you need a psychotherapist for?" blurted out Lola.

"Darling, out here, *everyone* has a therapist. All the stars go to Sylvia."

I had the impression that something wasn't quite right with Ramón. He seemed as tense as a violin string.

"What does a psychotherapist do?" Lola asked.

Ramón exchanged glances with Lou. "Oh, you know, being raised Catholic… You'll see that everything they taught you, all the guilt they stuffed into your brain… Well, out here, people are more uninhibited, more spontaneous. More authentic, you might say. And anyhow, this is 1926! It's time to let go of all that old-fashioned nonsense, for God's sake!" He stopped himself. "Or maybe not for *God's* sake."

"You don't believe in God anymore, Ramón?"

"Yes, of course I believe in God. I believe deeply in God. I feel God in the mysterious silence of the night, really feel His presence. I go to mass every Sunday, and once a month I go to a spiritual retreat at Retiro San Iñigo, in Los Altos… It's so peaceful there, you can really find your soul, your inner self. I believe in a God who loves me for who I truly am, Lola."

Ramón and Lou exchanged another furtive glance.

"What do *you* think, Mara?" said Ramón, suddenly turning to me.

I must have turned as pink as a flamingo. I wasn't expecting to be included in the conversation. Ramón was a big star with a bunch of hits under his belt—besides *Ben-Hur*, there was *The Red Lily*, *The Midshipman*—and yet, he was so considerate, so unpretentious. I mean, I was just…well, nobody in particular, and here he was asking my opinion. "I—I don't know," I stammered. "I think what matters most is how you behave yourself, how you treat other people…"

Lola stood up. "Where's the powder room, Lou?" Maybe she thought my comment alluded to her.

She was gone a long time, longer than seemed necessary. When she finally returned, she seemed unsettled. What could have happened between the drawing room and the bathroom, I wondered.

"I saw something…" she told me afterward. "Something upsetting. My head was buzzing, as though swarms of wasps had nested in my skull." She was so rattled, she wasn't sure she could make it back. "I focused on maintaining my body erect," she said. "One foot in front of the other. I inhaled deeply and held up my head, the way I'd learned in acting class. Control, I thought. I'm an actress. I'm in command of my movements."

After she left the powder room, she took a wrong turn and stumbled into Lou's bedroom. A cluster of photos on the wall caught her eye—photos of Ramón, all of them nude. Ramón in the shower, his back toward the camera. Ramón stretched out on a chaise longue, one knee artfully raised to shield his sex. Ramón facing the camera, fully exposed, staring brazenly out at the spectator. Ramón standing naked with a fully clothed Lou Samuel. And then, opposite the display of nudes, a large oil painting of a Christian martyr—she wasn't sure which one—a delicate young man tied to a tree, his hands fastened to a branch above his head to emphasize the contours of his body. Sensuous arms, gently rippling shoulders, supple belly, sinuous thighs, graceful legs. Everywhere shot through with arrows.

"My gaze rose from his feet to his face," murmured Lola. "His eyes… They were Ramón's eyes. The saint's face was Ramón's face. All those nude photos and then this, Ramón, the suffering martyr."

I bit my tongue. You have to understand, in those days, you didn't talk openly about…that sort of thing, even though it was pretty common in Hollywood. William Haines lived with his lover, Jimmie Shields, and was a one box office success all the same. Greta Garbo went everywhere with her girlfriend. Clara Bow kissed her female costar in *Maytime*. And *The Ten Commandments* showed a bisexual orgy. People whispered about lavender love affairs, lavender marriages. As long as it didn't get into the papers, you could get away with just about anything. Hollywood was tolerant. The general public was not. Folks in Boise or Duluth were not going to pay a quarter to see a movie that would shock the local pastor.

"Ramón must be…you know," Lola whispered.

I shrugged it off. I was in love with Gabe. All I wanted was to get married and have the kind of normal family I'd never had growing up. I was a mere mortal, and the games of the Hollywood gods didn't interest me.

11

Lola knew she should be overjoyed. *Joanna* opened in Mexico on March 6, at the Salón Rojo, to glittering reviews. She was listed third in the credits, and her name was spelled right. In *High Steppers*, Dolores Del Rio appeared right after Mary Astor, the lead, and now she'd completed two more new films. So, what was wrong? Why was she sobbing into her pillow at night?

"I don't know what the matter with me is," she confided. I was styling her hair for publicity shots for *What Price Glory?* Carewe wanted her looking very French and sexy.

"Hold your head up," I ordered. "Otherwise, I can't get your curls right."

She really was a celebrity now. Women imitated her clothes, and men hung photos of her in their workrooms. Yet, she couldn't shake the feeling that she was a feather in the wind with no control over her direction or destiny.

"Last night I woke up in the middle of the night," she whispered. "Jaime was snoring softly. He has this odor...like an old person. The moonlight was streaming through the slats in the blinds and cast a soft, sickly glow on his bald spot. I thought... God forgive me...how could I ever have been in love with this man? I pulled myself out of bed and fumbled toward the bathroom. I switched on the light and looked at my face in the mirror."

I know what she saw: perfect, smooth, luminous skin. Lofty forehead. Flawlessly arched eyebrows. Colossal eyes—rich and brown and seductive like expensive Belgian chocolate.

"What are you complaining about?" I said. "You're a household name, just like you wanted."

The studio publicity wizards had recast her into an exotic siren, and now she had a newly sculpted nose, slender and symmetrical, to go with her heart-shaped mouth, prettily puckered and pink even without lipstick. She was dark enough to market as a "female Valentino," but light-complected enough to get past the miscegenation laws that forbade showing mixed-race couples onscreen. The studios were marketing Ramón as a new type, not the traditional blond he-man played by actors like Wallace Reid, but the "Latin lover"—alluring and mysterious, but still Caucasian. Lola was the female version.

"I saw a wrinkle," she said.

"Ah yes," I said. "As Judas was to Jesus, so are wrinkles to a starlet!"

"Don't tease me, Mara!"

"You have a devoted husband, impeccable skin, a twenty-inch waist, and a spectacular career," I said. "Stop whining!"

I was anxious to finish up and leave. Gabe was going to take me to a baseball game that evening, and I was excited—not because I cared anything about baseball, but because we were going to double-date with his brother Vince and Vince's girlfriend, Julie. It meant something, I thought, that Gabe wanted to introduce me to his older brother.

"Sit up!" I commanded.

But her head kept drooping. She hadn't slept well. The fruits of a guilty conscience, I was sure. Jaime had become unbearably jealous, Lola complained, but who could blame him? Not only did Carewe cast Lola in sexy roles, but now the publicity was getting more suggestive. First National ran an ad for *Pals First* in which Lola appeared surrounded by the faces of six of the studio's handsomest male stars and the words, "Who is her next great love?"

Jaime was growing weary not only of Lola's screen image, but of Edwin Carewe's constant presence in her life. The sleazy gringo dictated her roles, her clothes, and her publicity shots. He even decided what parties she would go to—and with whom. Sometimes she went with her husband, but sometimes she didn't. Often she appeared on Carewe's arm. People whispered that they were having an affair, and I suspect that was exactly what Carewe wanted.

"Jaime tenses up every time the phone rings," she told me. "'It's for you, I suppose,' he says. 'No one ever calls me.' And then, in an accusatory tone, 'It's probably Ed.'"

Was Jaime's jealousy a sign of love or fear for his reputation? Maybe both. You have to understand that for a Mexican man of his class, an unfaithful wife was a disgrace. Jaime was, after all, a Martínez del Río y Viñent. Lola had confided that he was a dead fish in bed, and people were insinuating that he would rather make love to a boy than to his wife. Maybe Carewe planted those rumors. Who knows?

Carewe was growing weary, too—and he told her so. He was sick of waiting for her to leave Jaime. Her husband was dragging down her career, he said, and it was time for her to cut her losses and get rid of him, just as he was going to get rid of Mary Akin.

To be honest, I didn't really feel sorry for Lola. If she felt pulled in two directions, it was her own fault. Why had she let Carewe into her life—and bed—in the first place?

Four men crowded into the room. "We're ready for the shoot," they said.

Lola, Carewe, and I followed them into the photography studio. Carewe removed a little black beret from a costume bag.

"You play a French girl," he said, "so wear this." He plopped the beret down on her head. She struck a seductive pose. The beret slid down over her forehead.

"Shit!" bellowed Carewe. He turned to me. "Give me a bobby pin."

He fixed the beret in place and took a step backward to assess the effect. Again, Lola struck a seductive pose. "That's no good!" he groaned. "It casts a shadow over her forehead."

Lola looked as though she were ready to drop, but her drowsiness worked in her favor. It gave her a heavy-lidded, come-hither look.

Ed pushed the beret to the back of her head. It looked like the Pope's skullcap. "Oh fuck," he said. "That's worse."

"Here," I said. "Let me." I took the beret from Carewe and placed it at an angle on Lola's head, fastening it with two discreetly placed bobby pins. Now it stayed firm and didn't cast any shadows.

"Well, I'll be damned," said Carewe. "Who the hell are you?"

"The hairdresser," I said.

"Well, you've got a real eye for it, kid. Have you been doing Lola's hair all this time?" He stared at me as though I looked vaguely familiar. "You on the staff?"

"No, sir. I work for Miss Del Rio. But I'd love to—"

"Put her on the staff, Mike," he said to his assistant. He turned to me. "Go over to Makeup and Hair. Mike will take care of the paperwork."

Lola was beaming as though the whole idea had been hers. Finally! I thought. I couldn't wait to tell Gabe.

That evening, when he picked me up, Tía Emi didn't bother coming to the door.

"Does she still think I'm Jack the Ripper?"

"I think so," I giggled.

He gave me his hand, and we walked toward the trolley stop. I was twenty years old, and that was the first time I'd ever held hands with a boy.

12

Los Angeles, 1926
Independence Day

The red, white and green streamers dangling from the ceiling
fluttered in a breeze generated by strategically placed fans. A
banner announcing *¡Independencia mexicana, 16 septiembre 1926!*
crossed one wall of the ballroom, while another with the
words *¡Viva, México!* traversed the opposite wall. To the side
hung a huge panel emblazoned with *¡Grito de Dolores!* On the
platform under the independence banner, mariachis dressed
in black charro outfits with gold braid played "El corrido de
Macario Romero," their trumpets rising above the din of
the mingling guests. The music reminded me of when I was
little at Don Adalberto's, and the maids sang "The Ballad of
Miguela Ruiz" while they worked, but the guests were nothing like the women who smoked black tobacco and gossiped
in the servants' quarters of the estate.

I'd come to attend to Lola's hair, but she was busy with the
program directors, so she told me to go enjoy the festivities.
I wandered into the room reserved for special guests without
realizing I wasn't supposed to be there. Lola had lent me one
of her old evening gowns. I'd never worn a long dress before, and I was sure I was going to trip over the hem and fall
on my face, so I staked out a spot by the hors d'oeuvres and

stood there straining to hear the conversations over the blare of the brass coming from the ballroom.

Jaime and Ramón, both elegant in tuxedos, starched white shirts, and bow ties, stood nearby sipping tequila. "She looks stunning tonight, Ramón," Jaime was saying. "Have you seen her?"

"Not yet. Where is she?" Ramón eyed the door, as though planning an escape route.

"It's nice to be away from the studio crowd," murmured Jaime. For once, Carewe wasn't around, and he, her husband, could be Lola's undisputed champion, her escort, her *man*.

"It looks like Mexicans have taken over the industry," quipped Ramón.

Lupe Vélez, gorgeous in a shimmery white gown and a white fox wrap, smoked as she flung the tip of her fur playfully over the chin of her date, Douglas Fairbanks, her leading man in *The Gaucho*. Andrea Palma, another one of Lola's cousins from Durango, was lost in conversation with Richard Bennett.

"I'm only here for Lola," Ramón whispered. "And because I have to be on good terms with my *compatriotas*. I don't care anything about politics, but Mexico is one of the biggest foreign markets for US films. The studios want us to foster friendly feelings by shouting '*viva México*' for the cameras every chance we get."

I liked Ramón. On the one hand, he enjoyed the freedom Hollywood offered, but on the other, he recognized that it was all full of farce. He was honest. Besides, he was nice to everyone, whether they were Hollywood royalty or just plain folks.

A waiter appeared with a tray of margaritas. "Señores," he said, nodding to Ramón and Jaime. He was a muscular young man with high cheekbones, slick black hair, heavy features, and unexpectedly blue eyes. Ramón placed his empty glass on the tray and took a fresh drink. The waiter stood there, eyes lowered, then suddenly raised his gaze and aimed it straight at Ramón, who flinched and looked away.

"Mara!" he said, suddenly noticing me. "How nice to see you!" We'd only met once. I was surprised he remembered my name. "Come and have a drink with us," he said.

"I have to go backstage and put the final touches on Lola's hair." I hesitated. "To be honest," I said, "I'm having trouble walking in this dress."

Ramón burst out laughing. "Here," he said. "Take my arm. I won't let you fall."

The din rose to a roar as we stepped into the ballroom, and the musicians began "¡Mexicanos, al Grito de Guerra!" Jorge Peralta, president of the Mexican Independence Day commit- tee, took his place at the podium. Speeches. More music. More speeches. Guests of honor. Groups of schoolchildren singing "Adelita" and "Cielito lindo." Folk dancers performing the jarabe with voluminous twirling skirts. More speeches. More honored guests.

"And now, the moment we've all been waiting for!" pro- claimed Peralta. "*La Reina de la Fiesta*, the Queen of the Fi- esta!"

The audience hooted and cheered, and then hushed.

"*Señoras y señores*, the person I am about to present is no stranger to the Mexican community. Although very young, she is the star of countless films—*Joanna, High Steppers, The Whole Town's Talking*, and now the upcoming *What Price Glory?* But even though she has had incredible success here in Grin- golandia, she has never forgotten who she really is. She shares our values! Our devotion to God and family! Our sense of honor and dignity! She has never stopped being truly, authen- tically Mexican!"

The crowd whooped and applauded.

"And now to fete with us the independence of our great country," proclaimed Peralta, "our very own Dolores Del Rio!"

More applause. More cheering. The lights dimmed. The band played the opening music from *What Price Glory?*

"I'm leaving as soon as she's done," whispered Ramón. "I drove here myself. I never use a chauffeur. I love to drive."

Dolores, in a white silk voile Vionnet gown, biased-cut and flowing, glided across the stage like a sprite—her perfect hair, perfect eyes, perfect nose, mouth, and skin inspiring the women to throw kisses and the men to moan.

"Our daughter of Durango! Our national treasure! *¡Primera dama del cine norteamericano!*" intoned Peralta.

Ramón surveyed the hall, now clearly searching for an exit. A line of waiters stood along the opposite wall. The blue-eyed young man who had brought the margaritas was gawking like the others, but not at Lola. He was looking right at Ramón.

Lola took her place behind the microphone and, with her now customary poise and elegance, began to speak. *"Es un gran placer...nuestro adorado México..."* She blew kisses at the audience, and the orchestra played "Siete Leguas." Lola bowed and blew more kisses. Ramón squeezed my arm and turned toward the back of the room. I watched him struggle to make his way through the crowd to the doorway. The audience was going berserk, dissolving into a delirium of clapping and cheering. No one would notice him slipping away. I decided to follow. Maybe he could give me a lift to the trolley. I'd feel silly riding the trolley in an evening gown, but I was anxious to get out of there. I hiked up my skirt and took off.

The night was crisp and cool, as Los Angeles nights often are. The path to the parking area traversed a garden, and the roses formed a kind of welcoming committee for the olfactory senses with their sweet, heady perfume. Electric lights guided the pedestrian safely through the vegetation, yet paled against the glittering radiance of the diamond-studded dome above. Here, only fifty yards from the hall, all was still and serene.

Ramón ambled through the bushes, lost in his musings. At Lou's house, he'd said that he felt the presence of God in the mysterious silence of the night. In his early twenties, he'd flirted with the idea of becoming a priest. Watching him make his way over the path, I wondered if he sensed God's presence among the rosebushes. He slackened his pace, moved calmly, as though his spirit was suffused with a sweet tranquility.

A spark of light caught my eye. He must have seen it, too, because he paused. Something was flickering up ahead…a cigarette perhaps. It darted here and there. I peered into the darkness beyond the path and made out the silhouette of a man… no, three men. I sank back into the shadows, but Ramón kept walking. I followed him at a distance, still concealed. The men were conversing and smoking in a small, dimly lit courtyard between the path and the parking area. Ramón waved and smiled, then headed toward his automobile.

One of the men lurched onto the path and stood in front of him, blocking his way. I crept closer and recognized the waiter with the blue eyes.

"*Buenas noches,*" murmured Ramón, unruffled. Perhaps he was still half-lost in his meditations. He moved to the side to continue on his way.

"I know who you are," snapped the waiter.

Ramón smiled. He was used to people recognizing him. He probably thought the waiter was going to ask for an autograph. He reached into his pocket, maybe for a calling card.

The waiter grabbed Ramón by the wrist. "Keep your hands where I can see them," he snarled, yanking his arm so violently that Ramón let out a yelp.

"Shut up!" snapped the waiter. "Don't yell. Don't make a sound."

"Please let me go! You're making a mistake!"

"I said shut up!" snarled the waiter.

I was terrified, but even so, I tiptoed closer and crouched behind some bushes. If only I could help! I thought. But my feet were glued to the ground. Who knew what those men would do to me if they saw me? Who knew what they might do to Ramón?

"Hey, Riqui," said one of the others. "Don't overdo it."

"I'm just having some fun, Beto." He'd pinned both of Ramón's arms behind him and wrenched them upward. Ramón wailed.

"Listen, Mr. Ladies' Man! Mr. Latin Lover! Mr. Heartthrob of the Century! I know what you *really* are. You're an invert who prowls around at night looking for boys to ram their cocks up your ass, right?"

Ramón's knees buckled. "Please," he whimpered. "Please let me go. I need to urinate."

"Aw," sneered Riqui. "Baby needs to go pee pee." But he loosened his grip.

"Please!" cried Ramón.

"Listen to that, José," snorted Riqui, addressing the third man in the group. "He's begging! He wants it!" The men snickered.

José whipped around in front of Ramón and grabbed him by the crotch. This time, Ramón let out a scream. José squeezed. "You're a disgrace, Novarro! A disgrace to the Mexican race. A Mexican invert! It's disgusting!"

José bent over Ramón until he was practically kissing him. He was tall and wiry, with loam-colored eyes that were yellow where they should have been white, and a few broken teeth, which gave his mouth the look of an old saw. Scars crossed his right eyebrow and cheek.

"We have friends who are waiters in those bars downtown, those bars where fairies and hustlers hang out. They say you go there to pick up men."

I could smell the stink of José's breath from my hiding place. It was making Ramón gag. His chest was heaving. He was sobbing now, shedding fat teardrops as slimy and sticky as ruptured boils.

"Please stop," cried Ramón.

"Why? You know you love it."

The three men burst out laughing. In a split second, Ramón jabbed his tormentor in the ribs and took off. But Riqui was faster. He seized him by the shoulder and threw him to the ground. José jerked him back up and shook him like a rag doll. Ramón teetered, trapped between Riqui and José. In horror, he saw his tormentor bare his jagged teeth in a grotesque smile, then raise his fist behind his head. I saw it, too. But then it wasn't a fist. It had morphed into something else— a projectile of some sort, perhaps a grenade. It was moving toward him as if in slow motion. Then, crack! I grabbed my own jaw, unconsciously imitating Ramón, living his agony. Ramón's mouth was full of blood. I could taste it on my own tongue. Excruciating pain shot through his head, and mine.

When I opened my eyes, I realized that it was dawn, and I was lying on damp soil. I pulled myself up. I'd snagged Lola's evening gown on a thorn, damaging it beyond repair. I looked around for Ramón and panicked when I didn't see him. I found him lying facedown under a thicket, still unconscious. I knelt by him and called his name softly. He began to blink wildly. I stepped aside to avoid startling him. He raised his hand and placed it on his cheek. His temples were throbbing, and his jaw felt pulverized. I could tell just by looking at him.

How could one human being treat another that way just because he was different? I thought. Especially someone as kind and gentle as Ramón. I felt queasy.

"Ramón," I whispered. "Ramón! It's me, Mara."

He managed to roll out from under the thorns and pull himself into an uncomfortable crouch. His disheveled clothes—rumpled shirt, bedraggled trousers—were glued to his body with sweat and piss. To his horror, his pants were open.

He was struggling to remember the night before. Apparently all the other guests had exited through the front door instead of through the garden, and no one had seen him lying under the vegetation. Steadying himself against the courtyard wall, he inched himself up into a standing position. He inspected his body for broken bones and concluded that there were none.

He wondered out loud what time it was. Sunbeams radiated from the motionless sky. Ramón raised his wrist to eye level, but there was only skin where his watch should have been. He groped in his pocket. His billfold and cigarettes were gone, but his keys and the slim case where he kept his license and calling cards was still there. Naturally, I thought. The thugs weren't stupid. They wouldn't take anything that would link them to the crime. They wouldn't steal the car. If the police spotted a bunch of hooligans in a brand-new 1926 Chrysler Imperial, they'd be sure to suspect something and haul the guys in.

"Ramón!" I called.

He turned to stare at me—my runny makeup, my disheveled hair, my torn dress. "Mara!" he gasped. "I…I was attacked."

"I saw it all."

"You did? You saw it *all*?" he stammered, mortified.

"It was horrible, Ramón, just horrible. I wanted to help,

but I was so scared. There were three of them... I should have screamed, I realize that now. I should have thrown rocks at them or run to find a policeman! I'm ashamed of myself."

"Oh, querida! Of course you couldn't help me. But at least you're here now."

I assisted him to his car. I pulled myself into the passenger seat and waited to see what he would do. For a while he sat staring at the dashboard. Then he stuck his key in the ignition and drove to his apartment.

"Stay with me," he whispered. "I'm afraid to be alone."

He slept four or five hours, then showered. When he came back into the living room, I could see that he had scrubbed the blood off his lips and cheeks. I imagined him grasping the faucet to keep his balance, lathering his groins carefully, savoring the water running down his back and legs. Afterward, he tried out his voice to make sure it was steady, then called the studio and apologized for not showing up for work. He had a terrific fever, he explained, and had slept right through the alarm clock. The secretary believed him. After all, he had never missed a day of filming. He would be there tomorrow, he assured her, unless he was still ill.

"Now you call Lola," he said.

I told her a similar story. I had a fever, I said. Something was apparently going around.

Ramón went into the bathroom and applied a thick layer of theatrical makeup to his face to see if it would cover the bruises. Then we sat down with a cup of coffee. He picked up the newspaper and checked the crime reports to make sure there was nothing about the assault. He hadn't notified the police, of course. The studios hated negative publicity. If a star was involved in a mugging or an accident, studio executives would twist arms to keep it quiet. If the word *homosexual* was used in an interrogation, a star could lose his contract.

Fortunately, the only notice of the independence celebration in the press was in *La Voz de México*, the Spanish-language weekly.

Dolores del Río, epitome of Mexican womanhood, was the ideal choice for Queen of the Fiesta. Miss del Río embodies the most salient traits of the mestizo race: beauty, endurance, tenacity, loyalty, and faith. She is a Hollywood star who looks like us, speaks like us, and thinks like us. She is a symbol of Mexicanidad. It is with great pride that we celebrate her as one of our own.

13

Jaime jumped up and exploded in front of everyone. We'd just finished watching the director's cut.

"The first thing you see is her derriere," he complained. "She's leaning over a barrel, rolling it away from the camera. Of course, Flagg, who's billeted at her father's inn, gets ideas right away."

"That seems pretty harmless to me," said Ed. He was grinning at though he found Jaime's outbursts amusing.

"She leads him on. She swings her fanny back and forth, and he gets all excited."

"Well, what do you expect? He's a marine stationed in France during the war."

"He's full of tattoos and she's fascinated. Before you know it, she's all over him. Her father, Cognac Pete, tries to control her, but he can't, so he just tells her, 'Don't give anything away for free.' Another thing, Ed. The language is appalling. Fuck this, fuck that. It's a scandal."

"Why?" said Ed, still grinning. "Nobody can hear them. There's no sound."

"People can read lips" snarled Jaime. "I'm telling you, Ed, people know what they're saying."

"*What Price Glory?* is a war movie, Jaime. Victor McLaglen and Edmond Lowe are consummate actors. They talk like marines because they're playing marines. Don't forget these guys are in the middle of a god-awful war. They've seen their buddies get their brains blown out. So they let loose with a few *fuck*s and *shit*s, what's the big deal? That's what Raoul wanted, a realistic movie! The war scenes are brutally accurate. A stuntman actually got killed on the set! Vic and Ed lose themselves in their roles. It's called good acting, Jaime."

"Well, I don't like to see my wife playing a tramp!"

"Lola is perfect for the part."

"How is a Mexican woman from a decent Catholic family perfect for the part of a slutty French barmaid?"

"We've been through this a dozen times before. There's nothing Mexican about Lola's looks. She's exotic, unusual, striking. She could play any kind of foreigner. She has the energy and charm to play Charmaine and the sex appeal to sell tickets."

"Listen, Ed, my patience is wearing thin," shouted Jaime. "Don't you get what I'm saying to you? Is it because I'm speaking a language that isn't mine? Don't you realize that her conduct reflects back on *me*, on my family! Her contract says—"

"Don't tell me about her fucking contract. I didn't direct this film. Raoul Walsh did. He wanted her for this role, and I gave her to him. Don't forget I control her career. And *that's* what's in her contract."

"This isn't going to turn out well," I told Gabe when we met that evening for coffee. "Carewe is despicable. He talks about Lola as though she were a racehorse to be bought or sold or rented out."

Gabe wasn't as thrilled as I'd expected about my new position as staff hairdresser.

"I can't believe you want to spend more time with those

people," he said, sighing. "They're such phonies. It's one thing to do Lola's hair when she needs you, but now you'll have to be at Carewe's beck and call all the time."

"It's a lot more money. And besides, seeing how films are made is exciting!" It's true that I loved watching the actresses try on their costumes, and I loved doing their hair. It was fun being in the middle of it all. But even so, I was disgusted by Carewe's treatment of Lola.

Gabe shook his head. "I can understand how Jaime feels. I wouldn't want you prancing around in sexy outfits in front of the whole world."

I contemplated that for a moment. Should I be angry that he thought he should have something to say about my clothes, or should I be thrilled that he was beginning to adopt a proprietary attitude? It was 1926. Women had had the vote for six years already. They were wearing short skirts and going out to nightclubs on their own. They weren't letting men boss them around. But, I have to admit it, I liked that he was behaving as though I was his wife. When would he ever propose? I wondered.

"What do *you* think?" he murmured.

I smiled. Gabe and Ramón were the only men who ever asked me my opinion about anything. I'd kept Ramón's secret, and he considered me a friend. But this was different because…well… Gabe was special.

"I see why Don Jaime is annoyed," I said. "But I understand Lola, too. Her career is everything to her, and she does what she has to in order to get ahead." I paused. "She complains all the time that Don Jaime, who used to be so sweet and loving, has turned into a jealous, controlling husband."

He took my hand. I felt my body melt like warm honey.

"You're such a beautiful, smart girl, Mara. I…" He let go of my hand and lit a cigarette.

Damn! I thought. Say it, Gabe. Say: *You're a beautiful, smart girl, and I love you!* But he didn't.

"You have to understand," I went on, "Lola wanted children. The adoration of the crowds, the parties, the splashy photo spreads in movie magazines, I think all that fills a vacuum. But the kind of life she leads would never make me happy."

There! I thought, I've left the door wide-open. Ask me what kind of life I want, and I'll say a life with a nice husband and lots of kids. Then tell me you can give me that life, and ask me to marry you.

He took a drag on his cigarette. "You know, Mara," he said, "I want to get away from the studios. My father has been a joister his whole life, but I'm going to take a course in cabinet making and open my own shop. Vince is going to help me. These movie people... How can you stand working for Carewe?"

"It's not full-time," I said. "I still work at Marie's a couple days a week."

"I'm hoping you won't work at all when..." He caught his breath.

I loved styling hair, and working for both Lola and Marie part-time suited me fine. I met interesting women at Marie's and shared in the excitement of filmmaking at the studio. I kept up with all the latest hair fashions and heard all the Hollywood gossip. But Gabe was saying he hoped that someday I'd give it all up. That meant...that meant he was thinking about marriage, and marriage was more important to me than anything else in the world. Say it, I thought. Say: *I'm hoping you won't work at all when we're married!*

Gabe looked down at his cup. He began to fidget with his cigarette, then put it out, paid the bill, and got up to leave. I felt as deflated as a balloon the day after the party.

Lola and Jaime had abandoned their tiny Hollywood bungalow for a spacious hacienda-style home on Outpost Drive. Lola loved the Spanish arches and red tile roof, the elaborate gardens and multiple patios. A flagstone path led to the entrance, where a mosaic of the Virgin of Guadalupe welcomed guests with her calming presence. A staircase of blue and white Puebla tile led to the interior. Colonial paintings embellished the walls, and a huge chandelier of Taxco silver hung in the vestibule. The salon was adorned with velvet and mahogany furniture from Jaime's Durango estate. On the mantel sat a signed photograph of Queen Victoria Eugenia of Spain, who had given it to Lola when the couple visited Madrid on their honeymoon.

Lola sat brooding in the drawing room, a small spaniel at her feet. Her next film, *Resurrection*, was sure to cause a row at home. She was to play Katyusha, a Russian peasant girl who becomes the mistress of a prince. When he abandons her, she turns to prostitution. Jaime would have a fit.

The puppy stood on its hind legs and laid his head on her knee. Lola stroked its silky fur and scratched its ears. She'd named him Dimitri after the prince in the film, but now she thought that hadn't been such a good idea. Every time she called to the dog, Jaime would be reminded of Carewe's pull on her.

"Maybe we'll change your name, *cachorro*," she murmured, running her lacquered nails over the pup's tiny head.

"Yes," I said. "Change his name. The last thing you need is more trouble with Jaime."

Carewe had made a deal with United Artists. They would release *Resurrection*, but he would have full artistic control. *What Price Glory?* had been a huge hit, and he was determined that *Resurrection* should do even better. It would establish him definitively as Lola's director and Lola as *his* star. He was not about to lend her to Raoul Walsh or anyone else ever again.

Carewe was seeing to every detail of the production himself. The film was based on a novel by Leo Tolstoy, and Carewe had contracted an exiled Russian general to make sure the czarist uniforms were authentic. He poured over paintings of peasants for images of babushkas and even brought in Tolstoy's son Ilya to serve as a technical adviser.

Lola had invited me over to see the new house, but what she really wanted was to talk—and not about hairstyles. She'd made a decision about Jaime, she confided, only she didn't know how to tell her mother. There was no one else she could talk to, she said. She needed my advice.

Lola's mother moved in with Jaime and Lola right after they'd bought the new house, while her father stayed in Mexico because of his job. Now Doña Antonia whooshed into the drawing room, her pajama-like trousers swiping the heavy brocade chairs. Lola knew she couldn't hide her heartache from her mother much longer. Doña Antonia had always known how to read her like a script.

"Want some coffee?" Doña Antonia plopped down on a love seat. "What about you, Mara? I'll ask Esperanza to make us some." Doña Antonia had hired Esperanza as her personal maid in Mexico City, and she'd been with the family ever since.

"I don't want coffee," said Lola. I was sure Doña Antonia would notice she'd been crying. Her eyes were still puffy, and her nose was red.

"I have an idea," said Doña Antonia. "Let's drive down to the beach. You, too, Mara."

"I don't know, Mami," murmured Lola. "I really don't feel like it."

"Come on! Get your bathing suit," prodded Doña Antonia.

"Your father's *socio* Alejandro Bakovitch has a place in Malibu, a secluded property where no one will see you. He and his wife are out of town, and they told me I could use it. You love to swim, and you need to get away, at least for a couple of hours. I'll tell Alfredo to get the car ready."

The sky was a soft periwinkle blue. Feathery clouds dawdled above the seagulls. Rays of sunlight, glittering and irregular like a monstrance, reached outward as though to embrace the world. To the right, the Santa Monica Mountains. Clusters of wildflowers as yellow as egg yolks gleamed against swaths of gray-green chaparral. To the left, the watery fingers of the Pacific kneaded the air.

I sat in the front with the chauffeur. In the back, Lola and Antonia relaxed in quiet familiarity, with no need to fill every pause with chatter. After the rush and bustle of the movie set, the steady whir of the motor seemed to calm Lola's nerves. I turned around to look at her. Her eyes were closed. The purr of the engine had lulled her to sleep. Yet I knew she was uneasy. She had to tell her mother what she'd already told me, and it wouldn't be easy. For Lola, Antonia was the Madonna in Blue and Saint George the Dragon Slayer rolled into one. She was the queen of the Catholic Ladies' Auxiliary League, the censor who glowered if a neighbor wore her skirt above the calf to Mass. How could Lola expect her to understand?

The gates opened and Bakovitch's groundskeeper waved us in.

"Shall I ask the kitchen staff to prepare lunch for you and serve it in a cabana?" he asked.

"That would be lovely," answered Doña Antonia.

Lola slipped into her bathing outfit—yellow-and-white knit shorts and a matching chemise—and ran toward the sea. From the shade of the cabana, Doña Antonia and I watched her strong, even strokes. The Bakovitch servants set out a rectangular folding table and lay a white linen cloth on it, and then, with remarkable efficiency, porcelain dishes, crystal stemware, and silver dining utensils. By the time Lola emerged, her arms dripping with foam and her hair in a frenzy, she'd worked up an appetite.

We chatted while we devoured our chiles rellenos, but Lola and I both knew we were tiptoeing around the issue: Jaime, the sacrificial lamb. Finally, Lola could no longer bear it.

"Mamá," she said, her voice wavering. "I'm thinking of getting a divorce."

I got up to leave them alone.

"No, Mara," said Lola. "Stay. I'm not going to tell her anything you don't already know."

Doña Antonia chewed slowly, then took a sip of wine. Lola braced for the barrage of blame that was sure to come. She hadn't been a good wife. She'd sacrificed her husband (the lamb) to her career. She hadn't given him a child. *If you'd attended to your marriage,* como Dios manda, her mother would say. And then there would be a sermon about the sacred, *indissoluble* bonds of marriage.

But Doña Antonia just chewed and sipped. *"Tendrás tus razones,"* she said finally. "I'm sure you have your reasons." Their eyes met. I could see the tenderness in Doña Antonia's gaze.

She put down her knife and fork and signaled the attendant that they were ready for dessert. "We don't count calories in this family," she announced to no one in particular. "The only thing I'll say is this," she continued, after a long pause. "Don't rush into anything."

"It's just that Jaime isn't… I mean… He can't satisfy me."

"I understand," said Doña Antonia calmly, "but even so, take a trip together. Go far away, where Edwin Carewe can't distract you. You might come to some sort of…arrangement."

So Doña Antonia knew about Carewe. Lola bit her lip, and

I know what was going through her head: What must Mamá think of me? How disappointed she must be.

"I think Jaime may be like Ramón," said Doña Antonia. Lola looked stunned.

"We all know about Ramón," she went on. "He is as God made him. If Jaime is that way, too, you won't change him. But you have an image to uphold, and he has his family honor. If you decide to stay with him, I'll stand by you, Lola. And if you decide to leave him, I'll stand by you then, too. *Mi gatita* will never be alone."

Lola threw her arms around her mother's shoulders. "Gracias, Mami," she whispered. "No girl was ever as lucky as I am."

Gabe and I saw each other regularly for a couple of months— a Coke at the canteen, a baseball game, a party at a friend's house. Then, one evening late in the summer of 1927, he called me. "I have something to ask you," he said. His voice was steady. He sounded confident.

"Yes?" I held my breath.

"Could you come to dinner this Sunday? Mamá and Papá would like to meet you."

I knew what that meant, and I had to purse my lips to avoid shrieking with joy.

"Of course, your Tía Emi must come, too. They want to meet the whole family."

14

How can I ever forget those glorious days? Even now, sixty years later, I feel angels dancing on my shoulders when I think of January 1928. That was the month when Gabe and I were married! The month I became Mrs. Gabriel Estrada.

Dinner with his parents meant that Gabe had finally made up his mind. That was the usual procedure: dinner with the family, father's approval, formal proposal, wedding to which every living relative and acquaintance would be invited— *abuelito, abuelita,* Tía This and Tío That, first cousins, second cousins, even ninth cousins living in Oaxaca or Timbuktu.

The question was: *What to do about Tía Emi?* One *"me cago en la leche"* to Gabe's father, and the whole thing could fall apart.

"I told Papá she couldn't come," Gabe told me. "I said she worked for a costume designer and was busy all the time, but he wasn't buying it. 'You wouldn't be marrying just Mara,' Gabe's father said. 'You'd be marrying her whole family, and if her whole family is her aunt, we need to meet her.' I couldn't get out of it," Gabe apologized, "so I began to drop hints that Tía Emi was a little…uh…odd."

Gabe and I would go to mass in the afternoon, then go to Gabe's house, where Tía Emi would join us. I hadn't gone to church regularly since I was a child in Durango—Tía Emi had lost her interest in religion long ago—but Gabe came from a churchgoing family.

"Wear a decent dress," I told Tía Emi. "Remember to brush your teeth, leave your cigarettes at home, don't be late, and don't say 'fuck.'"

"Me cago en la leche," she growled. "You've gotten as uptight as a constipated goose."

We arrived at the house long before she did. Gabe's mother, Lupe, was a warm and welcoming woman in her forties, with jet-black hair combed into a chignon. His father, Gabriel, was more reserved—a solid, no-nonsense type who worked with his hands and looked you straight in the eye. During the week he cut wooden beams to reinforce floors and ceilings, on Saturdays he watched baseball, and on Sundays he prayed. He had no patience for bad behavior.

We were chatting in the kitchen when I heard a knock so timid that no one else noticed.

"That must be Tía Emi," I murmured. Lizards were leaping around in my gut. Gabe went to open the door.

In walked Tía Emi wearing a neatly tailored, drop-waisted burgundy dress, a headband with faux jewels, and chunky, low heels. I recognized the dress as Madame Isabelle's. The perfume, too—Poème Arabe by Lionceau. I'd bobbed her hair after the housedress-and-pigtail incident, and she'd lacquered it close to her head, à la Pola Negri. She looked normal. Attractive, even.

"Buenas tardes," said Tía Emi.

During dinner, she hardly said a word, although there were a few close calls. My hands went clammy, for example, when Don Gabriel started asking questions about family history.

"So, Emilia," he said in Spanish, "how exactly are you related to Mara? Are you her aunt on her mother's side or her father's?"

I expected her to say: *I'm actually no relative of hers at all. She's just some kid I got stuck with.* Instead, she pretended not to understand.

"Are you her father's sister or her mother's sister?" Don Gabriel insisted.

I held my breath. *"Su mamá,"* she said after a pause.

"He must think she's stupid," I whispered to Gabe.

"And her mother died during the Revolution?"

"Before," said Tía Emi, *"antes de la Revolución."*

I breathed a sigh of relief. It was a smart answer. It avoided questions like: Was she pro-Villa or anti-Villa?

Eventually, the conversation turned to baseball, and she sat quietly, laughing when the others laughed, shrugging when they shrugged. She didn't say *me cago en la leche* even once.

"Gracias," I whispered to Tía Emi when we got home.

"No seas cabrona," she growled. The politest translation I can offer is: "Don't be an ass."

Not long after that, Gabe appeared in Madame Isabelle's living room holding a tiny red box. He opened it and showed me a delicate silver ring with a turquoise stone.

"What took you so long?" I teased.

"I was saving up for the ring." He grinned sheepishly. "And for later…" He kissed me gently and we both started to giggle. That was the marriage proposal.

I can hardly remember the wedding. My head was in a whirl. I didn't have bridesmaids and all that. Lola wasn't there. She was on a publicity tour for *Ramona*, which was going to open in May. I wasn't angry because I knew she didn't set her own schedule. On Gabe's side, there were about five hundred guests: family, friends, neighbors, the girl who sold burritos after mass at church, the boy who brought the Spanish-language newspaper on Sunday, and all the guys on Gabe's construction crew from First National. I had six guests: Tía Emi, Madame Isabelle, Marie and her husband, Miss Kathy, and Mr. Edmond.

Afterward, we went back to Gabe's house, where his mother had cleared out her sewing room to accommodate us until we found a place of our own. The wedding was on a Sunday. On Monday, we went to work.

Early in 1928 I also got my cosmetology license. The year before, the Board of Barbering and Cosmetology had made licenses mandatory. You had to take a pretty hard test, but I studied and passed with no problem. I was proud of myself. Now I could get more money for my services. At the same time, Gabe and Vince started their carpentry business. Don Gabriel gave them some money, and they bought a little house near Sunset Boulevard. It cost over four thousand dollars! The house had four rooms and a shed in the back. In the front room, the boys would set up their store. One of the back rooms would serve as a workshop, while the other would be our bedroom. The fourth room was a kitchen. Vince would refurbish the shed so it could be his bedroom. There was no plumbing out there, so he'd have to come into the house to use the bathroom, but for the moment, it would have to do.

I was too busy setting up house to think much about Lola. She'd told me before she left to film *Ramona* that she was excited to be playing a tragic heroine instead of a whore, but she was nervous, too. The studios were ruthless, and if your film flopped, they would drop you in a minute. Scarier still, sound pictures were coming. The first talking movie, *The Jazz Singer*, had been released the year before, and Lola knew that there were plenty of young American actresses with perfect English pronunciation ready to replace her as screenland's hottest item.

Ramona wasn't scheduled to open until May, but requests for interviews came pouring in.

"Come with me," she begged. "I've missed you! And besides, my hair has to look good when I talk to the press."

"No, Lola," I told her. "I'm too busy now."

But Lola always managed to get what she wanted, and a few days later, I found myself accompanying her to the offices of *Star World Magazine*, where the gossip columnist Carla Myer was waiting with clamps and prongs and other instruments of torture to pry information from her prey.

It was a cool February morning, and Lola's chauffeur, Alfredo, steered the Studebaker through the West Hollywood Hills with expertise. The *Star World* offices weren't elegant, but they were located in a tony district favored by movie people. A pathway of cracked flagstones led to the small, drab stucco building. A wannabe building, I thought. A building that yearned for a new coat of paint and a glitzy sign over the door so it could compete with the really glamorous buildings in the neighborhood—the Elizabeth Arden salon, with its bright red awning; the Montgomery Properties Building, with its graceful faux-Greek columns; the Bank of America, with its imposing statues. Carla was just like the building where she had her office. Past her prime, in need of an overhaul, and envious of newcomers.

Carla shook Lola's hand and looked at me as though I were some peculiar object she didn't quite know where to put.

"I can wait in the hall," I said.

Lola nudged me into the office. "Mrs. Estrada is my assistant," she said. "She will accompany me." I smiled at the mention of my new name.

The office was small and grungy. Photos of movie stars covered the walls, and old copies of *Star World* were stacked by a tiny window that faced an alley. Carla pointed to two utilitarian chairs in a corner and nodded for us to sit down. She perched opposite, placing her ample tail on the edge of the seat and leaning forward, as if ready to pounce. She picked up her notepad.

"Usually interviewers meet me at the studio or a restaurant," said Lola. Her voice was clear and confident.

Carla shrugged to make sure we understood that the remark was of no interest to her.

"So, you play a half-breed in this movie," she began provocatively.

Lola smiled, opening wide her luscious chocolate eyes. "I see Ramona as a tribute to the indigenous peoples, a romantic *mixed-race* heroine who loves and marries an Indian man."

"She was Scottish in the novel by Helen Hunt Jackson," said Carla. "But I can see why they changed it. You can't show a white woman marrying an Indian."

"Ramona lives with her aunt, Señora Moreno, and a cousin named Felipe on a ranch in California, when California was still part of Mexico," Lola went on. "Ramona is…how do you say…? She is snobbed because…"

"Snubbed. She is *snubbed*," said Carla. "The thing is, Miss Del Rio," she went on. (Stars were always called "Miss," whether they were married or not.) "The audience knows that both you and your leading man, Warner Baxter, are white, so it's really not an issue."

"She is *snubbed* because she is a *mestiza*. You know, part Indian and part Spanish. Ramona falls in love with an Indian shepherd…"

"And he cheats on her?" Carla interrupted.

"No, they have a baby, but he and the baby die. And then Ramona…she goes kind of crazy… Felipe finds her wandering through the mountains. She can't remember anything, so he takes her home, and that's the end."

"So, they're both Indian. Felipe and Ramona, I mean."

"Ramona is the daughter of a Mexican and a pure Indian."

"But it's the same thing, right? How do you feel about playing an Indian? In your last film, *The Loves of Carmen*, you played a Spaniard, so this is something of a demotion."

"I'm Mexican," said Lola, ignoring Carla's remark. "I'm proud to play a Mexican woman who is the heroine of a lovely romantic story. I want to show Mexicans in a good way. I have some Aztec blood myself, as you can see. I'm not dark for a Mexican, but a shade darker than the average white American. I'm not ashamed of it, Miss Myer. I'm delighted. My skin tone reflects my heritage!"

"Your studio says you're a Spanish aristocrat!" Carla grinned as though she'd caught her.

"Ed Carewe knows I'm a *mestiza*," said Lola smoothly. "He's part Chickasaw himself."

Carla raised an eyebrow. Lola had told her something she didn't know. She paused, formulating her next question. "I hear you sing in this movie," she said finally.

"Yes, I do. It's United Artists' first movie with a synchronized score. It's not a talking film, but it has music, and I sing the song 'Ramona.'"

"And the rumors about you and Jaime? I heard you were getting a divorce."

Now I've got her! Carla must have thought. But Lola had been expecting the question. Reporters had been asking about her and Jaime for days.

"We're going to Hawaii for a vacation. Then, Jaime is going to New York to make a movie with RKO." Lola stood up. "I really have to be going now, Miss Myer," she said. "A reporter from *Photoplay* is meeting me at the Beverly Hills Hotel for coffee and an interview."

In other words, as Tía Emi would say, *"¡Me cago en la leche!"*

"¡Cabrona!" Lola whispered as we slipped out the door.

15

Years later, Lola would remember March 29, 1928, with a certain uneasiness. I know all about it because she told me many times.

Fixed in her mind were the tepid spring sunshine, the bright pink hibiscus in front of the Fairbanks-Pickford bungalow at the United Artists studio, the scent of jasmine in the air, the black open-throat dress with white lace trim that she wore, Charlie's sulking, and the soft lilt of Norma's chatter. Most of all, she remembered the sense of solidarity and friendship that brought them all together. And what came afterward.

The very name "United Artists" gave Lola a thrill. Artists who worked together. Artists who were united in their determination to control their projects rather than depend on the powerful commercial studios. D. W. Griffith, Charlie Chaplin, Mary Pickford, and Douglas Fairbanks were all veteran movie people with plenty of contacts and money, but that wasn't enough. They wanted a voice. They wanted their films to express their artistic vision. In 1919, they did something revolutionary: they formed United Artists. The plan was to produce five films a year, but it turned out to be harder than they'd thought. Feature films were growing more expensive, and artists are not necessarily shrewd entrepreneurs. It wasn't until they brought in producer Joseph Schenck, whose wife, Norma Talmadge, and brother-in-law Buster Keaton were box office sensations, that the experiment bore fruit.

Now the old friends had gathered on the lot to face together this terrible new monster that imperiled them all: talkies. Almost all of them were there except for Pickford, who had withdrawn at the last minute because her mother had died. There were a couple of new faces, too. John Barrymore for one, and, of course, Lola. Folks were anxious to know if the idols who enthralled them on the screen would lose their allure when they opened their mouths and produced sound. If it turned out that a dazzling vamp cackled like an irate hen, no one would want to spend a whole quarter to see her. And for actors like Lola and Ramón—foreigners with accents—the stakes were especially high. But Schenck had come up with an idea. It occurred to him that if UA's silent screen greats were to appear on the popular *Dodge Brothers Radio Hour*, fans would see they had no cause for alarm. The Dodge Brothers show aired on the new National Broadcasting Network, which included some fifty stations. The broadcast would be heard not only in homes, but also in movie theaters, by means of a fifty-five-city hookup.

"It'll be heard by fifty million people!" Lola had announced excitedly. "I wish you could go with me, Mara, but I know you can't. You have to be at Marie's. It's not that I'd need a hairdresser at a radio broadcast, but I'd love to have you there for moral support!"

"You'll be fine," I had said, kissing her on the cheek. "I'm sure you'll tell me all about it." And she did. I also read about it in the newspapers.

Looking prim yet stylish, Lola stood next to Fairbanks in the garden in front of the studio, waiting to enter. She giggled

nervously. Other stars, including English-speakers, had opted
not even to try to make the transition to talkies. Raymond
Griffith, one of the greatest silent comedians, had decided that
his career was already over. Mexicans like Ramón quaked at
the thought that their accents might make them unemployable.

Chaplin, the eternal clown, was uncharacteristically sub-
dued. "What are you going to talk about, Doug?" he said finally, addressing Fairbanks.

"It's not like you to deflect attention from yourself, Charlie," snapped Fairbanks. "What's wrong?"

"I'm scared shitless!" said Chaplin earnestly. "Mic fright!"

"What are *you* going to talk about, Lola?" asked Fairbanks.

"It's a secret!" Even now I can imagine her grinning co-
quettishly.

"I'm going to recite the 'to be or not to be' soliloquy from
Hamlet. Norma's going to talk about costume and fashion in
the movies. What's the big mystery, Lola?"

"Leave her alone," growled Talmadge. "I'm sure she has
something beautiful prepared."

"Of course," Lola told me afterward. "For me, it wasn't
only a matter of proving that I had a decent speaking voice,
but also that I could speak English without mangling it. The
whole world was waiting for me to fall on my face."

At last, Schenck guided them into the bungalow, where mi-
crophones had been set up. The members of the Paul White-
man Orchestra took their places. The odor of anxiety filled the
space. Chaplin wiped his mustache with his wrist, reminding
Lola of a kitten cleaning its whiskers. Norma Talmadge shifted
from one foot to the other—an edgy little two-step that made
her look like a cat on coals. Everyone knew this broadcast was
a potential career-killer. Only Barrymore looked calm.

Schenck gave the signal, and all of them entered the building. Dodge Brothers Company president Edward G. Wilmer

took his spot behind the mic. Instead of announcing the artists, he launched into a rambling discourse on the virtues of his latest model, "The Standard Six." The suspension...the breaks...the efficiency... On and on. Chaplin's face was as white as an unused chamber pot. The six-cylinder, L-head engine... A bargain at only $835... Lola began to squirm. She suddenly had to urinate, but at any moment Wilmer might wind it up and Schenck would signal her to step up to the mic. She couldn't take a chance and leave the room.

Shut up! mouthed Norma.

Lola nodded vigorously in agreement.

At last Wilmer sat down and Fairbanks got up. "To be or not to be," he intoned.

No one remembered what Chaplin said when he took the microphone because he began to stutter so violently that his words were lost in a barrage of "l...l...la...g...ge...uh...uh..."

"Dios mío," said Lola to herself. "Poor Charlie."

Lola's turn came toward the end. She forgot her desire to pee and adopted the air of a Spanish dancer. Chin up. Shoulders back. She stepped behind the microphone with exaggerated confidence and took a deep breath.

Unexpectedly, the orchestra began to play. The artists looked at each other. What was going on? The only one who wasn't flustered was Lola, who had clearly arranged the whole thing in advance. Her voice rang out, clear and crisp as a chime.

> *"Ramona, I hear the mission bells above*
> *Ramona, they're ringing out our song of love*
> *I press you, caress you*
> *And bless the day you taught me to care*
> *I'll always remember*
> *The rambling rose you wore in your hair..."*

I heard it on the radio. You could hardly understand a word she was saying, but what difference did it make? Her voice was lovely.

"By God," laughed Barrymore when the broadcast was over. "You beat the system, Lola! You were wonderful! People are going to fall in love with you all over again!"

But who knew what the critics would say?

In the morning, I went to Lola's house early and let myself in. She had given me the key so I could have easy access to her wardrobe, hair paraphernalia...whatever she needed. I was dozing on the sofa when she came downstairs. I'd have to leave for Marie's soon, but I wanted to be with her when the newspapers came in.

Lola kicked off her slippers and kissed me on the cheek. Luz entered the living room with the morning papers, which the studio had sent over. Lola held her breath. All the East Coast reviews and some from the Midwest were already in. A secretary had organized them, the most glowing on top.

One Atlanta newspaper called her performance "winning" and said they'd like to see more of her, but most of the reviews were horrendous—scathingly critical not only of her but of everyone. The *Chicago Tribune* was dismissive. "She sang a Mexican song," remarked Elmer Douglass. In a later edition of the same newspaper, Quinn A. Ryan noted her heavy Spanish accent and predicted that she would flop in sound films. Some critics even suggested that she hadn't done her own singing. They were even crueler to her colleagues. About Chaplin's stuttering monologue, *Variety* noted that, "Movie stars should be screened and not heard." Who could blame Charlie for being squeamish about talkies after that?

All day long, reports came in on the radio. Schenck made excuses: rainfall in the Northeast and ice storms in the Midwest had hindered reception. Some of the theaters had faulty receptors. Then, notices of audience revolt began to pour in. At the Fifth Avenue Playhouse in New York, Talmadge's ramblings about fashion had sent spectators over the edge. Crowds screamed, "Take her off the air!" After twenty minutes, management obliged. At Loew's Grand, spectators stomped their feet and yowled.

In the afternoon, during a break at Marie's, I called Gabe at the workshop. "I have to go over to Lola's right after work," I told him.

"You were just there this morning."

"I know, but the reviews of the radio broadcast are awful. She'll be a wreck. I need to calm her down, give her a back rub or something. She's my best friend, Gabe. I have to."

Gabe wasn't happy, but if there was one thing he understood, it was loyalty.

"Okay," he said. "Try not to get back late."

"It's not the end of the world," I kept telling Lola.

The phone rang. "I don't want to talk to anyone!" she called downstairs to Luz from her bed.

"It's Mr. Carewe, señora. He says it's *urgente!*"

"Tell him I went back to Mexico," wailed Lola. "Tell him I died."

"*¡Urgente, señora!*"

"Tell him to go to hell!"

"*¡Urgente, señora! ¡Urgente!*"

"Maybe you'd better take it, Lola," I said. "If it's bad news, better to get it over with."

Dimitri—she never did change his name—pitched sharp little barks at her. "I feel as though I were being pelted with stones," she moaned. She turned to the dog. *"Et tu, Brutus?"*

I accompanied her downstairs to the phone. "Stand right next to me so you can hear what he says," she ordered. "If he fires me, I want you to be there to pick up the pieces."

"Isn't it wonderful, darling?" Carewe's voice boomed through the receiver. He sounded as though he were doing a radio commercial for Black Cat stove polish. "Isn't it wonderful, darling! My oven shines like new!"

"What's wonderful, Ed? That Quinn Ryan says I have no future in film?"

"Who cares about Ryan? I'm talking about the song! 'Ramona' is flying off the shelves! The record stores can't keep it stocked! It's going to be an international bestseller. The movie was already going to be a success, and now the song is going to make it a smash hit!"

Lola breathed a sigh of relief.

"Listen," said Ed. "We have to celebrate. The minute you finish that turkey *The Red Dancer*, we should go away together. Just you and me."

"Are you serious?" Lola directed her gaze at Dimitri, who had followed us downstairs. "Did you hear that, *cachorro*? Ed has gone mad!"

The "turkey" Ed was referring to was Lola's current film project, *The Red Dancer of Moscow*, which he had tried to prevent. The story was too close to *Resurrection*, he argued. Another beautiful, destitute Russian dancer in love with a nobleman. Another film by Raoul Walsh. Ed ordered his lawyer, Gunther Lessing, to extricate Lola from Fox. The problem was, Lola didn't want to be extricated. She liked working with Walsh, and she was getting tired of Carewe's controlling ways.

"I can't go away with you, Ed," she told him, "even if you're right about *Ramona*."

Ever since Ed had divorced Mary, he'd pestered Lola constantly to take off with him on his yacht to some distant, romantic island, but what she really wanted was to end their affair.

Lola said goodbye and sat down on the sofa with her new

script. Dimitri stretched out on her lap, his nose hanging over one of her legs. She caressed his ears gently. He still had that sweet, pungent puppy odor. Lola scratched him on the head and he wiggled onto his back. "Tummy rub?" she whispered. "How can I learn the role of Tasia if I'm tickling your tummy?"

"Prison!" she intoned. "They've thrown the grand duke into prison! I must go to him!"

Dimitri perked up his ears.

"Not you," she said with a sigh. "You're not going to prison. You're just going out to the garden to pee. It's the Grand Duke Eugene who's in the clink!"

"Well," I said. "It looks like everything's going to be fine. I'll be off now."

16

I've pieced together this part of the story from what other people told me—Luz, Doña Antonia, Lola herself, and people like Carewe's lackeys—Max McClelland and the other guy, Edelstein. This is what happened:

Doña Antonia returned quite late from her mahjong game, but Lola wasn't home. She pulled off her gloves, then unbuckled her shoes and kicked them off. She lay down on the couch, confident that her new Debenham and Freebody knit suit wouldn't wrinkle. She had seen it in *Vogue* and imported it from London. She adored the long, slender line, the thigh-length jacket with the appliqué rose, and the extended lapel. Youthful, she thought. Stylish.

Dimitri snapped her back to the moment. He was whining and pawing at her foot.

"Stop that!" she snapped. "*¡Desgraciado!* You'll ruin my outfit and rip my stockings!" She sat up with a jerk. It was clear that the dog needed to go out. Where was everybody? "Luz! Esperanza!" she called. The house was empty. Jaime had moved out weeks ago. She got up and peered into the kitchen. Then she opened the door to the patio. Dimitri bounded out, desperate to relieve himself. Doña Antonia slipped into her shoes without buckling them and followed him into the garden.

When the dog had done his business, Doña Antonia went back inside and called me.

"I'm sorry, Doña Antonia," I told her. "I haven't seen Lola for hours." I was annoyed. It was the middle of the night, and I had to get up early for work.

She paced back and forth until morning, then called the studio.

"I don't know, Mrs. López," said the secretary. "We haven't seen Miss Del Rio today."

She hated that Americans called her Mrs. López instead of using her full name, López Negrete de Asúnsolo, but they had enough trouble with López, never mind Asúnsolo.

"Thank you," she said. "Do you by any chance know where she is?"

The secretary didn't. Doña Antonia sat down and tried to think what to do. She picked up a magazine. Photo after photo of Lola. Lola in a drop-waist chiffon dress. Lola in a floor-length gown. Lola in her Ramona costume with braids and a shawl. Doña Antonia was growing fidgety.

The phone rang. It was Luz. Señorita Dolores was in the hospital, she said. Señorita Dolores collapsed after dinner, and when Luz couldn't revive her, she called Ramón Novarro. Luz was composed and articulate, but before she could finish her story, Doña Antonia began to wail.

"Why didn't you call me immediately?" she howled.

"I didn't know where you were, señora," said Luz calmly. She was used to the hysteria of rich people. "Don Ramón came right away, though, and he took us to the hospital. Don Ramón is always dependable…"

"What about Alfredo?" Doña Antonia growled. "Where was he?" She'd forgotten that it was the chauffeur's day off.

"I know you want to go to the hospital," said Luz, still unruffled. "Would you like me to call Don Ramón's house again? If he isn't there, maybe they can send someone to drive you."

"First I'll call the hospital and see what I can find out."

Doña Antonia's eyes landed on Dimitri. "And why didn't someone let the dog out? The poor beast was ready to explode when I got home!"

"Esperanza and I accompanied Doña Dolores," said Luz. "We packed her nightgowns." Doña Antonia breathed into the telephone, as if waiting for a more complete explanation. Then she hung up. The phone rang again.

"It's Eddie," said the voice on the other end. "You need to come to the hospital. Lola is asking for you. I'll send a car."

When, an hour later, Lola's mother walked into the hospital room, she was surprised to see Lola sitting up in bed and surrounded by men. Ed Carewe was there, of course. He was always there. He'd convinced Lola to sign a contract giving him almost complete control of her career, which meant she was tied to him day and night, even though their affair was winding down.

"Oh, Toña, hi!" Carewe called when he saw her in the doorway. "Lola's fine. Well, she's going to be fine. The doctor says she collapsed from fatigue. Stress. Worry. You know, the business about Jaime. This is Harry Wilson, our publicist, Sam Edelstein, his assistant, and Jerry Montgomery, our marketer. And Max. You know our advance man, Max McClelland. We're figuring out how to spin it."

Antonia bent over her daughter and kissed her on the forehead. "*¿Qué te pasó, Gatita?* Spin it? What do you mean, spin it?"

"How we're going to present the divorce thing to the papers. We think this hospital stay could work to our advantage."

Lola's gaze floated from one to the other. She had the look

of a soldier who has just seen his best friend take a bullet between the eyes.

"Lolita, lie back and rest," whispered Doña Antonia. "Let them take their spinning into another room."

"Ha ha! Take their spinning... That's cute!" chortled Carewe. "No, Lola has to be here. She has to be in on the story. I mean, it has to be *hers*, Toña. She has to *own* it."

The plan was to distract fans from the impending divorce so that they didn't ask too many questions. "We don't want it to hit the papers," Carewe said. "It would be a disaster."

"You mean, Lola's illness?" asked Doña Antonia, incredulous.

"Of course not, Toña! That's not the problem, that's the solution!"

"What are you talking about, Eddie?" Doña Antonia was completely lost.

"The divorce, Toña! What else could we be talking about?" said Carewe. "We've sold Lola to the public as an upright married woman who plays a vamp but who in real life is a goddamn saint. But now she's getting a divorce! How is that going to look?"

Carewe turned to the others. "We should send out a press release about the illness right away, before all hell breaks loose about the divorce."

"Poor Lola. She collapsed from overwork!" chimed in Edelstein, whipping out a handkerchief and drying mock tears. "They'll love it! You'll see, people will send her flowers and get-well cards."

"Divorce is sticky in Hollywood," explained Montgomery. "It taints your image."

"Mary Pickford divorced Owen Moore," retorted Doña Antonia. "And her career survived."

"But Moore was an alcoholic. He used to beat the hell out

of her." Montgomery spoke slowly, as if explaining a difficult concept to a doltish schoolboy. "The public's sympathy
was with Mary, 'America's sweetheart.' You know, long blond
curls, doe eyes, all that. The trick is to get the hospital story
out before Lola and Jaime get divorced," said Montgomery.
"Then, when the divorce actually happens, nobody will even
notice!"

Once she returned home, Lola sat down and wrote a long
letter to Jaime, who had gone east for the filming of *From
Hell Came a Lady*, for which he'd written the story. *Ramona*
had opened in New York in May and was still drawing huge
crowds, but Jaime's film, which had premiered a few weeks
earlier with the title *The Woman from Hell*, was showing no
signs of life at all. The critics mostly ignored it. Moviegoers
stayed home. "I miss you," she said in her note. "I love you."
She placed a photo of herself in her Ramona costume in an
envelope and wrote Jaime's New York address on it. Hearing
Carewe and his men spin the story about her still unannounced
divorce while she lay in a hospital bed made her miss Jaime
more than ever. He might have different sexual preferences,
but at least he wasn't a callous bastard.

"I don't know what to do," she told her mother.

"Just wait," said Doña Antonia. "When the time comes,
you'll know."

"But I've always depended on Jaime."

"You'll be fine. Cats always land on their feet." Doña Antonia had thought about it a long time. She had been through
a war and survived. She knew her daughter's marriage was
doomed, but she also knew that people survived heartbreak
better than bullets.

When Jaime's answer came, Lola read the letter dry-eyed
and composed.

"It's a flop," he wrote. He used the English word *flop*: "*Es un* flop!" "I'm leaving New York, Lola. I'm thinking of going to Europe. Maybe to Germany. The film industry is booming there. Berlin is full of creative people." She could almost hear his voice quivering. "I've been a failure, Lola," he wrote. "I'm not the right man for you. I've let you down. It's better this way."

"Yes," she whispered, "I suppose it is." That evening, when she wrote her reply, she wished him luck, but didn't beg him to come back to Los Angeles.

17

Lola had made her decision.

"Please come with me, Mara," she begged.

"I can't, Lola. I can't travel right now." I was debating whether or not to tell her. Her only pregnancy had ended tragically, and I didn't want to bring back bad memories.

"Please, Mara!" She sounded miserable. "I can't do this alone."

"You won't be alone. Your mother is going with you."

"But I need *you*, Mara. You're like a sister to me."

Sooner or later, she'll have to know, I thought. I took a deep breath. "I haven't told Gabe yet, but I'm expecting," I said simply. "I can't travel."

She put down the sweater she was holding and looked at me. The color had drained from her cheeks. "Ex-expecting?" she stammered. "A baby?"

"What else would I be expecting, Lola? The trolley?"

She hesitated a moment. Then she burst into smiles and pulled me close. "Congratulations, *mi amor*! That's wonderful! Finally, I'll be an aunt!"

"Not only an aunt, but a godmother!"

She hugged me again, but I could tell she was struggling

to contain the tears. I'm sure it wasn't that she resented my pregnancy, not at all. I believe she was truly happy for me. But it must have hurt. This was the one area of her life where she felt she'd failed. After all, back then, a Mexican woman—especially a woman of Lola's background—was expected to marry and have children, not nurture a career. Doña Antonia had made it very clear that she wanted to be a grandmother, but Lola hadn't been able to make that particular dream come true. And now her marriage…

I watched her fold each piece of clothing carefully and place it in the suitcase. A black-and-tan Egyptian-patterned knit suit with a pleated navy skirt, a silk Georgette dress with embroidered sleeves, an ankle-length chemise dress, assorted shoes, gloves, and cloches.

"I tried, Mara. Truly I did. We took a vacation, the way Mami suggested. We went to Hawaii. But then, Jaime insisted on bringing back three 'houseguests'—men half his age who hung around the pool with him during the day and at night… who knows? At least he was in a better mood than before. As soon as they were gone, he left for New York. He needed some space, he said, at least, for a while. That's the last time I saw him."

I understood. I didn't judge Lola harshly anymore. Doña Antonia had grasped the reality of her situation long before I had.

"They'll be here any minute!" called Doña Antonia.

"I'm all packed, Mamá."

"*Está bien.* I'll have Alfredo get the bags."

Poor Lola, I thought. Despite all her success… She was staring at the wedding ring lying on the dresser. She gathered it up and wrapped it in a handkerchief, then tied it with a ribbon and put it in a drawer. She bit her lip to steady her chin. Soon they'd be on the road to Nogales, a border town part in Arizona and part in Mexico, known for divorces. She and Doña Antonia would go in one car, driven by Alfredo. Harry Wilson, her press agent, and Gunther Lessing, Edwin Carewe's crackerjack lawyer, would ride in another. Lessing would plead "incompatibility." She wouldn't stay to hear the final declaration.

Within a week, she would be a different person. She would no longer be a married woman, and the dream that had blossomed in the breast of a sixteen-year-old bride less than seven years before would be shattered for good.

18

Carewe wasted no time getting Lola back into the public eye. An extended absence from the limelight could destroy an actress's career, so when an invitation materialized to a party celebrating the success of *Ramona*, Carewe said yes. I went, too, of course. Lola's hair had to look perfect at all times.

"Can Gabe come?" I asked. I didn't like leaving him alone while I went off to a party.

"I suppose so," said Lola, "if he has a tux."

But Gabe had no interest in going. "I hate all that fawning and posing," he said. "Why do you want to go?"

"I don't," I said, "but it's part of my job."

"Well, make sure they pay you extra. You know, hardship compensation." He kissed me on the forehead, and I lay my head on his chest. Strong, sturdy Gabe, as solid as the beautiful teakwood cabinets he crafted in his shop. He laid his hand on my belly. "You're still not...?"

I giggled. "I didn't want to say anything yet."

"Oh!" He was beaming. "I'll light a candle to the Virgin. Stay away from the champagne, just in case."

"Promise!"

The plan was for me to arrive early and wander around,

making myself invisible. Lola didn't want me to enter with her entourage. She didn't want people to realize that she actually needed help to achieve that image of perfection. Periodically, she would disappear to the powder room and I would follow, she explained. She lent me a plain black evening dress.

I felt like a duck in a chicken coop. Society people, movie people. They were fascinating to watch, but I had nothing to say to any of them. The only person I knew was Max McClelland, the advance guy, who had driven me to the party. He was a fiercely ambitious man, but he'd taken a liking to me. I wandered around the room, my champagne glass filled with ginger ale, eavesdropping on conversations.

"She has an impossibly adorable navel," said a gorgeous blonde with a foreign accent.

"Greta, you are infuriating!" said a dark-haired woman—a colorful creature that seemed a cross between a radiant orchid and a keel-billed toucan, all magenta, turquoise, and ginger.

"It's true, Frida," said Greta. "It's a work of art, a finely chiseled marble bas-relief. She knows it, too. Why do you think she wears those midriff-baring blouses?"

"Are you in love with her?" teased Frida. "Are you going to be my rival for her affections?"

"Of course, darling. Why not?"

Greta looked enigmatically into her champagne glass. She watched the bubbles soar to the surface, then burst and fizzle like minuscule rockets. A smile crossed her lips. She turned away without uttering another word and drifted into the crowd.

The crème de la crème had gathered at the mansion of a hostess whose name no one bothered to remember to fête the success of *Ramona*. The house and gardens sprawled over two acres at the foot of the Hollywood Hills and boasted multiple levels, with balconies, patios, and a massive swimming pool.

Spanish wrought iron gates opened to admit the parade of vehicles that snaked up the driveway at least twice a month for parties. The room was abuzz with Hollywood glitterati— Greta Garbo, Joan Crawford, Ramón Novarro—a nonstop pageant of stars, directors, producers, designers, and hangers-on. The movie business was less than three decades old, but it had already produced an aristocracy.

The hostess was one of a handful of society wives who made a career of receiving movie people at their extravagant residences. Her taste was easy to define: anything less than too much was not enough. Paintings by van Gogh, Corot, Renoir, and "Darling, I really can't remember his name, but I paid a fortune for it." Chandeliers of cascading crystal, tufted sofas in pink and blue brocade, Chinese silk cushions, heavy marble coffee tables, intricately carved side tables covered with statues of naked boys carrying water pitchers, lutes, or dead animals. "Hollywood baroque," Gabe called it. He'd seen these interiors when he delivered cabinets to women like this.

That evening, the buzz was all about the reviews. Mordaunt Hall of the *New York Times* had called *Ramona* "an extraordinarily beautiful production, intelligently directed and splendidly acted." Actually, his words were: "intelligently directed and, with the exception of a few instances, splendidly acted," but the adman had performed a few nips and tucks before plastering Hall's quote all over the publicity posters.

In the spacious salon, a band was playing "Swanee River." Butlers pulled open the wide exterior doors so that guests could mingle in the patio and pool areas, bright with reflected starlight and outdoor lamps. The staff had installed a temporary dance floor in the farthest patio, where a second band played "Meet Me Where the Lanterns Glow." Photographers captured the glamour of the moment for the readers of *Photoplay*, *Star World*, or *Motion Picture*.

Two willowy blondes with astoundingly long legs and Marcel waves were sipping from fluted glasses. One wore a mauve, ankle-length gown with multiple ruffled tiers that emphasized the slimness of her hips. The other wore a free-flowing, Greek-style toga of a soft flaxen color, fastened at the shoulder with a diamond brooch and hemmed on the bias.

"Lola was the perfect choice to play Ramona," one of them was saying. "She has that—how can I say it?—that exoticness."

"So much better than Mary Pickford in the 1910 version. That's what they say, anyway. I never saw it, of course. I was just a child…"

The band in the salon was now playing "Sweet Georgia Brown." No one was dancing, but Max McClelland was tapping his foot in time to the music, causing his long black jacket to joggle and sway. Crystal clinked on china as uniformed waiters wove among guests offering trays of bacon-wrapped lobster, filet mignon skewers, and caviar on dainty, crustless slivers of bread. When the band switched to "Saint Louis Blues," several guests began to dance.

The woman called Frida edged her way over to Max.

"Darling!" he exclaimed. "What a surprise to see you!"

Frida tapped him on the ankle with her walking stick. "Why? Because I'm still alive?" She gave him a grin that exuded honey and acid.

"How are you feeling, dear?"

"Like shit, as usual. How about you?" Her long, frilly Tehuana skirts barely covered her bulky orthopedic shoes. "I don't see Jaime."

"Lola is coming with Ed."

"Of course she is. What does she need Jaime for? Her slimy director friend is much more useful to her now."

Max stared at her a moment. The flamboyant, plumed headdress, the delicate blouse all lacy and girly, the piercing brown eyes filled with bitterness and pain—the pieces didn't fit together. She was like some outlandish hybrid from Aztec mythology.

"It must have been hard on Jaime," mused Frida. "To follow his wife to Hollywood and then become Mr. Dolores Del Rio."

"It wasn't exactly like that."

"It's never *exactly* like that."

Suddenly, both bands stopped. A hush came over the grand salon, rippling over the gathering inside and then spreading out into the open air. Guests made their way back from the decks and gardens. Waiters disappeared silently into the kitchen. "She's coming," people whispered. "She's here!"

The musicians took up their instruments again, and strains of "Ramona" began to rise and swell. Frida sang under her breath, in her raspy croak: "Ramona, I hear the mission bells above / Ramona, they're ringing out our song of love."

"Shh!" scolded another guest.

Frida lifted her chin and glared at her rebuker through squinty eyes.

The massive front door opened. Exquisite, raven-haired, and wrapped in mink, Lola entered the room on the arm of a man in his forties, sharp-featured but balding. Of course I knew it was Ed, but somehow, it all felt so strange...so alien... it was as though I'd never seen him before.

The head butler announced: "Miss Dolores Del Rio and Mr. Edwin Carewe."

Oohs and ahs. Gulps and sighs. Lola allowed the fur to slip down her arms and then, with a dramatic gesture, handed it to Luz, who, in full servant's garb, was positioned by her side and waiting to take it.

Eastman cameras clicked loudly. Lola smiled beguilingly, first for one photographer, then another. Her one-shouldered

Poiret gown, with dropped waist and handkerchief points at the hem, was designed to show off her lovely back and arms, while her low, tight chignon highlighted her faintly olive complexion and her vaguely Indigenous features.

I stood in the shadows, fascinated. My eyes darted around the room. I caught sight of Ramón. A familiar face! I moved closer to him. He was standing next to the woman named Greta, who was picking at her plate of boiled shrimp and peering at the newly arrived couple.

"As usual, your cousin has taken their breath away," she whispered to Ramón. If he resented playing second fiddle to Lola this evening, he didn't show it. "Whiskey is so much better since Prohibition, don't you think, darling?" she teased.

"Absolutely," murmured Ramón. "Infinitely more potent."

Greta put down her dish and pulled a long, bejeweled cigarette holder out of her purse along with a pre-rolled cigarette. Frida appeared with a lighter and held up the flame. I was hoping the women would wander away so I could approach Ramón. It was uncomfortable having no one to talk to. Ramón was always kind and gallant. But Frida stayed glued to Greta's side, and Greta didn't move.

Lola smiled with rehearsed elegance at her admirers. She was twenty-four, with seven films under her belt, and she knew how to work an audience. Her laughter tinkled like diamonds on crystal. She squeezed hands and kissed cheeks.

Soft, purple shadows crept over the walls. The band drew out the notes of "Ramona," converting Gilbert and Wayne's score into a languid, achingly romantic love plaint. The scent of Chanel No. 5, the new fragrance from Paris, mingled with the aromas of colorful blooms that had been placed on tables and mantelpieces. Black-clad waiters stole like shadows through the crowd, offering delicacies, removing plates.

Glasses were refilled as though by enchantment. It all seemed magical. Gabe would hate this, I thought.

"Please," gushed the hostess, lifting a gem-bedecked index finger. "Please, Miss Del Rio would like to say a few words."

The murmur subsided.

"Please!" The hostess turned to face Lola, gazing at her as though she were a priceless Greek sculpture.

Lola opened wide her huge eyes and brushed an invisible strand of hair off her perfect forehead. Everything about her was impeccable—the eyes like elongated, upturned coffee beans, the ruby-red sweetheart lips. She inhaled deeply and prepared to speak.

"Ladies and yentlaymen…"

"Oh, fuck!" Max McClelland was positioned behind a large potted plant. Lola couldn't see him, but he could observe her every movement through the fronds. The guests close to him choked back snickers and guffaws. Sam Leighton, the speech coach, was standing slightly behind him, also out of Lola's line of vision.

"I wan' to tank jou…" Lola went on.

"Fuck it, Sam!" whispered Max. "I told you to work on her pronunciation!"

But Sam was doubled over in hysterics. The Scotch in his hand trembled dangerously, the ice smacking against the side of the glass. He clamped his teeth over his lips to keep from laughing aloud.

"Shit, man! I'm sorry, Max," whispered Sam. "I *have* been working with her, but she just can't shake that goddamn accent. Anyhow, I think it's kind of cute. What's the big deal, Max? She doesn't have to talk. All she has to do is be beautiful and mouth the words."

Some of the guests had turned to stare at the pair, clearly more interested in the spat than in Lola's speech. Max, lanky and large, with the jaw of a tyrannosaurus, towered over his collaborator, who stood less than five and a half feet tall. He looked as though he were going to bite Sam's head off.

"For *now* she can mouth the words, Sam, for *now*. But things are changing. The silents are on their way out. Talkies are the new thing."

"They'll never catch on." Sam wiped a drop of Scotch off his graying mustache.

"They're already catching on! Warner Brothers made a killing on *The Jazz Singer* last year. Lola's career is going to sink into a shithole if she doesn't learn to talk, and ours with it. It doesn't matter that she's gorgeous. Out here gorgeous girls are as plentiful as bumps on a syphilitic's prick."

"Look how popular the song 'Ramona' is, Max."

"Listen to her sing the lines, Sam! 'Ramona, when day is done you'll hear my call'...she says 'day' like 'dye' and rolls her *r*... You can't even understand her! It's okay for a song, but not for a movie role!"

"But in a sea of blondes, she stands out! Exotic is in!"

"And if that changes? What if next year exotic isn't in? Ed Carewe has invested a fortune in Lola, and we're Carewe's men. If he fails, we fail." McClelland ran his finger along the neck of his damp tuxedo collar.

The crowd applauded politely. Sam and Max wandered away. Lola was now mingling with the guests under Carewe's adoring gaze. I had to keep my eye on her. At any moment she could signal that she needed me. A few hairs had already come loose from her chignon.

I watched as Ed slid his hand gently down Lola's arm and placed his fingers on her minuscule waist, then guided her across the room to meet Al Jolson, star of *The Jazz Singer* and the most popular vocalist in America. She moved like the dancer she was, agile and graceful. A lilac mist. A whiff and a vapor.

It was all a fairy tale, a scene filmed in slow motion through a rose-colored gel. The guests moved languidly, stopping every few moments to gaze into nothingness as though posing for a magazine photographer. They glided from one conversation circle to another in choreographed movements. They were charming and witty and bored. The glittery gowns, the priceless baubles, the incandescence of the moon visible through the enormous glass panes—it all seemed too perfect, too beautiful, too idyllic. Even the trembling of the starlight in the swimming pool seemed staged. Everything was in motion and yet, everything was static. It was as though the film editor had decelerated the action to a still.

I turned to find Max standing next to me. "Let's call it a night," he said. "I'll give you a lift home."

"What if Lola needs me?"

"How many times has she needed you this evening?"

"Not once."

"I don't think she'll need you anymore tonight. It's pretty late."

I looked around for Ramón. I wanted at least to say goodbye, but he was gone.

When I got home, Gabe was dozing in the only chair we owned, the only piece of furniture besides the bed and the dresser that fit in our living quarters. How different he was from Carewe, McClelland, and all the Hollywood types. Strong and rugged, with the arms of a workman. *How lucky I am!* I said to myself. His eyes fluttered open when I threw down my wrap.

"How was it?" he asked.

"Awful, although I did see Greta Garbo up close, and also Frida Kahlo."

"Who's she?"

"It doesn't matter," I yawned.

"Since you're going to have a baby, we should start looking for a bigger place."

I was sorry he'd waited up for me. After all, he put in long, grueling days.

"How can we afford it, Gabe?" I said, slipping into my nightdress.

He stood up and pulled me close. "We've sold some nice pieces lately—a credenza, two wardrobes, a chest of drawers. I know I'll have to make more money, Marita. After all, soon you won't be working…"

"Right," I whispered, closing my eyes. "I can't wait!" I loved working, loved watching the directors and actors turn the words on the page into a real, tangible thing: a movie. It was magical. But now that a baby was coming, I was going to have to get used to full-time motherhood.

19

"I can't take it anymore, Mara. Ed is suffocating me. He wants me to marry him. Day and night, marrymeLola, marrymeLola. It just never lets up."

The solution, thought Doña Antonia, was a European tour. They left early in November. Lola didn't invite me to come with her because my baby was due in weeks. London was their first stop, and then Paris, where the press went wild because she could speak French. Reporters swarmed around her like bees around a goldenrod.

"Where is Mr. Carewe?" asked one.

"I'm not sure," demurred Lola. "He doesn't tell me everything." She paused and looked the man right in the eye. "Just as I don't tell him everything."

It was a whirlwind trip. Paris, Milan, Venice, Rome. Finally, Lola and Doña Antonia returned to the Savoy Hotel in London to prepare for the journey home. The Savoy was the first luxury hotel in London, complete with electric lifts and hot and cold running water in each suite. Lola was looking forward to spending a few days there before boarding the ship for New York.

One late afternoon, as they were navigating through the

spectacular art deco lobby, Doña Antonia noticed a shabby-looking man across the atrium. "Look," she whispered.

"Oh my God! It can't be," gasped Lola. She stopped and stared a moment, then took a step toward him. "Jaime!" she called.

Startled, Jaime looked up. "Oh! What…a surprise!" he stammered. "I'm here to see an agent. He might be interested in one of my scripts." His pupils were dull. He looked ill.

"That's wonderful," said Lola. "Come up to my suite. I'll order some tea."

"I really don't have time."

People turned to look at them—the glamorous movie star and the tramp.

"Come," she coaxed.

He followed her to the elevator, and she led him to her suite. He flopped down on the sofa and almost immediately fell asleep. In the end, he not only took tea, but supper and breakfast as well.

A few days later, Lola left for Los Angeles, and Jaime for Germany.

It was a dazzling winter morning, but Lola didn't know it because she was still lying in bed with the shades drawn. She'd gone back to work as soon as she'd returned from Europe, and she was exhausted. She opened her eyes and smiled at the ribbons of sunlight streaming through the blinds.

"Get up, sleepyhead!" I growled, pretending to be annoyed. "Don't you want to see your goddaughter?"

Dolores Emilia Estrada opened her eyes to the world on November 24, 1928, just as the doctor predicted, and from then on, punctuality was always one of her virtues. She had

Gabe's complexion and a few strands of russet hair. We called her Lolly.

"Get up!" I said again, holding out the baby. She called for Luz to bring coffee.

"Where are the papers?" she asked when Luz came in. "Why aren't they on my tray?"

"Oh…" Luz hesitated. "Doña Antonia told me to wait."

A moment later, Doña Antonia entered with a copy of the *Los Angeles Times*. She nodded to me, but didn't fawn or fuss over the baby. "I didn't want you to be alone when you found out about this," she said to Lola.

Lola took the newspaper and skimmed the pages. Suddenly, she recoiled. "Jaime del Río in a Berlin Hospital" read a small headline on page thirty-two. Jaime was dying of food poisoning in Germany, explained the article. A Spanish priest had flown in from Madrid to administer last rites. Lola yanked herself out of bed and threw on her clothes. "I need to send a telegram!" she exclaimed. "I need to tell Jaime to be strong! He needs to know I still love him! This is all my fault! I abandoned him! I drove him away!"

But it was too late. By the time her telegram arrived on December 7, Jaime was dead. The newspapers said it was due to complications of an infection. Gossips said it was a suicide precipitated by a broken heart.

20

Lolly was an easy baby, and I'd grown used to the routine and the tranquility of my life. The buzz and whir of Gabe's tools in the workroom. Lolly's gurgles and hiccups as she nursed. Daily visits from Doña Lupe and Tía Emi, both of whom were gaga over the new baby, even though Tía Emi tried not to show it.

"Shit and piss," she growled. "That's all babies are—shit and piss."

But she'd sit, eyes closed, in the rocking chair Gabe had made, humming the melody to "The Ballad of Miguela Ruiz."

Occasionally Lola would drop by. Her fancy, chauffeur-driven Studebaker looked out of place parked outside our little house, but Lola didn't seem to notice.

Her life was as topsy-turvy as mine was calm. Edwin Carewe was furious, she said. First she'd rejected his offer of marriage, and now she was working for his archrival Joseph Schenck, who wanted to buy out her contract. The truth is, I was divorced from all that now. I led a different kind of life now. Lola's world was no longer mine.

"Ed is suing me for damages!" she complained. "He's re-married Mary, so it's not that he still wants me for a wife, but he sees me as a traitor. He says I broke my contract with him! Fortunately, I have a good lawyer."

"Better yet, you have a good hairdresser!"

"What do you mean!" She was laughing.

"New life, new look!" I whipped out my scissors. "I'm going to bob your hair. A good style changes everything!"

I ran into Ramón Novarro on Las Palmas Avenue, where I liked to stroll with Lolly in her pram on warm afternoons. He lived in Santa Monica, so I was taken completely by surprise when I caught sight of him coming up the street. It was a lovely day, dry and temperate, perfumed by the scent of oleanders.

"What a surprise!" I exclaimed as soon as he was within earshot. "What are you doing in my part of town? And where have you been? In Europe?"

"You're the one with surprises!" He leaned over the pram to peer at Lolly, who was sound asleep under the frilly pink blanket Tía Emi had sewn for her. "What a little beauty! When did this happen?"

We chatted awhile about nothing in particular. "You're looking trim," I remarked. "Not like me. I'm a tub because of the baby."

"I've lost a few pounds. I'm working on a new film, *Devil-May-Care*. I play one of Napoleon's handsome young lieutenants, so, you see, querida, I can't be fat."

We'd reached the corner. "Want to get coffee?" he asked. He seemed to want to talk.

"It might be hard to maneuver this baby carriage into a coffee shop."

We sat down on a bench at the trolley stop.

"You know, Mara, the Mexican press ran a bunch of articles about what would happen to foreign stars once the studios started making talkies. According to them, both Lola and I are doomed. Maybe after *Devil* opens in December, I'll have to commit suicide." He was laughing, but I shivered. It didn't sound like a joke. "I need another hit like *Ben-Hur*, Mara." He sounded morose. "And now, my dear friend and business manager, Louis Samuel, just got married and bought a house in Los Feliz. Very fancy. Designed by the son of Frank Lloyd Wright."

"Married!" I didn't know what to say. I'd thought that Ramón and Lou were lovers.

"A girl named Grace. He's happy. I don't begrudge him anything."

We sat there awhile in an awkward silence. Ramón's personal life was not something I felt comfortable talking about. After all, it wasn't my place to have opinions about what he did in private. He was my friend, and I loved him. I didn't judge him. Still, I felt sorry about Lou. I could see Ramón was upset.

Motorcars passed, sending billows of black smoke upward into the grayish-blue sky. Horns honked. Trolleys clanged. The stink and the racket were beginning to give me a headache. "I have to get home," I said finally. "Lolly needs to nurse and be changed."

But he didn't get up. "She's still sleeping," he said, gazing at her pretty, caramel-colored face. "She looks like a little bonbon."

"She looks like Gabe."

"No, Mara. She looks like you." He smiled and took a deep breath. "Look, you asked me where I've been, and I'm going to tell you. After all, you already know all my secrets." He turned to face me.

"What happened that night at the Independence Day celebration… I've already forgotten all about it, Ramón."

"No, you haven't. Listen to me, Mara."

The previous weekend, Ramón had done what he always did when he was down. He threw a few things into a suit-case and got into his car. Then he pulled out onto the high-way, the old Camino Real, and drove north. The Los Angeles basin was hazy and heavy that day, but once he got out on the open road, the skies became crystalline. His route took him along the coast, where undulating ripples broke into waves that lapped at virgin beaches. Jets of water like greedy tongues reached, licked, then slackened and fell back. Those were his words: "greedy tongues." It was like a sacrament, he said—the sand and the sea, engaged in some primal erotic dance. The ocean had been thrusting its arms at the shore since the beginning of time. Reach and retract. Reach and retract. An eternal bolero. Ramón found the rhythms of this perpetual seduction calming, reassuring, and at the same time, exhil-arating. The god of the sea would reach out to the goddess of the sand whether *Devil* was a hit or not. The procreative and creative forces of the universe would continue to pulsate, bringing forth new life.

To the right, miles and miles of shrubbery covered the rocky terrain. Manzanilla, with its hearty oval leaves and bell-shaped flowers, some white, some pale pink, intermingled with chaparral. California lilac stretched out its boughs over-flowing with spiny clusters of purple blossoms. Farther north, pines of every type reached majestically upward, while giant sequoias towered over the cars on the road like colossuses.

As he drove up the gravel road to the retreat center, Ramón inhaled deeply and felt the tension drain from his body. The cross on the chapel came into view. Ramón had been visiting the Retiro San Iñigo for a couple of years now—every time he needed to renew his spirit and learn once again to find God in all things. It was a vast, sprawling, forested property with guest rooms in large dormitory buildings and niches for prayer in the gardens and woods. A spiritual seeker could walk the Stations of the Cross or commune with nature among the giant ferns and scruffy shrubs. The Jesuits had bought the property in Los Altos in the early 1920s with the intention to turn it into a kind of spiritual refuge, and in 1925, it opened its doors. Ramón found peace at San Iñigo as nowhere else.

He parked his car in the lot and walked to the chapel. "It was so quiet," he told me, "so absolutely still, that the chirping of birds and the buzzing of insects resounded in contrast."

Father Reynoso was waiting for him in the doorway. The two embraced—they were good friends by now—and the priest led him to his dorm room to get settled. He didn't need to explain the routine in detail—Ramón had made the *Spiritual Exercises* more than once already—but he did offer him a few reminders. He would spend his days in absolute silence, listening to God within. The Exercises, a system of prayer devised by Ignatius of Loyola, the founder of the Jesuit order in the sixteenth century, consisted of a series of meditations on passages from Scripture. The retreatant reads the passage, then pictures the scene in his mind, engaging all the senses, and finally, placing himself in it. By experiencing Scripture in this way—hearing the sound of Jesus's voice, smelling the scent of his skin, feeling the texture of his robe—the retreatant can connect with God and his own inner fears and longings in a profound new way. Once a day, Ramón would meet with Father Reynoso for a half hour to examine where the Spirit had led him. The Exercises always left Ramón refreshed and restored, and he was looking forward to embarking on the journey. His actor's brain began to rev up as soon as he laid eyes on the passage. It was like preparing a role. Words became image, and image became reality. His senses went into high gear. Jesus was there, his presence close and palpable, his embrace comforting, his gaze penetrating. Ramón smelled Jesus's sweat, washed the dust off his sandaled feet. It was powerful, mind-boggling.

As he sat in the chapel, conjuring up Jesus on the road to Emmaus, Ramón was overcome with fear that Jesus would never forgive him, that what he'd done was too awful. He'd gone to a drag show at Pinky's, taking the actress Elsie Janis along as a cover. He and Elsie had an understanding. She often accompanied him to speakeasies that catered to—he hated to say the word, even to himself—fairies, queers, poofs, inverts. That night at Pinky's, he was drinking heavily, when he caught the eye of a boy...such a young boy...sixteen or seventeen, maybe.

Walking back to his room in the intense stillness, he felt as though his senses were on full alert. He noticed the bees helicoptering over clover blossoms, a sparrow settling on the shoulder of a statue of the Virgin, the gurgle of the brook, and even fish darting to the surface. Without the distraction of everyday banter, he felt as though he were experiencing life for the first time. Beauty. Longing. Guilt.

"All the din and clatter of ordinary existence buffers us from the reality that surrounds us, and the reality within us," he told Father Reynoso. And then, he told him about the boy.

"This is where I need to be," he said to himself afterward, as he lay in bed waiting to fall asleep. "Not on a chaotic movie set worrying about how people like my pronunciation. Or my voice. Or my looks. This is where I really feel at home. Here, with God."

At last, Ramón was silent. I took his hand in mine and squeezed it.

"Thank you, Ramón," I whispered. "Thank you for telling me."

I got up and pushed the pram down the palm-lined streets to our house.

As a little girl, I'd had a crush on Ramón, and I was jealous of Lola for being his cousin. But what I had now was so much better. Ramón was a real friend, someone who confided in me. That's why I couldn't bear to see him hurt, and why what happened to him later, many years later, left me heartsick.

Less than a week later, everything changed. On October 29, the citizens of the world awoke to horrific headlines. "STOCKS DIVE!" screamed the *Los Angeles Times*. "BLACK TUESDAY!" blared the *New York Times*. "WALL STREET CRASH!" shrieked the *London Herald*. "DOW DIVES 508.32 POINTS!" screeched the *Philadelphia Inquirer*. But Lola checked *Variety* first. "WALL ST. LAYS AN EGG!" read the headline.

Once at the studio, she heard whispers everywhere: "lost everything," "suicide," "threw himself out the window." She began to grow jittery.

"What does it all mean?" she asked me when I came by in the afternoon for coffee.

She turned to her mother. "What does it mean, Mami?"

"I don't know, exactly," said Doña Antonia. "Maybe nothing. We've never bought stocks. All your money is in real estate. But we'll have to wait and see."

The next day, Lola wanted me to go to the studio with her. She was nervous, she said. Couldn't I go just for a little while? So I wrapped Lolly in a blanket and climbed into the Studebaker. Alfredo drove us to the United Artists lot.

"Max McClelland!" said Ruth, the makeup artist, by way of greeting. "You know, the advance man from over at First National."

Suddenly, I felt nauseous.

"Well, he always wanted to buy a house in Hollywoodland, in the Hollywood Hills. You know, the fancy commu-

nity up by the Hollywoodland sign. Well, he finally did it."
Ruth began applying foundation to Lola's cheeks. "Last night
he committed suicide, took out his gun and shot himself."

I felt my blood freeze and splinter. I sank into a chair to
keep from dropping Lolly.

"They say he invested all his money in stocks," Ruth went
on, "and now that Wall Street has gone to hell, he wasn't going
to be able to pay for that big fancy house with tennis courts
and a swimming pool. I guess he thought they were going to
snatch it all away, so he called it quits."

Lola was weeping quietly.

"Oh no!" exclaimed Ruth. "I shouldn't have told you! Now
you've messed up your makeup!"

21

San Simeon, July 1930
Soup Kitchens and Caviar

The country was in shambles. The guy with the little house and the mediocre job who had invested his meager savings in the stock market was now broke. He and millions of others like him had no money to buy food, never mind movie tickets. Factories and other businesses were slowing down production, laying off workers, reducing wages for those they kept. By 1930, four million Americans were out of work. A year later, the figure was six million. City streets were filled with breadlines. More and more people took their meals at soup kitchens. Farmers couldn't afford to harvest their crops because food prices had plummeted, so they left them to rot in the sun, while in the cities, people starved. One after the other, the banks failed. By 1933 thousands had gone under.

At first, Gabe thought we'd get through it. We didn't have stocks, we owned our little house, and Gabe had a bunch of orders for cabinets, bedposts, everything. But then, people started canceling. Why buy a fancy credenza for a house you might lose? People who had a little money spent it on a pork roast for their families, not on a new table. Lolly was toddling already, and we'd been talking about finding a bigger place, but now that was out of the question. Vince had been hoping to move out and marry Julie, but that plan was now on hold, too. Finally, Gabe had no more orders, which meant no more income.

"Don't worry, *mi reina*," he said. "I can always go back to the studio."

He'd taken to calling me *reina*, queen, when Lolly was born. She was his *princesa*.

"You hated working for the studio," I said. "There must be another way."

But there wasn't. There was no market for fine cabinets, and no businesses were hiring.

On the day he left to ask the personnel officer at First National for his old job back, Gabe put on his best overalls and brushed his teeth twice. One thing we had both learned from the movie crowd was the importance of image. He wanted to show he was clean, trustworthy, and ready to start right away.

But he was back before noon, crestfallen. "They're not hiring," he said.

"But they're still making movies!"

"They don't need me. Every poor slob who's out of work is begging at their door. And now there's the Okies."

I hadn't thought of that. Since the Okies had started pouring into Los Angeles, the studios had plenty of labor to pick from, and the personnel guys would much rather take a white carpenter from Oklahoma than the likes of Gabriel Estrada.

"They've set up camps by the studios. They live in tents and cook over open fires. And they're there first thing in the morning offering to do anything the studio people need— run errands, drive cars, build sets, whatever. You can't blame them. They were starving back home, so they pulled up stakes and moved west."

Lolly had stumbled over to Gabe, and he picked her up and

held her against him. He breathed in her sweet baby scent and kissed her on the back of the neck.

"Maybe I could go back to work," I said. "I'll ask Marie." I loved staying home and caring for Lolly, but the thought of returning to the hustle and bustle of the salon was also appealing. On the other hand, I thought a new baby might be on the way, and spending time in a shop filled with fumes and smells might not be such a good idea. Still, we really needed the money. Our situation was getting desperate. I was torn.

"I don't want you to go back to work," murmured Gabe. He squeezed his eyes shut and pulled his lips back as if to let out a scream. Lolly started to squirm, and I took her from him.

"Maybe just a few days a week," I said gently. "The thing is, Gabe, you need a license to fix hair, and I doubt many Okie women have one, so they won't be able to compete with me."

"No one can compete with you," he whispered. He kissed me on the lips and took Lolly back in his arms.

I didn't think it was a good time to tell him that I suspected I was pregnant again.

Marie said she'd had to let hairdressers go, but if things picked up again, she'd let me know right away. "Maybe two or three times a week," I said.

Lola, on the other hand, was delighted to have me come back to work for her. She even offered me a raise. Gabriel slumped over his worktable.

"Who will take care of Lolly?" he said, when I told him.

It seemed logical to me that since he was home and without work, he could take care of her, but I knew better than to suggest it. He was a Latin man, after all, and he had his pride.

"What about Tía Emi?" I suggested.

"Your Tía Emi is—"

"I know, but she knows how to take care of a baby. We don't have many options."

"If she still has her job with Madame Isabelle, we can't ask her to give it up."

"I could drop Lolly off at Madame Isabelle's in the morning. I grew up crawling over skeins of thread and scraps of cloth, and I turned out okay."

"Better than okay," said Gabriel, smiling weakly.

But he wasn't comfortable with having Tía Emi care for Lolly. He arranged to take her to his parents' house every morning. Señora Lupe still had children at home. One more wouldn't faze her, she said. In fact, it would be nice to have a toddler around again.

While most of us were struggling, for Marion Davies, life was good. Davies had met newspaper tycoon William Randolph Hearst while she was performing in the Ziegfeld Follies, and she soon became his most grandiose project. Hearst formed Cosmopolitan Pictures for the sole purpose of producing films starring Davies, and he made arrangements with Paramount and MGM to distribute them. He bought the Cameo Theater in San Francisco and renamed it The Marion Davies Theater. From his office on Market Street, he could see the pink neon letters blinking and winking her name, a continuous reminder that he, like God, could create stars. Davies didn't have to worry whether people like us could afford a movie ticket because her success was guaranteed. Hearst financed her films whether they made money or not. He even produced newsreels publicizing her social activities—flamboyant spectacles over which she presided like a queen. But his most magnificent contribution to Marion Davies's renown was San Simeon, a sprawling 127-acre estate.

The centerpiece of San Simeon was the Castle, which had been inspired by the Church of Santa María Mayor in La

Ronda, Spain. It was surrounded by smaller palaces and pa-
vilions, some of which Hearst had transported from Europe,
stone by stone, and set in reinforced concrete using modern
engineering methods. An avid traveler, Hearst had combined
different architectural styles he'd admired in Europe. The
Castle featured fifty-six bedrooms, sixty-one bathrooms, and
nineteen sitting rooms. All the details were in the newspapers,
and I still have the articles. "Chaotic luxury," is how they described San Simeon. The magnificent chandeliers were pow-
ered by electricity from the private power plant Hearst had
installed for his own use. The grounds boasted tennis courts,
an airfield, and the largest private zoo in the world. Zebras
and giraffes and a host of other exotic animals roamed the
grounds. Acres of woods were filled with redwoods, oaks,
cedars, and Italian cypresses. The gardens, kept by an army
of gardeners, burst with color all year long—bougainvillea,
California poppies, azaleas, calla lilies, cyclamen, and roses of
every variety. Hearst had imported antiques from all corners
of the planet—delicate Venuses, handsome Adonises, Russian
Orthodox Madonnas, and Indian Shivas.

Why so much luxury? Because Marion's parties were fabulous affairs that lasted for days and brought together the most
powerful tycoons, the most influential politicians, the most
popular movie stars, the most successful artists. Everyone who
was anyone was invited, and Dolores Del Rio was definitely
someone.

When Lola told me about the invitation, I didn't pay much
attention. She was always going out to fancy parties. I'd do her
hair beforehand, but I no longer accompanied her. However,
this time, she made it clear, she expected me to go. Never
mind that I had a family. She was a movie star, and she was
single. She wasn't used to thinking about childcare or how a

husband might feel about being left alone. There was no way out of it. We needed the money.

"Lola is going to a shindig at San Simeon," I told Gabe one afternoon. "She wants me to go with her."

"Where's San Simeon?"

"On the coast. In the Santa Lucia Mountains, about 250 miles north of here. I'd be gone for a few days."

He sighed. "I suppose Lolly could stay with Mom," he conceded gloomily. "I could stay there, too." In those trying times, sometimes you had to say yes when you really wanted to say no.

Lola packed as though she were making a monthlong excursion to Paris. She stuffed her suitcases with gowns, slacks, shorts, and bathing suits. I threw a couple of loose-fitting sundresses into a valise. I was vexed. I'd never been separated from Lolly for more than a day.

"You should bring a bathing suit," she said airily.

"Why?" I said. "I can't swim."

"Oh," said Lola, looking puzzled. I suppose in her world, everyone knew how to swim.

On Friday afternoon, we picked up tickets at the Glendale Station for the private train that would take us to San Luis Obispo. From there, transportation would be provided by automobile.

I tried not to gasp when I saw our private compartment.

It seemed like a moving hotel room, with beds, an armchair, a secretary fully stocked with writing materials, and glass-doored cabinets with books and magazines. Brocade curtains covered the windows, and fine paintings hung on the walls.

In the dining car, we had our choice of filet mignon, lobster, or just about anything else, but I didn't feel like eating. I knew that Gabe would be having chicken enchiladas at his mother's house—if he was lucky. Any kind of meat was a luxury. I considered not ordering, but then it occurred to me that it might be a while before I could enjoy another meal this good, so I had a steak and French fries.

The train pulled into San Luis Obispo around two in the morning. A caravan of elegant cars, each with its own chauffeur, was waiting to take the guests up the coast. Lola dozed for a few hours in the back of the Mercedes-Benz, but I couldn't sleep. I imagined Lolly in the old crib where Vince had slept, then Gabe, then Señora Lupe's three younger children. Did Lolly miss me? I wondered. It was the first time she'd slept away from home. Was she scared?

Around eight, Lola opened her eyes. I raised the black shades on the windows, and we both gazed out onto a magnificent panorama. As the car climbed the narrow mountain road toward the estate, we marveled at the sprawling gardens vibrant with flowers, the terraced parks dotted with villas, and the pools glimmering in the morning sunlight. In the distance, the grandiose white marble Spanish-style Castle gleamed like a jewel.

At the entrance, we were met by Antonio and Sheila, Lola's personal valet and maid for the duration of the stay.

"Or did you bring your own maid?" asked Sheila, looking me up and down.

"Mrs. Estrada is my assistant," Lola said. "She will take her meals in our suite."

Sheila looked annoyed.

She and Antonio escorted us to our lodgings, an actual Italian villa surrounded by plots of silver lupine, hydrangea, and snapdragon.

"We will bring your breakfast shortly," said Antonio, handing her a menu. Lola looked at the long list of exotic dishes and opted for her usual egg and toast.

"What about you, Mara?" she said.

"The same," I said. I was thinking about Gabe eating dry cornflakes at Señora Lupe's kitchen table.

"Afterward, you may want to explore the grounds or engage in one of the many activities available to our guests—tennis, golf, archery, badminton, croquet, swimming, boating, or horseback riding. If you need anything, you have only to ask. Lunch is served at one." Antonio bowed and left. Sheila stayed on awhile, fussing over Lola's clothes.

After breakfast, Lola threw on a wrap, and we headed for the beach. Miles of milk-colored sand stretched along the water's edge. Tiny pebbles and fragmented shells made ripples in the shallow drifts at the shoreline. Lola ducked into a cabana to put on her bathing costume, then ran toward the ocean and plunged in. I stood at the water's edge and then waded in up to my calves. The salty water felt prickly against my skin.

I watched Lola propel herself beyond the breakers with strong, decisive strokes to the placid waters farther from shore. She paddled on her back awhile, drinking in the sunshine, then swam parallel to the beach, pushing herself hard, racing the boats on the distant horizon.

I tried to feel grateful. After all, Lola had given me my old position back, a job I desperately needed to keep my family afloat. Yet…the carefree way she was enjoying herself…all this pomp, all this wealth, when so many people were struggling… It just seemed wrong. But something else was bothering me, too. I'd tried to push it out of my mind, but it stung. She'd introduced me as her assistant. Whenever we went to an interview or photo shoot or a party, I became Mrs. Estrada, her assistant. Never her *friend*. Maybe Tía Emi had been right all along. I could be her playmate when there was no one else around, but I could never really be her friend. Girls like Lola just didn't have friends like me.

Sunbathers dotted the beach. Some lay on chaise longues,

others gathered in groups to chat or play cards. Cabanas lined the periphery, providing shade and privacy. To one side, under a large awning, was an elaborate buffet replete with fruits, juices, and breads of every type.

"That swim gave me an appetite!" called Lola, running toward me through the foam.

She threw on her wrap, and we headed to the table, where she reached toward a pyramid of strawberries arranged to look like giant red gumdrops.

"They look delicious, don't they?"

We both turned in the direction of the voice. The man standing next to us looked as though he'd stepped out of an advertisement for the film, *The Great Gatsby*, which had come out a few years before. He was dark-haired and unspeakably handsome, with the kind of elongated, heart-shaped face, perfect nose, and full, sensuous lips that casting directors die for. It looked as though a costume designer had put together his outfit—a casual white linen suit, light blue vest, and loose trousers. A blue handkerchief peeked out of his breast pocket. Either he's an invert or an artist, I thought. And then, maybe he needs a fine crafted cabinet for his house. Gabe could make him one, and he looks like he could afford it.

Lola smiled. "I *was* eyeing those strawberries, but it's almost time for lunch, so I think I'll wait. I hear that lunch at the Hearsts' is an elegant affair."

"It is. I hope you're hungry." He had the melodious voice of a movie Lothario.

I waited for her to introduce herself, and then me, her "assistant." But she didn't. "Well, I'd better go get ready," she said, pivoting and nudging me toward the road.

"I hope I see you again," he called after her. She did not turn around.

I washed and styled her hair, then helped her get dressed

for lunch. After she left, I picked up the receiver and tried to figure out how the telephone worked. I fumbled around in the drawer of the table where it stood. A pencil. A notepad. A phonebook. A Bible. A card with instructions on how to use the phone. I wondered if it would be okay to call Los Angeles. I'd have to go through the operator and wait awhile until she made the connection. It might be expensive. Who would pay for the call? The Hearsts were fabulously wealthy, but they might not like their guests' hairdressers making long-distance calls. I dialed 0 for the Hearst operator. I told her I wanted to call a different city. She sounded as though it were the most natural thing in the world and connected me with the Los Angeles operator, who connected me with Señora Lupe's house. Gabe's mom sounded surprised and happy to hear my voice. Lolly was fine, she said, not to worry. "Enjoy yourself!" she said, as if I were on vacation. "Gabe's at the workshop." He spent every day in the workshop, even though he had no orders to fill. I called the house. Gabe sounded tired. I listened for some hint of recrimination in his voice, but no, there was none. I told him about the buffet. "Eat a lot!" he said. "Now's your chance!"

I realized that Lola hadn't ordered lunch for me. How did one order lunch, anyway? I called the operator again and told her I wanted to eat. "Of course," she said, and connected me with the kitchen. Wow, I thought, things are certainly easier when you're rich!

I expected Lola to come back around three, but it was past five before she pushed open the door, all smiles.

"You can't imagine what a fabulous day I've had!" she announced.

I must have rolled my eyes or shook my head, because she stopped in her tracks.

"Oh," she said softly. "I've done it again. What did *you* do today, Mara?"

"I took a nap," I lied. What was I going to say? I spent the afternoon moping around?

I felt ridiculous. Here I was, in a beautiful villa, surrounded by luxury, atop a majestic hill with views of paradise, and I was sulking. Gabe was right. I should just enjoy it. Why not? It wasn't going to last, so why not relish the moment?

"How was the lunch?" I asked.

"Well, the dining room was enormous," she began. "Waiters in white jackets escorted us in and took us to our places along an enormous antique table that William Randolph brought from some medieval European monastery. The host and hostess sat at either end, each with a preferred guest. I sat next to Marion, and that man we saw this morning by the beach buffet was seated next to Hearst. Suddenly, I looked up, and guess who was staring at me!"

"Mr. Handsome from the strawberry pile."

"Well, I asked Marion who he was. 'Ah,' she said, 'That's Cedric Gibbons!'"

Lola stared at me, waiting for a reaction. "Who's Cedric Gibbons?" I said, finally.

"Only the artistic director of MGM, Mara. He was one of the founding members of the Academy of Motion Picture Arts and Sciences. He's the one who designed the Oscar!"

"And he threw himself at your feet and asked you to marry him, right?"

"He just won an Oscar himself for *The Bridge of San Luis Rey*, and he's not even forty!" She lowered her voice, as if confiding a secret, even though there was no one else in the room. "Marion says he's one of Hollywood's most desirable bachelors."

I shrugged.

"Well, after lunch, I set off to explore the artwork in the Castle. Every room is like a museum, Mara. I was staring at a huge painting of a delicate young man tied to a tree, with his hands fastened to a branch above his head to emphasize the contours of his body. Sensuous arms, gently rippling shoulders, supple belly, sinuous thighs, graceful legs. Everywhere shot through with arrows. I was sure I'd seen it before."

"At Lou Samuel's place," I said. "In the bedroom. A nude, with Ramón's face. I remember it left you rattled."

"That's right..." She was pensive. "Cedric came up behind me. 'The Martyrdom of Saint Sebastian,' he said, 'the patron saint of homosexuals.' I didn't quite know what to say, but now that you mention Ramón..."

She spent the following couple of days with Gibbons, exploring the grounds, admiring the wild animals... I don't know what else. I went to the beach and lay in the sun.

"Lola," I said, as I helped her pack to go home. "Why don't you ask Gibbons if he needs a credenza? Gabe could use the work. And if not, maybe he could get him a job at MGM."

"I don't know, Mara," she said. "I mean... I just met Cedric."

"Lola, are we friends? Really, truly friends?"

"Of course, Lola. You know that."

"No, I don't. You always introduce me as your assistant, not as your friend. And now, when I ask you for a favor...because, frankly, Lola, we're desperate...you hesitate."

She looked as though I'd slapped her in the face.

"Gabe needs work, Lola. If you're my friend, you'll help me."

"I *am* helping you! I gave you back your old position, didn't I?"

"But I don't know how long I can continue." I could hear my voice quivering and struggled to steady it. "I'm pregnant."

She looked stricken. "Pregnant?" she said, finally. "Again?"

I didn't expect her to say "congratulations," or "that's wonderful," but her reaction stung. I started to cry.

"Oh my God, Mara," she said. "I'm sorry." She put her arm around me. "Of course, I'll help you," she murmured, "because you're my oldest, dearest friend."

And she did, too. Within a week, Gabe was on the carpentry crew at MGM.

When I'd told Gabe I was expecting again, he stood staring at me a moment. Oh no, he must have been thinking, another mouth to feed. But all he said was, "Another gift from God, *mi reina*." Then he kissed me on the forehead.

22

Los Angeles, Santa Barbara, the Highway, Summer 1930
Bumpy Roads

I stared at the glittering oval on her finger and wondered: Is she doing the right thing? It had all happened so fast! After San Simeon, they were together constantly. His yacht. Her film opening. His club. Her pool party. Excursions up the coast, to the mountains, to Baja, to Catalina Island. Cedric seemed so right for her in so many ways. She was twenty-six; he was thirty-seven—a much smaller age gap than between her and Jaime. And he was a Hollywood animal. He knew the ropes and how to navigate studio tar pits. For Jaime, the movies were a dream. For Cedric, they were an industry in which you worked your way up.

Even though he'd been born in Dublin, Cedric was one hundred percent American. He had graduated from the Art Students League in New York and then, for a few years, sweated like a lackey in his father's architectural office, where he learned about design and the value of knowing the right people. In 1915, he cut loose and linked up with Edison Studios. When he'd already left his mark on over a hundred films, Sam Goldwyn recruited him. Jaime had struggled with screenwriting for years, but never created a successful script. Cedric was now supervising art director for MGM, with scores of films under his control. In other words, Jaime was a failure; Cedric, a superstar.

They did have something in common, though. Like Jaime, Cedric loved cars. He drove a red Duesenberg Model J. The Duesy was his baby. Before getting behind the wheel, he put on a pair of white gloves and didn't take them off until he put the Duesy to bed. And like Jaime, Cedric loved art, but while Jaime had the superficial understanding of painting and sculpture of an educated dilettante, Cedric was an actual artist, a leader in the new art deco movement. Chrome and glass and black or white marble. Open spaces and rectilinear motifs. Cedric was introducing the new style into his films, inspiring moviegoers to try it in their homes.

With Jaime's death, Lola was free in the eyes of the Church, which hadn't recognized her divorce. But now that she was a widow, she had every right to marry. Cedric was Catholic, so they'd be able to have a traditional wedding with a priest and a mass, which thrilled Doña Antonia. Cedric was rich and would surely get richer, which thrilled Don Jesús Leonardo. The Depression had left most of Hollywood's high rollers in a ditch, but Gibbons kept on making films and making money. Even though Lola was a big star and earned a fortune, said Don Jesús Leonardo, she still needed a man to take the reins.

Cedric took Lola to all the best restaurants, the most elegant parties. He was smart, handsome, ambitious, charming, and witty, and he was a gringo. This time, her parents thought, she'd gotten it right.

This last point—being a gringo—was important because things were changing in Hollywood. Newspapers carried stories about Stalin's plans to abolish private property, and, while many in the artsy set agreed with his goals, the governing class was growing nervous. Communism was a real threat, and there was talk of deporting immigrants with possible Communist connections. Foreign actors were suspect, especially Mexicans, because Mexico had been a hotbed of radicalism for decades, and artists like Diego Rivera were hard-core Communists. With a husband like Cedric Gibbons, Lola's parents knew Lola would be safe. In spite of his Irish birth, Cedric was as American as bland vegetables and overcooked chicken.

And yet, I still wondered, was she doing the right thing?

"I hate to give this all up," Lola murmured, looking around her patio.

It was three days before the wedding, and I'd come over to visit, as I often did on my days off.

Lola had designed the exteriors of the house on Outpost Drive herself, surrounding the pool area with California wildflowers—golden stars and hyacinths, poppies and meadowfoam. Cacti of every size and shape stood in pots around the patio, and orange and lemon trees dotted the garden. But soon the sprawling hacienda-style residence would be up for sale.

Cedric had built a magnificent art deco mansion on Kingman Drive—a futuristic, multilevel spaceship in plaster and chrome. The floors were shiny and white, almost clinical. The stairs, terraced and carpetless, were bordered by metal rails—extended square tubes that seemed like they would smudge if you looked at them too intently. The chairs and sofas were low and long, with silver-colored arms and white leather seats. No place here for one of Gabe's beautiful walnut cabinets, I thought. I would have loved to see Cedric's reaction if Dimitri pooped on the floor.

Cedric's decoration was minimalist. A metal vase with a solitary red rose, which his valet replaced daily. A Lalique statuette. A poster showing a costume for Diaghilev's Ballets Russes. A large painting consisting of a single red squiggly line. I wondered if Lola was going to become just another decoration in Cedric's perfect art deco house—a colorful bird-of-paradise in an antiseptic white cage.

Lola didn't seem as excited as you'd expect a bride-to-be. Had she sensed in Cedric the same delicateness that she'd seen in Jaime? There were rumors that Cedric liked men, but gossip hovered around about so many people in Hollywood.

Lolly was shoving a push-toy over the flagstones. No one would have to teach this child the meaning of the word *play*, I thought. I felt the baby in my womb kick and flutter. It was playing, too.

"I'm going for a swim," Lola announced.

Lolly looked on fascinated as Lola threw off her wrap and dove in. It was all I could do to keep the baby from flinging herself into the water. Dimitri began to bark anxiously.

"You silly dog! Don't worry, I won't drown!" called Lola. Dimitri ran around the perimeter of the pool, yelping desperately. Just like Jaime, I thought. Always wanting to protect her, except that Dimitri knows better than to leap in where it's too deep. But what about Lola and her marriage to Cedric? Was she leaping in over her head?

"I'm exhausted," groaned Lola, pulling herself out of the pool.

"Maybe..." I ventured. "Maybe it's too soon, Lola. You haven't known Cedric very long. Maybe you should wait awhile."

She shook her head. "Mami has already made all the arrangements." She sounded more resigned than enthusiastic.

On August 6, 1930, at 5:40 in the afternoon, Lola and her parents pulled up to Santa Barbara Mission. Gabe had bought a secondhand Ford to get to work, and we followed them to the church. Doña Antonia was glowing.

Don Jesús Leonardo helped Lola out of the car. *"Estás bellísima, hija,"* he exclaimed.

She did, indeed, look especially ravishing. Her gauzy white dress. Her fur-cuffed jacket. Her cream-colored cloche. Her dainty, beige shoes, which gave her the height she needed to reach the brim of Cedric's hat. Everything was perfect.

The church rose between the vast ocean and the Santa Ynez Mountains, its towers gleaming like crystal against the clear blue sky. The lobe-like petals of the ash trees reminded me of huddling fairies. Franciscan friars were tending the mission's renowned rose garden, just as they had for nearly a century and a half. The extraordinary aqueducts and water treatment system constructed by Chumash Indians were still functional.

The air was lifeless, even for August. No nippy breeze caressed Lola's cheek or cleared her head.

"Why did I wear this cloche?" she complained to no one in particular. "It's so tight, I feel as though my skull were in a vise. And this jacket with fur-trimmed cuffs? I'm suffocating!"

Cedric, dapper in a dark cinched suit and a gray felt hat, was waiting by the door of the chapel, smiling radiantly.

Beads of sweat were forming along the edge of Lola's cloche. "He loves me as no man has ever loved me before," Lola murmured, as though trying to reassure herself.

The Mass was lovely, the reception, tasteful. Afterward, kisses goodbye. Congratulations and thank-yous. Finally, it was over. Lola and Cedric climbed into the Duesy and headed for the highway. They planned to honeymoon in Monterey to avoid spending too much time away from work. Gabe and I took off for his parents' house to pick up Lolly.

The road was bumpy. Gabe drove slowly to avoid unsettling our unborn baby. I imagined Cedric and Lola in the Duesy, Cedric guiding the automobile expertly along the coast, through San Luis Obispo and Santa Barbara on the scenic roads. Soon they would be in Monterey. I'd seen pictures...the spectacular views, the wharf, the yachts, the little sailboats all lined up, their colors flying... An ideal honeymoon spot. Relaxed and cozy. I dozed off thinking about Lola and Cedric holding hands, watching the sunset over the water.

But that's not what happened. Before Cedric had driven a half hour, nausea was making Lola's head bobble like a puppet's. She pitched forward, almost hitting her skull on the dashboard.

Doña Antonia called me at daybreak. Lola was in the hospital with a severe kidney infection.

"The doctor says she's suffering from overwork," Doña Antonia told me. "She's near collapse. She needs bedrest, Mara. I need for you to come and sit with her."

Come and sit with her? I needed to work! Marie's business had picked up a bit, and I'd promised to be at the shop three days a week in spite of the fumes and bad smells.

"Of course, Doña Antonia," I said. "I'll come in my free time." Naturally, I wanted to go, but the imperious manner in which Doña Antonia had commanded it rubbed me the wrong way. Even so, I answered diplomatically. After all, I needed the job that Lola had given me. I couldn't afford to anger her mother. But no, it was more than that. I was truly worried about Lola.

This is a bad sign, I thought. An ominous beginning to an ill-starred marriage.

By fall, Lola was back on her feet, and in the spring she flew off to Hawaii to make *Bird of Paradise*. I stayed home. Gabriela Mariana had been born on December 15, 1930. Marie offered me four days a week at the salon—somehow, women always find a few dollars to get their hair done—so now, Señora Lupe had two baby girls to take care of.

"Keep them out of public parks," Gabe admonished his

mom when we dropped them off each morning. "And don't go anywhere near a public pool. The polio epidemic…"

"They're too little for a pool."

"And keep them away from other kids. Even cousins."

Gabe was a worrier, a mother hen as much as a father rooster.

I didn't see much of Lola after she returned from Hawaii. She was busy with her new husband and her new life. She'd convinced Cedric to move out of his glass-and-chrome spaceship and into her house on Outpost Drive, but I no longer felt comfortable visiting. There was something about Cedric… something too suave, too perfect. Lola and I did talk on the phone sometimes, but she seemed to still be in a funk.

She'd just signed with RKO to make *Flying Down to Rio*. However, people weren't flocking to the movies anymore. Contracts were no longer pouring in, and Lola's name was hardly ever in the newspapers.

On the other hand, Ramón's name was in the press all the time, not only in *Photoplay* and *Star World*, but even in the *Times* and the *Examiner*—but for the wrong reasons. Ramón was going through a bad time. His last film, *In Gay Madrid*, had flopped like a whale in a swimming pool. Worse still, his old friend Lou had used Ramón's money to play the stock market and lost most of it in the crash. Ramón took possession of the new house that Lou had bought, although instead of moving in, he went back to Santa Monica to live with his large and chaotic family and escape the polio epidemic sweeping the country. He also started drinking heavily.

What put Ramón in the headlines was the accident. He'd gotten royally drunk at one of Marion Davies's parties and crashed his car. The studio executives did their best to keep it quiet, but reporters jumped on the story like wolves on a stray lamb. Ramón's career was already floundering, and now this.

There was nothing I could do to help Ramón, and besides, I had my own problems. Lola had been away in Hawaii, and filming hadn't yet begun on *Flying Down to Rio,* so I wasn't making money doing her hair. Once in a while, Gabe would get a request for a cabinet or a table, but most of our income came from his salary from MGM and my tips from the shop— hardly enough to cover groceries. And now this new disease was lurking in the shadows like an ogre, swooping down on innocent children and leaving them paralyzed. We sat up all night worrying.

23

Los Angeles, 1932
Gossip

Lucille Carver was the wife of a bank executive and one of Marie's standing customers, with an appointment every Thursday afternoon at two o'clock. She wore French-cut suits and a mink stole with the animal's head, tail, and feet hanging on either side of her shoulders, even in the summertime. I had the chair right next to Marie's, and it was fun to listen in on their conversations when I wasn't engaged with my own customers. Mrs. Carver loved the movies. She had just seen *Bird of Paradise*, and now she was chattering like a squirrel in mating season.

"Johnny is so dreamy," she began. "He's on a yacht in the South Pacific...all in white, a real sailor, bronzed skin, golden hair."

"How can you tell?" asked Marie. "Movies only show black and white."

"But you can imagine. You can see the blue skies, the white tails of the sharks..."

"Sharks?"

"The yacht is sailing close to an island, and a bunch of islanders approach in pontoon boats."

"What's a pontoon boat?"

"Kind of like a raft held up by buoys. Anyhow, the point

is, they're friendly people and they've come to greet the foreigners. The sailors throw them stuff, and they dive for it."

"What kind of stuff?"

"My God, Miss Marie, stop asking questions so I can explain this to you! A cap, a pipe, that kind of stuff. Suddenly, sharks come. One of the sailors wants to shoot the closest shark, but the captain tells him not to because he might hit one of the natives. Listen, do you think this color is too dark for me? I usually go for a lighter shade, but they're showing dark in the magazines...like Hedy Lamarr."

"I think it's okay, but look at this one. It's not so auburn. So what happened with the shark, Mrs. Carver?"

"Well, Johnny tries to catch it by throwing out bait tied to a hook. But then, and this is the really scary part, he gets his foot caught in the loop of a cable."

"So do you want to go with this color, or do you want something a bit more reddish?"

"This one's okay. So then, all of a sudden, he goes flying overboard!"

"Right into the shark's teeth?"

"Well, almost. But then Luana, the chief's daughter, dives into the water and saves him! She cuts the rope and pulls him to safety. When he opens his eyes, she's blabbering away, telling him everything that happened."

"That's Dolores Del Rio, right?"

"Oh, she's so gorgeous, Miss Marie..."

I hadn't seen *Bird of Paradise*. We had no money to spend on the movies, but Mrs. Carver not only had the quarter for a ticket, but also plenty of time to read *Star World* and *Photoplay*. With her small head and closely cropped hair, she didn't look that different from the dead mink hanging on her shoulder.

I didn't mention that I knew Dolores Del Rio. Lucille Carver was Marie's customer, and it would have been improper for me to butt in. Besides, she probably wouldn't have believed me.

"Anyhow," she went on, "he doesn't understand a word she's saying because she speaks a different language, but she gestures and moves around, so he gets the idea. The way he looks at her, Miss Marie, you know they're going to…you know! Joel McCrea is so sexy! So chiseled and…manly. In this movie, he wears a sarong. A *sarong*! He's bare-chested and, oh, you could just die… Well, pretty soon, he and Luana are meeting under the stars. One night, she swims out to him completely naked. You just catch glimpses of her, but you can see she doesn't have a stitch on. She's so slim and gorgeous, with such a tight little behind. He jumps over the side of the boat…"

"Naked?"

"He keeps his briefs on. Too bad. He swims after her and catches her. At first, she doesn't want him to touch her, but he kisses her on the mouth. It's clearly a new experience for her. She keeps pointing to her lips and saying some foreign word. She wants him to kiss her again. He'd like to keep her forever, but she can't go back to the States with him because she's engaged."

"Engaged!"

"Her father promised her to the prince of another island, a repulsive guy who drools every time he looks at her. Her father arranged a fancy wedding, where she has to dance in the middle of a circle of fire, and…you won't believe this, Miss Marie… Dolores Del Rio dances practically naked! I mean, she has a grass skirt on—it doesn't cover much, to be honest—but nothing on top!"

"And nothing on top?" Marie gasped.

"Well, a lei covers her boobies," said Mrs. Carver. "You can see from the back that she doesn't have on a bra, but you don't actually see her nipples. She looks so exquisite, Miss Marie. Flawless lipstick, smooth eyebrows, high cheekbones. And get this! Perfectly bobbed hair! As though she'd just walked out of this beauty shop!"

"Ha ha, that's funny! On a South Pacific island?"

"Anyhow, at first, she can't get into it. But then, she catches sight of Johnny smiling at her through the bushes, and she just goes wild. She gyrates like a stripper!"

Just like Lola, I thought, pushing the limits.

"Well, Johnny runs out and grabs her and carries her away. The prince is furious! He and the other natives run after them, but Luana and Johnny have already escaped to another island."

"And then they live happily ever after."

"No, not at all. At first, it looks like everything will be fine, but then, she hears the volcano erupt on her father's island, and she knows she must go back to her people. They believe that they can only keep the volcano from destroying their village by feeding it a beautiful young woman. Luana runs away and Johnny takes off after her, but the natives attack and wound him in the shoulder with a spear. The natives are prepared to sacrifice both the lovers, but the sailors from the yacht rescue them."

"Whew! And then they live happily ever after?"

"Oh, for heaven's sake, Miss Marie. You know a white man can't marry a dark-skinned woman!"

"But Dolores Del Rio is Spanish! It says so in all the movie magazines."

"Well, in the movie she's Polynesian, and she can't marry Joel McCrea. So she throws herself into the volcano!"

"Don't cry, Mrs. Carver. You'll ruin your makeup."

The following week, Mrs. Carver came in with a copy of *Star World*. I kept the magazine.

Del Rio Named World's Most Beautiful Woman!

Dolores Del Rio is the most beautiful woman in the world! Medical experts, artists, and designers all agree: Lola is perfect!

Some readers expressed surprise that these men chose a foreigner who, although technically white, exemplifies a sultry, dark kind of beauty. However, most see her as the answer to male Latin lovers such as Ramón Novarro, now gracing the silver screen in A Night in Cairo.

Del Rio, the pert Spanish star of Bird of Paradise, *established herself as an erotic icon when she swam naked in the film with the luscious Joel McCrea, then lolled in the grass with him, she apparently wearing nothing and he in the tiniest of white briefs. Indeed, some church groups protested that the scene pushed the limits of decorum. But in today's Hollywood, anything goes! Viva Hollywood!*

Rumor had it that Lola was washed up after her former paramour, Edwin Carewe, remade Resurrection *as a sound film and chose Lupe Vélez to star in it. The earlier silent version directed by Carewe had starred Del Rio as the beautiful Katyusha Maslova, and fans widely viewed Carewe's choice of Vélez as a slap in the face to Del Rio. However, it's hard to keep a good woman down, especially if that woman is the most gorgeous creature in the world!*

Now Del Rio has hired Oliver Hendsell, Hollywood's top acting coach, to get her ready for her new role as the Brazilian bombshell Belinha de Rezende in Flying Down to Rio, *directed by Thorton Freeland and costarring Gene Raymond.*

And by the way, if you've got a zillion dollars and want to bask in the shadow of beauty, Del Rio's fabulous house on Outpost Drive is on the market, as Lola is now living in the gorgeous art deco home that her husband, Cedric Gibbons, designed for her. Gibbons had promised to move into the sprawling hacienda-style mansion Del Rio shared with her mother, but in the end, the couple decided it was just too big.

24

Hollywood, 1933
Shattering Glass

It wasn't the first time I'd visited Lola at her husband's avant-garde monstrosity, but it was the first time since her marriage that we'd had a chance to sit down and really talk. Sometimes I'd stop by to drop off a hair ornament or trim her bob, but I'd never stay long. I really didn't feel comfortable in her house, especially when Cedric was home. He seemed so... I don't know...cold and aloof. But she'd called me and said she needed to talk, so I gathered up the kids and jumped on the trolley.

Lolly and Gabi were scampering through the kitchen, playing with wooden toys Gabe had made for them. A giraffe on wheels, and a miniature vacuum cleaner. Gabe hadn't wanted me to bring the girls to Lola's. We'd seen photos in *Life* of the iron lung—a huge ventilator that seemed to swallow people alive—and the thought of one of our children stuck in that thing... It was just so awful. We'd heard that researchers were working on a polio vaccine, but for the moment, there was no protection. According to the newspapers, the disease was spread through contact with infected people, and contagion was worse in the summer.

"Please don't take them," Gabe pleaded. "It's nearly June, and it's warm. If anything happened..." He was almost in tears.

Gabe wanted the girls isolated at home or at his mother's house, but that day, Doña Lupe had a doctor's appointment. I promised to keep them away from everyone—no playing with the gardener's children, no kissing Lola—and to come home right after the visit. No park. No pool. No market.

Lola's kitchen was pure white with a bowl of fruit in the center of the table for color. Cedric had rented a yacht to take her to Hawaii for a long vacation, she was saying. She'd loved filming *Bird of Paradise* there. She adored the calm, silver waters to the southwest of the Big Island, the feel of sea spray on her skin, and the salty, briny smell of the sand.

"It's magical," she gushed. "Jets of water seem to shoot from mouths of invisible fish, then hover over the surface, iridescent and dazzling, as though flash frozen!"

I thought: *Iridescent* and *dazzling*? *Flash frozen*? Where'd she get that nonsense?

She went on and on. The prickle of sunrays on her skin! The flowers!

"You just can't imagine, Mara! Everywhere riots of hibiscus—red, pink, yellow, white. Orange heliconia, its fingerlike petals stretching toward the sky. Shell ginger, like tight white braided sugar dipped in raspberry jam."

"'Fingerlike petals stretching toward the sky'?" I teased. "Really, Lola? Did you memorize a travel brochure?"

She ignored me.

"The sharp, sweet scent of rosewood and the tickle of wild grass under your feet!"

All of a sudden, she turned to face me. "I suppose that means I'll have to sleep with him," she blurted out.

Ah, I said to myself. So that's it.

Lola bowed her head. "I'm sorry, Mara." Her voice quivered. "I didn't mean that."

I looked away. "Yes, you did," I said under my breath.

"I've pushed the question out of my mind for months. But now there's just no way to avoid asking myself. Why does the thought of sleeping with Cedric repulse me?"

She'd insisted on separate bedrooms from the start, pleading exhaustion and illness. Her health issues—kidney infections, mostly—had been in all the papers.

"Why did you marry him, if you find him revolting? You knew you'd have to have sex."

"At first, I thought it'd be okay. But then... I couldn't tell anyone, Mara, not even Mami. But I had to tell you. There's no one else I can trust. There's something about Cedric... something strange. Oh, he's always the perfect gentleman. He never pressures me." She put down the toast she was nibbling. "But..." She hesitated. "He doesn't seem that interested in me. He says all the right things and touches me in all the right places, but it's like...it's as though he were an actor performing a role."

"Why did you marry him, Lola?" I asked again.

She shook her head and forced a smile. "I don't know what's the matter with me," she whispered.

"You should be happy, Lola. You're the most beautiful woman in the world, you have a new film coming out, and you're not yet thirty!"

She winced, and I realized that I'd said the wrong thing. I shouldn't have mentioned her age. Almost thirty. Thirty was the crisis age, the career-killing age for any Hollywood celebrity. Ramón was in his thirties, and he was clearly on shaky ground. And Lola's career was beginning to teeter, too. *Bird of Paradise* had certainly raised eyebrows, but so far, it hadn't made much money, in spite of the hype over the swimming scene.

Dimitri bounded in and began to romp around with the children. I felt a knot in the pit of my stomach.

"Lola," I said firmly. "Could we get Dimitri out of here? I promised Gabe I'd keep the children away from everyone."

"He's a *dog*, for God's sake, Mara." She was clearly irritated. "They can't contract polio from *him*."

"It's just that…he could have been around someone who… what I mean is, he could be a carrier. I can't let anything happen to the girls." I felt my eyes well up. "Gabe would…"

"Gabe would what?"

"Gabe would die."

She looked at me as though I were an amateur actress who was botching her lines. She didn't shoo Dimitri out the door. Instead, she picked up the script of *Viva Villa!*

"Look," she said. "They just sent me this new script. I'd play Teresa, the beautiful sister of Don Felipe, who introduces Pancho Villa to the ideals of the Mexican Revolution."

"Could we please put the dog in the garden, Lola?"

"Listen to this, Dimitri," she said, turning to the dog. She began reading. "I once thought Pancho Villa was a hero, a great man!"

Dimitri looked up at her and yawned.

"That's what I thought," she laughed. "It's a stupid script. But listen, what if I say it this way?" She took a deep breath and put on her thickest Mexican accent: "I once t'ought Pancho Villa was a eero, a grret mahn!"

Dimitri flopped down on the floor, rolled over, and closed his eyes.

"You're right, Dimitri. This script is an insult to Mexico. I'm not going to do it. From now on, you'll be my script adviser, okay, Dimitri?"

Dimitri sprang up and went to look for his ball.

"Goodbye, Lola," I said, scooping Gabi up into my arms, while Lolly scampered along beside me. "I hope you work out your problems."

Lola blinked as though awakening from a dream. "I'm sorry, Mara," she breathed. "Of course, I'll put Dimitri outside."

She reached for the dog, knocking over a glass of orange juice. It crashed to the floor, spraying glass in every direction. Gabi started to wail.

"Oh, Mara, I'm sorry! I'm so sorry!"

That's how these movie people are, I thought. They offend you, then think they can make it all better with an apology.

But Lola was sobbing. She really was sorry. She was checking Lolly's bare little legs for splinters of glass.

"Don't touch her, please," I said dryly. "Gabe doesn't want the girls to come into contact with anyone."

"Of course." She yanked away her hand. "I understand." She pulled herself up. "I really am sorry, Mara. It's just that I've been so upset…"

"It's time for us to go," I said, this time more gently. "The girls need to nap." And then I added: "Go ahead and take that trip to Hawaii with Cedric. Try to relax and have a good time. And as far as *that* goes…the sex thing…it will take care of itself."

25

The trip to Hawaii had cleared her head, Lola told me when she called again. She understood things better now, and not just regarding her and Cedric. She'd done some thinking, come to some realizations, and now she was ready to get back to work. William Dieterle was going to star her in *Madame Du Barry*.

"And you know, Mara, I can't trust anyone else with my hair. Please!"

Marie wasn't happy about my taking a couple of weeks off, but she finally agreed. I told Lola she could count on me.

I'll try to piece together what happened that day, the first day of filming, as Lola walked to the lot. I wasn't with her because I was already in her dressing room, getting ready to pin up her hair, but she described it to me more than once. Anyway, this is how I imagine it.

7:15 a.m.

Tiny pebbles press against her soles. Sharp, irregular pain radiates from the balls of her feet to her arches. At times, it's so intense that Lola wants to scream. The bottoms of her dainty sandals seem to be made of film.

"Oh God," she moans. "This is hell!" But she has to keep

walking. She can't be late for the seven thirty shoot. She limps along the construction path that leads to the set, choking back tears and struggling to block out the throbbing. It's like treading on a hobnailed roller. "Serves me right," she mutters. *Vogue* was showing strappy sandals worn over sheer silk stockings. They'd looked adorable on the page, but they turned out to be instruments of torture.

Actually, though, the foot pain is the least of it. For weeks now, she's been haunted by something else, something less tangible. By sounds. By words that bruise. Words that seem to float on the breeze, at first almost inaudible: *"Foreigner! Mexican!"*

A whisper. A suggestion. *"Foreigner! Mexican!"*

She stops and shakes off her sandal. Her feet pulsate from the balls to the heels. The seam of her stocking cuts into her flesh. She turns her toes under and stretches her arches, a move she uses to relieve foot cramps from dancing. She glances behind her and sees a cluster of chorus girls giggling and twittering. Are they gossiping about her? she wonders. No, they don't appear to notice her. The reproach seems to come from elsewhere—from the trash cans, from under the benches, from around the bushes. *"Foreigner! Foreigner! Mexican!"*

Lola stops and looks for a place to sit down. She has to get off her feet, if only for a moment. She finds a bench, slips off her sandals, and massages her toes.

"Foreigner! Mexican!"

What has happened? One minute she's the erotic icon of Hollywood, the next, just some wetback!

She digs her thumb into her outer heel. She needs to understand what's happening to her career. After *Bird of Paradise*, gossip columnists started writing that she was box office poison—incapable of drawing an audience and making money. If she doesn't make money, the studio will have no use for her.

Cedric has tried to reassure her. No one has a quarter for the movies these days, he says. Besides, all those prudish ladies in the Midwest are handing out leaflets in the church vestibule condemning the immorality of Hollywood.

"People are still going to theaters," she counters. "After all, they're going to *your* movies! What's happening is that the country is turning xeno...xeno..."

"Xenophobic. That's the word you're looking for, darling. I don't think you need to worry," he always reassures her. "You're still the industry's Latin sweetheart."

He sounds patronizing. She hates it. It's easy for him to laugh it off, she thinks. He's just won an Oscar for *The Merry Widow*!

Cedric just doesn't get it. A new narrow-mindedness is taking root. Politicians. Certain intellectuals. Even industry insiders. Cedric is white and at the top of his career. He's oblivious to the racism creeping into the media. She's dark, at least by white standards, and hypersensitive. It's hardly subtle, she thinks. *Photoplay* has been printing articles all year about how foreigners are overrunning Hollywood. Why so many foreign extras? complain fans. "I do wish these foreign actors would watch their accents!" says a letter to the editor in *Photoplay*. Another reader grumbles: "Americans can play Frenchmen, Spaniards, or Russians just as well as foreigners!" Furthermore, "these foreigners have no sense of decency! That Austrian hussy Hedy Lamarr romps around naked in *Ecstasy*!" But what about the all-American Clara Bow? thinks Lola. You can't get more naked than she is in *Hula*!

Demands for censorship are growing. Sexy and sultry are being replaced by all-American apple-pie goodness. *Wholesome* is the word of the day. Films like *Bird of Paradise* are being derided as Hollywood filth.

7:18 a.m.

If she runs to the set barefoot, Lola thinks, she'll tear her stockings. "This is a punishment," she tells herself. "I've betrayed my upbringing, God, and even Sister Madeleine."

She imagines the old French nun sitting in a movie theater, staring at the screen, as Lola's naked body glides through liquescent celluloid and slithers like a water snake under the froth and foam of the waves. *"Bon Dieu!"* Sister Madeleine chokes back the words. *"Mais c'est affreux! C'est scandaleux!"* In spite of her aching feet, Lola laughs.

Even though *Bird* bombed, RKO took a chance and signed her for *Flying Down to Rio,* and at least that one made money. A silly film. Thoroughly predictable. Thoroughly successful! But Carla Myer's review in *Star World* had her worried.

The amazing new dancing team, Fred Astaire and Ginger Rogers, flew across the floor like fairies. Whether swaying to the samba or pulsating to a mambo, the couple kept spectators' eyes riveted to the screen. In one extraordinary scene, Miss Rogers flies through the clouds sitting astride an airplane. In another, a bevy of gorgeous chorus girls dances on the wings. Dolores Del Rio, who plays a Brazilian society girl, was lovely, as always.

"Was lovely, as always?" That's all she had to say about me? thought Lola. What about *my* dancing? What about *my* acting? In the whole damn review, only one sentence! The supporting actors stole the show! The whole country was in love with Fred and Ginger.

She glances at her watch. It's after seven twenty. She'll be late. Warner Brothers has given her one last chance: the starring role in *Madame Du Barry.* She can't just waltz onto the set any time she pleases like a spoiled diva. But her feet refuse to be forced back into the sandals.

At this point, I'm already on set. I've prepared the powdered wig with fore-tresses piled high and delicately placed mouton curls along the sides. All I have to do is pin up Lola's hair, place the wig on her head, and secure it with bobbies. But where is she?

Somewhere on the grounds, struggling to calm her nerves, it turns out. Workmen are sawing and hammering, and the noise makes Lola's head throb. She smells the odor of fresh stucco and burning paper mingled with the acrid stink of sweat. Her sweat. She showered and perfumed her body in the morning. How could it be that she smelled like a panhandler? What if someone stands close to her? What will they think? The exquisite Dolores Del Rio reeks like a rotting carcass!

7:26 a.m.

"Move!" she orders her body. She forces herself to stand. She hobbles forward, then collapses back onto the bench.

Is it because I'm Mexican? she asks herself. Is it because people say that Mexicans are Communist agitators?

She's seen photos of American workers standing in breadlines. In the newsreels she's seen activists urging out-of-work men to take back the factories by force. "Fight—Don't Starve!" they scream. She's seen mounted cops smashing heads with nightsticks, releasing tear gas, making mass arrests, and sometimes even killing demonstrators. The newspapers say all this violence is the fault of foreigners. Foreign agitators. Foreign workers who take Americans' jobs. Foreigners like her.

Lola forces herself to focus on walking. She shoves her swollen, inflamed feet into her sandals and takes a step. A stone like a nail cuts into her sole. She ignores it and pushes on.

7:31 a.m.

Dieterle is positioning the cast for the Versailles ball scene. "Louis XV, here. Girls, there." Scores of extras with skirts like inverted pastel beach umbrellas move into place. Lola flings off her shoes. The dresser fastens her crinolines. I pin her wig in place. Dieterle is busy with Reginald Owen, who plays Louis. He is showing him how to walk up the stairs so that the cameras can achieve both the long shot of the palace and the short shot of the king emerging from the crowd into the center of the frame. The film is all frills and froth, but it's what audiences want, and Dieterle aims to please. He's one of those Germans who, like his friend Marlene Dietrich, escaped the rising tide of Nazism back home. Dietrich had made it big with films like *The Blue Angel* and *Morocco*. Dieterle was convinced he could do the same.

He's ready for Lola. I push her onto the set. She crawls into Owen's lap and mouths teasingly, "To me, you're not a king, you're just a man."

"The folks will eat it up," laughs Dieterle. "Just leave a second more after 'not a king.' Very coquettish, very insinuating, very suggestive."

"To me, you're not a king…you're just a man," Lola repeats breathily.

Once the day's shooting is over, I accompany Lola back to her house. The girls are still at their grandmother's. Lola goes into the kitchen and dumps her sandals into the garbage.

"*Madame Du Barry* won't save my career, will it?" she says. "It's rubbish."

I shrug.

"There's a lot of bad feeling about Mexicans right now," she says. "There's always been resentment, but now it's intensifying. I hope things don't get rough for Gabe at MGM."

"He hasn't said anything," I say. "But I've heard words— *beaner, wetback*. I'm nervous, too. I'm especially nervous for the children. They're dark, like Gabe."

"Mara, do you think that in ten years anyone will remem-

ber drivel like *Madame Du Barry*? At least, *you're* doing something important."

"Combing out ladies' hair?"

"Raising a family, creating something for the future."

It's the first time I've ever heard her say anything like that.
Suddenly, I realize how deeply she's hurting.

"You have a family," she says. "I have nothing."

I look around at her Lalique statues, her chrome furniture,
the expensive avant-garde paintings on the walls, her husband's Oscar standing on the mantel. What can I say? It's true,
I think. She has nothing.

26

I don't know why Lola insisted that I meet her new friend
Marlene. Maybe she wanted to shock me—Marlene was famous for her outrageous behavior. I admit I was curious. Everyone was talking about the German bombshell who'd come
to Hollywood with the director Josef von Sternberg and taken
the country by storm with *The Blue Angel.*

The maître d' whisked us across the crowded dining room
toward a small private area at the back of the restaurant.

"No one will bother you back here," he whispered conspiratorially. He seemed to see himself as the protector of imperiled movie stars.

"Thank you, Andrés," said Lola.

"The others are here already," he added, showing us to
our table.

Marlene, wearing a man's suit and bright red lipstick, put
down her whiskey and stood up to embrace Lola. "Darling,"
she murmured. "I've been dying to see you. This is Astrid,
my dresser," she added, nodding at the willowy blonde sitting
next to her at the table.

"And this is my friend Mara," said Lola. For the first time,
she hadn't introduced me as "my hairdresser" or "my assistant." I felt a ting of satisfaction.

Astrid was staring at Lola intently.

"Ah! I knew it!" snapped Marlene with mock indignation. "You vant her all to yourself."

"Want, not vant, you Kraut!" Astrid snapped back.

"Kraut! Look who's calling whom what! Der pot is calling den *Wasserkessel* black! Okay *want*. I can say it right!"

"Lola doesn't know what is a *Wasserkessel*," hissed Astrid. "You have to say 'kettle.'"

"What a *Wasserkessel* is, not what is a *Wasserkessel*. Your English is just as bad as mine, *mein Schatz*!" Marlene turned to Lola. "The Swede is quite endearing, once you accept that she's the center of the universe."

"The German is so charming that if you gave her a dollar for every friend she makes, you'd come back with change!" snorted Astrid.

"I'm not getting into a battle of wits with you, my love. You're an unarmed combatant!"

Lola seemed amused by their banter. "Girls, stop!" she twittered. "You're going to make me pee from laughing."

"Isn't she adorable, Astrid? Let's go back to my house after dinner, Lola," Marlene murmured. "I'm tired of fucking Astrid. I need a change."

"You, too, Mara!" piped in Astrid. She winked and puckered her lips.

I wasn't used to that sort of foolishness. I didn't know what to do.

The sommelier brought the wine menu. He gazed at us a moment without speaking.

"What are you staring at, Norman?" snapped Marlene. "Have you never seen so many beautiful women in one room before?"

"It hasn't escaped me, madame, that I have before me the most beautiful women in the world," said the waiter smoothly.

"Except for this one," Marlene said, tweaking Astrid on the cheek. "This one is no great beauty, but terrific in bed. Her name is Astrid Petersen. You can have her if you want her."

The young man's cheeks turned pomegranate. He lowered his eyes.

"Wine, ladies?" he stammered finally.

He raised his eyes and caught my gaze. I nodded in commiseration. What would Gabe think? I wondered. Solid, steadfast, church-on-Sunday Gabe.

Marlene was groping Lola's knee under the table. "Norman, I'll have another whiskey on the rocks. And wine, Schloss Johannisberg Riesling Bronzelack Trocken Rheingau."

"Clement," said the sommelier stoically. "My name is Clement, not Norman."

"I'll have…" gasped Lola. "I'll have a glass of mineral water."

"Me, too," I echoed.

"*Mein Gott,* Lola. When are you going to get over all those upper-class Mexican Catholic inhibitions? There are lots of delicious things to try. Relax. At least have some wine."

"My cousin Ramón once told me the same thing."

"Well, he's right. How is Ramón, by the way? I saw him in *Mata Hari*, with the bitch."

I'd heard that back in Berlin, Marlene and Garbo had had an affair that ended badly, and now they weren't speaking to each other.

"He and Greta were great together," said Lola. She was trying to be diplomatic. "The movie was a huge success. The censors hated it, of course."

"So shocking!" sneered Marlene. "Sex between unmarried people! What's the matter with these Americans? All this puritanical *Scheiße*."

"Yeah," giggled Astrid. "Marlene and I aren't married, at

least, not to each other." She nibbled gently at Marlene's neck. Clement looked away, clearly uncomfortable.

"Poor Norman," snickered Marlene. "Have you never seen two women kiss before? Didn't you see me in *Morocco*? I wear men's clothes and kiss a woman!"

"Will Madame also be having the Riesling?" he asked, turning toward Astrid.

"Depends on what I have for dinner."

"Of course."

Clement backed out of the room with his head bowed, as though taking leave of a king.

"You've hardly said a word, Mara," said Marlene. "Lola says you're also from Mexico. I wouldn't have guessed."

"From Durango," I said after a pause.

"Are your parents still there?"

I hated when people asked questions like that. What was I supposed to say? That I had no idea who my parents were?

"They died in the Revolution."

She looked puzzled.

"The Mexican Revolution."

"Ah, and how did you come to Los Angeles?"

"With my aunt Emilia. She raised me."

"Your mother's sister?"

Now what was I going to say? That I didn't know? "Yes," I said, "my mother's sister."

The waiter came in with the menus.

"I recommend the trout," said Marlene.

"I'll have steak," countered Astrid, defiantly.

"Have whatever you want, darling. I can afford it."

"And a French cabernet."

Marlene turned to me. "Have a whiskey, Mara. It'll relax you."

"I don't think so," I said.

"Why not? It's legal now. No more Prohibition."

"No," I said firmly. "I'm pregnant."

I felt my whole body turn to rime. It was as though an icy fog had descended on the room.

"Another one?" hissed Lola. "You already have two!"

I stared at the silverware.

"They don't ration them out like bread loaves during the war, darling," purred Marlene.

"Why didn't you tell me?" sniffed Lola.

"I just found out myself," I whispered.

"Why should she tell you?" interrupted Marlene. "If she and her husband want another baby, that's their business."

Lola had become as pale as the tablecloth.

"It's nice to have a child," Marlene went on, "as long as someone else takes care of it. I have a daughter, you know."

"No," I said, "I didn't know."

Lola looked from Marlene to me. I thought she might suddenly dissolve into a puddle.

"My husband, Rudy, takes care of her. My husband, Rudolf Sieber. And the nanny."

The waiter brought the food. Marlene smiled seductively at Lola. I choked down my trout.

"Do you think there will be a war in Europe?" Lola asked.

Marlene sat upright. "What brought that on?" she asked, unexpectedly edgy.

"People are saying that there might be a war. Attitudes toward foreigners are changing. There's a new nationalism, a new…a new xenophobia."

"Of course, there will be a war. Hitler is a madman."

"Well, we'll be safe here in Hollywood," murmured Astrid, tweaking Marlene's wrist.

But Marlene was no longer in a playful mood. "He's destroying the country. He had himself declared the *Führer* and he's dismantled all of Germany's democratic institutions. And Astrid is wrong. No one will be safe."

"But the Americans won't get involved, will they?" I asked. A horrifying thought passed through my mind: Was I going to bring a new life into a raging conflagration?

"He's stoking hatred by saying that business interests in Europe and the US are in cahoots with the Jewish community. So yes, America could get involved. It might get really ugly." She'd become somber. She lifted her fork to her mouth mechanically, without savoring her trout.

Waiters picked up the dishes and brought in dessert menus.

"That one's cute," whispered Astrid to Marlene. "Let's invite him to our orgy tonight!"

Marlene ignored her. "Two tyrants, Stalin and Hitler, both with insatiable appetites for power and both willing to sacrifice their people to their own mindless ambition," she said after a pause. "Of course, there will be a war, Lola. I lived through the Great War, and I can tell you it was ghastly."

I remembered the streets of Mexico during the Revolution. Laborers mowed down like dogs. Shit and blood in the gutters. Madero.

"We've seen carnage," I said softly.

"My God!" moped Astrid. "Who wants to talk about war? Bring back Norman…or Clement…or whatever his name is."

"If we do go to war," said Marlene matter-of-factly, "I'll become a soldier and fight against Hitler! And when we march into Hamburg, I'll fuck all the girls, and when we sleep in trenches, I'll fuck all the boys! It will be marvelous!"

Marlene was struggling to maintain her aura of outrageousness.

The waiter brought our desserts and the sommelier brought a list of after-dinner liqueurs.

Marlene stabbed at her flan as if she were attacking with

a bayonet. Lola picked daintily at her raspberries sauvignon. I glanced at my watch. It was only 9:05. Maybe I could be home by ten.

"I have an idea!" blurted out Marlene, clearly trying to force a mood shift. "Let's go visit Ramón! I haven't seen him in ages. Ramón is always—what do you say?—a can of laughs."

"I think it's 'a barrel of laughs,'" said Lola.

"A barrel? What's that?"

"A big...how do you say it? A big container. A vat."

"Finish your *Apfelkuchen*, Astrid," ordered Marlene.

"I can't go," I said. "Please just drop me off at home. I promised Gabe I'd be back early."

"We'll just say hello, and then I'll take you home," said Lola.

It was nearly ten o'clock when we got to the graceful, Mayan-style house on Valley Oak Drive—the house Lou Samuel had bought with Ramón's money, and that Ramón now occupied. It was completely dark.

"How strange," said Lola. "Usually he floods the front with light."

"Maybe he's not home," said Astrid.

"Or he's busy with one of his boyfriends," snickered Marlene.

"He could be in the back, in the swimming pool," suggested Lola.

"Hey, Ramón!" squealed Astrid. "Come on down." She pressed on the bell.

It took five or six minutes, but he finally opened the door. He reeked of alcohol, and his eyes were spinning like pinwheels. Lola took his wrist and tried to ease him over to a sofa, but he yanked away and lurched against a wall, then burst into tears. The sleeve of Lola's silk dress was suddenly wet and sticky. She looked down and saw that it was covered with tears, snot, and vomit. Ramón collapsed onto the sofa, trembling.

"Take off your clothes," Marlene ordered Lola. She wasn't being playful.

Lola went into the bathroom, slipped off her dress, and threw on one of Ramón's dressing gowns. She placed the dress in a bag she found in the kitchen and took it out to the car.

When she returned, Ramón was sprawled out on the sofa, his head in Marlene's lap. He was mumbling something about "jail." Marlene was patting his forehead with a damp cloth. At that moment, she looked...well...maternal.

"Calm down, *Liebchen*," she murmured. "Tell us what happened."

"They're going to send me to jail," Ramón whimpered.

"Nobody's going to send you to jail," whispered Marlene, stroking his arm.

"Look at the paper on the kitchen counter!"

Lola disappeared into the kitchen and fetched the paper. It read: "Summons to appear..."

"I don't know anything about this," sobbed Ramón.

"I do," said Lola coolly. "It's about a police raid at the Sacramento headquarters of the Cannery in July."

"The Cannery? I don't even know what that means."

"The Cannery is an Agricultural Workers Union. The people who put the vegetables and fruits in cans that wind up on the shelves of American markets are called 'canners.'"

"Canned vegetables are disgusting," piped up Astrid.

"The police found the names of some of us on a list in the office of the union secretary. It had your name, mine, Lupe Vélez's...mostly they're going after Mexicans, but James Cagney was there, too. People suspected of trying to unionize California's agricultural workers."

"I know nothing about that stuff," whispered Ramón. "Nothing! ¡*Nada!*"

"It's a Communist witch hunt," said Lola. "Writers, actors—anyone suspected of 'un-American' leanings. Celebrities and labor activists, mostly."

Gabe and I weren't either of those things, and I wasn't worried about being summoned. All I wanted was to get out of there. "Lola," I said. "I have to go home. If you want to stay with Ramón, I can call a cab."

"And then there was that screening of *¡Que viva México!*, the Eisenstein film we all went to. They say it's a Communist propaganda film. Someone was watching and writing down the names of the attendees."

"Really, Lola," I said. "I promised Gabe I wouldn't get back late. I'll have to ask you to lend me some money, though. Ramón, where's your telephone?"

Ramón was still curled up on Marlene's lap, eyes half-closed.

"Nothing's going to happen, Ramón," whispered Marlene. "Let your lawyer handle it. Or the studio. Just tell them you never gave money to any Communist organization."

"Exactly. That's what I did," said Lola. I remembered Lola had once mentioned that she'd been summoned, but she didn't make a big deal of it. It was all resolved within weeks.

"Tell them you could never support the Soviet Union," quipped Marlene. "The Soviets criminalize men going to bed together."

Ramón began to sob.

"Marlene!" snapped Lola.

Astrid bent down and kissed him on the forehead. Lola massaged his wrist.

"Ramón," I said. "Could I please use your telephone?" I looked around the room. "Just tell me where it is so I can make a quick call."

"Look, Ramón," said Lola, "MGM is not going to let them brand you a Communist. They have too much money invested in you. Warner Brothers is going to intervene for me. They'll demand the government produce proof and there isn't any, so that'll be the end of it."

"It will be fine, Ramón," murmured Marlene. "You'll see. Everything will be fine."

"Ramón..." I began again.

"All *right*," hissed Lola, "I'll take you home."

It was nearly eleven thirty when I stuck my key into the keyhole. The front room was dark except for the dim beam of a night-light. Gabe was sitting in the rocker with Lolly on his lap.

"Oh," I whispered, "I had the most awful evening. First..."

"Where have you been?" snapped Gabe. It wasn't the reception I'd expected.

"I went to dinner with Lola and that German actress, just like I told you." I was taken aback. Gabe was never cross with me.

"Lolly is sick. You should have been here instead of wasting time with those mindless movie people."

"What's wrong?" I bent down to take her out of his arms, but he held her against him.

"Fever, vomiting, sore throat."

We both knew what the first symptoms of polio were. I felt my blood turn to sand in my veins.

"She had an awful headache after dinner. She cried for hours. She finally fell asleep about a half hour ago. Don't wake her."

"Oh God," I whispered. "Did you call Dr. Restin?"

"He said he'd come first thing tomorrow morning. You'll have to stay home. I have to be at the studio by seven tomorrow. If I'm late, they'll dock my pay."

"Lola wanted me to..."

"I don't care what Lola wants. I'm tired of Lola and Cedric and the whole lot of them." He was trembling.

"I'm sorry, Gabe. I'm sorry I wasn't here. I thought…"

"If it turns out that Lolly has…that disease," he interrupted, "you can't be around her…because of the baby. Gabi can't be around her either. I don't know what we'll do. And the money for the doctor. Where…?" His voice broke.

He pulled himself up and carried Lolly to her bed. Then he sank back down into the rocking chair, buried his face in his hands, and sobbed.

27

Hollywood, 1934–1938
Worries

I didn't like Dr. Restin, even though people said he was a good doctor. He had a face like a paper bag, and fat, gnarly fingers that reminded me of raw ginger. Still, he came when you called. He trudged to the door, his black doctor's bag in hand, smelling of antiseptic and musk. He always greeted me with a curt *"Buenos días,"* which annoyed me. There was something sanctimonious about the way he said those two words, probably the only two words he knew in Spanish. It was as though he thought he was doing me a favor.

"Good morning," I said. "Lolly is still asleep."

"Well, wake her up," he ordered. "I don't have all day." He followed me into her bedroom—the room that had once served as the store where Gabe and Vince sold furniture and wooden bric-a-brac.

I watched him reach under her little nightgown and knead her pudgy legs. His knuckles were hairy and damp. I looked away.

He flipped her over like a pancake, hiked up her skirt, and stuck a thermometer in her rectum. Lolly let out a shriek and started to wail.

"She's ill," I whispered. "Can't you be a little gentler?"

He looked at me as if I were a toad and pulled out the thermometer. "Fever," he said, glaring at it. "I need more tests. Get her to the office this afternoon. You can pay me then."

I felt such loathing for the man that my stomach began to churn. Still, he was a doctor, and Lolly was ill. I had to obey. Gabe had taken the car, and the thought of traipsing through town with a sick child and a three-and-a-half-year-old on the trolley was daunting. I went to the phone and dialed Señora Lupe's number. If I could at least leave Gabi with her, I could manage. But there was no answer.

I called Madame Isabelle's house and asked to speak with Tía Emi.

"She left for the studio about a half hour ago," the house-keeper told me.

Who else was there to call? I'd never be able to reach Gabe at MGM. Then I remembered that I was supposed to give Lola a haircut in the morning and that I hadn't canceled yet. I picked up the receiver again.

"Lola," I said, when she came to the phone. "I'm sorry, but…" I explained about Lolly.

"Why didn't you call me right away?" she said. "I'll take you to the doctor."

"Don't you have to be at a rehearsal or something?"

"No," she said. "Not this afternoon."

We arrived at Dr. Restin's office at one thirty. The drab yellow waiting room reminded me of a jail. No color. No toys. A few old, dog-eared magazines for the moms—*Photoplay, Star World, Modern Sewing*—but nothing for the children. Two small windows with iron grating. A dull beige carpet, the kind that doesn't show the dirt. Gabi sat on Lola's lap.

Dr. Restin poked Lolly's belly and jabbed a needle into her buttock. He squeezed her thighs and calves until she wailed. He made her stand naked in front of him and walk across the room to check her posture and balance. Then he picked her up like a sack of grain and plopped her onto the examining table. He opened her legs and prodded her genitals. She was only six, but she was embarrassed. He flung her over as he had in the morning and stuck his finger into her rectum. She scrunched up her face. Tears were flowing down her cheeks. I felt her agony, but what could I do? He was the doctor.

"I'll call you tonight," he said, when he had finished. He wrote a prescription and handed it to me. "You can get it at the Rexall on the corner. Pay the receptionist for the office visit and this morning's house call on your way out."

I had five dollars for the doctor, but hadn't counted on the medicine.

"Don't worry about it," said Lola. "After all, Lolly's my god-child." She looked somber, worried. We walked to the drug-store, and Lola gave the pharmacist the paper, then slipped a bottle of pink gooey liquid into my hand. I didn't see how much she paid, and she wouldn't tell me.

On the way home, she said, "I'm sorry about last night, Mara. About making you get home late. I wasn't thinking clearly. I've been worried about something…but what matters now is Lolly. Let's get you and the girls home, and we can talk about it some other time."

I didn't say anything. I was grateful she wasn't going to tell me about her problem. I appreciated her taking me to the doctor—I don't know how I would have managed without her—but at the moment, I had more than I could handle with my own worries.

"By the way," she said, as we climbed out of the car, "when is the baby due?"

"Oh," I said, "not until late summer. Around the end of September."

"Ah," she said. "Congratulations." She smiled and squeezed my hand. "I suppose Gabe is hoping for a little son."

"Yes," I said. "He is."

That night, we ate dinner in silence, trying not to glance at the telephone. We finished around seven, and Dr. Restin still hadn't called. Gabe sat down next to the phone with his hands clenched so tightly that his palms bled where his nails dug into the skin. We waited. I washed the dishes. We waited. Lolly had slept all afternoon and was still sleeping, but Gabi needed her bath and a bedtime story. Finally, around eight thirty, the phone shrilled. Gabe answered. He listened to the voice on the other end of the line without responding, without flinching, without betraying the slightest emotion. Then, finally, he smiled and hung up.

"Dr. Restin doubts it's polio," he said. "He thinks it might be some kind of an influenza. But at least, it's not...*that*."

I felt like I'd been carrying a boulder on my shoulders and an army of angels had flown in through the window and lifted it off.

Gabe took a deep breath and lit a cigarette. "Holy God, thank you," he said, looking upward, as though he could see through the ceiling, into heaven. "My mother's been at church all day, praying." He exhaled slowly. "And Dr. Restin, what a wonderful man he is. What a wonderful doctor!"

I bit my lip. "Yes," I said, even though I thought he treated children like dishrags. "Lola's the one who paid for the medicine," I added. "I didn't have enough money."

Gabe looked as if I'd insulted him. "I'll pay her back," he said.

"No," I said. "She won't let you. She wanted to do it. After all, she's the godmother."

Gabe pulled me to him. I felt his strong, firm workman's arms around me, and his heart beating in his broad, smooth chest.

"I was so scared," he whispered.

"I know," I said, and I understood that I'd been forgiven.

◇◇◇◇◇

It turned out to be a nasty flu, one of those bugs that make you feel like you've been hit on the head with a plank. I stayed home with Lolly until she'd finally shaken it. Lola called once or twice a week to ask about her. Did she need more medicine? Toys? Books? Games? I always said no, even though money was tighter than ever, and we could have used some help.

Our daughter Lupita, named after Gabe's mother, was born on September 22, 1934, but I had to go back to work. We were struggling to pay the bills, and even Gabe realized that we couldn't make it without two incomes. By mid-October, we'd fallen into a routine. Gabe dropped the children off at his mother's, took me to Marie's, and left for the studio. I'd have rather worked for Lola because she paid more, but Lola didn't have any projects at the moment, so she rarely needed me.

Usually when she called, it was to ask about Lolly, but one day she said, "I have to see you! It's urgent!"

I didn't know what to think. Was Lola ill again? Had something happened to Doña Antonia? I knew I had to go. After all, hadn't Lola come right away when I'd had to take Lolly to the doctor? I phoned Gabe and told him to pick up the girls after work and took the trolley to Lola's after my last customer. She was waiting in the doorway as I walked up the path.

As soon as I set my foot in the door, she whisked me into the parlor. "This is what he said to me," she blurted out. "He said, 'Face it, Lola, your career is over! *Madame Du Barry* was a flop! We can't sustain losses like that year after year!'" She was trembling.

"Who are you talking about, Lola?" I took a seat on the chrome and leather couch.

"I told him that it wasn't my fault! It was Hays! And he said, 'Hays is the new reality, Lola. The Motion Picture Production Code sets the guidelines. We had to take out the sex.'

You saw the rushes, Mara. It was just cute sex. Nothing really bad. *Madame Du Barry* is a comedy, so what did Hays expect? And then he puts on this great big important voice and says, 'As president of the Motion Picture Producers and Distributors of America, Mr. William H. Hays can expect whatever the hell he wants! Mr. Hays has decided no sex, no tits, no pubic hair, no hanky-panky. And that's not all—no bad language, not even *Christ* or *hell*.' But the cuts ruined the film, Mara. Do you realize what they're doing? Starting July 1, 1934, you had to get a certificate of approval for every film before you can show it in the theaters."

She was pacing back and forth like a tiger.

"Well," I said, "when you make your next film, you'll know from the beginning what you can and can't do. That way, you won't run afoul of the codes."

"Who knows if I'll ever make another film! The *Du Barry* reviews are awful. Look at this one, from *Photoplay*, 'you (the viewer) are mentally requesting the privilege of wringing Miss Del Rio's lovely neck in some of her gushy and quixotic moments.' And from *Star World*, 'An all-time low for Dolores Del Rio. Probably her worst film.'"

I sighed. I didn't feel much sympathy for Lola. I was too worried about paying the electricity and phone bills. "You're a big star, Lola," I said. "One bomb is not going to ruin your career."

"Nobody's is going to pay money to see a leading lady whose neck you want to wring."

"This will blow over, Lola."

"He says the Breen Office wrote to him that *Madame Du Barry* was full of crudeness and adultery. Furthermore, Breen thought it might get us into hot water with France to show the French king so…well, horny. Mr. Warner had no choice but to cut the naughty parts."

"What's the Breen Office?" I hadn't understood half of what she said.

"Joseph Breen is Hays's chief censor. The guy in charge of expur—how do you say it?—getting rid of tits and pubic hair."

"Expurgating."

"And then he says to me, 'I'm nothing, Lola. I'm just a hired hand, a studio manager who carries out Jack Warner's orders. But I'm telling you, it's going to get harder and harder. Breen won't let anything sneak through. Even film advertising has to be squeaky clean. They held up Rita Hayworth's new film because the ads focused too much on her patooties.' And this is the worst thing of all, Mara, the most *hurtful* thing of all. He says, 'Anyway, studios are looking at young talent, kids like that girl in *The Gay Divorcee*, with Fred Astaire and Ginger Rogers. The blonde kid, you know… Grable… Betty Grable…terrific legs.'"

"So you were talking to Jack Warner's studio manager. What do you care what he thinks, Lola? He doesn't make the decisions."

"'*I* have terrific legs,' I said to him. 'Yeah,' he says, 'but let's face it. You're thirty already. She's only eighteen. You know how they are. Always looking for fresh flesh.'"

I stood behind her and massaged her shoulders. He was right, this studio manager. She was thirty—old for a Hollywood star. Worse still, she didn't have the frothy blond glamour or the blue eyes of a Betty Grable, a Jean Harlow, or an Olivia de Havilland. Tastes had changed. Maybe Greta and Marlene would make it, with their fair, northern looks, but exotic brunettes had fallen out of fashion. Ramón hadn't had a hit in years. Hollywood was looking for the bouncy, flaxenhaired "girl next door" and the square-jawed, pale-skinned cowboy.

Lola had calmed down. The ranting was over. She rang for

Luz to bring in some lemonade and snacks and sat for a while, her chin in her hands.

"You know," she said finally. "It's time for me to make some changes. I'm tired of making silly films like *Madame Du Barry*. Ever since I came to Hollywood, they've been casting me as the sexpot, the empty-headed Mexican who swims naked and wiggles her ass. And it's the same for all us Mexican actresses. Did you see Lupe Vélez in *The Half-Naked Truth* and *Hot Pepper*? That's how they see us, Mara, half-naked and hot! I've hardly had a serious role since *Ramona*!" She shook her head. "I hate this, Mara. I want to be a *real* actress!"

"You *are* a real actress, Lola," I insisted, but she looked away.

"At the Eisenstein screening—we were talking about it at Ramón's house, remember?—I met a Mexican director, Emilio Fernández, who envisions a new kind of cinema, a cinema that deals with real people and real problems. Problems like social injustice, poverty, that kind of thing. Ramón says that now that he's been cleared of 'un-Americanism,' he's going to leave MGM and try his hand at directing. Maybe it's time for me to make some changes, too. The truth is, they don't want us here, so maybe I should…" Her voice trailed off as she poured herself a glass of lemonade.

By the time Lola got another film offer, I was expecting our fourth child. It was 1937. Twentieth Century Fox cast Lola as a German spy who makes the dangerous mistake of falling in love with her prey in Daryl Zanuck's new film, *Lancer Spy*. Yes, once again, she would play a sexy foreigner, but the topic was relevant and trendy. "A sure bet," said *Star World*. "German spies are the rage."

And no wonder. War was coming. Nazi Germany and Fascist Italy had just created the Axis. Then Germany signed a pact with Imperial Japan to oppose the Soviets. I remember all those things. I had three little girls and a baby on the way. Would war come to Los Angeles? I had nightmares.

But Lola didn't seem concerned. Her mind was elsewhere. She and Cedric continued to play the charming celebrity couple, attending parties and avoiding questions. After *Lancer Spy*, she was mostly out of work. His career was skyrocketing. Hers was fizzling. They had nothing to talk about, so they went to parties and pretended to be in love.

However, changes were on the horizon. Big changes.

In the meantime, Alejandra—we called her Lexie—was born on October 20, 1937. I hadn't given Gabe the son he wanted, but he never uttered a word of reproach. All he asked was that we name her for his grandfather, Vicente Alejandro.

28

He wasn't exactly handsome. His fleshy face was almost infantile, like that of a toddler who hadn't quite lost his baby fat. Yet there was something manly about him, something sensuous—the way he moved his hands, the way he puckered his lips. He exuded primal energy.

He had the shrewdness of a panther, yet the playfulness of a retriever pup. His pudgy cheeks didn't fit his swagger, but the combination of childlike vulnerability and raw sexuality seized women off guard and made them quiver.

"Who is that?" He'd caught Lola's eye across the room, and she'd looked away, trying hard not to appear interested. After all, he was a kid, maybe twenty-one or twenty-two, she thought, while she was a married woman in her thirties.

"Isn't he darling?" Marlene waved at him. "What do you say we share him?"

He grinned at her, and Marlene sent him her most salacious come-hither look, the one where tongue crosses upper lip slowly and suggestively.

"That's Orson Welles," she said, "the scandalous reader of H. G. Wells's *The War of the Worlds*."

"You mean the radio program about an alien invasion?"

"*Ja, natürlich.* The one they performed last Halloween. He made up a bunch of fake news bulletins describing the attack step-by-step. No commercials. So realistic that people didn't realize it was fiction. Scared half the country to death. The kid directed and narrated it. Amazing, isn't it?"

Marlene blew smoke rings into the air.

"It looks like he's coming over here. Pretend like you're a fan. I hear he has an ego as big as Czechoslovakia."

"Miss Del Rio," Welles said smoothly. "I've been in love with you since I saw you in *Bird of Paradise.*" He took Lola's hand in both of his. "It's such a pleasure."

Lola felt her feet turn into two stiff, cold fish.

"And, Miss Dietrich," he murmured softly, "I've always been a fan of yours, too, ever since I saw you in *Blonde Venus.* You were extraordinary."

Marlene smiled sweetly. "Cary Grant was extraordinary. I just did what I do."

"Those scenes of you swimming in the ocean, Miss Del Rio. So fluid, so agile. I was breathless. It was like being in the presence of something divine."

"Oh look! There's Gary!" said Marlene, winking at Lola. "Gary Cooper. I haven't seen him in ages." She lowered her voice. "We slept together when we made *Morocco,* but he left me for Lupe Vélez, or maybe he was with Lupe before me. I'm really not sure."

Lola and Orson watched Marlene's blond locks disappear into the throng of finger waves and Marcel curls.

"Let's leave and go someplace quiet," suggested Orson.

Lola hesitated. She remembered Jaime, Edwin, Cedric... The smiles, the sweet flattery, the coaxing. *I can't let this happen again,* she thought. *Not now. Not with this boy.* But there was something about him... He was so intense, so polite, so adorable...

"Alright," she said finally. "Where would you suggest?"

Orson Welles was only twenty-four years old—not twenty-one or twenty-two as Lola had thought, but still a baby—and already a Broadway star. He'd become a sensation four years earlier, when he played Mercutio in *Romeo and Juliet*. In 1937, he'd created *Caesar*, a revolutionary adaptation of *Julius Caesar* that had the New York critics practically delirious. A child prodigy! A wunderkind! But it wasn't until *The War of the Worlds* that Orson Welles became a household name. Everybody in Hollywood said he was smart, arrogant, and a smooth-talker. Everybody whispered that he knew how to get what he wanted, and he wanted everything.

Afterward, Lola would tell herself: I should have known.

They drove to the beach, took off their shoes, and walked along the water's edge, the tongues of the tide lapping at their toes. A puny moon glimmered faintly through a misty sky. It had drizzled during the day, and now the air was clammy and uncomfortable—unusual for Los Angeles. Lola let her hand fall into Orson's and felt calm and safe. The jetty in the distance was barely visible. It appeared to Lola like some lumbering prehistoric animal immersed in a ford.

Orson told her about his production of *Macbeth* with an all-Negro cast—well, in those days we said Negro, not Black—and his musical, *The Cradle Will Rock*, about greed and political corruption. He was planning to direct a film on the same subject, he said, *Citizen Kane*. He was sure it would cause a scandal because some really important people would be exposed for what they were—hypocrites, liars, and thieves! Lola found him fascinating, but, she kept asking herself, was she making a mistake? She could feel herself falling in love, yielding to his spell, but how could she let her emotions run away with her? Hadn't she been through this all before?

"We should get back to the party," she said finally.

"I have to see you again." There was an urgency to his voice.

"I don't know…"

But she did know. She wanted to see him again.

"Tomorrow night?"

She hesitated a moment. "Okay," she said. "Tomorrow night."

They saw each other the next night, and the next, and the next after that. Sometimes they'd go to some glitzy get-together at a fancy hotel, but usually they'd just grab a bite and then walk on the beach.

"Let's swim," he whispered one evening after he'd had dinner at the Beverly Hills Hotel.

"I don't have a bathing suit."

"You don't need one. You like to be naked in the sea."

Orson stopped and pulled her to him. "Lola," he whispered. He slipped his hand around the small of her back. His skin smelled of musk and seawater.

"What about Virginia?" she asked cautiously.

"I'm going to divorce Virginia, just like you're going to divorce Cedric. Virginia Nicolson is a struggling, two-bit actress. She's made one film, and it was a flop."

"The Hearts of Age."

"Did you see it?"

"No."

"Neither did anyone else."

"That's hardly a reason to divorce her, Orson."

"That's not the reason I'm divorcing her, darling Lola. We've grown apart. Just as you and Cedric have grown apart."

"It's just that… This is happening so fast. We just met a few weeks ago, Orson…"

"Seize the moment, my love. You know, carpe diem."

His hands were working their way up her vertebra. He

ran his tongue over her ear, making her spine tingle. His sex bulged against her, and she became aware of her own gasping desire.

"We should find a motel," she breathed.

"Why not here? There's no one around."

"Out in the open? Someone could come."

"No one will come. We'll go over there behind those rocks. If it starts to drizzle, I'll cover you with my body, *mi* Lolita. Not a drop will touch your silken skin."

Lola allowed him to lead her to a rock formation that would shelter them from view. He eased her back gently onto the sand, careful to place his shirt under her hair. Suddenly his lips were on her throat, her chest, her breasts. His tongue gently caressed her nipples. Lola felt as though Popocatépetl were erupting in her belly. She had never felt such passion with either Jaime or Cedric or even Ed. This was a different kind of lovemaking—an adventure, a voyage of exploration.

The sand prickled her backside. She giggled, embarrassed. "I think sand ants are eating my rump!"

"Ah, then I'll have to bathe your sweet little ass with borax," laughed Orson, sliding his trousers under her bottom. He slipped off his shorts. "I hope they don't bite my prick!"

"What about me? Can I bite it?"

She closed her eyes and felt him sink into her body deeper, deeper, as though he had reached her very soul. A sense of plenitude engulfed her as their bodies rose and fell to the rhythm of the surging sea.

"It was divine," she murmured. I'd stopped by to give her a fancy barrette she wanted for a dinner party. She invited me to stay for lunch and told me the whole story.

"It's too soon," I said. "You're still married to Cedric. You're still living in his house."

"It's over," she said. "I'm going to file for divorce. I love Orson."

"You hardly know him, Lola."

She glowered at her plate. I could feel the storm coming. I pushed on anyway. "Why would you be attracted to a man so much younger than yourself? Did you ever wonder?"

"No," she snapped. "I never wondered. Love comes when it comes."

I should have let it go at that, but instead, I said, "Is it because he makes you feel like a young starlet?"

In an instant, her face transformed. Her color rose. Her nostrils flared. Her lips stiffened. She jumped up and glared at me.

"You're just jealous!" she cried.

"Of what, Lola? You told me that I had everything—a husband, a family."

"That was before Orson. You're jealous because I have a bombshell of a young lover, and you're stuck in the house with your brats, or at that stinky beauty shop for housemaids."

I realized she didn't mean it. She was upset because she knew that her escapade with Orson was all wrong. Because she was in her thirties. Because her career was floundering. Because her marriages had failed. Because she'd never have children. I understood all that, but still, it hurt.

"I'd better go now," I said. I hated to leave Luz's delicious *arroz con pollo* on the plate. We never had *arroz con pollo* at home. We couldn't afford chicken.

"Yes," she said, "you'd better go now."

I showed myself out.

29

Hollywood, December 1939
The Truth about My Mother

I'd heard Tía Emi threaten to kill people. I'd heard her snicker at inept thugs, highfalutin society ladies, and Mr. Edmond's pseudo-Frenchness. I'd heard her sing, and I'd heard her laugh. Strangely, I'd only heard her cry once—that time when I told her I might take a screen test. Tía Emi was not a crier, but when I walked into Madame Isabelle's sewing room that day in December accompanied by four little girls, I found her sobbing.

"Está muerta," Tía Emi whispered. "They finally got her. She's dead."

I took a Kleenex out of my purse and handed it to her. "Who's dead?" I asked.

Two-year-old Lexie grabbed the Kleenex with her tiny fingers and dabbed at Tía Emi's eyes.

"Your mother!"

I stared at her. "Why are you crying *now*? She's always been dead. I mean, ever since I was a baby, you've told me she was dead."

"But it wasn't true. I told you that because…" Her voice drifted off.

"Why?"

"Because it was easier."

"Easier than what?"

Lolly and Gabi were leafing through pattern books, and Lupita was organizing spools of thread by color. Lexie was snuggling in Tía Emi's arms.

"Than explaining things. But she wasn't dead. She was hiding. She's dead now, though. He killed her."

"Who killed her? Who is…was my mother?" I was trying to keep my voice low so the children wouldn't hear.

Tía Emi began to sing to Lexie.

*"Duérmete mi niña, duérmete mi amor
duérmete pedazo de mi corazón."*

"Please, Tía Emi, tell me who she was. I have a right to know."

*"Esta niña mía que nació de noche
quiere que la lleve a pasear en coche."*

"How do you know she's dead? Who told you?"

*"Esta niña mía que nació de día
quiere que la lleve a la dulcería."*

"Did someone write to you? Can I see the letter? There must be a return address on the envelope. Let me have it."

*"Duérmete mi niña, duérmete mi amor
duérmete pedazo de mi corazón."*

Lexie had dozed off. Tía Emi closed her eyes, and for a moment, I thought she'd fallen asleep, too. But then, she suddenly exclaimed, "His brother did it! He's been waiting for years, and he finally caught up with her. That gun-toting weasel!"

In my mind, I saw a giant weasel with enormous teeth and a revolver in its claws. Under different circumstances, it would have made me laugh.

"Who is *he*?" I demanded. "What's his name?"

"As mean as a trapped crocodile."

"What's his name?"

But she refused to say anything more.

"Alright," I said, trying to sound calm. "Don't tell me his name, but at least tell me *hers*. I don't even know the name of my own mother."

But she'd clammed up.

On the way home, I felt jittery. I can't say I felt sadness over my mother's death. I'd thought she was dead all along, so Tía Emi's revelation didn't really affect me. No, it wasn't sadness I felt, but a kind of low-grade fear lodged like a stone in my gut. All these years, Tía Emi had told me I was in danger, and I'd thought she was being ridiculous. But if someone had killed my mother, then maybe he'd come after me, too. And my little girls! I shuddered.

I debated whether to tell Gabe. I didn't want to worry him, but on the other hand, we had no secrets from each other. And if the children really were in danger, he should know.

A day went by. Then another. Then a week. Then a month. Nothing happened. Tía Emi didn't mention my mother again. When I asked her, she just shrugged. I began to think that maybe she'd made the whole thing up. I decided not to tell Gabe.

30

Mrs. Carver settled in her usual chair, with her usual cup of coffee, and her usual cigarette. As always, I was working at the next station, combing out the curls of an elderly lady who was beginning to doze off.

"Remember that Spanish movie star?" Mrs. Carver had a copy of *Star World* on her lap.

"Lupe Vélez? I saw her in *The Girl from Mexico*. She was so funny, I understand they're going to make a sequel."

"Not that one, Miss Marie. The one who swam naked in *Bird of Paradise*. I used to really like her."

"Oh, Dolores Del Rio. Gosh, Mrs. Carver," said Marie, "I haven't seen her in a couple of years. I don't know if she's even making movies anymore."

"Well, I saw her photo in *Star World*. She was at a party, all dolled up like Lady Astor's pet horse. She had on this low-cut chiffon gown and a kind of tiara. She still has those gorgeous, high cheekbones and her makeup is always perfect. Well, you'll never guess who she was with!"

"Isn't she married to Cedric Gibbons?"

"She is, but she was with Orson Welles! Carla Myer...you know, the reporter for *Star World*...she says the marriage is shaky and they'll probably get a divorce. Listen, don't cut it too short this time, Miss Marie. Roy likes it long."

"I understand. A woman has to please her husband. I keep mine shoulder-length because of Rick. I was never such a Dolores Del Rio fan. There's a new one, now… Rita Hayworth."

"Yeah, same type as Del Rio, but not so…you know…dark. But I loved some of Del Rio's movies."

"Wasn't she once involved with Edwin Carewe?"

"She was, but didn't you hear? Carewe committed suicide about a week ago. I saw it in *Star World*. They said that even though some newspapers reported it as a heart attack, it was really a suicide. They called him the 'discoverer of Dolores Del Rio.' According to the article, Del Rio went to the funeral and sobbed all the way through. Gibbons was sitting right behind her."

"Those movie people, they just go from one lover to another. It's disgusting."

I didn't say anything. I never do. It was better that Mrs. Carver didn't know I knew Lola. If she did, she might not have talked so freely, and I liked to hear the gossip, especially about Lola. I liked to know what people were saying about her. The truth is, I was still a little miffed about the way she'd treated me the last time I saw her. Maybe that's why Marie's comments didn't bother me. Anyhow, I knew that Gabe felt the same way about movie people.

31

The telephone jangled. Lola had decided not to spend the night at Orson's because she wanted to sleep late, and Orson had to get up at the crack of dawn. He was at work on his first feature film, *Citizen Kane*, and he had an early appointment at RKO to discuss some ideas with Herman Mankiewicz, his cowriter. However, Lola had no movie projects, and she was tired. By then, she was living with Orson, but she'd rented a small apartment off Sunset Boulevard for times when she wanted to get away and be alone.

The phone clanged again. *"Por Dios,"* she groaned. "Who's calling at this hour?"

It was probably Orson, she thought. Maybe he wanted to run an idea by her, or maybe he just wanted to tell her how much he loved her. He'd been so insistent lately, ravaging her with kisses the moment he came through the door, pulling open her blouse, grabbing at her breasts. The gentle lovemaking of their first encounters had transmuted into raw appetite.

He called incessantly. "I just had to hear your voice," he would say. "I called you before and you didn't answer! Where were you, Lola?"

"I was out by the pool with my mother," she would say

when she didn't want to tell him the truth—which was that she just didn't want to talk to him. "We didn't hear the phone. I'm sorry, darling."

The phone rang a third time, and Lola reached for the receiver.

The voice on the other end was distraught, but controlled. "Just now," it said. "Just a while ago. The doctor said it was a heart attack."

"Why didn't you call me right away, Mami?"

Lola ripped off her nightgown and tossed on a shirt and slacks. Then she called me.

"Mara, please, I need you. I'll pick you up in ten minutes. Wait for me in front of your door." She'd forgotten that she'd practically thrown me out of her house... Cedric's house... the last time I'd visited her, about six months before. But I didn't hold grudges...not for long. I knew Lola was going through difficult times—no work and an inappropriate lover she felt uncomfortable about, even though she said she didn't. He was too young for her, and she knew it. Someday he would leave her for a new starlet with baby-soft skin, and she knew that, too. I asked Gabe to take the older girls to school and Lexie to his parents' place.

"I thought you'd decided not to jump and run every time Lola snapped her fingers," he said reproachfully. "She hasn't called you in months!"

"She says it's an emergency. We've been friends for so long, Gabe. I really have to go."

He shrugged and didn't say anything more.

I dressed and went outside to wait. In less than ten minutes, Lola drove up in the Cadillac she'd bought herself for her birthday, and we headed for Santa Monica, where her parents had lived ever since her father moved to the States from Mexico. She told me about her mother's phone calls in the car.

We found Doña Antonia sitting in the shadows, shades drawn, reciting the rosary. Lola collapsed onto the sofa next to her and prayed with her through choked tears: *"Dios te salve, María. Llena eres de gracia..."* I stood there watching them. I hadn't said the rosary in years. "Catholic peyote for old ladies," Tía Emi always said.

"I brought Mara with me for moral support," Lola told her mother. "Where is he?"

"In his bed. Dr. Contreras is making arrangements to transport the body to Mexico so he can be laid to rest in the family plot." She paused and stared at her rosary beads. "The same place I will lie when my time comes."

"Oh, Mami. No, don't talk about such things."

"The Lord calls each one of us to Him when He wills."

Lola sat down next to her mother and laid her head on her shoulder, but Doña Antonia pushed her gently away. She had her own grief to deal with. She'd been married to Jesús Leonardo Asúnsola over thirty-five years. There had been ups and downs and long separations, but still, he'd been her life's partner. Now he was gone. That had to sink in. It would take time.

Lola held out her hand to me. "Thank you for being here with me," she murmured.

Hand in hand, we walked to the bedroom. Don Jesús Leonardo looked as though he were sleeping serenely. His puppet lines had softened. His forehead was smooth and moist. Lola eased herself onto the chair by his bed and watched his chest, as though expecting him to suddenly inhale. I sat on a stool by the vanity and listened to the drip drip drip of the faucet, the buzz of a bee outside the window, the hiccoughing inhalations of Lola's breath. Everything was as before. The drip, the buzz, the expanding and contracting of her lungs. The continuum of the universe. Only hours before, Don Jesús Leonardo was

part of all this. Now he was gone. The thread between life
and death was so fine, I thought, so fragile.

Lola was no longer crying. It was as if her tears had coag-
ulated in her chest. I was stopped up, too. I felt as though a
wad of glue were wedged under my breastbone.

Doña Antonia came into the room. "Go get some rest,
Gatita," she said. "We will have a memorial service here in
Los Angeles, and then the funeral in Mexico."

She placed her arm around Lola's waist. They'd forgotten
I was there.

They stood together immobile, like the painting of the Virgin and Saint Anne in our parish church. Mother and daughter
embracing, a single, inseparable unit. Light filtered through
the window, illuminating their faces. Two women, one still
young, the other aging, both with pained expressions, comforting one another. Mother and daughter united in grief.

I sat there watching them. A dull ache was growing in my
breast. Lola was right when she said I was jealous. I *was* jealous, but not for the reasons she thought. Not of her fame and
money, not of her spectacular love life. No, I was jealous of
her closeness with her mother.

My own mother had recently died, and I felt nothing. How
could I feel anything? I didn't know her. In a way, I didn't even
believe in her existence. She was some mythical figure. Saint
Anne was more real to me than her. Saint Anne had a face
and a family and a story. My mother didn't even have a name.
And my father God only knew who he was. Lola and Doña
Antonia had come together to share their sorrow because a
man had died, a real, flesh-and-blood man, Don Jesús Leonardo, father and husband. They remembered his touch, his lips
on their foreheads. They remembered his smile, his anger, his
passionate political opinions. They remembered his pride in
Lola's first successes. Now they had the comfort of weeping

together. But I... I didn't have a father. I was like Jesus, *sin pecado concebida*. Or maybe conceived in pure sinfulness—in a drunken orgy, a chance encounter, or a rape. Who knew?

I turned away, counted my blessings. I had Gabe, the kind of strong, devoted, caring husband Lola had never had, and four beautiful little girls. My envy seemed petty and pointless. I pushed it out of my mind.

Lola was quiet as she drove me back home.

"You're a true friend," she said, when we got to the door. "I don't know how you put up with me, but I'm glad you do. I couldn't get through things like this without you."

32

Hollywood, 1940–1941
Bombs

For months, newspaper headlines had screamed updates in 72-point font. One after the other, territories fell to the Axis. I saved the clippings.

May 10, 1940. Nazis occupy Luxembourg.

May 14, 1940. Netherlands surrenders.

May 28, 1940. Belgium surrenders.

June 10, 1940. Italy enters the war, allied with Germany.

June 21, 1940. Italy invades southern France.

June 22, 1940. France signs armistice agreement. Germany occupies northern France. Nazis occupy Paris. The pro-Axis Vichy capital is established in the Auvergne.

September 13, 1940. Italy invades British-controlled Egypt, launching the attack from Italian-controlled Libya.

September 27, 1940. Germany and Italy sign a pact with Japan.

October 15, 1940. Charlie Chaplin releases *The Great Dictator*!

The talk in Hollywood wasn't about the Italian invasion of Greece. It was about Chaplin's first talkie. Until then, he'd bucked the trend and made only silents, but now he was creating a splash with a new film designed to stir up controversy. Chaplin used his amazing plasticity and comic skills to hone a piercing caricature of Adolf Hitler. He played both the brutal yet clownish dictator of Tomainia and the gentle Jewish barber who looks just like him.

"Well, at least someone is making hay on this war," muttered Orson.

"The ballet he does with a balloon globe is simply amazing, don't you think, darling? He's so graceful and agile. The way he uses his body to create humor is extraordinary." Lola was lounging by the pool, gorgeous in a baby blue wrap.

"If villainy can be funny, I suppose so," grunted Orson. "I don't find the image of Hitler playing games with the world very funny."

I was spending the afternoon with them at Orson's house in Bel Air. I'd worked until late the night before, and Marie had given me the day off. Lolly, Gabi, and Lupita were in school, and Lexie was with Doña Lupe. I'd been looking forward to stretching out on a chaise longue and relaxing for a few hours, but Orson was in a foul mood.

Luz brought out a lunch of cold meats, but Orson started with the wine. The sun shone white and angry, and there was no breeze to tame its fury.

"What's the matter with you, darling?" said Lola. "You've been so gruff lately."

Orson disappeared into the house and emerged a few moments later, smiling.

"I'm sorry, Lolita. *Citizen Kane* leaves me so drained, I just can't think straight," he said. "But I just took my medicine. I should be okay now. Anyhow, Mank wants to make it a straight-out biography, and I have to make him see that he's being too...well...too literal. This isn't a biography of William Randolph Hearst. I mean, it's not *just* that. It's an American story, the story of what happens to men when they get too successful too fast, and then think they can control everyone around them."

"Well, Herman Mankiewicz will just have to realize that you're the one in charge. After all, it's your film. You're the producer, the director, and the star. He's just the coscreen-writer. RKO has faith in you, Orson. Just put your foot down."

I nibbled on some ham and sipped my ginger ale. Orson went on and on about how he'd given Mank notes, which Mank had ignored, and how Mank was so drunk half the time that he didn't know what was going on.

Lola leaned over and kissed him. Orson ran his lips gently over her neck. "I love you so much. You give me the mettle to carry on. I want this to be a beautiful film, the most beautiful film ever made. All the newest cinematographic techniques. Exquisite lighting. Stunning shadow angles. I know you understand."

"Of course, I understand."

He unbuttoned his shirt and ran his fingers over his chest. "Kiss me here," he murmured. "Right here on this little mole."

His body stank of sweat and alcohol masked imperfectly by Brummel Eau de Cologne.

"Not now," Lola demurred. "I'm sure Mara—"

"Oh, Mara won't be shocked." His tone was slightly mock-ing. "She knows all about sex. You think she made those four kids with the Holy Spirit?" He winked at me, and I turned away.

Lola pretended not to hear. She began to fidget. "I'll ask Luz to make us some coffee."

"I'm going to pour myself a drink," said Orson. "I'm beat." He went back inside.

He was drinking more than before, Lola whispered, and he was taking a lot of medicine. It seemed to calm him down and put him in a better mood, she said, so there was probably nothing wrong with it. She'd heard stories about people becoming addicted to certain medicines, but she was sure that Orson was smart enough to keep things under control. But still...so much alcohol, so many drugs... It was worrisome.

Orson returned holding a Scotch.

"Come on," he teased, tugging on her blouse. "I feel better now. Let's go swimming."

"I'll go put on a bathing suit. You brought a suit, didn't you, Mara?" She'd forgotten I didn't know how to swim.

"You don't need a bathing suit."

"But Mara is here!"

"She's seen you naked before. Anyhow, you swam naked in *Bird of Paradise* in front of a couple of million people." There was a nasty edge to his voice.

Orson's moods were getting on my nerves. I got up to leave.

"Mara!" she called after me.

"Let her go!" I heard him say as I slipped through the gate.

By mid-February 1941, they were both divorced. Lola had made just one film since the previous year, *The Man from Dakota,* a silly comedy set during the American Civil War about a beautiful woman who helps two Union spies sneak into the South to gather information. Audiences loved it. The news from Europe was horrifying, and people needed a laugh. The studios kept on churning out movies, even though times were tough for working men and women, and everyone was sure we'd be drawn into the conflict abroad. Orson didn't seem overly concerned with Lola's career. *Citizen Kane* would soon be released, and that's what had him holding his breath.

"I was thinking," Lola said to me one day as I was combing her hair into ring curls around her face. "Maybe it's time for me to go home. American audiences don't like foreign actors anymore, except when we play nonsensical characters in trivial films. And now, even those roles are drying up. What is there for me here? In Mexico, people still see me as a star."

I understood the situation. Lola was nearly thirty-seven already—old for a movie star. She had no work and no prospects. Audiences wanted fresh young faces. Even Betty Grable, at twenty-five, was considered past her prime. Girls like Veronica Lake, with golden hair and long legs, were snapping up the roles.

"What about Orson?"

"I love him madly, and he says he loves me," she insisted. "Yes, he's impetuous, but that's his charm. He has a vigor and vibrancy, and yes, he makes me feel young."

"But?"

"For now, he adores swimming nude with me in the moonlight and making love under the stars. But he's a decade younger than me, Mara. What about when I'm forty-five and he's still a virile young star surrounded by flaxen-haired babies?"

I could have said "I told you so," but I didn't. I didn't want to be cruel.

A few days later, the three of us were having breakfast together, Lola, Orson, and I, at Orson's house. Usually, he left early for the studio, so I hadn't expected him to be home.

Lola was pouring coffee. "What if I went to Mexico for a while?" she ventured. I noticed that her hand didn't waver. She sounded completely unruffled, as though she'd said, *What if I went shopping for a few hours this afternoon?*

But Orson snapped to attention. "Just like that? Out of the blue? *Kane* opens in a month!"

"It's just that… I've started to feel out of place here. I'm tired of being 'the female Valentino,' the Latin actress, the Mexican. Frida de Rivera wrote to me…well, it's Frida Kahlo, now that she's divorced. She says that in Mexico, they're proud of me—local girl makes good, that sort of thing—and I thought... I mean, Frida has contacts..."

"I have contacts, Lola. I can help you here. Anyhow, how can you even be thinking of such a thing? We're going to be married! Or don't you love me anymore?" I noticed that he had mentioned the opening of *Citizen Kane* before their impending marriage.

"Of course, I love you, darling." She stood up and wrapped her arms around him. "I just want to...scope out the possibilities. After the opening of *Kane*, of course." She didn't say anything about marriage.

The phone rang, and Orson went into the other room to answer.

"You've been in contact with Frida Kahlo?" I said a little reproachfully. "You never mentioned it."

"She wrote to me a while ago. She sent me one of her paintings. I thought it was a gift, but then, a couple of days later, she sent me a bill!" Lola burst out laughing. "I guess she needs the money, now that Diego has divorced her. The painting's still in the crate. Cedric wouldn't let me hang it...it didn't fit in with his decor...and here, well, who knows how long we'll be together..."

Orson appeared in the doorway, his eyes spinning out of their orbits. Sweat was dribbling from his hairline to his temples and onto his chin.

"The bastard!" he roared. "I never even mentioned him in the press releases. I said it was a story based on the legend of Dr. Faust. I swear, the words William Randolph Hearst never appeared. And now the son of a bitch is trying to squash the whole project! The best goddamn film ever made in Hollywood, and he's trying to crush it! That miserable motherfucking, cock-sucking bastard!"

He picked up a vase from the table and hurled it against the wall. It exploded into a chrysanthemum of splintering crystal.

"Orson!"

I sat there, trembling. I don't think Lola had ever seen him in such a rage. He wasn't the same man she'd described making love to her on the beach, in the moonlight.

"Shit!" he screamed, spewing saliva over the table. "Who does the fucking asshole think he is? I was right to make this film! I was right to expose him for what he is! A tyrant! An autocrat who thinks he can control the world, the same as Hitler! I had to expose the son of a bitch! I had to show people who he really is!"

"You knew you were taking on Goliath with this film," said Lola.

But Orson didn't hear her. He'd gone to the bedroom to take his medicine.

This is what happened: *Citizen Kane* had previewed for a small group of publications early in January of that year, 1941, and the critics had liked it. However, celebrity gossip columnist Hedda Hopper had burst in uninvited, and in the time it takes a bullet to tear from a revolver into a victim's heart, she alerted the Hearst organization that the bratty kid director Orson Welles had made a film shamefully defaming the great newspaper magnate, William Randolph Hearst. Then she sat down at her typewriter and banged out an article calling the film "vicious and irresponsible," and Hearst a "great man." She made Welles look like a reckless thug who was dragging the name of a national hero through the mud. Louella Parsons, Hopper's rival in the gossip business, worked for Hearst, and blew a gasket when she found out that Hopper had seen the film before she had. Worse yet, her boss was furious because he hadn't been forewarned about any of it. Hopper, in the meanwhile, continued her full-frontal attack on Orson. *Citizen Kane* was "appalling," she said. It was "disgusting."

However, Hopper wasn't content with going after Orson. She had it in for Lola, too. She described her as a bauble that hung around the neck of powerful men, and she ridiculed her for appearing in public with Orson before she'd ended her marriage to Cedric. Lola felt like a fawn besieged by wolves.

Parsons demanded a private screening and threatened a lawsuit to prevent the film's release. All the ballyhoo would have been great publicity if Hearst hadn't quashed any mention of the film in his newspapers. No ads. No reviews. Nothing. And Hearst controlled half the papers in the country. Orson knew what that meant. It meant no business. No wonder he exploded!

A couple of weeks after that breakfast—it must have been sometime in April—I was back at Lola's to style her hair. I was just combing it out when Orson barreled through the bedroom door.

"I'm going to call RKO right now! They have to release *Citizen Kane* on time! According to *Variety*, it's going to be delayed!"

Lola and I exchanged glances. Orson was like a line of recurrently detonating grenades. You knew the explosion was coming, but you never knew exactly when or how bad it would be.

"Yes, darling, you should call George," said Lola softly. "You can't let them bully you."

"Damn right I'll call George Schaefer! He's the one who should have told me. Why do I have to find out stuff like this from some movie rag! Anyhow, as head of RKO, he has a duty to protect me! Ha, Hearst thinks he's going to ruin me! I'm going to ruin *him,* that greedy pig! He thinks his trashy newspapers can destroy Orson Welles? Well, he's about to

see what my film can do to a rapacious, no-good bastard like
William Randolph Hearst!"

"George Schaefer is no fool," Lola told me after Orson had
stormed out of the room, "and RKO has a lot of money invested in *Citizen Kane.* He'll call together a crack legal team,
and if the lawyers say Hearst can't sue RKO for libel, they'll
release the film on time."

Lola was right. Not only did *Citizen Kane* open on May
1 at the RKO Palace in New York, but Schaefer unleashed
the most lavish publicity campaign in RKO's history to en-
sure its success.

The critics went wild. "An Astonishing Picture!" trumpeted
the *Hollywood Review.* "A first-class film of potent importance
to the art of motion pictures," proclaimed *Variety.* Here's the
article by Carla Myer of *Star World.* I've kept it with me all
these years. Mostly I just saved stuff that had to do with Lola,
but this picture was especially significant to me because I'd
been in on so many of Orson's explosions leading up to it. I
knew the backstory, let's say.

*Citizen Kane will make movie history, and not just because the
lighting and camera angles are spectacular! I attended a screening
last night and can report that director Orson Welles's use of deep
focus cinematography to create depth is breathtaking. But what's
going to bring American audiences to theaters is the scandal created by Welles's depiction of tycoon William Randolph Hearst.*

*The story begins in Xanadu, the mansion of publishing mag-
nate Charles Foster Kane (played by Welles himself), who ut-
ters one final word before dying: "Rosebud." The story revolves
around the quest of reporter Jerry Thompson (William Alland)
to discover the meaning of that word. His investigations reveal
how Kane took over the New York* Inquirer, *using yellow
journalism to destroy his enemies, and launched the Spanish*

American War for his own profit. When he becomes involved in an extramarital affair with a third-rate singer named Susan Alexander (Dorothy Comingore), her career becomes his obsession. Remind you of the Marion Davies story? Well, it's no wonder that Hearst is up in arms!

According to reliable sources, Hearst actually planted a fourteen-year-old girl in Welles's hotel room and stationed photographers outside to take pictures when the director walked in! What a scandal that would have been! Fortunately for Welles, he got whiff of the trap and stayed away!

Now Radio City Music Hall has refused to screen the film. Everybody is afraid of big bad Hearst! RKO had originally delayed the official release, but it opened at the RKO Palace on May 1, in New York, as planned, and in Los Angeles on May 8. It will be shown in local theaters throughout the country beginning in September.

In the meantime, Welles appears in public frequently with the lovely Dolores Del Rio on his arm, even though the ink has only just dried on her divorce papers.

Lola ignored the jab from Myer and went shopping. Movie openings always mean parties, and the bashes RKO planned for *Citizen Kane* would be over-the-top.

RKO executive Arnold Hausen had built a posh Bel Air villa for his new bride, and now he was going to give a shindig there for the most important film RKO had ever made. He wanted it to be in every non–Hearst newspaper, magazine, and gossip rag in the country. Lola knew what her role demanded. She would arrive on the arm of the director and star, and she had to shine.

Gabe understood that I had to do my part. Lola depended on me to look her best, and besides, we still needed the money, especially now that the girls were older. Mercifully, they weren't babies anymore. Lolly was twelve already, Gabi was nearly eleven, Lupita almost eight, and even little Lexie was four and enrolled in nursery school.

The night of the party, I kissed Gabe good-night and tucked Lupita and Lexie into bed.

"I'll probably be back late," I told Gabe, "but I'll take the car so I can leave before it's over. Don't wait up."

"Okay," he said. "I know this affair is important to those empty-headed friends of yours, so go and enjoy yourself."

"I doubt I'll enjoy myself," I said, "but I'll try to nab some éclairs for you and the girls."

I got to Orson's house about seven thirty in the evening and rushed to Lola's room. I had already done a day's work at Marie's, made dinner for Gabe and the children, and put the little ones to bed. My feet were aching, but I dutifully combed Lola's hair into long, relaxed curls.

Luz zipped up Lola's gown, a strapless black silk Chanel sheath. Lola pulled on the long black gloves that just covered her elbow, then slipped into jeweled, high-heeled sandals. She posed in front of the mirror.

"Too bad I don't smoke! A jeweled cigarette holder would look great with this outfit!"

"What do you want me to wear?" I asked her wearily.

"Look in my closet. Take whatever you want."

After four pregnancies, I no longer fit into most of Lola's gowns, but I finally found a high-waisted lace number with an ample skirt.

I followed Lola and Orson to the Hausen estate in my own car and felt like a duck in the wrong pond as the valet looked my old Ford up and down and took the keys.

The instant Orson entered the ballroom, reporters and guests descended on him like locusts. I eyed a waiter carrying hors d'oeuvres. I tried the shrimp canapés, the smoked

salmon on toast, the stuffed mushrooms, and even the caviar. I wished there was some way I could sneak a few into my
purse, but those kinds of hors d'oeuvres begin to ooze and
smell pretty quickly. Maybe I'd have better luck with the dessert buffet, I thought.

I caught sight of Lola, and I walked over and stood beside
her. "Your hair still looks good," I whispered. The reporters were no longer swarming around her. "Where's Orson?"

She shook her head. "I don't know," she said. "He disappeared into the crowd. Look, there's Marlene and Erich!"

I knew who Erich was. Erich Maria Remarque was the
handsome German author whose novel, *All Quiet on the Western Front*, had come out in 1928 and enraged the Nazi warmongers with its pacifist message. I looked in their direction.
Marlene smiled and waved, and then she and Erich came
over to us.

"Erich, *mein Schatz*," she said, "go get Lola and Mara some
drinks, will you?" As soon as he was out of earshot, she turned
to Lola. "I don't want to upset you, darling," she whispered,
"but look over there."

Orson, drink in hand, was telling a story—apparently a very
funny one—to a pert blonde showgirl who appeared to be
about eighteen. She was wearing a red silk evening gown with
an impressive décolletage and seemed cemented into a forward
lean. Orson wasn't even coy about gaping. He looked as if he
were going to pour gin into her cleavage and then lap it up.

"That's the way he is," said Marlene matter-of-factly. "That's
the way they all are."

Orson looked up and saw Lola. He tore himself away from
the décolletage and was suddenly standing next to her.

"I feel faint," murmured Lola. "I'd like to go home."

"But, darling, we just got here."

"Mara will drive me. You should stay. After all, tonight's your night."

Lola glanced over at the girl in red, who was staring at Orson. Her lips blossomed into a smile, and she blew him a kiss. He beamed like a fat tabby who had just nabbed a sweet little blond mouse.

"If you're sure you don't mind," he said.

The parking valet must have been astonished to see the glamorous Dolores Del Río climb into a shabby Ford next to her bedraggled hairdresser. I was home before eleven thirty.

"I expected you after midnight," Gabe said. He was reading the war news in the *Examiner* when I came in.

"Lola didn't feel well, so we left early, but I did manage to sneak out some little cakes." I pulled squashed Napoleons, brownies, and cookies out of my purse.

"Let's save them for the girls," he said.

"Let's eat two of them ourselves!" I teased. "Get out the champagne!"

He opened the fridge and took out a couple of bottles of beer. We laughed and cuddled and drank Schlitz until we dozed off in each other's arms.

33

"Turn on the radio!" shouted Gabe. "Out in the street, everyone's in a panic, and at the studio, nobody's working. They're all talking about some sort of attack!"

I got up and turned on KNX.

"We are at war with Japan!" thundered a voice. "Japanese war planes pummeled Pearl Harbor this morning at 7:55 a.m. Hawaiian time. The attack lasted 110 minutes, until 9:45 a.m. At least fifteen hundred are known to be dead, although the toll will surely rise."

Oh God, I thought. Those poor people. And then I thought: What if California is next?

At a time like that, you think about the people close to you. I called Tía Emi first. "We got through one war. We'll get through this one," she grumped. She didn't seem particularly concerned. I called Lola at Orson's house, but there was no answer. I tried her apartment, but nothing. Finally, I dialed Doña Antonia's number. Lola picked up.

"What are we going to do?" she kept saying. "What are we going to do?"

"What *can* we do?" I murmured. "We have to wait and see what happens."

"Mami says we should get out of Los Angeles. Orson is busy working on *The Magnificent Ambersons,* so he doesn't need me for the moment. Los Angeles is a target. Why not take the girls and drive to Palm Springs with Mami and me?"

"Just like that? The girls are in school!"

"The girls are in *danger,* Mara!"

I considered it a moment. "I'll have to talk it over with Gabe," I said.

But Lola's mind was already made up. "Mami is right," she said. "Orson doesn't need me now. I'm beginning to think he's never needed me." She paused. "He's acting strange. He prowls around all night and nods off during dinner. He complains of headaches all the time. And, Mara, every time someone raises an eyebrow or smiles funny, he blows up." She lowered her voice. "He wants sex at the oddest hours and then falls asleep just as things are heating up. People at RKO don't want to work with him. I think it's the Dexedrine."

"What's Dexedrine?"

"The pills he takes. I think they're making him *loco.*"

In the end, the girls and I didn't go to Palm Springs, and neither did Lola. For one thing, Lola decided to finally go back to Mexico. For another, Gabe was drafted.

I'll tell you about Lola first because it's easier to talk about. Lola had been talking for a while about returning home, and now that people were saying that Los Angeles could be Japan's next target, this seemed like the right time to make a move. She thought that possibilities might open up for her in Mexico because President Roosevelt had named Nelson Rockefeller the new Coordinator of Inter-American Affairs, and Rockefeller had made a deal with the Mexican government: Mexico would make anti-Nazi, pro-American movies, and in exchange, the US would provide the Mexicans with cel-

luloid and forty-five million feet of virgin movie film. It was
a coup for the Mexican picture industry.

Now Rockefeller wanted Orson to go to Brazil and make
the same deal with the Brazilians, and now there was nothing
to keep Lola in Hollywood. No fiancé. No career. Nothing
but a bunch of dreary cocktail parties and the chance that her
house would be bombed to smithereens.

She and Doña Antonia left for Mexico early in 1942. There
was still no air service between Los Angeles and Mexico City,
so they took the train. I didn't hear from Lola for a month or
two after that. There was no phone connection, and the mail
was unreliable. Besides, I didn't even have her address. Maybe
I'll never see her again, I thought. Maybe she'll stay in Mexico
forever. It was a painful idea, but the war was getting to me.

I didn't think they'd draft Gabe. After all, he was thirty-
eight and the father of four. I knew they were taking men
as old as forty-five, but in the way the mind has of painting
things the way you want them to be, I convinced myself that
he was safe. Then the letter came.

He's a carpenter, I told myself. They'll put him to work
building camps or maintaining rigging. They won't stick a
rifle in his hands and expect him to kill Germans.

The first time I saw my beautiful, muscular husband in
uniform, I cried—but maybe not for the reason you think.
We'd heard about Nazi bombing raids in England and atroci-
ties in France. In my head, I heard the explosions. I closed my
eyes and saw the Dorniers flying low, dropping their loads
over London houses, stores, and schools. I imagined those
blond blue-eyed British moms, with their little British kids
and their playful British pugs—one moment they're sitting at
the table eating scones and cream, the next, they're dust. I saw
the newsreels—handsome young men, most not over twenty,
lying lifeless in the mud, some without an arm, some with-

out an eye. A minute before, their adrenaline was pumping. They were thumping their chests and shouting war cries. I'd seen war before. I knew what war could do. So yes, I cried because I was scared. But that's not the only reason.

I cried out of joy, too, because I could see how proud Gabe was. He puffed out his chest and strutted around the workshop, so thrilled to wear the uniform and serve his country. If anyone had any doubt about whether men with names like García or Sanchez or Estrada were real Americans, I thought, here was the proof that they were. Some five hundred thousand Mexican Americans served in the war. Most of them were guys like Gabe, guys who were born in the United States and were itching for the chance to show that they were just as American as the Smiths and Joneses. Once they proved what they could do, the House Committee on Un-American Activities would lay off investigating folks just because they had a Spanish surname—at least, that's what we all believed. They'd stop seeing people like us as foreigners, Communists, traitors. Those people who tormented Ramón and made it hard for Lola to find decent roles, when they saw how our men fought, they would change their tune.

In fact, it was beginning to happen already. President Roosevelt was courting the Latino communities. A new poster was circulating, alongside "Uncle Sam Wants You" and "Rosie the Riveter": "Americans All!" it trumpeted. "¡Americanos Todos! Luchamos por la Victoria!" If people accepted that we were all American, then discrimination would end for sure.

But when the time came for Gabe to leave for Fort Leavenworth, all my enthusiasm leaked away "like a slow fart," as Tía Emi would say. I felt crampy and weak. I didn't want to get up in the morning. Still, I knew that Gabe had to go. Stories were trickling into the news about medical experiments and gas chambers. Stories that made your blood run cold. Children fed to dogs. Women douched with acid. If Hitler didn't like Jewish people, he wouldn't like Mexicans any better, I thought. He fed lots of people to the flames just because they weren't Aryans, and if he got to California, we would be next. That's why Gabe needed to join the fight—because if Hitler won, he would annihilate us, too. Gabe had to fight not just for his country, but for his family, his girls.

They sent him to North Africa, where the Allies were trying to wrest the French territories from Vichy control. But the Vichy government counted on German support, and the battles were bloody. Sometimes I'd awake during the night to hear Nazi boots in the workshop or guttural *r*'s in the kitchen. I'd mistake the glint of Gabe's saw for a bayonet. I'd slip into the girls' bedroom to make sure they were all safe in their beds.

I read the newspapers obsessively. June 1942: "Allied Troops Take Midway." January 1943: "Red Army Defeats Germans in Stalingrad!" The newspapers made it sound like one Allied victory followed another, as if American troops were in no danger at all. Then the gold stars started appearing in people's windows. Every day there were more of them, more mothers and fathers who had lost a son.

I felt as though I were sinking into a tar pit. I couldn't breathe. I couldn't think. Every day, I dropped the girls off at school, then headed for Señora Lupe's to keep her company for a while before going to work at Marie's. Señora Lupe wept, trembling and moaning. Both Gabe and Vince were far away, at war.

"*Mis chicos, mis hijos…*"

I wanted to reassure her. I wanted to say, *They'll come home safe and sound before you know it*. But I couldn't, because in a war, you never know.

I worked as many hours as I could at the beauty shop. Work got me through the day. I forced myself to concentrate. I couldn't mix up the dyes or the permanent lotions. I couldn't make pin curls when the patron needed barrel curls. You might think that women didn't go to the beauty shop during the war, but it was just the opposite. Their husbands and sons were away fighting, and they felt miserable. Now more than ever, they had to remind themselves that they were human, that they were women. So they had their hair styled and put on red lipstick, then went off to their factory jobs or to their empty homes and cried.

34

Today you can just pick up the phone and call another country, but it wasn't like that back then. There was no telephone service between the United States and Mexico, so, aside from a note or two—the mail sometimes went through and sometimes didn't—I didn't hear from Lola until the following year, when she made a quick trip to Los Angeles to tie up some legal matters concerning the sale of her property.

We met at the Biltmore, where she'd taken a suite. She hugged me and asked about the children. Then she looked at me the way you look at a calf that's about to be sacrificed for your Sunday dinner and whispered, "Have you heard from Gabe?"

I know she was trying to sound concerned, but her delivery was a bit melodramatic. The truth is, I doubt she ever even thought about the war, because a moment later, she launched into a description of her exploits in *la capital*. I did this. I did that. Me, me, me. She was the same old Lola. I had to smile. I appreciated the distraction.

"I only had to look around me to be certain I'd made the right decision," she was saying. She'd heard stories about Orson's shenanigans in Brazil—the drinking, the drugs, the women. She knew she had no future with him and no future in Hollywood either. Her future lay in Mexico, where a vibrant cultural scene offered countless possibilities.

"Frida and Diego gave me a birthday party almost as soon as I arrived," she gushed. "The *crema y nata* of Mexican society were there. Artists, politicians, writers, directors! Even the Chilean poet Pablo Neruda, who whispered love poems in my ear. The muralist Orozco begged me to pose for him, and the poet Salvador Novo hinted that he'd love to write a screenplay for me. Frida and Diego remarried, you know, and they were twittering and cooing like lovebirds—lovebirds with barbed claws!" Lola burst out laughing.

But my mind was on Gabe. I didn't know exactly where he was, and things were uglier than ever in Europe. In my head, I saw little children clutching teddy bears marching toward gas chambers.

"Frida was wearing an elaborately embroidered apple and apricot Tehuana dress, a bright purple woven silk shawl, and a white flowered headdress. You should have seen her, Mara. And Diego, for once he was wearing a suit that fit him."

I didn't want to pop her balloon, so I sat and listened.

"'I am thirty-seven years old today, and I am embarking on a new adventure!' I said, and I raised a glass of champagne!" She grabbed a teacup from our table in the Biltmore lobby and pretended to raise a glass.

She was actually thirty-eight, but what did I care? I kept quiet.

"A new career! A new life!" she intoned. "Now I will become the actress—yes, actress, not just celebrity—that I've always wanted to be. This is something I can only do in my own country. In my own language. Among my own people."

I could see the crowd applauding and cheering. I could hear the cries of *"ándale!"*

We both knew that what was going to open doors for her in Mexico was her star status in Hollywood. In Mexico, they didn't know that Hollywood considered her a has-been. To Mexicans, she represented the glitz and glamour of Gringolandia.

"Mexico is entering a period of tremendous creativity," Lola told me with great earnestness. "You and Gabe just have to come visit when he gets back. I have a beautiful new house I've named La Escondida, and there's plenty of room. *This* is the year for the Mexican artist!" she went on. "President Roosevelt has asked Nelson Rockefeller to plan a huge exhibition to be called 'Twenty Centuries of Mexican Art' at MOMA."

"What's MOMA?"

"The Museum of Modern Art in New York. Rockefeller is the president. The exhibition will include some five thousand examples of ancient and modern art. Our greatest painters will all be represented—Diego Rivera, José Clemente Orozco, Miguel Covarrubias—and, by the way, they were all at my birthday party!"

Overhead, a plane was flying low. I shuddered at its rumble, imagined it dropping bombs on the Biltmore. I imagined the entire hotel exploding, the elaborate crystal chandelier dropping on our heads and shattering into a million pieces. Who will take care of the children if I die? I thought. Oh God, I said to myself, don't let it bomb the schools.

I was trembling, but Lola didn't notice. "Mexican directors like El Indio Fernández are creating a new, socially relevant cinema, Mara. They're not making stupid little comedies like *Flying Down to Rio*. They're dealing with real social issues… poverty, prejudice—"

"I have to be going, Lola," I interrupted.

"Well, let me just tell you this. I was dancing with Diego, and suddenly, he whispered, 'Lolita, you know I love Frida, even though she's a pain in the ass. But it's you I'm interested in now.' Well, I didn't say anything. I thought he was going to make a pass, and I didn't want to get angry, not at my birth-day celebration."

"I have to pick up the children, Lola," I said.

"But just listen to this, Mara. He said, 'The Revolution in-spired a surge of artistic innovation in Mexico. Murals, sculp-ture, novels… It's stronger than ever now, Lola, and you can be part of the movement. Emilio Fernández is becoming a respected director in Mexico, and he's going to launch some really big projects. He wants you to star in all of them. You are the essence of Mexico—glamorous, elegant, and *mestiza*—and you have that Hollywood allure. You'll bring Mexican cinema to a new level. This is your time, Lola!' Can you be-lieve it, Mara?"

I gathered up my things and got up. The airplane had passed.

"That's wonderful, Lola," I said. I was happy for her, really I was, but how could I think about Mexican cinema when Gabe was stuck in some hellhole, bombs bursting, blood and mud flying, men moaning? I could smell the sopping earth, the guts and shit, and yet, I had no idea where he was, in a trench in Algiers or in the Libyan desert. "How's your mother?" I asked, not only to change the subject, but because I really wanted to know. I was fond of Doña Antonia.

"She left the party early," said Lola, suddenly dejected. "She gets tired easily. She's slowing down, Mara. Furrows are forming in her forehead. The skin on her cheeks is still firm, but it's losing its juice."

"We're all getting older," I said. "Except you." It was true. My once-slim hips had widened, and my breasts had grown heavy, but Lola was as trim and firm as ever.

"I'm…I'm afraid for Mami," she stammered. "I keep think-ing: What would I do without her? I'd be all alone."

Of course, that was the real issue. Not Doña Antonia's wrinkles, but Lola's fear of being alone.

"Well, there's something else I have to tell you before you go!" she went on. "I was dancing with Orozco when a young man pulled me aside. 'Someone is here to see you,' he whispered. 'His name is Orson.'"

"Orson!" I exclaimed! "Orson was in Mexico?"

"I found him in the corridor. He was standing next to a potted ficus, head bowed, contrite. He reminded me of a pale, blubbery walrus. 'Orson,' I said. 'I thought you were in Brazil!' He said he'd heard I was back in Mexico and had come to apologize for the way he'd behaved. 'Take me back,' he begged. 'You know I love you.' He looked pathetic."

"Well, I hope you said no," I said.

"I put my arms around him and gave him a squeeze, then stepped away. 'It's over, Orson.' I told him. 'I have to get back to the party. I want you to leave.' He cried awhile, said he couldn't live without me. 'I wish you happiness,' were the last words I said to him. I walked away and didn't look back."

"I'm proud of you," I said. And I meant it.

35

Something in Señora Lupe died the day we heard that Vince had been killed in action. She didn't stop breathing or moving, but her soul left her body.

Don Gabriel read her the telegram, a terse government communication: "We regret to inform you…" Vince's wife, Julie, had brought it over in the morning, but Don Gabriel waited until his own tears were dry before taking his wife's hand in his and telling her the news. She hardly cried. Instead, she went outside and sat on the front porch and stared into the night sky as if she could see her first-born son rising up to heaven.

Lolly and Gabi took it like adults.

"Uncle Vince was killed in action," I told them simply. They both had school friends who had lost fathers, uncles, brothers, cousins. They seemed to think it was inevitable.

"They'd better not lay a finger on Daddy," Lolly said after a long pause.

"Or what?" murmured Gabi. "You'll grab a gun and go kill a bunch of nasty Germans?"

Later, I heard Gabi sobbing into her pillow.

The little ones didn't even try to act brave. Nine-year-old Lupita burst into tears. "Uncle Vince!" she screamed. "Uncle

Vince!" Six-year-old Lexie, who always took her cues from her older sister, followed suit.

I sat down and lit a cigarette. We were all thinking what only Lolly had dared to say: What if Gabe was next?

I have to admit that I was close to tears most of the time. Whenever I heard about an Allied offensive, even in a place far away from where Gabe was...where I thought Gabe was, because you could never be sure... I would break down. For example, when the Americans invaded Guam, I had nightmares for weeks about snipers aiming for Gabe, even though I knew he wasn't in the Pacific. I started to smoke. The doctor wanted to give me some kind of barbiturate to calm me down, but I was afraid. I'd seen what drugs had done to Orson.

In the afternoons, after work, we visited Señora Lupe. She was drifting backward. "Hurry and get ready for class, Vicente!" she'd call. "You don't want to be late!"

"What shall I do about the little ones?" I asked Don Gabriel. "Señora Lupe is in no state to take care of them after school, and Tía Emi is busy with her sewing all day." I didn't want to say: *Tía Emi isn't fit to look after them*.

"I can take care of them," said Don Gabriel.

"Vicente!" called Señora Lupe. "Wash your hands! It's almost time for dinner!"

She'd set a dish for him at the table.

"But you're still working, Don Gabriel," I said. "How can you take care of them?"

He shrugged and looked away. "I'll make a space for them in the workshop. They can play or do homework. They'll be safe. I won't let them near the tools."

"Vicente!" Doña Lupe called again. "Wash your hands and comb your hair for dinner! *¡Ese niño!*"

"Why doesn't she set the table for Gabe?" I asked quietly. "She knows he's still alive."

Somehow, I felt comforted.

In the end, I didn't leave the girls with their grandfather. I didn't want them in the workshop, with sawdust everywhere and nails lying all over the floor. Tía Emi agreed to pick them up from school and take them to Madame Isabelle's. It wasn't ideal, but in hard times, you have to rely on family, and Tía Emi was the only family I had.

With time, Señora Lupe began to think that Vince and she were both children. "Vicente!" she would yell. "Give me back my doll."

"What's the matter with Abuelita?" asked Lexie. "Why is she talking funny?"

"She's ill," I explained. Lexie nodded and went out to play.

Sometimes Señora Lupe would open up the refrigerator and peer inside. "There's no ice cream!" she would scream. "Vicente, you ate it all! You're so mean! Not like...not like my other brother...what's his name?"

"Gabe?" I'd ask gently. "Do you mean Gabe?"

"Ah, yes, Gabriel. Do you know him?"

At first, I'd try to explain that I was his wife, but she didn't understand. "Let it go," said Don Gabriel. "She's happy in her own world. Don't complicate things for her."

"Who are you?" she asked Lexie one day. "Are you in my class? Do you want to play with my toys?"

Lexie burst out laughing.

"You're mean!" screamed Señora Lupe. "You don't want to play with me! You broke my doll!" She stamped her foot, then turned to me. "Who are *you*?" she cried.

The newspapers talked of collateral damage—unintended deaths: people caught in the cross fire; civilian victims of a raid on an enemy stronghold. They printed the numbers: Allied deaths, 54; Axis deaths, 112; collateral damage, 198. But those numbers didn't include people like my mother-in-law,

Guadalupe Estrada: women whose grief over the death of a
son sinks them so far into depression that they emerge in another dimension, in a world where they're little girls again
and don't have sons who go to war.

It didn't last long. In mid-April, Señora Lupe had a stroke
and died.

It was a blessing, really, because she never knew about Gabe.

My darling husband, the kindest, gentlest man I've ever
known, was killed in action in Tunisia, during Operation
Torch, May 1943.

How can I describe how I felt? Like a nail had been ripped
from my finger. Like the skin had been pared from my face.
Like an awl had pierced my gut. My beloved, my lover, my
Gabe. I had no words to express my grief...and my fear. I was
alone with four young daughters, no husband, and no money
except for a small widow's pension.

"You'll manage," said Tía Emi. "I never had a man to depend on, and I managed." She threaded a needle with a steady
hand. "You have a job. You have a roof over your head. You'll
survive. Women have been through worse."

What could be worse than losing your soul mate? My Tía
Emi was an old maid, I thought, with no understanding of
what it meant to bury a husband.

I walked to the telegraph office and wired Lola: "Gabe
KIA. I need you."

She responded within hours: "Pack your bags and come to
Mexico with kids."

"You'll be free of me at last," I told Tía Emi. "I'm going
to accept Lola's offer. I can't stand to be here without Gabe. I
need a complete change."

"Who says I want to be free of you?"

"Well, you took me in for no reason. I was a constant burden to you."

"Who says for no reason? I promised your mother." She turned and stared at me. "You can't go back. It's dangerous. He killed your mother, and he'll come looking for you, too. And maybe even your kids."

"That's ridiculous!"

"He wants vengeance."

"Who was my mother anyway? I don't even know her name! Who is this man? I need to know her story. Otherwise, how can I believe you?"

"Her name was María."

María? I thought. In Mexico, everyone's name is María. I'm María Amparo. Lola is María de los Dolores. Tía Emi is María Emilia. Even men had names like José María. She'd told me absolutely nothing.

"What are her surnames?" In Mexico, people usually used two, the father's and the mother's. "At least tell me one of them."

Tía Emi hunched over her sewing. The needle went in and out of the cloth, in and out.

"Well, if you won't tell me anything concrete, I refuse to believe you," I shouted. "I need to get out of Los Angeles. I can go back to being Lola's personal hairdresser. The children can go to school there. They know enough Spanish."

"*No!*" yelled Tía Emi, suddenly adamant. "I promised your mother!"

"Who the hell are you to tell me no?" I yelled back. "I am nothing to you!"

I thought she wasn't going to answer me, that this confrontation would end as all the others had, whenever I asked about my mother. But then she said quietly, "You are something to me. You are my niece. Your mother was my sister."

It took a moment to sink in. I'd always called her Tía Emi, but she'd always said she wasn't a blood relative.

"So my mother's surnames were Rojas-Moreno, like yours?"

"No," she said. "We had different fathers."

"Then what was her last name?"

Tía Emi squinted at her needlework. Her fingers had grown knobby and rough from pinpricks—she never used a thimble—but they glided over the fabric like a seagull flying low over water.

"Why would anyone want to kill her?" I asked cautiously.

Tía Emi kept on stitching.

She's talking nonsense, I thought. By the end of the week, I'd made up my mind. I wired Lola: "We're coming." I told the girls to pack their bags.

I hadn't counted on them having their own opinions. After all, they were children. But Lolly resisted. She was in high school, she argued. She had friends. She had plans. I tried to soothe her with promises of a new life, visits to Tía Lola, the chance to meet movie stars.

"I don't want to meet movie stars," she retorted. "Papá hated movie stars. He only put up with Tía Lola because of you! Why can't I stay with Tía Emi?"

"Me, too!" Gabi piped in.

"We're not babies anymore. We can take care of ourselves! We'll go to school during the day, and afterward, Tía Emi can teach us to sew."

I gaped at them. They *were* babies, not quite fifteen and thirteen years old.

Tía Emi thought it was a wonderful idea. "You shouldn't go at all," she grumbled, "but since your mind's made up, you'll travel more easily with just the two younger ones. You always were as stubborn as a pregnant donkey." She scowled. "And don't get knocked up down there," she added. "Those men can be real bastards."

I almost laughed, but the idea of being with another man was too painful.

I'll only stay for a while, I thought. Just until my head clears and I figure out what to do.

I gave the keys to our house to Tía Emi. "You can live here," I told her. "You can convert the shed into a sewing workroom."

"Yes," she said. "Fewer disruptions that way, and when you come back—if you come back—your house will be here waiting for you."

"*Gracias, Tía,*" I said.

PART III

36

Xochimilco, 1943
El Indio

A pasty black sludge like decaying excrement seeped through her dress. The stink. The flies. She wanted to retch. She swallowed hard and squeezed her eyelids, but her gut continued to heave. Her skin was clammy. A shiver shot through her right arm, causing it to jerk upward.

"Keep still!"

She kept still. She didn't want to provoke him. The last time he'd lost his temper, he'd nearly struck her.

"Lower your head!"

Her cheek was almost in the muck. Filth was oozing through her blouse now. She felt as though she were swimming in a giant latrine. Her body was trembling violently. She was going to vomit. He would scream at her. Maybe he would even raise his hand, but she couldn't help herself. She couldn't control the throbbing in her entrails. It was beginning to drizzle. Her hair was damp. Grime covered her skin, causing it to smart.

She felt rather than saw them coming. The pounding of feet. A veritable stampede. The charging extras were causing the ground and her skull to vibrate. She felt as though someone were hammering an anvil in her head.

"Cut!"

At last, I thought. At last, he'll give her a ten-minute break. Filming on location in Xochimilco was a nightmare.

He squatted next to her, his heavy boot nearly striking her eye.

"Ha! Now you look like a real Mexican!"

Lola reached for the towel I held out to her, but Emilio grabbed it.

"Don't wipe your face. I like you like this, dirty and down in the shit. You wanted to get back your true identity, didn't you? You didn't want another vapid Hollywood role. You wanted something more authentic. You wanted to play an Indian. Now you know what it feels like to be downtrodden."

Lola held her tongue but grasped at the towel. "I need to change," she said finally. Her voice was raspy from the damp.

"You can't change. We have to keep working."

"I'm going to catch a cold."

"Listen, querida," he snarled. "This isn't Hollywood. Here you can't play the star, the big-shit prima donna. Here, you have to do what I say. I'm the boss, even if I am nothing but a *pinche Indiecito*. Here, you don't give the orders, *I* do. And don't go thinking that just because we're fucking, you have any special privileges. So, go take a piss and be back in ten minutes."

Lola pulled herself up. He was a tyrant, worse than any two-bit Latin autocrat, but this was the project she'd chosen. He was right, she thought. She'd wanted to play a woman of the people, and now she was doing it. This was an important project, a film that embodied Revolutionary values. She wiped off the mud with the towel as best she could.

She'd fallen for Emilio Fernández—everyone called him "El Indio"—almost from the beginning. He was just her age, but that's all they had in common. He'd been born in Coahuila, the bastard son of a Revolutionary general and the descendant of Kickapoo Indians. He prided himself on his Indian roots, and he cultivated the image of a coarse peasant melded with that of a hard-drinking soldier. It wasn't a phony image. His father had fought in the war and imbued Emilio with its Communist ideals. El Indio's reverence for the earth, he had inherited from his mother. In 1923, he'd joined the uprising led by Adolfo de la Huerta against the government of Obregón and got himself thrown in jail, but he was brash and wild enough to escape. He snuck across the border and wound up in Los Angeles, where he'd worked in a laundry, a bar, on the dock, and in Hollywood studios as a stonemason. Eventually, he found work as an extra in the movies. We all knew El Indio's story. He was proud of it. He told it over and over.

Fernández had the classic, rugged good looks of a Mexican rogue—olive complexion, slick-backed hair, a thick mustache over full, sensuous lips, and perfect white teeth. He exuded the same urgent sexuality as Orson, but without the schoolboy affectation.

The boulder that fell on Fernández and changed his life was Sergei Eisenstein's *¡Que viva México!* He'd seen fragments of it at a special Hollywood screening—the same one Lola and Ramón had attended—and felt a jolt of arousal he compared with lying next to a beautiful, naked woman. The lighting, the mood, the *image of Mexico*, and more than anything, the *message*! A new Mexico, free of the exploitation and class-consciousness that had plagued the country since its inception. He could hardly believe that Eisenstein, a foreigner, had made that film. Fernández wanted to take Eisenstein's techniques, his passion, and his vision to the Mexican screen. He had to leave Hollywood and go home.

In 1933, Mexico granted amnesty to its exiled dissidents, and he returned. The Americans were making films in Mexico, insipid musicals and melodramas, trash that made him gag. What Mexican audiences needed, Fernández decided, was a new cinema—serious films that spoke to the people of their own reality, films that ignited their aspirations. He needed to do with celluloid and actors what Diego Rivera did with paint.

But breaking into the business wasn't so easy. In Mexico, Fernández puttered around the studios doing this and that. His good looks ensured that he got acting roles, but that wasn't what he wanted. Finally, he took fate into his own hands and wrote *La isla de la pasión* and directed it himself. It was the story of an island under the control of a small detachment of soldiers who are forced to confront their individual passions when the Revolution prevents their leaving.

"Patriotism and sacrifice," he told anyone who would listen. "Those are *my* passions!"

He got his big chance when Agustín Fink of Films Mundiales asked him to direct *Flor silvestre, Wild Flower*—a story about class conflict and exploitation, right up Fernández's ally. Lola played Esperanza, the wife of a ranch owner's son with Revolutionary beliefs, played by Pedro Armendáriz. It turned out to be Fernández's breakthrough film.

El Indio was pitiless during the filming of *Flor silvestre*, and Lola wound up telling him to go to hell and walking off the set. She'd vowed never to make another film with him. However, right before it opened, Doña Antonia gave an elaborate party. Always ready to create a spectacle, Fernández showed up uninvited, carrying a wad of napkins on which he'd written the script of *Xochimilco*. He threw it at Lola's feet, then knelt down before her.

"I had no money to buy a gift," he announced dramatically. "But this is for you. It's your next film."

Lola glanced over the script and burst out laughing.

"You hate it!" moaned Fernández, pounding his breast in pretend desperation.

"I haven't read it yet! I'm laughing at your histrionics!"

That night, Lola read the script for *Xochimilco*, one napkin at a time, lying in bed next to him. She'd never been with a man like him before, a man who reeked of pulque and tobacco and had the manners of a swamp crocodile, but whose creative vision was flawless. Everything about him surged from some demonic inner passion. Working with Gabriel Figueroa, the greatest cinematographer in Mexico, he produced films as visually gorgeous as Orson's and as meaningful as the Revolution itself. He'd seduced her with his genius. Lola found him irresistibly raw, tough, rough, and genuine.

"I love it," she told him, after she'd finished reading.

The protagonist, María Candelaria, was a real tragic heroine, a woman who was misunderstood but held her head high. Lola had never had a role like this before. She had the feeling that María Candelaria would spur her career in a wonderful new direction. And besides, Pedro Armendáriz, whom she adored, would once again be her leading man.

But now, dripping wet and ready to gag in Xochimilco, she was no longer sure she was willing to take orders from a foul-smelling, would-be revolutionary from a hovel in Coahuila, just so she could play the lead. She respected El Indio's extraordinary talent, drive, and artistic sensitivity, but she hadn't counted on his raw brutality. She'd never before had to deal with constant insults and physical abuse.

I wrapped a clean towel around her shoulders and walked beside her in silence to the makeshift latrines beyond the filming area.

"I don't know about this project," she said after a while. "I wanted to be part of a movement, to do something worthwhile. Working with Emilio gives me that chance, but I just can't allow myself to be constantly mistreated."

At the latrines, I wiped her face with a damp towel. Neither of us realized that Doña Antonia had followed us up the path, but there she was, a bottle of lavender water in hand.

"Come," said Doña Antonia. "Sniff this. It will calm your nerves…and your stomach."

Lola shook her head. "Oh, Mami, did you see how he…?"

"Yes, I saw everything."

Lola took a deep breath. "I don't think I can take much more of this…and yet, I know he's not going to change. If I want to make this kind of film, I'll just have to put up with it."

A few minutes later, we started back down the path to the chinampas.

Doña Antonia knew that her daughter and Emilio Fernández were lovers, and she hadn't opposed the liaison. She believed that Lola needed male companionship, and she and Emilio shared a passion for this new kind of cinema. Relevant cinema they called it. *Cinéma engagé.* But Doña Antonia had begun to fear for Lola's safety.

By the time Lola got back to the bog, Fernández had already positioned the actors and was standing next to Pedro Armendáriz, fidgeting with a cigarette and tapping his foot.

"You're late!" he snarled.

"I just went to the bathroom and came right back!"

"Must have been an avalanche of a crap, because you've been gone for fifteen minutes."

Lola turned radish-colored.

"Why do you always have to embarrass her in front of the cast and crew?" I muttered under my breath. Lola glared at him.

"Places!" he shouted.

Lola's flimsy peasant skirt was still soaked, and her legs felt as raw as if they'd been rubbed with sandpaper.

"I said, 'places,' prima donna! Didn't you hear me?"

He raised his hand. Sweat oozed from his armpits. It seeped through the threads of his homespun white shirt, turning the underarms a brownish yellow and exuding a rancid odor. His deep brown eyes were gleaming. He placed his hand carefully on her shoulder and shoved. She wobbled in the slippery sludge but regained her balance.

"I heard you!" she hissed. "Don't push me!"

Suddenly, a scalding, throbbing sensation shot up her jaw, and she let out a shriek. She hadn't seen it coming. The slap had been so swift and unexpected that this time she couldn't steady herself. She toppled and fell to the ground. Armendáriz gasped and reached out to help her up. Lola fingered her cheek. It felt as though someone had scorched her flesh with a sizzling iron, she told me afterward. Fernández sneered, and Armendáriz shook his head in disgust.

Lola considered what to do next. They'd been shooting an important scene that would come at the end of the film. The furious townspeople are charging through the streets, forcing María Candelaria to run toward the chinampas, where she falls into the mud. Lola took a deep breath. She would get through it, she told herself.

"We're going to do the pig scene over," announced Fernández. The steady drizzle that had dogged them for days was turning into a real rain.

"I'm not doing the pig scene over," moaned Lola. "At least, not today."

"Why are we doing the pig scene?" asked Armendáriz. "I thought you said we didn't need any more footage with the pig. Anyhow, the pig is dead."

"Obviously, we can't do it over," sniggered Fernández, "but she hates the pig. I just said that to make her squirm."

The plot of this film wasn't complicated: a journalist urges an aging painter, played by Alberto Galán, to recount the story of a painting—a female nude—that he keeps hidden in his atelier. Flashback to Xochimilco, 1909, the year before the Revolution. Indigenous people inhabit the picturesque hanging gardens, cultivating flowers and vegetables to sell. Reading the script, you could imagine the beautiful tableaux that the expert hand of Gabriel Figueroa would create. Glistening canals among the chinampas. Gaily decorated rafts heaped with vegetables and flowers. Moonlit landscapes. Pristine lagoons.

But for María Candelaria, Xochimilco is hardly a paradise. Because she's the daughter of a prostitute, her own people shun her for being "unclean" and prevent her from making a living selling flowers. María and her sweetheart Lorenzo, played by Armendáriz, raise a piglet, which they hope will grow up to produce offspring that they can sell for a profit, but Don Damián, a cruel mestizo shop owner who wants María for himself, kills it to prevent them from marrying. When María becomes ill with malaria, Lorenzo steals medicine to cure her, but they catch him and send him to prison. María agrees to model for the painter to get money to have Lorenzo released, but she refuses to pose nude, so he paints only her face and completes the painting with the body of another woman. When her neighbors see the painting, they assume that María is a whore just like her mother and become enraged. They charge through the streets until they corner her and then stone her to death.

Not your typical Hollywood "happy ending," right? Well, the thing is, Lola hated the pig. She found it disgusting. She couldn't stand to touch it. The day they filmed the pig scene, about a week before the latrine incident, she almost vomited.

"Pick up the goddam pig!" Fernández snarled. "Hold her to you like you wanted to give her a teat! Look at her. Tender eyes, Lola. Motherly love. Even though you don't have any babies of your own, you can imagine."

That was cruel, I thought. She'd accepted long ago that she couldn't have children, but he didn't have to rub her nose in it.

"Now nestle your cheek against her little face. Pretend she's your baby. That's right. You're bursting with love. Get over your aristocratic aversion to farm animals and pick her up!"

On the pig's fatal day, Lola braced herself. Fernández stood about ten feet away, pointed his pistol and fired. The animal writhed a moment, then collapsed.

"We'll do the scene where Don Damián shoots the pig from

his doorway later, in the studio," said Fernández impassively. "We'll do the ones with the dead pig now. Pick it up, Lola."

Lola forced herself to pick up the limp little body.

"Get down on your knees. Cradle it in your arms. A dead baby."

Fernández wanted a pietà effect, with Lola and Armendáriz forming a triangle over the pig, suggesting the Holy Family. It was a warm, humid day. After about fifteen minutes, the cadaver began to stink and attract flies. Creatures crawled up Lola's arms and stung her skin. By the end of the shoot, her body was a swollen, itchy mess, and she was close to tears.

That's why she balked when he mentioned redoing the pig scene.

"Don Emilio," whispered Antonia. "Lola is exhausted, and it's beginning to rain hard."

Lola hadn't seen her mother tiptoe into the filming area. She usually watched from a distance, never interfering with the work, never even speaking.

As swift as lightning, Fernández raised his hand again, only this time, Lola and I both saw it. Lola scrambled to her feet, but she was too late. With a lightning-swift swing, he threw the full weight of his body into the thrust. He caught Doña Antonia on the temple, inches from the eye.

"My God, Emilio!" screamed Armendáriz, grabbing Doña Antonia under the arms to keep her from hitting the ground.

Lola was ashen. Her hands were trembling. Doña Antonia groaned. She would have collapsed if Armendáriz hadn't caught her.

"We are leaving!" Lola shouted. She clutched her mother's arm and headed toward the car.

"If you walk away, you'll never work in México again!" screamed Fernández.

"We'll see about that!" she retorted. "Who's the Hollywood star, me or you?"

There, she's gone and done it, I thought. She's thrown her Hollywood fame in his face. It was the worst move she could have possibly made. Now he'll feel honor bound to take revenge.

Armendáriz accompanied us to the automobile. He eased Doña Antonio into the back seat and held her hand until she calmed down. I climbed in next to Lola.

Armendáriz was as sweet as Fernández was coarse. Armendáriz was always a gentleman and always professional, arriving on time with his lines perfectly memorized. Besides, he was every bit as handsome as Fernández. Too bad he's married, I thought. He'd be a perfect partner for Lola.

"Shall I go home with you?" asked Armendáriz. "I can help you put Doña Antonia to bed."

"No," Lola said. "Mara will help me. But thank you, Pedro."

"Lola," he added, "you should change clothes. You're soaked." It had started to pour. "Nobody's going to film anymore in this rain. In the meantime, Emilio will cool off."

But she had no intention of waiting for him to cool off. She started the motor and pulled out of the lot.

When we got to Lola's house, I helped Doña Antonia to bed and asked Esperanza to bring her a hot tea. Then Lola and I went into the living room. Curled up on the sofa with Fiesta—Dimitri had died a few months before—Lola took stock. She wouldn't go back to work for Fernández, even if he begged her, she said. She'd begun the project full of enthusiasm, but enough was enough. She scratched the Chihuahua behind its ears.

"I wonder who he'll get to play María Candelaria," she mused. "Maybe Katy Jurado. She'd die for a part like this."

"But, Lola," I said gently, "you should have known."

"I knew he was violent, Mara, but I thought he cared for me. Now I see that for him, I'm just a tool. If I don't jump and bow every time he opens his mouth, he tries to demolish me, like an old car that no longer runs properly. I thought

that with this film, my career would soar again. I was so excited! I even started writing my name the Spanish way again,
with a lowercase *d* and an accent on the *i*: d-e-l R-í-o. Now
I'm back where I started. With nothing."

By the time I got home, Lupita and Lexie were back from
school, and Felipa, my housekeeper, was scrambling eggs.
Every day, Felipa picked up the girls and brought them home
for the midday meal, then walked them back to school and
picked them up again at six for supper. She scraped the eggs
onto plates and served them with warm tortillas. Yes, I could
afford a live-in maid. Help was cheap in Mexico in those days.
Felipa slept in a small room off the pantry. I liked her because
she was dependable and quiet. She understood that sometimes
I needed to be alone. She wasn't intrusive.

I read the girls a story in English—I was trying to maintain their language skills—and tucked them in. Then I went
into the kitchen and picked up a cold tortilla left over from
their *cena*. The kitchen was empty. In my mind, I could see
the table in our little house in Hollywood—Gabe at one end,
me at the other, two little girls on one side, two bigger girls
on the other. I could hear the laughter, the teasing.

"Lolly thinks that David Richards is cute! She wrote his
name on her notebook!"

"I did not!"

"You did, too!"

Gabe laughs. "My little girls are growing up!" he says.

Now he would never see them graduate, never attend their
weddings or the birthday parties of their children.

When it came to men, Lola was dumb. I wasn't. I'd chosen a wonderful man—a calm, gentle, hardworking man. But
now I was no better off than she was.

37

Frida's kitchen was redolent with cinnamon and chili and chocolate. The fragrances filled our nostrils, making us light-headed. To Lola, they brought back memories of girlhood in Durango—her little dog Siroco bounding through the patio, Sunday afternoons trotting on her pony side by side with her Papá, maids chattering gaily in a dialect of Nahuatl as they dusted and swept, the cook Inocencia whipping together a *queque de chocolate* and then letting Lola lick the bowl. To me, they conjured up memories of Don Francisco's kitchen, Tía Emi shaving slivers of *chocolate de metate* for cups of rich hot chocolate with cinnamon.

Every inch of the kitchen was filled with knickknacks. A perky pottery crocodile painted with orange and blue cross-hatch. Two vividly decorated dog dishes. In the corner, on the floor, an oversize Talavera flowerpot with red, blue, green, and yellow papier-mâché flowers.

I'd jumped at the chance to meet Frida Kahlo. I'd seen her at parties in Los Angeles, but I'd never actually spoken to her. But now Lola was on her way to Frida's and had asked me to come along. She was feeling miserable after the blowup with El Indio, and she thought Frida might put her in contact with other directors. Frida knows everyone, she kept telling me. Frida will know what to do.

Perched on a stool in the kitchen, Lola watched as Frida stirred the sugar and a few drops of balsamic vinegar into the batter.

"Want to taste?" teased Frida. She rubbed her finger along the side of the bowl and stuck it in Lola's mouth. "Suck, *mi amor*," she murmured, making her voice throaty and seductive.

"Mmm," Lola purred. "That's good."

"I can give you more," whispered Frida.

"What about you, Mara?" she added, as an afterthought.

"I…" She turned away before I could answer.

Frida's life had been a series of operations, braces, and plaster casts, but this afternoon, she didn't need to wear her corset. A specialist was going to fit her for a new contraption, and her doctor wanted her muscles to relax.

Frida grimaced as she twisted toward the counter.

"Does it hurt?" asked Lola.

"Of course it hurts," snapped Frida, suddenly irritated. "You think I like living in a straitjacket?"

She was limping badly, but she managed to get to the cupboard and pick out the ingredients one by one. Flour. Powdered cocoa. Sugar. She was making a one-layer Mexican chocolate cake with a chocolate glaze.

"Let me help you," insisted Lola. "I can get those things for you."

"Sit down," barked Frida. "It's good for me to move. If I wanted help, I'd call one of the maids." She lit a cigarette, then put it down and fished the food coloring out of a drawer. She placed a plate of strawberries and five bowls of creamy icing on the counter. "I'm going to dribble drops of color into each one, see?"

Lola watched her without saying a word. She knew that

sometimes the pain made Frida snap at people, and she didn't take her mood swings personally. But I was taken aback by Frida's behavior. One minute she was gushing all over you. The next, she was hissing like a cat with its tail on fire.

Frida mixed the coloring into the icing. "One green, one red, one yellow, and one I'll leave white. I'm going to make a Mexican flag. The yellow is for the serpent. I'll put the strawberries around the edge and drip chocolate on them. You're so quiet today, *mi amor*. What's going on?"

"Can I help with the strawberries?"

"No, you cannot. You're an actress. I'm the artist, and this cake is my canvas."

"I used to work in the kitchen of Francisco Madero," I blurted out. "My aunt was a cook there. I know how to ice a cake."

Frida turned and looked at me as though she'd never seen me before.

"Come on, *amiga*," she said to Lola. She'd forgotten all about me again. "Something happen with El Indio?"

"Damn it, Frida," laughed Lola. "Why do you have to be so perceptive?"

"Ha!" roared Frida. "Of course, I'm perceptive. I have to sense Diego's oncoming tantrums before he has them. It *is* El Indio, isn't it? Is he having trouble getting it up?"

"Nothing like that. He's furious with me. I walked away right in the middle of filming." Lola bit her lip. "He's a brute, Frida! He slapped me. And not only me, my mother, too!"

Frida shook her head. "What a fucking moron," she said. "We ought to go over there and cut off his balls. We'll take that one with us, too," she said, nodding at me.

"He hit her in front of the whole cast and crew!" I piped up.

Frida reached across the counter and squeezed my hand, as though I was an old friend.

"He treats me like a peon!" complained Lola. "I loved that

film, Frida. I loved the story. Now he'll reshoot all my scenes with another actress. He'll never let me come back. And I don't want to go back. He tortures me, makes me carry around a dead pig swarming with flies and infested with maggots just to show he can. He wants to humiliate me!"

Frida stood next to Lola and pulled her close. "Poor thing," she murmured, running her hand over Lola's hair.

"I heard that afterward, Emilio went to a *pulquería* and got drunk, then started shooting off his pistol all over the place. I can't stand it anymore, Frida! But what if I never work again in Mexico?" she moaned.

"Cry," whispered Frida. "Cry. It will do you good." She began to stroke Lola's back, softly at first, then more insistently, massaging her muscles with her fingers, fiddling with the lace on her blouse.

"Frida," Lola gasped. "Frida, don't."

"Calm down, precious. Relax. Look!" She stuck her finger into the chocolate glaze and drew a mustache on Lola's mouth. "Now you look like Errol Flynn in *The Sea Hawk*!"

Lola burst out laughing.

"You don't like it? I'll have to lick it off!"

Frida passed her tongue over Lola's lip, gently, methodically massaging with the point of her tongue. Then she covered Lola's mouth with her own. I didn't want to watch, but I couldn't take my eyes off them.

Frida moved to the counter and stuck her finger back into the bowl. She drew a mustache on her own face. "Recognize me? I'm Clark Gable in *Gone with the Wind*! Now it's your turn to lick it off, querida."

Lola hesitated. I wanted to melt into the ground and disappear between the cracks of the tiles. What should I do? Should I slip out the door and try to find a trolley? I wasn't familiar with the San Ángel area. I might get lost.

"Come on, sweetheart!" Frida coaxed.

She ran her tongue along Lola's neck, then bit her earlobe ever so lightly. Lola closed her eyes and rested her head on Frida's shoulder. She let Frida slither her fingers under her blouse and along her back. Then Lola picked up her head and began to lick the chocolate off Frida's face. Frida dipped her hand in the bowl and wiped it over Lola's mouth and cheeks. They were devouring each other ferociously now. Frida yanked open Lola's blouse, pulled off her brassiere and covered her body with icing.

I sank back behind the door, terrified that Frida would catch sight of me and drag me into their game. What would Gabe say if he knew? I wondered. Gabe, straight as a dowel and as old-fashioned as a gimlet. I wanted to hold his hand, to squeeze it, to be reassured that certain things were not okay. And yet, Frida's nonchalant way of breaking the rules—there was something so…why not say it?…appealing, even liberating about it. I was embarrassed to think those thoughts. And yet, I couldn't help myself.

Frida pulled off her own Tehuana blouse and stood in front of Lola, waiting for her to assess her body.

I tried not to gasp. I'd seen Frida's nude self-portraits—for example, *The Broken Column*, which she was working on at the moment. In that painting, Frida stares directly at the public as though daring people to feel sorry for her. Her body, supported by a corset, is crumbling. Nails penetrate her torso and face, and yet, her flesh is tight and youthful, her breasts high and firm. There is a beauty about her. But this Frida, the Frida who was standing there in the kitchen, was battered and disjointed, with flaccid arms, droopy breasts, and greenish-purple splotches where the corset had dug into her flesh.

"Not such a pretty sight," snickered Frida, as if reading the deception in Lola's gaze. "Well then, let's cover up this nasty mess!"

Frida thrust her entire hand into the chocolate and rubbed it all over her chest. Then she dropped her skirt and her surprisingly plain, serviceable underwear to the floor, and continued rubbing chocolate over her body. Lola unbuttoned her trousers and stood there in her lacy panties until Frida yanked them to the ground and spread chocolate cream all over Lola's body.

Lola was giggling hysterically.

The chocolate was gone, so Frida plunged both hands into the colors.

"What if one of the maids comes in?" asked Lola, suddenly horrified.

"Oh, the maids won't come in," gurgled Frida. "They know better."

Suddenly, Frida caught sight of me cowering by the door.

"Mara!" she cried. "Come and join us!" She stretched out her hand to me.

I froze. "No," I stammered. "I...I can't..."

"Of course you can! It's fun!"

"Leave her alone," murmured Lola, grabbing Frida's outstretched hand.

The two of them were lying on the floor, squealing and howling. I hurried down the hallway toward the front door. I had no idea how I'd get home, but then, I remembered what Tía Emi used to say: "If you're a donkey, all you can do is bray, but if you're a person, you can ask directions."

A heart-stopping scream pierced the corridor. It was Lola. I turned and ran back toward the kitchen. Frida was propped up on her elbow, while Lola struggled to grab a dish towel to cover whatever parts of her body she could.

Diego was standing over them, silent, eyes bulging, lips glistening. Frida was still exploring, tiptoeing her fingertips over Lola's belly. Mortified, Lola sat up, pushing Frida away, but Frida pecked at her shoulder with her green-red-frosted mouth.

The corners of Diego's mouth began to twitch. He grabbed the edge of the counter as though to steady himself, and then, as if he could no longer hold it in, he roared with laughter.

"Ha ha ha, *¡qué bello!*" he kept saying. "*¡Qué belleza!* How beautiful!"

He turned and lumbered toward the door. "Have fun, girls!" he called back over his shoulder.

Lola covered her face with her hands. "Oh God," she wailed.

"Stop it," snapped Frida. "You're carrying on as if we'd done something shameful. There's nothing shameful about it."

She took Frida's hand and led her to the bedroom, where they washed. Frida crawled into bed. She'd grown melancholy. She lit a cigarette and closed her eyes.

"I need a shot," she whispered. "You there, what's your name?" She was squinting at me.

"You know my name," I said quietly.

"Morphine. The pain is unbearable. Do you know how to do it?"

"No," I said.

"What about you, Lola? I could teach you."

"You've taught me enough for one day," said Lola.

Frida smiled wanly. Lola sat on the bed and held her hand.

"Listen…uh… I'm sorry… I can't remember your name… My head."

"Mara," I said. "My name is Mara."

"Mara, be a darling and get me that bottle of pills over there. The green one, right near the ashtray. I need three of them. And pour me a glass of water from the pitcher on the dresser."

"It says, 'Take two twice a day with meals,'" I said, reading the label.

"Well, I need three right now," she snapped.

"Maybe we shouldn't have..." murmured Lola.

"Sure, we should have. It got your mind off El Indio and mine off my body."

The pills were taking effect. She was dozing off.

On the way home, Lola was quiet as she drove down Insurgentes. "It never happened," she murmured, as I got out of the car. "What you saw this afternoon never happened."

"I know," I said. "It never happened."

38

Mexico, 1943–1944
Time

The morning after our visit to Frida's, I arrived at Lola's house before dawn. Charlie was snuggled up on her comforter, so sound asleep that he didn't budge when I tiptoed in and shook Lola awake.

Charlie was the long-haired, snow-white Chihuahua with pointy, perky, pink ears Lola had bought to keep Fiesta company.

"Come on, sleepyhead!" I coaxed. "You wanted to drive to Taxco today to buy some silver doodads for the house. You told me to come at five o'clock so we could get an early start. I'll get coffee. Don't bother Luz."

She yawned. "Of course," she said. "What else have I got to do?"

A few minutes later, I came in with coffee and warm *bolillos* for both of us. I didn't bother to open the curtains. It was still dark out.

"Por Dios," Lola moaned. "Marlene once told me that fame was like sex. It's fun while you're doing it, but it doesn't last. So, what now? Once people find out I've lost my contract with the studio Emilio works with, Films Mundiales, no one will hire me."

"Come," I said, "let me give you a new hairdo. It will make you feel better."

Dawn was breaking. Sunlight trickled through the window on either side of the heavy curtains. It settled on the bed and the cabinet, creating radiant stripes across the comforter and highlighting the grains of wood of the mesquite furniture.

An hour later, Luz was calling softly at the door. "Señorita Lola! A message just came for you from the studio."

Luz entered and pulled aside the heavy curtain. Light flooded the room with a healthy morning glow.

Lola took the note that Luz handed her on a tray adorned with a small silver vase and a perfect button rose. She tore open the envelope. The note was from Pedro Armendáriz. Films Mundiales had demanded that Fernández apologize. Lola read the message five times before its meaning sank in. The filming was going to continue, she said. The studio had made Fernández promise to behave himself from then on.

"Should I go back, Mara?" she asked. But we both already knew the answer.

Doña Antonia tapped gently on the door and walked in. She hugged me and then sat down by Lola's bed.

"Well?" She raised an eyebrow and waited.

"They want me to be at Xochimilco tomorrow morning, bright and early. Emilio is going to apologize in front of everybody."

"Will you go?" asked Doña Antonia.

"Yes, of course I'll go," said Lola, without hesitation. "I want to see this film finished as much as anyone. You should be there, too." She handed her mother the note. "They had to do this, Mami. Too much money is at stake to abandon the project."

"Good, because…" Doña Antonia pursed her lips. "Have you heard about Orson?"

"What about Orson?"

"He just married Rita Hayworth. I didn't want you to hear it from anyone else. I knew you'd be upset."

"Rita Hayworth? The one the American newspapers are calling 'the new Dolores Del Rio'?" She sighed. "I'm not upset. I'm glad to have him out of my hair."

Well, maybe that wasn't completely true. She didn't love Orson anymore, I knew that, but to be replaced by a younger woman, and one who was so often compared to her…

"Well," I said. "I guess we won't be going to Taxco today after all."

"No, I guess not," she said. "I'll have to spend the day getting ready for the shoot."

When the cast and crew gathered again at Xochimilco, Fernández apologized begrudgingly, and he remained civil throughout the rest of filming. The movie opened late in 1943. They changed the name from *Xochimilco* to *María Candelaria*. It was the main character, argued the marketing team, who would seduce audiences. Both Lola and Fernández held their breath. People were beginning to talk about the "new Mexican cinema," which would put Mexico on the map as a leader in the film industry. If *María Candelaria* was a success, the reputations of the star and the director would skyrocket.

As for me, I was more interested in the newsreels. Allied troops were making progress, according to the clips. They had landed on the beaches of Salerno, near Naples, and it was just a matter of time before they moved north to take the capital. If only Gabe were here to see this victory, I thought.

Reviewers loved the film. "Look," Lola said, handing me a couple of newspapers. "Efraín Huerta says beautiful things about my acting and Gabriel's cinematography. Blanca Hernández says my portrayal of María Candelaria will make people see Indians in a new way."

"It's a wonderful film," I said, kissing her on the cheek. I meant it. In spite of the misery Fernández had caused every-one, he had real vision.

The film was a sensation not only in Mexico. Soon US au-diences were flocking to theaters to see it. The appetite for Spanish-language films was exploding in American cities, which were magnets for newcomers from all over the Spanish-speaking world. It was released in September 1944, in Los Angeles, without dubbing.

Lolly wrote that she and Gabi had seen it with Tía Emi, and viewers wept when the Indians stoned María. "The only bad thing," she wrote, "is that Tía-Abu coughed during the whole show, and people kept turning around to give us dirty looks." The girls called Tía Emi *tía abuela,* "great-aunt"—*tía-abu,* for short.

Lolly sent me reviews from *Star World* and the *Los Ange-les Times.* Carla Myer wrote that Dolores Del Rio (Carla still spelled it the American way), had "rekindled her career in Mexico" and had played the lead in *María Candelaria* "flaw-lessly." The *Times* said that even without translation, the mean-ing was completely comprehensible, thanks to the wonderful acting of the star, Dolores del Río, "a great actress."

"You'll see," said Frida, one afternoon when she stopped by to drop off a painting. "The gringos will be begging you to go back to Hollywood."

But the truth is, Lola didn't want to go back. She was already working on a new film, *Las abandonadas,* and was convinced it would be her best. Her character, Margarita, ages from a young girl to a decrepit old woman—a challenge for any actress.

"Another film with El Indio?" said Frida. "Are you trying to self-destruct, querida?"

"There's a scene in the bordello where Margarita is working. A handsome, kindhearted general, played by Pedro, comes in and sees her at the top of the staircase and instantly falls in love with her. We did so many takes… I had to walk up and down, up and down the steps. Afterward, I felt ready to collapse."

"But you're happy," said Frida.

"Yes," said Lola. "I'm happy."

It wasn't a sudden thing. I'd been toying with the idea for a while. Lola's career was soaring, and she really didn't need me anymore. I missed Lolly and Gabi, and I wanted us to be all together again. In the summer, I thought. When the school year ends. But, as they say, *El hombre propone, pero Dios dispone*. Little did I realize that fate had already made the decision for me.

A few days after Lola finished filming *Las abandonadas*, Felipa handed me a letter as soon as I got home. It was from Lolly. Even though she swore she wrote once a week, the mail service was horrible, and letters often got lost or stolen. When one finally arrived, I savored it. I stared at it and held it, smelled it and kissed it, before I ripped open the envelope. I lit a cigarette and sat at the table to read.

Dear Mom,

I hope this letter gets to you, because I have some big news! I won the Essay Prize at school, and my teachers are going to recommend me for a special Teacher Training program at UCLA! I could start in the fall of next year, right after I graduate. I know you want me to get a job as soon as possible because with Dad gone and all, we really need the money, but this is a big chance for me, Mom, so please, please, PLEASE say yes. There is no tuition fee for residents of California, but you have to pay $39 for "incidentals," whatever that means. I'll work at Marie's in the summer as a shampoo girl, and if I save up my tips, I should have enough for the first year.

Gabi wants to work for Madame Isabelle after she graduates, and she is already making patterns and simple dresses. She's really good at it. She says that as soon as she starts getting paid, she'll give me a dollar every week to help me pay for college. Don't tell her I told you, but she has a crush on a boy named Zach Mattaboni. She's just a baby, though, every week she's in love with someone new, so I don't think you need to worry about it.

One piece of news that isn't so great is that Tía-Abu Emi coughs constantly, just like a sputtering old motorcar, and I'm worried she's got TB or something. She refuses to see a doctor. She gets up at 5 every morning and takes the trolley to work, but she's so exhausted by the time she gets home that she skips dinner and goes right to bed, so Gabi and I eat alone.

Gabi sends her love. We miss you. I hope you'll be back for my graduation. Tell Tía Lola to come, too! Give her our love. I hope she's making lots of movies. I read in Star World *that your friend Marlene Dietrich is entertaining the troops over in Europe, and that she became an American citizen. I also read that Cousin Ramón's last movie was a big flop.*

I love you, and I miss you,
Lolly

I put the letter in my purse to read again later. I knew I'd read it over and over until the edges frayed. It gave me a warm feeling just to hold it in my hands. My little Lolly! My baby girl! She was already going into her senior year in high school. And now she was planning to go to college and become a teacher! How proud Gabe would have been of his girls.

"I'll go home next year, after the release of *Las abandonadas*," I said to myself. "That will give me time to dispose of the apartment and the furniture."

But then, a telegram came from Lolly: EMI ILL HOSPITAL. COME HOME.

39

Mrs. Carver settled back in her chair while Marie brushed out her hair. I plopped down on a sofa in the waiting area, near enough so that I could hear their conversation.

"You know what I really love about *Keep Your Powder Dry*?" Mrs. Carver was saying. "The way three women join the WACs and, in spite of their different backgrounds and petty jealousies, learn to appreciate each other and work together. I mean, a socialite and a housewife who—"

"I didn't see it, Mrs. Carver."

"Well, Lana Turner plays Val Parks, this flighty society girl who—"

"I'm not in the mood for movies these days, Mrs. Carver."

"Oh, of course not. Your son… But it wouldn't hurt you to get out a little bit, Miss Marie. Something like *Anchors Aweigh* with Gene Kelly and Frank Sinatra. It might help you get your mind off things. Lots of music and dancing. By the way, I saw something in *Star World* about that Spanish girl I liked so much."

"What Spanish girl? You like this color, Mrs. Carver? I think it makes you look younger. What I mean is, it gives you a brighter look."

"Yeah, well, that's a lost cause. You can make it as blond as you want, I'm still going to look like a hag. I can't remember her name."

"I'm the one who looks like a hag, worried day and night about my boy Bobby and my husband. Just because Hitler committed suicide doesn't mean it's over. Bobby is still out there someplace in the Pacific... I haven't had a letter in months. I just... I just can't..."

"Don't cry, Miss Marie. Bobby will come back before you know it. Why don't we go out to the movies Saturday night? My husband wouldn't mind. I mean...if he were here instead of in Germany. We could see something like *A Tree Grows in Brooklyn,* with Dorothy McGuire. They say this new director Elia Kazan is terrific."

"It's about Irish people in Brooklyn. How good could it be? Anyhow, Rick...he's in a hospital somewhere in France... I just found out. I—I'm sorry, Mrs. Carver... With my husband over there and Bobby God knows where... Have you heard from Mr. Carver?"

"No...but I think the fighting is mostly finished in Germany."

"God, when will this war be over!"

"You really need to get out, Miss Marie. Oh, I remember now. Her name was Dolores Del Rio. Let's go see *Meet Me in St. Louis.* You love Judy Garland!"

"I'm sorry, Mrs. Carver. My friend Mara Estrada just came back to Los Angeles. Her husband was killed in North Africa. You remember her, don't you? She used to work at the station right next to mine. There she is, there in the waiting area. She's coming over on Saturday night. Maybe we can...console each other." Mrs. Carver turned to look at me, and I waved.

It was strange being back at Marie's. Everything was familiar, yet different. The same chairs were in the same places.

The mirrors, the hair dryers, the rows of mannequin heads with their wigs and falls, the trays of brushes and rollers, the shelves with dyes and permanent wave lotion. Even most of the patrons were the same. Mrs. Carver still came in for her weekly wash and set on Thursday afternoons. But the photos showing off the latest hairstyles had changed. Now the models wore pageboys or soft, fluffy curls. A framed picture of Alice Faye, with a high pompadour and long, lose ringlets had replaced the photo of Joan Crawford, with tight coils at her temples and a cloche. But the biggest difference was that now, instead of Miss Mara, I was Mrs. Estrada, an unemployed war widow receiving a small pension, and that instead of working at the station next to Marie's, I was leafing through magazines like a patron.

I'd left Mexico as soon as I could. I broke my contract with Films Mundiales to attend to Lola's hair until she was done filming *Bugambilia*. I let the apartment go and yanked the kids out of school. But back then, you couldn't just jump on a plane, like now. It took a couple of days to get from Mexico City to Los Angeles. By the time I arrived, Tía Emi was out of the hospital.

I was home for good, I decided. Tía Emi had converted the shed where Vince once lived into her sewing room. Gabi had transformed Gabe's old workshop into a bedroom for Lupita and Lexie and the furniture store into a bedroom for her and Lolly. I shared my bed with Tía Emi. Once, all four girls had shared the bedroom with Gabe and me. Then when Vince married Julie and moved out, Gabe had the shed outfitted with plumbing and electricity so that Lolly and Gabi could use it as a bedroom. Now all the girls were back in the house, each with her own space.

We were a family again, except that…we weren't. Not without Gabe. As we sat around the table—me at the head, Tía

Emi at the foot, two girls on each side—I felt gratification, yes, because we were all together, but also a hollowness, as though some vital organ were missing. All over the nation, families sat down to dinner with an empty plate on the table, an empty chair at the head. Women learned to sleep next to an empty pillow. They went to the beauty shop and had their hair done up in victory curls in memory of a husband, a lover, a brother. Grief is like a tick that latches on to you, lacerates your flesh, and drains your energy. Yet you learn to live with it because you have to.

The war ended on September 2, 1945. The whole neighborhood danced in the street. People cheered, screamed, and waved flags.

"The boys will be home soon!"

It wasn't a moment of joy for me, though, and not only because Gabe would not be home soon. Something awful happened that day, something that would make me see things in a different way.

The girls had joined the ruckus. Lupita and Lexie, in the pert red, white, and blue pinafores Tía Emi had made for them, held their flags high and hopped up and down like jumping beans in a warm hand. A man approached them—a tall, muscular man with close-cropped hair and a square jaw. I thought he was going to say something about how brave they were to carry on while their father was gone.

"What pretty little patriots," he would say. "What valiant little girls!"

Instead, he said, "What the hell are you two shouting about?"

The children looked at him uncomprehending, wide-eyed.

"The fighting is over," said Lexie.

"What do you care?" he snarled. "It wasn't your war! You're Mexican!"

What did he think? That because my children had their father's dark complexion and high cheekbones, they weren't American?"

"Their father died in North Africa," I said quietly, "fighting with the US Army."

"I bet!" he snarled again and spat on the ground.

"Come on, girls," I said. I grabbed them by the hand and went to find their sisters.

"Fucking Mexicans!" he called after me.

Lolly and Gabi were dancing with soldiers on a neighbor's front lawn.

"Come!" I called to them. "We're going home!"

But Lolly and Gabi had lived for too long without parents to pay attention. Lolly waved me away. I didn't see either one of them again until late that night, when the festivities began to die down.

"Fucking Mexican?" No one had ever called me that before. I felt as though I'd come home to find my house had burned down. It was as though I were looking at my furniture, my walls, my kitchen sink through a smoky haze. As though everything that was mine wasn't really mine. My husband had died in combat, wearing the uniform of the US Army, and some moron had called me and my girls "fucking Mexicans"!

Tía Emi just shrugged when I told her.

"What did you expect?" she said, coughing through cigarette smoke. "You think you're one of them, but you're not. You'll always be the daughter of an *indiecita*, a Mexican—"

"What? A Mexican what?"

"Maid," she said, squashing her cigarette in an ashtray. "A Mexican maid."

"Who was she?"

But Tía Emi picked up her sewing and pursed her lips.

For a few days, I raged. Why did my husband give his life

for this country, if all I was to its people was a fucking Mexican, the daughter of an *indiecita*?

But I didn't have a lot of time to sit around feeling sorry for myself. I had to lick my wounds and get on with my life.

Marie agreed to take me back. Now that the war was over, all the women in America wanted victory curls, and her salon had waiting lists for appointments. I worked long hours. After all, if Lolly was going to go to college, I'd have to support her another four years.

And then I began to think: Lolly will go to college! She'll become a teacher! I may be the daughter of a fucking Mexican maid, but I have my own house and car, a cosmetology license, a steady income. All this wouldn't be possible if I hadn't come here. I remembered something my ninth grade teacher once told us: "It's not where you're from, it's where you're going." I took comfort in those words. I began to feel proud. Now, more than ever, I needed to find out who my mother was. I needed to see just how far I had come. My mother may have been poor, but she was someone. I come from somewhere, I thought, I have no reason to be ashamed.

A few months later…it must have been early in 1946…a letter came from Mexico. There was no name on the envelope, but I recognized the handwriting as Doña Antonia's. Why would Doña Antonio be writing to me? I wondered. Why not Lola? Was something wrong? Was Lola ill? I had a queasy feeling as I slit open the flap.

I didn't keep that letter, but I do remember what it said. *María Candelaria* had been nominated for the international film festival in Cannes! "Pack your bags, Mara!" wrote Doña Antonia. "We're going to France, and Lola wants you to come with us—all expenses paid, of course. And bring along plenty of bathing suits! After all, we'll be in Cannes!"

I thought about it. France! All expenses paid! It was the chance of a lifetime!

But I couldn't just take off and go abroad. What about my children? What about my job?

"No," I said to myself. "These people can just leave town at the drop of a hat. They have nothing to think about beside themselves. But I have responsibilities."

I sat down to write Doña Antonia: "I truly appreciate the invitation, and I'm so sorry to decline, but..."

40

Now that the war was over, we were getting gruesome news from Germany. We wouldn't have believed it, if we hadn't seen the images. Newsreels showed soldiers wheeling piles of skulls and bones out of colorless buildings, the debris of war. Inanimate things that had once been human beings, children who played and sang songs, adolescents who dreamed, as my own daughters now dreamed, of becoming someone important—an actor, a doctor, a teacher, a fashion designer. People who prayed, as I still prayed. People with stories. Somebody's brother. Somebody's daughter. Somebody's neighbor. My overactive imagination conjured up gut-wrenching scenes. The hulking storm trooper in his thick black boots, crushing infants underfoot, dragging a small child still clinging to her doll out from under a table. I could feel her terror. One moment, the world was safe, with milk and kuchen and a mother's soft touch. The next, the world was a chaos of shrieks, bullets, exploding skulls, and blood-spattered walls. I remembered Lola once told me that, back in Durango, a strange man had entered her room at the outbreak of the Revolution, and she'd been terrified. That invasion of their property was what made her parents decide to leave Durango. Doña Antonia had borne her away in a laundry basket, but the children hiding under tables when the Nazis kicked down their doors weren't so lucky.

I didn't go to France with Lola, but after the festival, she flew from Paris to New York, and then to Los Angeles to visit Ramón and me and other friends. Her descriptions of the devastation were heartbreaking. France was in shambles— misery and disease everywhere. She had seen it on the drive from Paris to Cannes—disoriented Jewish refugees trudging along the roads, searching for their loved ones, needing shelter and food.

The movie industry was in ruins, but for that very reason, Lola explained, the Cannes Film Festival had to go on. Artists had to continue producing beautiful, creative things—films, paintings, music, dance. Otherwise, evil would triumph. We were back at the Biltmore, Lola, Doña Antonia and I, sipping coffee and eating sweets that Lola was going to pay for.

"You think a bunch of film people partying on the Riviera is going to save the world?" I said smugly.

She thought about it a moment. "Good old Mara," she said, laughing. "Always there to prick my balloon and send it zigzagging back to earth. You're right, of course. We're not going to save the world. The best we can do is infuse our films with a sense of human dignity and hope they'll have a positive effect."

"You've grown up," I said, surprised. "You're actually making sense."

"It's just that, when you think of what the victims of war endured, those clashes with Emilio, the humiliations, the hours in the mud, all that seems insignificant."

"Yes," I whispered, "when you think of what people went through in the camps."

She caught her breath. "And you, Mara...losing Gabe..."

She fumbled with her napkin before going on. "You don't think I'm doing enough, do you, Mara? Making movies, I mean. It's not enough."

I shrugged. "To wipe out evil? No, of course not."

She stared across the room, crestfallen.

"At least, movies like *María Candelaria* make people aware of injustice," said Doña Antonia.

I smiled. Doña Antonia was sixty-six years old and had just traveled halfway around the world, organizing Lola's wardrobe, making sure she got her beauty sleep, staying up past midnight to keep Lola's fans entertained, even hosting parties. Her midriff had grown pillowy, and the gentle furrows over her brow were now deep and jagged, like slashes made by a knife blade, but she was still defending and protecting her *gatita*.

"Tell me about the prize!" I coaxed, hoping to lighten the mood.

She perked up immediately. "I was so nervous," she began. "A win for *María Candelaria* would mean we'd all return home in triumph. I wasn't a candidate for best actress, but even so... By the time the ceremony began, my hands were shaking! I looked around the room at the other guests. You should have seen the clothes the women were wearing, Mara. Long, sweeping floral prints. Iridescent white silk floor-length sheaths. Shimmering strapless evening dresses pulled tight at the waist into a bow. I wore a midnight blue, chiffon tunic, cut on the bias, over an ankle-length crepe skirt. And Aztec jewelry. A heavy gold chain with a turquoise-incrusted amulet in the form of Tepoztecatl, the Aztec god of wine and pulque."

"Slit to the thigh!" piped in Doña Antonia. "You should have seen how that skirt fluttered when she walked!"

Ah yes, I thought. The clothes. It's always about appearance.

At the presentation of prizes, Lola sat between Pedro and

Doña Antonia. Next to Doña Antonia was Emilio, pretending not to care about any of the hoopla. Lola struggled to keep her breathing even. Every announcement was preceded by music, entertainments, and sweaty brows. Every award was followed by speeches and sighs. It should have been me, some of the artists were probably thinking as they applauded for the winners. On and on it went. Best color. Best animation. Best cinematography. They had a chance at this one, Lola thought. Gabriel Figueroa was a master cinematographer. The rafts on the iridescent waters of Xochimilco. María Candelaria's perfect jaw. The buzzing marketplace. The lifeless pig framed by the hunched-over bodies of María and Lorenzo. Gabriel produced images bathed in light and shadow with the deftness of a Renaissance painter.

"The winner is Gabriel Figueroa, for *María Candelaria* and *Los tres mosqueteros*!" announced the presenter.

"I almost peed!" giggled Doña Antonia, with uncharacteristic abandon. "Gabriel was beaming so widely that his moustache quivered."

"I thought *Los tres mosqueteros* came out four years ago," I said.

"Yes," explained Doña Antonia, "but there was no festival between 1942 and 1945 because of the war, so they recognized it in 1946."

By the time the Mexican contingent quieted down, the master of ceremonies was already on to Best Actress—Michèle Morgan for *La Symphonie pastorale*. Best Actor went to Ray Milland, for *The Lost Weekend*. At last, they came to the winners of the Grand Prix. Drum rolls, squirming in chairs, clearing of throats, deep breathing, squeezing of hands.

"*María Candelaria!*" announced the presenter.

"The applause was overwhelming!" squealed Lola. "Emilio stood up, looking very serious. He couldn't pretend he thought

it was all silly anymore. His film *María Candelaria* had made
the New Mexican Cinema a movement of international importance. He smiled and bowed, then moved forward through
the hall to accept his award. He didn't gloat or wisecrack. For
once in his life, he behaved appropriately."

"Well," I said. "You did it, Lola. You're a world-famous
actress! You have everything you've ever dreamed of."

"Not quite," she murmured. "Not everything."

No, I agreed silently. Not everything.

41

Mexico City, 1947
Seek, but You May Not Find

Naftalí Rodríguez, Lola's agent since she'd made *Las aban-donadas*, was trying to be as gentle as possible.

"The thing is," he told her, "we just can't continue making the kind of films you did with El Indio." He lit a cigarette and slumped over his desk. "They were beautiful," he went on. "Exquisite. All of them. I think that *Bugambilia* and *Las abandonadas* were your best work. But try to understand our position, Dolores. The Americans want to make movies in Mexico. During the war, the gringos were cooperative. They helped us develop our industry by supplying celluloid and technical assistance because they wanted us to make pro-Ally propaganda films. But now they're trying to squash us. We can't let it happen. The Ávila Camacho administration tried to do what it could to help us by imposing minimum quotas on Mexican productions and buying theaters that would show only Mexican films. But it's hard for us, Dolores."

"I can't go back to making those mindless musicals I made in Hollywood."

"That's what the public wants, and now that El Indio's group has disbanded, we couldn't make artsy films even if people wanted them. Armendáriz isn't even in Mexico now."

"Pedro allowed himself to be seduced by Mary Pickford,

but he might find himself playing butlers and chauffeurs up there. At least he didn't burn his bridges with Emilio. He can always come back."

"Our studios can no longer afford to make the kind of extravaganzas that Emilio loves."

"Would you be happy if we got together again—Emilio, Pedro, Gabriel, and me?"

"I don't see how. You've all gone your separate ways."

"John Ford, the American director, has a project. He wants us all in it. It's a film based on Graham Greene's *The Power and the Glory.*"

"Who's Graham Greene?"

"A British writer whose novels deal with faith struggles, moral issues…"

"That stuff doesn't sell."

"This will. It's about a Catholic priest in some Latin American country where religion is forbidden. He doesn't name the country. The priest is on the run from the government."

"Everybody will know it's Mexico. Even now, thirty years after the Revolution, priests have to sneak around in regular clothes without their collars. So who's this priest?"

"He doesn't have a name. He's anonymous during the whole film."

"Great. Any other bright ideas?"

"There's this other guy, also on the run, who comes to town—a vicious thug they call El Gringo, and he's got this beautiful Indian girlfriend."

"That's you."

"That's me. We decide to help the priest escape. We get him to a safe place, but then, a police mole convinces him to go back to the town because, he says, El Gringo is mortally ill."

"And needs the priest to give him last rites. Viaticum."

"Yes, exactly. Did you read the book?"

"And then the police arrest the priest and put him to death, right? I didn't have to read the book. It's obvious."

"After he dies, the people feel tremendous grief."

"And they wail and carry on, especially because before they shoot him, he forgives his informant, just like Jesus did. 'Forgive them, Father, for they know not what they do.' Luke 23:34. I went to Catholic schools. Didn't you?"

"Of course."

"Then everyone sees that God isn't dead because the people believe in Him. I like it, Dolores. But I don't know about an American film. Who plays the lead?"

"Henry Fonda."

"Henry Fonda is Jesus Christ and the bad guys are all Mexicans? Typical. Who does Pedro play? The gringo?"

"He plays the police lieutenant. Ward Bond plays the gringo."

"In English, right?"

"Yes, of course in English. Henry Fonda doesn't know Spanish. But it's not an American film, Naftalí. He's going to make it in Mexico. Emilio is going to coproduce."

"What studio?"

"Ford's own studio, Argosy. RKO will distribute."

"You know how this will look, Dolores? Like we've sold out to the gringos!"

Suddenly, Lola turned to me. "What do you think, Mara?"

"I think it's a great idea," I said to support her. I mean, what was I supposed to say?

I was in Mexico for a couple of months with Lupita and Lexie, staying with Lola at La Escondida. Lola had bought us tickets on Mexicana Airlines, and the girls were more excited about the airplane ride than about being back in Mexico.

Of course, I was squeamish about leaving Tía Emi alone in the house again. What if she burned it down with a cigarette? Or what if her lungs gave out? Who would rush her to the hospital?

"So what's the worst thing that could happen?" growled Tía Emi. "I'd die, and by the time you got back, I'd already be breakfast for worms."

In the end, Lolly and Gabi convinced me to go. They promised to watch over Tía Emi, and Don Gabriel said he would check in regularly. We left at the end of June, as soon as the school year was over.

"Why?" Naftalí asked now. "Why is it a great idea?" He was squinting at me from behind thick, frameless eyeglasses.

I wasn't expected to answer, of course. My job was to accompany Lola to meetings, or wherever else she wanted, and to make sure her hair and wardrobe were in order. As for John Ford, in Lola's mind, he was a giant, but all I knew about him was what everybody else in Hollywood knew. He'd made mostly Westerns, filmed on location in Monument Valley. He was known for his majestic long shots. Rugged men rode across vast plains, specks against breathtaking landscapes, "just as we are specks in God's fathomless creation," he once said in an interview. His heroes were loners, often played by Fonda, who was considered the embodiment of the tough, independent he-man. Ford was known to be a nasty director who goaded his actors to their limits and once even brought John Wayne to tears. But rumor also had it that he could be kind, that he often made secret donations to the needy and once even financed an operation for a desperately ill woman.

"Okay," Naftalí said finally. "If that's what you want."

Ford would shoot *The Fugitive* in Mexico because he wanted to make it as authentic as possible, but he wouldn't name the location because he didn't want problems with the Mexican government. Of course, Mexicans would know it was about the state of Tabasco, where the brutal atheist governor, Tomás

Garrido Canabal, had persecuted priests relentlessly, killing scores of them. Ford was already in Mexico making preparations, and Lola was going to meet with him the following day.

"I want you to come with me," she said, when we got back to her house.

"No," I said. "I promised to take the girls to Xochimilco for a picnic."

She wasn't pleased, but she didn't say more.

To be honest, I hadn't gone to Mexico just to babysit Lola's new bouffant hairdo. I had other plans. However, it wasn't going to be possible to carry them out with two young girls in tow. I had to leave them with someone, but I needed to be careful. I didn't want anyone to know what I was up to. It occurred to me that Luz might be willing to watch them, but then Lola would ask questions. I didn't know where to reach Felipa, and anyhow, by then, she was certainly working for another family.

But I couldn't take the children with me. It might be dangerous. In fact, even going alone could prove dangerous if it was true, as Tía Emi always said, that someone was after me. I certainly didn't want to leave my girls orphans, but, on the other hand, I'd lived in Mexico before, and no one had tried to kill me. Of course, it was easy to remain anonymous in the capital. In Durango, someone might be on the lookout for me.

The day Lola met with Ford, I did, in fact, treat the girls to a picnic in Xochimilco. I packed a basket, and we took a boat tour around the floating gardens and listened to a mariachi playing "Cielito lindo." We visited the church of San Bernardino and saw the famous Niño Dios. By the time we got home, Lola was back.

She launched into her report the moment we walked through the door. "He wore a patch over one eye and dark glasses to protect his delicate vision. He was smoking a pipe.

He has a long, oval face like a hard-boiled egg. His hair is a silver fawn color, and he wears it very short, military style. It looks like the bristles of a dirty scrub brush!"

She'll be talking about him for hours, I thought. She was enthralled with Ford. He hardly smiled, she said. Instead, he clamped his teeth down on his pipe and growled, a low, droning growl like that of an annoyed lion. Lola loved his intensity, his no-nonsense determination. He was nothing like the prima donna directors she'd dealt with before.

"'The damn studios!' he roared. And then he said, 'Excuse me, Miss del Río. I don't allow my men to swear on set in the presence of ladies, and here I am swearing myself. It's just that Hollywood…it all makes me so mad.' He took a puff on his pipe. 'Greed!' he growled. 'They're all dominated by greed. All they think about is profits. You can't make beautiful films anymore because the only thing that matters is money. That's why I started Argosy. I wanted to control my own productions.'" Lola imitated his deep, raspy voice.

"I appreciate his dedication," she told me, "and I'm anxious to get back to making films that are more than entertainment. We're going to start rehearsals in a few weeks, querida, and I'll need for you—"

"I'll only be here until the end of August," I interrupted, losing patience. "School starts right after Labor Day. I can't keep the girls out of class. And by the way, Lola, I wonder if I could leave them with Luz for a few days next week. I have… I have something to do, and I can't take them."

"Oh?"

"I ran into an old friend, and we'd like to spend some time together. He has a place in Guanajuato…an old colonial house…" It was a lie, of course, but I knew the suggestion of romance would intrigue her.

"Anyone I know?"

"No."

"Well, Gabe has been gone for four years now, Mara. It's time for you to get on with your life. I'll tell Luz." She winked at me and went on talking about Ford.

A few days later, I kissed the children goodbye and caught the bus for Durango. I wore a plain black pleated skirt and a lightweight burgundy sweater—not the kind of thing you'd wear for a tryst, but Lola had gone out by the time I left the house, so I didn't have to explain. To avoid attracting attention, I wore no jewelry, not even earrings. I carried only a small suitcase with fresh underwear and two clean blouses.

It was a long trip—about ten hours. The bus was a rolling junk heap glued together with masking tape and chewing gun. Half the windows were broken, and the seats were hard and narrow. The passengers were mostly campesinos on their way home from the markets in the city, some with leftover goods—ears of corn, avocados, tomatoes, even chickens, goats, and lambs. The odor of animal shit and cigarettes was overpowering, in spite of the shattered windows. We stopped a couple of times to pick up passengers, or so that we could use the stinking, overflowing toilets or buy food in some dilapidated cantina.

The jerky ride was made worse by my pogoing nerves. I hadn't smoked since we'd moved back to Los Angeles, but I fished a cigarette out of one of the packs I'd bought specially for the trip and lit it. Of course I was edgy. For one thing, I didn't even know who I was looking for. What was I going to do? Approach strangers and ask, "Do you know a woman who looks like me, except older?" For another, what if Tía Emi's stories were true? What if someone recognized me and reached for a pistol? As the bus rolled into the station, I half expected to be met with a barrage of gunfire.

I climbed down and stretched my stiff limbs, then looked

around at the place where I was born. Nothing about it was familiar. The flophouses around the bus station were downright fetid, but I walked along the road until I finally found a relatively clean inn. A breakfast of coffee and dry sweet rolls or tortillas was included in the price. I went to bed and fell asleep almost immediately.

In the morning, I took off on foot toward town. Everything seemed strange, almost otherworldly. I sensed eyes squinting at me from behind doorjambs and whispers wafting over crumbling walls. *It's just my overactive imagination*, I kept telling myself. Suddenly, footsteps, heavy and uneven, approached from behind, and I caught my breath without slackening my pace. The irregular thwacks on the ground were coming closer. I picked up my stride, and he picked up his. It wasn't my imagination. I could smell his breath—putrid and close. He was gaining on me. I felt as though I were suffocating. I expected a hand like a claw to clutch my shoulder at any moment, but then, he...no...it was a she...pushed past me, shoving me against the wall as she plowed ahead—a heavy, unwieldly farmwoman pulling a goat on a tether.

In a doorway, an old woman was shucking corn. I might as well start somewhere, I thought.

"Excuse me," I said. "I am looking for a woman... I don't know her name, but she's the sister of Emilia Rojas-Moreno. She used to live here."

My voice sounded alien to my own ears, and my question, absurd.

The woman looked at me blankly, and I realized she didn't understand Spanish. I smiled and said, *"Tlazohcamati,"* "thank you," one of the very few words I knew in Nahuatl.

In a little plaza, I came upon a group of five or six women who appeared to be about Tía Emi's age. Brown, braided Indians with leathery skins. Earlobes deformed by heavy earrings.

Yellowed blouses. Faded, woven shawls. Stinking cigarettes or pipes hanging from their mouths. Tía Emi would look like these women, I thought, if she'd stayed here. Like them, her hands were gristly and her complexion, coffee-colored, but she wore her graying hair in a bob, and she sewed pert little shirtwaists for herself. She wore cardigans, not homemade shawls, and shoes, not huaraches.

Tía Emi's name was María Emilia Rojas-Moreno. Tía Emi had said that she and my mother had different fathers, but, I thought, perhaps they shared a maternal surname.

"I'm looking for a woman," I began. "María Moreno. The sister of Emilia Rojas-Moreno." The women jabbered in dialect a moment, then shrugged.

Toward evening the following day, I spied a group of men and women in a different tiny plaza adjacent to a church. One of them strummed a guitar, and another tapped a makeshift drum. They were singing some of the old Revolutionary ballads I'd heard as a child—"Adelita," "Juana Gallo," "Corrido a Pancho Villa," "Miguela Ruiz."

"My aunt worked on an estate around here. It burned down during the war," I began when there was a lull in the singing.

"Campesinos set fire to it!" one of the men corrected me.

My heart leaped! These people knew about the estate!

"Bien hecho!" chimed in one of the women. "They had it coming!"

"You knew Don Adalberto and Doña Verónica, the owners?"

"No," they replied, one after the other.

"Then how did you know that *peones* burned down the hacienda?"

"We burned down all those filthy, fucking estates that the *terratenientes* used to break the backs of the poor slobs who worked the land."

The guitar hummed. The voices rose. *"Si Adelita se fuera con otro..."* *"Don Pedro amaba a Miguela..."*

They were all gawking at me. Of course they were. In those days, it wasn't so common for a woman to roam through town unaccompanied. Don't forget, women couldn't even vote in Mexico until 1953.

If only I knew where the estate was located, I thought. Then I could visit the local church and look at the baptismal records.

"All those little parish churches were destroyed during the war," the owner of the inn told me, when I explained my plan to her, "but you might try the cathedral."

My third full day in Durango, I thumbed through the cathedral records. I figured that my mother was probably born around 1890...maybe a little earlier...but there were no entries in the books from between 1880 and 1930. I left disheartened.

I planned my return trip so that I would arrive back at La Escondida while Lola was out. I didn't want to answer questions. The 6 a.m. bus would get in at about 4 p.m. By the time I caught a taxi and returned, Lola would be done with her siesta and back at the studio going over the script with Ford.

For once, everything worked out as anticipated. The house was quiet when the taxi dropped me off in front of Lola's elegant wrought iron gate. I tiptoed in, bathed, and changed clothes. I played paper dolls with the girls—they'd brought two books of Katy Keene from the States—and gave them their supper. Then I went to bed.

I looked like a ghoul when I came in for breakfast—sunken eyes, droopy mouth, skin like skim milk. I'd been too upset to sleep.

"How was it?" asked Lola cheerily. "Mami's got a boyfriend," she whispered conspiratorially to Lexie and Lupita. "In Guanajuato."

Lexie glared at me, mortified.

"No, I don't. It...it's not what you think, Lola."

I should just tell her the truth, I thought. But I was ashamed. I was an orphan, an abandoned child, the bastard of some maid. How could I talk about these things to Lola, whose own mother was so adoring? It was too painful.

"What about Ford?" I asked. "What's he like to work with?"

As I knew she would, she instantly forgot about Mr. Guanajuato and launched into an account of her day with Ford. He didn't live up to his reputation as a hard-ass, she said. He treated her with respect, and El Indio, following his example, behaved himself. Best of all, she was once again making a serious film with Pedro and Gabriel.

A few days before the girls and I returned to the States, Lola walked into my room while I was packing. She was wearing a tight, deep green sweater of the type that makes church ladies hyperventilate.

"That top leaves nothing to the imagination," I teased.

She laughed. I was folding Lexie's skirts and shorts and placing them carefully in the suitcase, but I could feel Lola's eyes on me.

"If you really had a boyfriend in Guanajuato, you'd have told me all about him, right, Mara? After all, we're best friends...sisters..." She put her arm around me. "What's going on?" she asked gently.

How could I not tell her?

"If you can find out the names of the estate owners," she said, after she'd heard the whole story, "Mami might be able to help. She knew all the important families in Durango."

"All I know is their first names, Adalberto and Verónica," I said.

"Talk to Mami."

Lola began folding Lexie's shirts and placing them in the suitcase. She kissed me on the cheek. "Remember," she murmured in my ear, "in the future, no keeping secrets from big sister!"

We arrived back in California a week before Labor Day. Lolly started her sophomore year of college, although she almost didn't. She hadn't been able to save up the thirty-nine dollars the university required for "incidentals." She put every five-or ten-cent-tip she got at Marie's in a big glass jar, but all the coins only added up to about eight dollars. Gabi gave her two dollars from her earnings as Madame Isabelle's assistant, and I'd managed to put aside ten dollars as well, but it just wasn't enough.

In the end, it was Tía Emi who saved the day. She'd lived with Madame Isabelle rent-free for years, and then she came to live with us. She made her own clothes, even her underwear, and I cut her hair. The only things she spent money on were taxes, shoes, cigarettes, and an occasional movie ticket for the Rialto *cine en español*. With no expenses, she'd managed to save up thousands of dollars, and instead of hiding it under the mattress, as you might expect of an uneducated woman raised on a hacienda in the middle of God knows where, she opened an interest-bearing account at Bank of America. Madame Isabelle had shown her how.

"Keep those *centavos* you put together working your little asses off," she told Lolly and Gabi. "I'm going to write a check."

And she did. It was the first check she ever wrote. (Well, actually, I wrote it, and she signed it. Tía Emi wasn't so good at writing.)

"My niece is going to be a teacher," she announced to anyone who would listen. "She's going to stand up in front of a bunch of white kids, and they'll have to pay attention and do whatever she says. Otherwise, she'll beat the shit out of them."

A few days after *The Fugitive* opened, Mrs. Carver brought a copy of *Star World* into the shop. I flipped through it on my break and came across this article by Carla Myer:

Dolores del Río Returns to the Silver Screen in Ford's The Fugitive
Carla Myer

The Fugitive *opened on November 3, and my feelings are mixed. With hardly any dialog, the film depends on star Henry Fonda's superb acting skills, which, as wonderful as they are, cannot carry this grim tale of Revolutionary Mexico's persecution of priests. Director John Ford is known for gorgeous imagery, but here, mood and cinematography overwhelm the story.*

The Hollywood grapevine has it that Fonda himself doesn't care much for The Fugitive, *and I can see why. The story is plodding, the script meagre, and the symbolism heavy-handed. Fonda's character, the last surviving priest in an unnamed country that is obviously Mexico, represents Jesus, and his nemesis, a criminal known as El Gringo (of course!), is the devil. I will not spoil the ending for those of my readers who want to brave 104 minutes of tedium, except to say that there are no surprises in this film.*

On the other hand, it is a pleasure to once again be writing about Dolores del Río. (She used to write her name Del Rio.) It has been about five years since she starred in Orson Welles's disastrous Journey into Fear, *her last picture in English until now, and she has certainly developed as an actress since then. In* The Fugitive, *she plays an unnamed Indian woman who has a baby by a savage police lieutenant (Pedro Armendáriz). In one overwrought scene, he laughs viciously when he corners mother and infant in a church. A believer, del Río's character has the priest baptize her baby and tries to help him get out of the country.*

There are positive elements to report, to be sure. Richard Hageman has composed a score that captures the atmosphere of Mexico, although at times it seems a bit clichéd. Del Río's acting, while sometimes strained, is admirable. Gabriel Figueroa uses the camera like a paintbrush, shooting del Río in his black-and-white pallet as though she were the Mona Lisa. *Every angle shows off her ageless beauty. Although she must be over forty, kneeling in church with her infant daughter, she looks about twenty-six, thanks to Figueroa's magic. (And perhaps to a plastic surgeon. A little bird told me she's had some work done.) Gabriel Figueroa and Dolores del Río bring out the best in each other. He knows how to caress her impeccable, heart-shaped face with the lens, how to use light and shadow to bring out her sculpted cheekbones and her neat, vertical nose, and she, of course, knows just how to pose.*

With its clumsy, transparent Catholic symbolism, The Fugitive *may not attract non-Catholic moviegoers or make a lot of money for its producers. It is a shame that Dolores del Río chose such an awkward vehicle to make her comeback in the US.*

I laughed at the bit about a "plastic surgeon." Of course Lola had a few nips and tucks. Who in the movie business hasn't? But did that vixen have to mention it?

I debated whether to send the review to Lola. Maybe she'd like to read that onscreen, she looked about twenty-six, I thought. But then, I reflected a moment longer. What about that comment about plastic surgery?

"No," I said to myself. "She doesn't need to see that."

42

I first read about this in *Photoplay en español*. The American movie magazines didn't give the incident much space, but KSPA, the Spanish-language radio station, aired an interview with actress Columba Domínguez, who called Lola *"loca, chiflada, tirana,"* and a *"mujer horrible, cruel, y totalmente demente."* That got everyone's attention. Much later, Lola told me her own version of the story:

After she'd finished filming *The Fugitive*, Lola left for Argentina to film *Historia de una mala mujer... The Story of a Bad Woman*, an adaptation of Oscar Wilde's *Lady Windermere's Fan*. In Buenos Aires, she worked with the director Luis Saslavsky, a handsome and refined man just a year older than herself, who knew how to bring out the best in his actors without insulting or abusing them. Eva Perón was so delighted to have a famous Hollywood actress as a guest that she fawned over her like a princess.

Lola returned from Argentina elated. *The Fugitive* had been a disappointment, but the Saslavsky film had made her a Latin American—not just a Mexican—star. Mexico and Argentina were the two most important movie-producing countries on two continents, and Lola dominated both markets. She was constantly in demand, and now Emilio Fernández wanted her for a new project—one that would once again bring together the old team despite Naftalí's prediction. Everything was perfect. What she hadn't counted on was Columba.

How to describe Columba Domínguez? Huge brown eyes. Luscious black hair. Elongated oval face with high cheekbones. Full lips. The same fine features as Lola, but twenty-five years younger. Emilio repeatedly cast her as an Indian, even though she looked no more Indian than Lola. She'd won a few prizes, and her star was on the rise. By the time Emilio featured her in *Pueblerina*, he was sleeping with her.

His new film, *La malquerida, The Unloved*, was based on a play by the Spanish writer Jacinto Benavente, but Emilio set it in rural Mexico. In an exquisite act of cruelty, he chose Lola and Columba as the two female leads. Lola and Columba— yesterday's lover and today's. At first, Lola hardly thought about it. She no longer had feelings for Emilio, and besides, he had mostly behaved himself during *The Fugitive*. Lola was sure that by now, El Indio realized that she was not a woman to be bullied. She accepted his invitation without qualms.

"Here's your costar," snickered Fernández, handing her some photos.

Lola looked at the publicity shots and felt an unexpected pang. "It wasn't jealousy," she told me. "How could I be jealous? After all, I was the number one star." Columba stared out from the page with a liquid gaze, her perfectly formed, elliptical face framed by a simple white kerchief. Columba looked identical to Lola a quarter of a century before.

Once filming started, Lola realized that she was in for a rough time. She'd been looking forward to the project, but now this slinky little minx had thrown a wrench into the works.

"He wouldn't even let me call him 'querido' on set," Lola

told me, "but Columba planted kisses on his mouth every chance she got."

Lola was to play Raymunda, an uptight widow recently re-married to the handsome Esteban, played by Pedro. Columba was her knockout daughter, Acacia, who wiggled her shapely ass whenever anyone was looking. Of course, Esteban falls for the younger woman.

"What a cruel way to tell me what I already know," Lola sighed. "That I'm getting old."

On the day she lost her temper, they'd been filming since early in the morning, and everyone was exhausted. Emilio egged the women on, deliberately building up tension.

"You're still beautiful," he whispered to Lola, just before the shoot began, "only Columba is more beautiful and so much younger. And she's more—how shall I say it?—agile. You know, for the things men need." Lola looked away and pretended not to hear.

Emilio turned toward Columba. "She has what you want," he teased. "Now take it away from her! Lights! Camera! Action!"

Columba glowered at Lola as if she were prey. "You had to go and marry him!" she hissed, reciting her line with un-canny conviction. She shifted her weight forward as though ready to pounce. Emilio smiled broadly. He was getting ex-actly what he wanted out of the two women.

Columba glared at Lola with fury and loathing. She wasn't acting. At Emilio's signal, she arched her back with feline grace. Lola stood in front of her, partially turned away from the camera. "That's no way to speak to a mother!" she screamed.

Columba's face hardened. "You're not acting like a mother! You're quarreling with me over a man! He doesn't love you anymore, Raymunda! The one he wants is *me*!"

"I felt as though she'd spat at me," Lola told me later. "I

grimaced. Columba wasn't talking about Esteban, she was talking about Emilio."

Lola's temples began to throb. A dizzying rage almost threw her off-balance. Instinctively, she raised her hand and let it fall with such force that her wrist and fingers smarted. Columba let out a bloodcurdling scream that wasn't rehearsed. She staggered backward, falling to the floor.

"Cut!" yelled Emilio. "That was perfect! A perfect slap! No need for another take!"

Columba held her cheek. It was swollen and bloody, and it was going to bruise.

"She did that on purpose!" Columba cried. "She cut me with her ring!"

"No…" stammered Lola. She looked down at her hand. She'd forgotten she was even wearing a ring. "No…" It was an old-fashioned diamond wedding band that her mother had given her. "I didn't mean to," she stammered. "Really, Columba."

Emilio helped Columba to her feet and examined the cut on her cheek. "Go home, darling," he murmured. "You have to rest."

He turned to Lola with a sneer. "She's really gotten to you, hasn't she?"

"It was an accident, Emilio, really. I didn't mean to…"

"Of course you did, but it doesn't matter. That scene was flawless. The only thing is, it's going to cost us time. Columba won't be able to work again for at least another two days."

"Well, you were back in Los Angeles, Mara, and I had to talk to *someone*," Lola explained when I saw her again in Hollywood, "so I went to see Frida.

"I'm playing the *mother* of a *grown woman* in this film," Lola told her friend. She thought Frida would understand. After all, Frida had put up with Diego's escapades with younger women for years.

But instead, Frida just said: "So?"

"So! Emilio thinks I'm old!"

"That's all you have to worry about?" snickered Frida. She took a swig of tequila. "I'm putrefying. My flesh is rotting off my bones."

"We're all dying," retorted Lola.

"Well, what do you want? You're old enough to be the mother of a grown woman."

"But I just played the mother of a newborn in *The Fugitive*."

"That was two years ago."

Propped up on a chair in her studio, Frida reminded Lola of one of those skeleton puppets children play with on the Day of the Dead—the ones that stand upright when you hold the strings, but collapse into a pile of sticks when you slacken your grip. Frida's hair hung loose and stringy on her shoulders. The colorful headdresses that usually adorned her braids lay in a basket on her dresser. Her ebony unibrow crept over her forehead like a caterpillar, dense and messy, with stray hairs like tiny feet extending in all directions. Her nose, a mass of miniscule spiderwebs, dripped incessantly. She must have caught the revulsion in Lola's eyes.

"It's as though I were already dead and being consumed by organisms," she said.

Lola didn't answer.

"Yes, I look like a slug," she said matter-of-factly, lighting a cigarette. "I'm afraid Diego doesn't love me anymore. Not the way I love him."

Lola paused. "I'm sure in his own way..." she began tentatively. She was sorry she'd snapped at Frida.

Frida threw the lit cigarette on the floor. "In his own way!"

she screamed. "He's fucking María Félix! I'm sure you know all about it!"

"No," said Lola calmly. "I don't."

"Liar! Everybody knows about it! It's in all the papers!"

Lola focused on the painting on Frida's easel. She'd seen self-portraits that captured Frida's pain before—images of Frida in her Tehuana dresses, tears streaming down her cheeks, Diego's likeness implanted squarely on her forehead to show that he was lodged in her mind. But this one was different. Frida looked wan and haggard. Her hair hung wild and unadorned around her face, stray strands encircling her throat as if to strangle her. No vegetation, no monkeys, no brightly colored blouses. No other figures but the cameo of Diego on her forehead. Only the red of Diego's shirt, repeated in her dress and lips, offered any respite from the dominant grays and browns and washed-out greens. The wretchedness of Frida's emotional state was evident in her somber face, unmade-up, naked, resigned.

"Philandering son of a bitch," whispered Frida. She lit another cigarette.

"I'm sorry, Frida. Really, I didn't know."

Frida sat for a long while, staring into space. She appeared to be asleep, even though her eyes were open. Ashes were falling from her cigarette, but she made no effort to snuff it out.

"Sorry!" she screamed suddenly. "Sorry! Do you know what it means to be married to a man like Diego? He is a genius! A marvel! I don't care who he fucks! Diego is too enormous a man—*man* isn't the right word—Diego is too colossal a phenomenon for just one woman. He's like a river that must overflow its banks! The banks don't suffer because the river overflows. I don't suffer because Diego fucks around! Even when he fucked my own sister, I didn't care! Diego is a *god*! Do you understand? I am blessed to have such a husband! And *husband* isn't the right word either, because *husband* implies he belongs to me and only me, but Diego is too vast...too vast..." Frida picked up the bottle of tequila and hurled it at the wall. Shard-filled liquid ran down the surface and over the floor. She was on drugs, thought Lola, just as Orson had been on drugs when he'd smashed a vase against the wall years ago.

"Tula!" howled Frida to the maid. "Come pick up this mess!" She had worn herself out. She slumped in her chair, forlorn. "If you want to look younger, you could always have plastic surgery," Frida said dryly.

"If I have any more plastic surgery," quipped Lola, "instead of to a regular doctor, I'll have to go to a pediatrician!"

Frida smiled and blew her a kiss. "You're still stunning, Lola. Play the beautiful, classy older woman, and don't let them get to you." She acted as though her outburst had never happened.

Just as Emilio had predicted, Columba had to take two days off. Or maybe, thought Lola, Emilio had shut things down to make her look bad. He wasn't above wreaking havoc with everybody's schedule to make some petty point.

It was just as well. Doña Antonia hadn't been feeling well, and Lola wanted to stay home with her. She tucked her mother under the silky sheets and dainty hand-knitted coverlet she'd bought for her in France and brought up a broth that Luz had made.

"I didn't mean to hit Columba that hard, Mami," she told her mother. "Or maybe I did. She and Emilio flaunt their affair! They go out of their way to humiliate me. Emilio keeps reminding me that I'm getting old, and the truth is, it's not easy for me to play Columba's mother."

Doña Antonia sank back into her pillow and closed her eyes. Then she took a shallow breath and recited her favorite passage from Ecclesiasts.

"To every thing, there is a season, and a time to every purpose under heaven: A time to be born, and a time to die; a time to plant, and a time for uprooting what has been planted..." Then she said: "I have a feeling you're about to enter a new, exciting, and wonderful season of life, Gatita."

43

"I'm sure I'll croak before she gets that diploma," Tía Emi said, bringing a cigarette to her lips. "Ha! All those white children will have to—"

"Don't croak," I said. "Maybe if you'd stop smoking..." People didn't associate smoking with cancer until a decade later, but still, I suspected cigarettes couldn't be good for her.

"Bah! I've been smoking since I was a little girl, and I'm not dead yet."

"On the estate in Durango?" I asked. "That's when you started? Or before then?"

"There was no before then. I was born there."

"Ah! And my mother, too?"

She clammed up.

Tía Emi wasn't a morbid person, but lately she talked often about "croaking."

"Tough as a bull's prick," she hooted. "That's why I didn't die back then, when I was in the hospital. I'm tough as a bull's prick. But now I can feel her coming, La Catrina, la Señorita Muerte."

She'd sit in the yard and hem the girls' skirts, but she couldn't concentrate for long. Sometimes she'd fall asleep, and the cloth would slip from her hands. Or the cigarette would drop from her mouth. Oh God, I thought. What if she starts a fire? Sometimes she'd have a fit of coughing so violent that her whole body would shake, and I feared she really might die. What if she died before telling me my mother's name? How would I find out who I really am?

But I pushed those selfish thoughts from my mind. Tía Emi was the only parent I'd ever had. She'd been good to me and my girls. I didn't want her to die. I loved her.

She did die, though. Not long after Lolly began the teaching program that would, Tía Emi thought, enable her to beat the shit out of unruly white kids. My aunt faded away in her sleep without even bothering to say goodbye.

"I didn't want to disturb you," she would have said, if she could have sent a message from beyond the grave. "You were busy sleeping."

She left a will. Madame Isabelle had told her she had to put her last wishes in writing, and since Tía Emi hardly knew how to write, Madame Isabelle typed up her statement and had Tía Emi sign it in front of a notary.

She left me everything she had: $43,862.84.

"So my great-nieces can go to college if they want to," she wrote in the will, "and my niece María Amparo can buy a bigger house."

She never told me the names I was yearning to know, but she saw to the children's education. She was a nearly illiterate seamstress, but she understood that learning opened doors and bestowed power, and she wanted to be sure that her great-nieces could beat the shit out of any white kid who got in their way.

Tía Emi's death left me feeling like an empty laundry bag. I dragged myself around the house, unable to grasp that she was really gone. Her sewing machine was still in its place, with neat boxes of pins, measuring tapes, scissors, and swatches of fabric lined up on a little table nearby. Her bedroom slippers lay by the bed. Her toothbrush hung in its holder. Her Spanish-English dictionary, hardly opened, sat on the dresser.

Lola wrote to me in the late spring. "Come spend the summer with me," she said. "You need a rest. Leave the girls at home. They're old enough."

They weren't old enough, of course. Lola had never had children, so how could she know that a twelve-year-old and a fifteen-year-old should not be left alone for an entire summer?

Lolly had begun working as an assistant at a nursery school, and Gabi, who had just graduated high school, had replaced Tía Emi as Madame Isabelle's full-time assistant. She was planning to enroll in a design program at Otis College in the fall while continuing to work part-time.

"Madame Isabelle is getting old," Gabi told me. "I need to learn other facets of design so that when she goes..."

I agreed, and I was overjoyed. Paying tuition wouldn't be a problem. I had the money now.

"I'll have to bring the younger ones with me," I wrote to Lola. "Unsupervised girls can get into a lot of trouble."

At the end of June, we packed our bags. Lola was waiting for us at the airport, looking as sunny as the sun-drenched streets of the capital. The city had changed in the two years since my last visit. A trolley system had been installed. Construction of the new Federal District Building had been completed. Automobiles zipped here and there, although campesinos with donkeys could still hold up traffic.

La Escondida was as I remembered it, except that Lola had enlarged the patio and added a couple of chaise longues for sunbathing.

Luz kissed the girls and made the usual comments: "My,

how you've grown! You're already señoritas!" The girls settled
into their room, and before long, we could hear them jumping up and down to the music on the radio.

Lola was getting ready to film *La casa chica*, a tearjerker
about a married doctor who falls in love with a medical student and sets her up in an apartment. *"Casa chica"* refers to a
man's second household, his mistress's house. Lola was looking forward to working with the director Roberto Gavaldón,
but first, she was going to take a break, she told me. She was
exhausted.

"Let's go to Acapulco," she said one morning. "We could
both use a change of scenery."

"I'll tell the girls to pack their swimsuits."

"No," said Lola, "leave the girls here. Luz will take care of
them. She loves them. You don't have to worry."

We left early on a Monday. Lola's chauffeur, David, drove
her sparkling new Chrysler, made in Mexico.

Lola had booked us a suite in a luxury hotel on the beach.
In the morning, we got up a little after dawn and headed for
the ocean. The sand was luminous. Gauzy clouds dotted the
sky. Lola breathed in the salty air. She loved the beach in the
early morning, before the sunbathers arrived. She loved to
amble along the water's foamy edge. It quieted her nerves.

I watched her from the shade of a large pink-and-green
beach umbrella. She was digging her toes into the moist sand
when she became aware of a man observing from nearby. I
saw him, too. Lola was used to having men's eyes on her,
but there was something about the intensity of his gaze that
made her self-conscious. He was not particularly handsome.
He was balding and had a rather flabby chin, a hooked nose
and a Clark Gable moustache over thin lips. His tall, reedy
frame gave him the air of a slightly disjointed scarecrow, and

yet, he had a winning grin—warm and affable. He waved at her, and she stopped.

"We've met!" he called in Spanish, as he walked across the sand toward her.

He was dressed casually, in loose gray trousers and a red polo shirt, but very stylish. He carried his huaraches in his hand.

"Have we?" They'd moved closer to me, and I could see the deep lines around his eyes, furrows that extended into his temples and upper cheeks.

"Lew Riley," he said, holding out his hand.

"I can't quite remember..."

"Los Angeles, I think. Perhaps the Hollywood Canteen... you know... Bette Davis's project to help the war effort. Everyone went there. You must have gone, too."

"I was back in Mexico by 1942, so I don't think so. Maybe a party..."

"At the Yacht Club! Have you been there?"

"Oh yes! Have you?"

"I own it!"

Lola smiled. "Ah! Now I remember. Your brother Beach introduced us."

Lew and Miles Beach Riley were the sons of a wealthy Pennsylvania businessman who had made millions with Union Carbide. After their mother died, the boys visited Mexico and fell in love with a sleepy little fishing village called Acapulco. They decided to stay and eventually opened the Club de Yates, which soon became the place to be and be seen.

But Lew also loved film and was fascinated with Hollywood. He and Lola knew the same people and quickly became involved in an animated conversation. She'll be busy all morning, I thought. She needs a man. She never goes to a party or an opening without an escort. She always has to be hanging on some guy's arm.

I closed my eyes and dreamed of Gabe...sweet and gentle, strong and safe. "There will never be another like him," I said to myself. "I'm not like Lola. If I can't be with Gabe, I'd rather be alone."

Lola and Lew strolled together along the shore. Words wafted toward me on the breeze... *Marlene... Greta... Bette... Cary.* I dozed awhile, then opened the picnic basket the hotel had provided and fished out an enchilada dripping with sauce, along with a dish, flatware, and napkins. I took out a copy of John P. Marquand's *Point of No Return* and began reading.

Before I knew it, the sun was hanging low and faint in the sky, and Lola and Lew were approaching slowly, hand in hand. Lola's portion of our lunch lay untouched in the picnic basket.

"Let's go back to the Club for supper," suggested Lew.

I wasn't sure whether I was included in the invitation, but then Lew said, "I'll bring a friend. I'm sure Mara will find him interesting."

"You know, Mara," Lola confided as we walked toward the hotel, "it just occurred to me that today, for the first time in years, I felt completely at ease with a man. Lew is so knowledgeable and entertaining. I laughed with him and cried with him, all in one day. I can't remember a time when I've been happier." Her face glowed with excitement.

"Take it slowly, *amiga*," I told her. "Don't be too quick to jump into the fire." Or, I thought, you'll wind up like a suckling pig on a spit with a celery stalk up its ass. I laughed to myself. I was beginning to sound like Tía Emi.

Lew was ten years Lola's junior, even though he looked older, and she'd had enough experience with younger men to know such relationships could be treacherous. Why, I wondered, does she want to do this again? Didn't she learn her lesson with Orson?

That evening, Lew was waiting for us at the Club de Yates

in a white dinner jacket with a black bow tie. Lola wore a mauve silk cocktail dress with a halter top and a deep décolleté. I was underdressed, but pretended not to care.

"Mara," said Lew suavely, "I'd like you to meet my friend Dutch Janssen."

I smiled and held out my hand.

"My real name is Erik," said Lew's friend, "but everyone calls me Dutch. My parents were born in Amsterdam."

He had soft blue eyes, blond hair that was turning white at the temples, and an easy grin. Lew offered us drinks, then led us to the Captain's Corner, an ample table in a premier spot next to the window, with a magnificent view of the sea and the yachts moored at the dock. A waiter brought champagne in an ornate ice bucket.

I can't remember what we talked about, but I imagine Lew and Lola reminisced again about Hollywood. What I do remember is Dutch's beautiful smile, his attentive gaze, his mellow voice. He was soft-spoken and courteous. I forgot I was wearing plain white linen slacks and a sailor blouse. I laughed at his jokes and told him about Tía Emi, who never spent a penny on herself but left us a small fortune—at least, it seemed like a fortune to me—when she died. He squeezed my hand.

"I'd like to see you again," he whispered when we said good-night.

"I don't think so," I murmured. "I'm leaving for Los Angeles soon. So no," I said softly.

"I'm sometimes in Los Angeles," he insisted.

I smiled and squeezed his hand back. "No," I whispered.

That night, I had the hotel room all to myself. I didn't see Lola again until the following afternoon, when I caught sight of her frolicking in the waves with her new love.

44

Los Angeles, 1949–1951
Discoveries

We returned home at the end of the summer, and I still hadn't learned anything new about my mother. Doña Antonia promised to ask around, but without the surnames of the owner of the hacienda, she had nothing to go on. She didn't remember anyone called Adalberto or Verónica.

I settled back into my usual routine at the beauty shop. Marie wanted me to take over as manager. She was tired, she said. She had to slow down.

"I really can't," I told her. "Maybe in a couple of years, when Lexie's in college."

"She's not a baby," snapped Marie.

Marie had changed, and I knew why. Her son, Bobby, who had been stationed in the Pacific, came home traumatized. At least he came home alive, I thought, but still, I felt sorry for her. She'd been a wreck while he was away, and now that he was back, she was still a wreck—short-tempered, bleary-eyed, given to crying jags.

"I'll see what I can do," I said. "Gabi has her driver's license now. Maybe she can take her sisters to school in the Ford, and I can take the trolley. We'll work something out." In the end, though, I didn't take the trolley. I bought myself a new Chevy.

"Thank you, Mara," she whispered. "Shell shock is awful…
and now Rick…well, he just can't face what's happened to
Bobby. He's started drinking. I just can't…can't take any more.
I'm sorry I was cross."

I handed her a Kleenex.

"Tell you what," she said, sniffing back the tears. "You can
have my best customer, Lucille Carver. She'll talk to you for
hours about the movies."

She stumbled over to the row of big black dryers lined up
against the wall, their hoods bent over chairs like kindly, pro-
tective giants. They were resting now, but during our busiest
hours their roar could split your eardrums. She slumped down
under one of them and stared into space.

That Sunday afternoon, the girls and I piled into my new
Chevy and drove downtown to the Rialto cinema, where
they were showing *Doña Perfecta*, starring Dolores del Río.

"Tía Lola!" squealed Lexie when she saw her on-screen.

After the show, I took the girls to dinner at Mario's—a real
treat for them because we almost never ate out. In spite of the
money I'd inherited from Tía Emi, I was frugal. After all, I
still had to educate the younger girls, and besides, I thought we
might have a wedding in our future. Lolly's boyfriend, John,
had gotten his degree in electrical engineering and was already
making good money working for Westinghouse, and Lolly was
teaching—not in the lily-white school Tía Emi had envisioned,
but in a barrio she herself had chosen. She was happy, she said.
Those were the kids who needed her most, and she was making
a difference in their lives. But she didn't know how long she'd
continue, because she and John were planning to get married.
My God, I thought, in a few years I might be a grandmother!

"Wow," said Lolly, biting into her pizza. "Tía Lola still
has it!"

"Has what?" asked Lupe.

"*It*. You know, pizzazz, sex appeal."

"No, she doesn't," retorted Lupe. "She's old!"

"She's only forty-seven," I said. "Two years older than me."

"Exactly!" mumbled Lupe. "Old!"

But Lupe was wrong. Lola looked wonderful and yes, sexy. Perfect skin, smooth and taut. She was gorgeous, even queenly, as Doña Perfecta, in her mantilla and brocade dresses.

"I read she got thirty-five thousand pesos for this film," piped up Gabi. "She and María Félix are the highest paid actresses in Mexico!"

I sighed. "Eat your pizza."

The shop was closed on Sundays and Mondays, which gave me time to tackle a task I'd put off for over a year: going through Tía Emi's things. She'd left her sewing machine, fabrics, and pattern books to Gabi, but her workspace was still piled high with boxes of costume jewelry, photos, even newspaper clippings, which was surprising, given that she could hardly read.

"Probably most of that junk can just be thrown out," said Gabi as we sorted through it. "Who needs a bunch of mismatched earrings and crumbling newspapers from thirty years ago? And by the way, I'm happy to drive Lex and Lupe to school, and I'll be very careful. Don't worry about it."

I kissed her on the cheek.

We pulled down each of Tía Emi's precious boxes one by one. Gabi was right. Most of Tía Emi's stuff was rubbish. We threw away nearly all of it. Some of the photos were interesting though: me as a little girl at Don Francisco's house, me in my school uniform standing in the plaza where I learned what *play* meant, Gabe and me at our wedding. I had no idea who had taken those photographs. One in particular caught my eye: a group of men and women, all mestizo or Indian, lined up in two rows. I stared hard at the image. It was faded and frayed, and at first, I didn't recognize anyone, but then, I made out a familiar face. Tía Emi as a young woman, maybe seventeen or eighteen years old!

I turned the photo over. The names of all the people in the photo were listed in two lines, apparently in the same order in which they appeared. The old-fashioned handwriting was hard to decipher, but I finally made out *Mª Emilia*. There were no last names. At the top of the photo, a line read: "Household servants of the hacienda of Don Adalberto Morales y Pardo."

My heart skipped a beat. Adalberto Morales y Pardo. Now I knew the name of the hacienda owner.

I'd seen other photos like this in the archives in Mexico. Large landowners often had their staffs photographed so that if one of the domestics disappeared with a piece of the household silver or some other valuable, the hacendado could prove that the thief was his retainer. I squinted at the names again. The one next to María Emilia was crossed out. I could just make out an *M* at the beginning and the tail of another letter that extended below the line. *Mª Angélica? Mª Alejandra? Maya? Maruja?* I turned the photo over and stared at the girl standing beside my aunt. She was young, maybe fifteen or sixteen. She looked a little like Tía Emi, but I couldn't be sure.

None of the other photos was of particular interest, but a newspaper article, dated December 28, 1910, caught my attention. Like the photo, it was faded and faint, but with some effort, I was able to decipher most of it. "On Wednesday, December 28, the estate of Don Adalberto Morales y Pardo, in the area of Canatlán, was destroyed in a fire in which the whole family perished. Arson is suspected. Witnesses testify that peons and household servants from the estate fled the grounds..." I gasped. Now I knew not only the name of the landholder, but also the location of his property!

By then, telephone service existed between Mexico City and Los Angeles, but making a long-distance phone call was

complicated—you couldn't just dial a number, like now—
and astronomically expensive. I opted for a telegram instead.

Mrs. Carver hardly batted an eyelash when Marie explained
to her that I would be taking over as manager.

"I'd like Miss Mara to be your hairdresser," she said, as
though she were doing Mrs. Carver a big favor. "I'll be working fewer hours from now on. I have to… I have a lot of responsibilities at home."

"I understand," said Mrs. Carver. "No one came out of the
war unscathed." She squeezed Marie's hand. "You've been a
good friend for over fifteen years," she said. "I'm sure Miss
Mara and I will get along just fine."

She sat down in my chair. For a moment, she was silent,
but then, she launched into a description of *A Streetcar Named
Desire*, starring the incredibly handsome Marlon Brando. "Oh
my God," she breathed. "I couldn't take my eyes off him."

After a while, Marie came over to make sure everything
was going smoothly.

"Listen," Mrs. Carver said to her, "isn't it weird that they
changed that famous sign in the hills from *Hollywoodland* to
Hollywood? The Los Angeles City Council decided to make it
official because this area has been called Hollywood for ages."

"I guess so," said Marie. "Frankly, I don't care one way or
the other."

Mrs. Carver was pensive for a moment.

"To be honest, neither do I," she said finally. Then she settled back into her chair and began to leaf through *Star World*.

The following week, Lola telegraphed me that her mother
had heard of the Morales y Pardo family, although she didn't
know them personally. She believed that the owner, his wife,
and their children had all died in a fire, but there might be
relatives. She'd ask around.

I wrote a letter thanking her. Now there was nothing to
do but wait.

45

A stinging rain drenched the mourners. A typical July storm, with drops that smarted like nails. Lola took Lew's arm and wedged herself under the umbrella. Londres Street was replete with admirers who had come to pay their last respects. Some sobbed uncontrollably. Lola and Lew inched toward the Casa Azul, the house where Frida first opened her eyes and where she closed them forever.

I followed at a distance. Doña Antonia had located a distant relative of Don Adalberto's, Elvira Pardo y López de Irizarry, and I'd returned to Mexico for two weeks to investigate.

But then, Frida died.

In the Casa Azul, Frida lay on her four-poster bed, looking as if she had just fallen into a deep and tranquil sleep. She was dressed in a black Tehuana skirt and a huipil—a loose, white, Oaxaca-style tunic embroidered with red and yellow flowers. Her left foot, pasty and limp but with vivid crimson toenails, jutted out from under her petticoats. Her right leg had been amputated the previous year due to gangrene.

"My body is putrefying," she'd said. "Soon the rest of me will rot."

However, lying there among red roses and bows, Frida

did not evoke decay but exuberance and life. The hues of her tunic harmonized with the flowers and ribbons woven into her braids. She wore a ring on every finger, just as always. Long, dangling earrings hung from her lobes. Elaborate necklaces rested on her throat and chest—pebbled collars of textured silver, ropes of silver and jade beads. Frida was as dazzling in death as she'd been in life.

"Where's Diego?" Lola whispered to Frida's sister, Cristina. But Cristina was too choked with tears to answer.

"He locked himself in his room," said a woman I didn't recognize. "He doesn't want to see anyone. He's too upset."

"That's Emma Hurtado, Diego's new lover," whispered Isolda, Cristina's daughter, without a trace of irony. "She's also his agent."

What? I thought. Diego's hiding in his room, disconsolate, but is already sleeping with another woman?

In the late afternoon, Frida's sisters removed the expensive jewelry from her corpse, leaving only a necklace from Tehuantepec and some tin baubles. Then funeral workers placed her body in a coffin to transport to the National Institute of Fine Arts to lie in state. David, Lola's chauffeur, drove Lola, Lew, and me to the Institute, where the coffin, surrounded by bouquets, rested on a black cloth with a placard that read: "Magdalena Carmen Frieda Kahlo y Calderón de Rivera, July 7, 1910–July 13, 1954." Frida had actually been born in 1907, but claimed 1910 as her birth year to identify more closely with the Revolution.

Frida's admirers streamed by, most weeping, some too suffocated by grief to weep. Diego had come in and now stood by the coffin. Friends from Diego's days as a Communist militant patted his shoulders and comforted him.

"She's not dead! She's not really dead!" Diego wailed. "We can't cremate her like this, not while she's still alive!"

Andrés Iduarte, director of the Institute and an old class-mate of Frida's, had given permission for her to lie in state, but had forbidden political speeches or paraphernalia at the event. The cavernous hall was adorned with flowers and keepsakes, but no party flags or symbols. Occasionally groups of mourners burst into one of Frida's favorite corridos—ballads of love and loss—but nothing radical.

Suddenly, a man erupted from Diego's circle and threw an enormous red flag with a hammer and sickle over the casket. Iduarte glared. "How dare Rivera play political games at his wife's funeral! The flag has to go!" he barked. Then, lowering his voice, "It's illegal to display that flag! I'll lose my job!"

But Diego stood his ground. "I am a Communist," he thundered, "and Frida was a Communist! The flag stays!"

Iduarte was beside himself. He got on the phone and placed calls to every public official he could think of, but no one was reachable. At last, former president Lázaro Cárdenas took his place in the honor guard beside Frida's coffin and gave permission for the flag to remain. Cárdenas was a national hero. He had the last word.

"This is a farce," I whispered to Lola. "Pure spectacle!"

"Of course! Frida would have loved it!"

"We should have known Frida's last hurrah would be filled with drama," said Lew, taking Lola's hand in the car. "I didn't know her very well, but well enough to expect a spectacular closing scene."

"I just can't believe she's gone. She was just forty-seven years old, three years younger than I am."

Lew kissed her fingers, and she smiled feebly.

She'd finally found the right man, I thought. I was pleased for her. Lew had moved into La Escondida shortly after I'd returned to Los Angeles, but they kept the arrangement quiet because Mexican society still frowned on unmarried couples

living together. The last thing she needed was to have her re-
bounding career sabotaged by gossip columnists. She seemed
calmer now, more at ease with herself. She accepted that she
would have to share the title of First Lady of Mexican Cinema with María Félix and play older characters, but her face
was still in the magazines. She'd won an Ariel for best actress
in *Doña Perfecta*, and, although there were fewer film offers
than before, she was working. Best of all, Lew was at her side.
Good, I thought. She deserves to be happy.

"We should get some sleep," Lew said after supper. "Tomorrow will be torturous."

"Frida always loved to be the center of attention," whispered Lola without sarcasm, "and tomorrow, she will be."

It was still pouring the following day. Muddy rivulets
formed in the streets, and the sky growled like a lion, creating a soundtrack of background noise. The marble steps in
front of the Institute were slippery and treacherous, and Lola
held on to Lew as she tottered toward the entrance. I grabbed
a handrail.

Inside, hundreds of mourners had gathered around the coffin singing Frida's favorite Revolutionary ballads. The same
crowd as the day before, only more. In a few moments, the
throng separated so that the coffin could pass. Diego and his
friends hoisted it into the air and gingerly carried it out into
the deluge.

The spikelike drops of the previous day had given way to
plump, juicy globules that crashed and exploded on the slick,
smooth stone. Diego struggled to keep his balance. His enormous shoes splashed and sloshed like otters on a riverbank.
The men took the stairs one step at a time, teetering, then
shifting their weight, wobbling, and transferring the bulk of
the casket from this side to that. One step, then another, then
another until they reached the sidewalk, where the hearse was

waiting to take Frida to the shabby crematorium at the Panteón de Dolores.

The atmosphere inside was asphyxiating. Frida's family, friends, and Communist cronies crammed into the tiny space. Outside, hundreds of mourners crowded under umbrellas or covered their heads with rebozos. In the anteroom lay Frida, crowned in red carnations. Carlos Pellicer read a poem he had written for her, and then the mourners burst once more into song.

Adiós, Mariquita linda
(Goodbye, lovely Mariquita)
ya me voy con el alma entristecida
(I'm going away, my soul dejected and sad)

The doors of the oven opened. Diego clenched his fists and tightened his jaw. Frida's sister Cristina began to sway back and forth as if she were going to faint. Isolda clutched her chest, fighting back nausea. Lola wept with the controlled elegance of a leading lady, grasping Lew's arm, but without emitting a sound. Every eye was fixed on the cart holding Frida's body— its slow, relentless movement toward the flames. Suddenly, everyone started grabbing at Frida's hands as if to hold her back.

"Don't go, Frida!" wailed a heavyset woman in black.

"Adiós, Fridita linda!" moaned a spindly man with a mustache.

They were crowding around her, in spite of the heat from the furnace, and pulling off her rings or tearing at her flowers. They wanted mementos—a piece of tin jewelry, a ribbon, a snippet of lace, anything at all. They wanted to show their children and grandchildren that they possessed something that had once belonged to Frida Kahlo.

Lola trembled, and Lew put his arm around her. In Hollywood, Lola hadn't known Frida well, but once she returned to

Mexico, Frida had behaved like a true friend, introducing her to people who could help relaunch her career. Frida was temperamental and unpredictable, but she could also be extraordinarily generous. Lola loved her. I could see she was suffering.

The cart continued its laborious journey. Cristina started to scream uncontrollably. "I'm sorry for all the things I did to hurt you, Frida! I'm sorry I wasn't a better sister! I'm sorry I slept with Diego!"

"Stop, Mother!" cried Isolda. "Stop!"

A gust of heat from the oven thrust Frida up into a sitting position. Her hair burst into flames, creating an aureole around her face. Her lips parted into a smile. The mourners gasped. Although she still had flesh, her cheeks were sunken, and her eyes were bulging and eerie. Then, she disappeared into the crematorium.

After what seemed like a long while, the furnace opened its doors and thrust what remained of Frida Kahlo de Rivera from its bowels. The powdery ashes shimmered like silver. They had preserved the form of her skeleton. Cristina buckled, then collapsed on the floor like a wad of rags, but Diego took out a pad and sketched this last image of his wife. Then he amassed her ashes and tied them in a cloth, which he placed in a small cedar box.

"I want to leave now, Lew," Lola whispered.

"There'll be a reception. It won't look right if you're not there."

"I can't take any more. There will be so many people, Diego won't even notice."

She took his arm, and they went out into the rain. I followed close behind. Lola was so engrossed in her grief that she'd forgotten I was there. The cool, clean air felt good on my face. I have to admit that I hadn't known Frida well enough to feel much of anything.

46

A few days after the funeral, I had lunch with Doña Antonia at her house next to La Escondida. It was less cluttered than Lola's place, more traditional in design. Heavy, Spanish-style furniture distributed sparsely about the parlor. One lordly, silver-framed mirror above the sofa.

Esperanza brought us roast chicken and rice. Doña Antonia had to be careful with her diet, she explained. She had to avoid cholesterol and salt. I watched her pick up her napkin and spread it over her lap. Plump blue veins were visible under her thinning skin, and brown spots, some as large as dimes, dotted the backs of her hands. Esperanza served the lemonade, her arms trembled slightly. We're all growing older, I thought. Ladies and maids alike.

Doña Antonia said grace, crossed herself, and took a breath. "About your family," she began. "I've asked around but I haven't been well."

"I understand," I said.

"However, I've located a woman Doña Elvira. I spoke to her on the phone, but I really didn't understand much of what she said. She lives here in the capital."

I was relieved. I had no desire to make the long trip to Durango, even though now, I could afford to hire a car.

I spent a while figuring out exactly how I would frame the story I was going to tell the woman Doña Antonia had contacted. Finally, Lola's chauffeur drove me to a once-tony part of Mexico City, where Doña Elvira lived in a substantial but not spectacular colonial house.

A maid answered the door in traditional garb—a black dress with a white apron and mop cap of the kind that hadn't been used in Mexico for decades. She looked to be about seventy and rather frail.

She showed me into the parlor, where another elderly lady sat, this one even more fragile looking.

Doña Elvira held out her hand without getting up.

"Laura, bring us some coffee and sweets," she commanded.

"*Sí, señora,*" said Laura. "I'll tell Obdulia to make a fresh pot and put together a tray."

A few minutes later, she tottered in with a large silver platter with a coffeepot, porcelain cups, and a selection of cinnamon, coconut, and almond cookies. The fragrance was divine. They must have been freshly baked.

I explained my mission to Doña Elvira, about Tía Emi and my search for Emi's sister, my mother. I asked about the girl in the photograph whose name had been scratched out. Doña Elvira, leaning forward in her seat, seemed to be hanging on to my every word. But then I realized she had fallen asleep! She was sleeping with her eyes open!

"Doña Elvira!" I called. "Did you hear me?"

She snapped to attention. "Yes, dear?"

"The hacienda…"

"Oh, they're all dead."

"Do you remember Don Adalberto and Doña Verónica?"

"Who?"

I repeated my story.

She stared at me, confused. "Who are you, dear?"

"Do you remember a seamstress named Emilia Rojas-Moreno?"

"Dead! They're all dead! They died a long time ago! Dead! Dead! Dead!"

I thanked her for the coffee and cookies and got up to leave. She watched me pick up my purse and turn toward the door. Then, without warning, she let out a shriek.

"Laura! Laura!" she screamed. "This woman is a thief! She wants to steal my silverware!"

She pulled herself up, and, with an agility of which I wouldn't have believed her capable, she grabbed a fork and lunged at me. Before she could thrust it into my cheek, Laura grasped both her arms and eased her back into the chair.

"There there, Señora Elvira. This nice lady only came to visit. She doesn't want your silver."

I made a beeline for the door. David was slumped down in the driver's seat, smoking. He apparently hadn't expected the meeting to be so short, but the moment he saw me stumbling down the path, he leaped out of the automobile and opened the door.

"Señora, wait!" called someone behind me.

I turned and saw that it was Laura.

"Apologies, señora," she said. "Señora Elvira is not always like that, but lately it happens more and more often. I just wanted to say, I think I might be able to help you."

"In what way?" I was inching back toward the car.

"I knew the Morales y Pardo hacienda. I worked on a neighboring estate, on the hacienda of Don Gustavo Kehlmann. Don Gustavo and Don Adalberto were friends, and the Morales y Pardo family sometimes visited with their children and some of the staff."

"Oh?"

"I was Doña Paulina's personal maid and wasn't up on much of the gossip, but I did hear that Pedro, Don Gustavo and Doña Paulina's youngest son, was quite smitten with a laundress from the Morales hacienda. So smitten, in fact, that Don Gustavo asked Don Adalberto to let her come and work for him. In those days, servants were like sewing needles. If you lost one, you could replace it without too much trouble, so it's not surprising that Don Adalberto said yes. That's probably the girl whose name was scratched out on the photo you saw. They scratched it out because she no longer worked there."

"Do you remember her name? You worked together in the same house."

"I never knew her name."

"Thank you, Laura," I said, "and thank you for saving me from being stabbed with a fork." I turned back toward the car, but then I thought of something else.

"One other thing, Laura. Why did you leave the Kehlmanns?"

She hesitated a moment. "Something awful happened. One morning, Pedro's servant went in to open his curtains and found him dead!"

"Dead? How did he die?"

"I don't know, señora. Some disease, maybe. Perhaps a heart attack. All I can tell you is that his mother was so disconsolate that she moved back to Mexico City to live with an aging aunt and uncle. Naturally, as her maid, I went with her. I never returned to Durango."

"And the laundress?"

"I don't know what happened to her."

"Where is Doña Paulina now?"

"She died of grief, señora. Not long afterward."

My head was spinning. When I'd seen the photo of the

Morales-Pardo servants, I thought I detected a resemblance between the girl whose name was crossed out and Tía Emi. Was she Tía Emi's sister—and therefore my mother? The old ballad came back to me: "Don Pedro loved Miguela—" Was it about Pedro Kehlmann and the laundress?

"Thank you, Laura," I said. "You've been very helpful. Uh, the laundress," I called as she entered the house, "do you know if she had any relatives?"

She turned around, looking puzzled.

"I don't know, señora. I really don't know anything about her."

She went into the house and closed the door.

47

Lola was down in the dumps and so was I. Let's start with Lola.

The Golden Age of Mexican Cinema was over, she said, and the junk the studios were making—cheap tearjerkers and silly comedies—was nothing like the beautiful films of the forties—*Flor Silvestre*, *María Candelaria*, those films.

"Today's audiences want foreign stuff, or else soppy Mexican melodramas," she complained. "There are more American, Italian, and French movies in Mexican theaters than Mexican."

"She's been in a funk for weeks," Lew confided. "She didn't make a single picture last year except a botch-up mess called *Señora Ama*, directed by her cousin Julio Bracho."

"Well," I said. "*Gatitas* always land on their feet. I'm sure something will come up."

"We do have our production company," said Lew. "I was thinking we could work out something for Lola through that. Falmouth Theater in Massachusetts is always asking me to do a project with them."

A few years before, in 1953, Lew and Lola had launched Producciones Visuales to provide the material paraphernalia for film and theater productions. It had seemed like a good investment at the time, but so far, nothing much had come of it.

"You mean theater?" said Lola when Lew mentioned it to her one day as they were having lunch on the patio. "I'm a movie actress. I can't do live theater."

"You can do anything you set your mind to, Lola. Maybe it's time to try something new."

She laughed and kissed him on the forehead. "You know, darling, I think you're right."

She got up and went inside, then rummaged through her desk and pulled out her phone book.

"What are you looking for?" Lew asked.

"The phone number of Stella Adler. If I'm going to be a stage actress, I'd better learn technique, and Stella Adler is the best acting coach in the business."

I hadn't been back in Mexico for two years, not since Frida's funeral and my visit to Doña Elvira—two remarkable years during which I managed Marie's beauty salon, planned Gabi's wedding, attended Lupita's graduation from nursing school and Lexie's from high school, and helped Lexie with her college applications. None of my daughters would be a hairdresser, like me. None of them had opted for cosmetology school. Best of all, I became a grandmother! Lolly and John had had their first baby the previous June, and I took a leave from Marie's to care for little Nicholas, the sweetest ball of giggles and talcum powder you've ever seen. By then, Marie's son, Bobby, was doing better, and she was once again able to manage the shop.

So why was I down in the dumps? With all the activity back home, I hadn't been able to return to Mexico to continue my search. Now that I was here, though, I planned to spend a week in Durango interviewing people who might remember the Morales-Pardo family, examining birth and death records, and ploughing through newspaper archives in search of information about the fire. Most important, I had to find out more about the laundress who had stolen Pedro

Kehlmann's heart. Was she really Miguela Ruiz, the betrayed lover from the ballad?

Lew and Lola were leaving for Acapulco in Lew's car, so Lola asked David to drive me to Durango. I'd told Lola about my visit to Doña Elvira's, and she understood how urgent it was for me to find out more about the mysterious laundress. David dropped me off at the Hotel Carlota, a grandiose colonial-style building with sweeping, arched windows, graceful balconies, and a massive front door of carved Mexican oak. How different from my last trip to Durango, I thought, as I looked around my bright, sunlit room.

I reviewed my to-do list: examine the church records in Canatlán, check the archives of the local newspaper, interview anyone who had known the Morales-Pardos or the Kehlmanns. In the morning, David drove me to Canatlán, but as I'd been told, the birth and death registers had been badly damaged during the Revolution. I did see that Gustavo Kehlmann had died in 1932, and that he was survived by one son, Mauricio. There was also mention of a son named Gustavo, who had died in the Revolution at age twenty-four, and another son, Pedro, who had died in 1906, at the age of twenty—it didn't say how. In the Landholders' Registry, Gustavo Kehlmann's property was listed, but there was no inventory of his belongings or photograph of his servants.

In the morning, I set off for the library to have a look at copies of old newspapers. "For local news and gossip," said the librarian, "you might want to check *La Verdad*. It's more a monthly scandal sheet than a newspaper, but you might find what you're looking for."

What I found was mostly a mixture of political news and local gossip: June 1906. Labor unrest erupts in the haciendas, more than twenty peons killed and many more injured. July 1906. The mutilated body of Don Esteban Mendoza y Montenegro found dead in the coal bin of his manor. Authorities suspect his wife and her reputed lover, Bernardo Ortiz, the family physician.

But then: Pedro Kehlmann y Mendoza, youngest son of Don Gustavo Kehlmann y Abdendaño, was found stabbed to death at his father's estate. Don Gustavo blames the laundress Miguela Ruiz, and has sworn to kill her and every member of her family.

So, I thought, Pedro Kehlmann hadn't died of a heart attack or a disease. He had, in fact, been murdered by Miguela Ruiz. Laura had lied, but why? I thought back to the photograph of the Morales y Pardo servants. The name that had been scratched out began with an *M* and had a letter that extended below the line: Miguela. I shuddered. If Miguela was actually my mother, that meant I was the daughter of a murderess. No wonder Tía Emi believed my life was in danger. Gustavo Kehlmann had sworn vengeance. But why hadn't he gone after Tía Emi? I wondered. He probably didn't realize the two women were sisters. After all, they didn't have the same last names.

If only I could remember the *corrido*. That was the key. *"Don Pedro amaba a Miguela. / La persiguió noche y día."* I closed my eyes. Little by little, I pieced together the first stanza.

Don Pedro amaba a Miguela
(Don Pedro loved Miguela)
La persiguió noche y día
(He pursued her night and day)
La agarró sola en la cuadra
(When he saw her alone in the stables)
La tumbó y dejó con cría
(He knocked her down and left her expecting)

La tumbó y dejó con cría. What ever happened to the baby? I wondered. Was I that baby?

48

Instead of heading back to La Escondida, David drove me to Acapulco, where the famous New York acting coach, Stella Adler, had already begun preparing Lola for her new role as Anastasia.

"Your little dog Fiesta is playing in the garden," Stella was saying. "She chases her tail. She wrestles with the hose. She jumps up on the decorative rock by the flowerbed, but her little claws slip and slide on the stone until she tumbles off. She picks herself up and scampers across the lawn because she's heard Lew's car roll into the driveway. You're smiling. You see her. I can tell by the way your face has brightened. Now a shadow approaches, a man. He is creeping across the garden, looking this way and that to see if anyone is watching. He approaches Fiesta. She begins to yap playfully, and he crouches down to pet her. He says soothing words to her, running his hands gently over the fur behind her neck. Then, suddenly, he grabs her by the scruff of the neck and bashes her head against the rock, splattering blood and brains all over the flowerbed."

Lola gasps, screams, and recoils. Tears gush out of her eyes as she presses her hand to her mouth. She is trembling. "No," she whispers. "No!"

"That's it! That's what I'm looking for!"

As though in a daze, Lola stares at the woman standing before her. Then she smiles. "Oh my God, Stella!"

"That's the difference between movie acting and the stage, Lola. In film, you can count on the camera to capture the emotion, to show a close-up of the tear in your eye or the sweat on your brow, which, of course, can be put there by a makeup artist wielding an eyedropper. But onstage, you have to play your role in a different way."

"I just can't believe what I felt when you described that horrible scene."

"Now, think of the real Anastasia. She witnessed the Bolsheviks massacre her entire family. What did she feel? Seeing a scene in your mind is the same as seeing it in reality in terms of the emotional response it elicits. How did you react when you saw Fiesta murdered? Think of your mental state. What did your body do? Your hands? Your shoulders?"

Lola shook her head and pursed her lips. Stella lit a cigarette and waited for Lola to regain her composure.

"Now, remember when your father died. What did you feel?"

Lola shook her head again and swallowed. "No, Stella, I can't."

"Do you think remembering your father's death would help you to play this role better?"

Lola knew she was supposed to say yes.

"No," she said resolutely. "No, I don't. I think it would paralyze me entirely. I'd get too upset. I'd lose control of my acting."

Stella fixed her gaze on the sea. A syrupy sun oozed light through the massive picture window of the Yacht Club ballroom. "Yes," she said finally. "You're exactly right. Memory work is of limited effectiveness because actors must be able to play characters whose experience is way outside their own. As I've said before, 'The ideas of the great playwrights are almost always larger than the experiences of even the best actors.'"

It had been a grueling morning. Stella Adler had agreed to come to Acapulco to coach Lola for two weeks, to the tune of $750 a class. An exorbitant fee, but in Lola's view, worth it. Naturally, I had no idea who Stella was when Lola called me in Durango and told me she wanted me to meet "the best acting coach in the world," but during the days that followed, Lola and Lew filled me in on her remarkable story.

The daughter of two luminaries of the New York Jewish theater, she'd been acting since she was five. A sassy blonde with a pert nose and a disarming smile, she'd starred in a slew of Broadway plays and Hollywood films, but what really interested her was the art of acting. She'd seen the great Russian actor-director Konstantin Stanislavski in the 1930s and was knocked off her feet by the power of his performances. Stanislavski was new. He was dynamic. His method for training actors was like nothing she'd ever heard of. Until then, acting coaches concentrated on voice training and movement, but Stanislavski thought that the actor had to go beyond the physical. He proposed a new method, the "art of experiencing," which required actors to explore their subconscious in order to find feelings similar to their character's. When Lee Strasberg launched the Stanislavski movement in New York, Stella joined him. Then, in 1934, she left for Russia and on the way back, spent five weeks in Paris studying with Stanislavski himself.

In 1949, she opened the Stella Adler Studio of Acting. By then, she had abandoned the Stanislavski method and developed techniques of her own. She'd trained talented young actors like Marlon Brando, Judy Garland, and Elizabeth Taylor, and that's why, when Falmouth Theater contracted Lola to play the lead in *Anastasia*, a new play by the French writer Marcelle Maurette, Lola knew whose number to dial.

"Okay," said Stella, brushing her blond curls off her temples. The heat was oppressive in spite of the sea breezes. "What's this play about?"

"Well, Russian expatriates living in Berlin decide to make a killing by circulating the story that Anastasia, the youngest daughter of Tsar Nicholas II, survived the Bolshevik attack on the royal family. They choose a suicidal amnesia victim to impersonate Anastasia, but she plays her role so well that it's not clear whether she's the real Anastasia, a talented scammer, or a delusional nobody convinced she's royalty."

"That's the plot, but what's the play really about?"

Lola thought for a while. "Maybe about the ability of a person to believe what she wants to be true. I'm not really sure..."

"But as the actress, you have to decide, because that will determine how you play her."

Lola gazed out the window. Gulls floated through space like large petals borne by the breeze. Their cries harmonized with the lap of the waves, creating a gentle sonata. Garlands of light fell across the sand.

I was spellbound watching the two of them. At fifty-five, Stella Adler had spent fifty years in the theater and spoke with authority. Yet, she seemed to be a warm, practical woman. Except for her outsize earrings and glittery rings, her clothes were simple. That day, she wore a plain white button-down shirt and a full yellow skirt, cinched at the waist. Nothing pretentious. With Lola, she was frank and matter-of-fact.

Lola was in her fifties, too, and here she was, taking instruction, learning new techniques, starting over. By the end of the first evening, she was exhausted.

"What did you think?" she asked me.

"Amazing!"

"Come, let's go for a swim." She knew I didn't know how to swim. She'd be doing the swimming while I lounged.

We left Stella dozing on a chaise longue on the balcony, slipped into our bathing suits, and took off for the ocean. The salty water always invigorated Lola and sharpened her mind, but I sensed anxiety buzzing in her gut like a swarm of bees.

"You're brave," I told her as we walked to the beach. "It takes courage to try something new."

"You're beginning something new, too," she said. "You're investigating your roots."

"It certainly brings me no comfort to think I might be the daughter of a legendary murderess," I said. "What will I tell my daughters?"

"We'll think of something," she laughed. "By the way, I just got a letter from Ramón. He's trying new things, too. He hasn't had any movie roles lately, but he's doing television, taking singing lessons, even doing summer stock, just to keep performing."

"You've got to hand it to him," I said. "He's a trooper!"

We'd reached the sand. Lola threw down her things and ran toward the water. I stretched out in the shade of an umbrella and listened to the ceaseless splashing, the cries and caws, the wind whining like a violin—the sounds of eternal life. The beach symphony would continue long after both of us were nothing more than a memory. Would it really matter if Lola relaunched her career...or, for that matter, who my mother was? But for now, we had to live in the moment. Lola had to prepare her next career move, and I had to decide how do deal with Miguela Ruiz.

There were still so many unanswered questions. If Gustavo died in 1932 and his eldest son predeceased him, who killed Miguela? Was it Mauricio, his second son? And why had Laura lied about Pedro's death? The pieces just didn't fit together. I hated the idea of returning to Doña Elvira's, but I knew I had to speak with Laura again.

Unfortunately, it would have to wait for another trip. Summer sessions at LA schools were about to begin, and I'd promised to watch Nicholas so Lolly could go back to work. On Saturdays, I would attend to my regular customers at Marie's. Mrs. Carver, who had switched her day from Thursday to Saturday, was due for a cut and color.

49

Massachusetts, Mexico City, Los Angeles, 1956
Transitions

The night before *Anastasia* opened on July 6, Lola lay awake watching shadows cross the ceiling like crows in flight. She knew that this performance had to be a success, or her career would really be over.

"Sleep during the day," Stella told her over the phone, "so you arrive at the theater rested."

Lola took a mild sedative that afternoon and felt better after her siesta.

But she needn't have worried. The reviews were fabulous.

She called me a few days later. "My room is filled with flowers and telegrams!" she told me.

I'd seen photos in the magazines. Lola in a navy dress with a sailor collar, designed to convey youth and innocence. Lola in an elegant white dress with a ruched bodice and a daring décolleté, designed to convey opulence and royalty.

"I'm no match for Marilyn Monroe," she said, "but I didn't look so bad. I only wish you were here to do my hair and give me moral support, Mara!"

But, as they say, only the sea is eternal, not fame. In September, the American papers were still writing about *Anastasia*—only not about the Falmouth production. A film with the same name, starring Ingrid Bergman, was set to open in December, and the critics were already buzzing that Bergman was Academy Award material. The play finished its run, and Lola returned to Mexico. She wanted to do more live theater in her own country and in her own language, but no offers materialized.

In mid-December she called, breathless with excitement. "I have news!" she blurted out.

I thought maybe she'd heard something about Miguela Ruiz.

"I just got a letter from Jean Sirol, the French cultural attaché. I'll read it to you.

December 14, 1956

Dear Miss del Río,
On behalf of the Ambassador of France to the Republic of Mexico, it is my honor to invite you to the Film Festival of Cannes, which will take place in May of next year, as a member of the jury to select the most outstanding films and film profession-als of 1956."

"That's wonderful," I said, trying not to sound too disappointed. "Congratulations, Lola."

"Well, this is one role where María Félix can't upstage me! Even if she someday gets to be a judge at Cannes, I'll always hold the honor of being the first woman!" She paused. "It would be terrific if you could come, too, Mara. I want my hair to look perfect, and you've never been to France. Besides, it would be so much more fun if you were there."

I would have loved to go to Cannes, but for the moment, it was out of the question. "Lolly just had her second baby," I said, "so I can't be away that long, but I could go to Mexico before your trip to help you get ready."

"I'd like that," she said.

50

Cannes, La Escondida, Los Angeles, 1957
The Ballad of Miguela Ruiz

I flew to Mexico in early April. Lola's head was swimming
with dreams of parties and passionate discussions about French
New Wave cinema with Jean-Luc Godard and François Truf-
faut. Exciting things were happening in Europe, she told me.
New Wave directors were abandoning the old-fashioned,
novel-inspired stories of previous generations and concen-
trating on social issues.

I'd decided to wait until after Lola had left for Europe to
contact Laura. One thing at a time, I told myself. Step by step.

The Mexican newspapers followed Lola's every move. In
Cannes, reporters surrounded her, their pencils grinding. Photographers followed her, their cameras clicking. Everywhere,
people fawned over her. The Begum Aga Khan, grandmother
of the Aga Khan, invited her to spend a few days at her villa.
Her fellow jurors even named her vice president of the festival!

Jean Cocteau, one of France's greatest writers and directors,
shepherded her around the city. With his long, thin, starched
body, he looked like a wafer on legs, one that could crack at
any moment, but the French intelligentsia worshipped him.

Every day the jurists watched screening after screening,
taking copious notes on the films. Miss del Río was drawn

to the war stories, reported *El Excélsior*, not the depiction of horror, but the face of human suffering. "Miss del Río opines that the director Andrzej Wajda has shown brilliantly the effects of violence on ordinary people struggling to resist the Nazis," wrote *Photoplay en español*. "When people understand what war is," Miss del Río argued to the jury, "they will strive for peace. Film has an important role to play in avoiding these catastrophes."

I was thrilled for Lola, truly I was. She was back in her element. But I couldn't spend my days reading movie magazines. I was preparing for my visit to Laura. How did she explain the discrepancy between her account of Pedro Kehlmann's death and the newspaper's? And who killed Miguela? "I don't want to call first," I told Doña Antonia. "I don't want to tip Laura off that I'm here and give her time to concoct some story…"

"You're right," said Doña Antonia. "It would be best just to knock on the door. Surprise her, but don't be confrontational. Don't make her feel like you're trying to catch her in a lie."

A few days later, David drove me to Doña Elvira's, but left me at the corner as a precaution. I came around the side of the house, then tiptoed up the steps.

"Be cheerful, not threatening," Doña Antonia had advised. I rehearsed the scene in my mind. "Laura! How nice to see you! I wondered if we could chat in private a moment."

I knocked. It took a while for Laura to answer. She looked haggard. "Laura!" I began. "How nice to see you!"

She glowered at me, a wolf ready to attack, then clutched my shoulder and shoved. I tottered, struggling to regain my balance. One step backward and I would go plummeting downward onto the hard stone, maybe crack my head. I grabbed the wrought iron handrail. She lunged and whacked my knuckles, but I held on. I'd thought she was frail, but I was wrong. I reeled toward her just as she attempted to slam the door in my face.

"I need to talk to you!" I rammed the door back against her. In spite of the throbbing in my temples, I tried to make my voice reassuring. "I don't want to hurt you, Laura. I just want to ask you a few questions." Once again, she lunged at me. I caught her arm and held fast. "Stop," I whispered. "Stop."

"What do you want?" she hissed. "The old lady is sleeping."

"Good, because it's you I want to talk to." I pushed myself into the house. "Let's go somewhere quiet."

Sullen, she led me to a small sitting room off the parlor. "Sit there," she commanded, as if giving an order to one of the parlormaids.

"How did Pedro Kehlmann die?" I asked, getting right to the point. I'd tried to follow Doña Antonia's advice to be gentle, but perhaps a direct approach would be more effective. "You told me he died of an illness, but the newspapers say he was murdered."

She pursed her lips. "I don't know," she said finally.

"What about the laundress who worked for the Kehlmanns? You had to know her name. You were both servants in the same house. You knew that Pedro was after her."

"I really don't remember, *señora*," said Laura. Her voice was once again soft and steady. She had reverted to her role of perfect lady's maid. "I served Doña Paulina. I had nothing to do with the others. I had my own room next to Doña Paulina's suite."

"Does the name Miguela Ruiz ring a bell?" I asked.

The color drained from her already pallid cheeks. Her hand trembled ever so slightly.

"No," she said after a long pause.

"Why did you follow me out to the car to feed me a pack of

lies the last time I was here?" I said, making my voice sharp. "I was on my way out! Why didn't you just let me leave?"

"I wanted to stop you from snooping around," she blurted out. "I thought that if you thought Pedro had died in his sleep, you'd let it go!"

"So Miguela Ruiz *did* murder Pedro Kehlmann," I murmured.

"No," said Laura. "She didn't."

I stared at her. "According to the newspapers…"

"She didn't kill him." Tears were streaming down her rutted cheeks.

"Laura!" called Doña Elvira from upstairs. "Laura! Obdulia!"

I stood up to block her exit. "You're not going anywhere until you explain this to me," I snapped. "I have the right to know what happened."

She glared at me through her tears with those lupine eyes. "I have to go! She's calling me!"

"Obdulia can go. I have the right to know," I repeated. "I'm Miguela Ruiz's daughter."

I expected her to fly into a fit. Instead, she said simply, "I know."

"You know?"

"Of course. You look just like him. Fair complexion, brown, wavy hair. I knew the moment I laid eyes on you."

"Like *him*? Like Pedro Kehlmann?"

"They were Austrian. Don Gustavo was born in Mexico, but his family was from Salzburg. So many foreigners settled around Durango. Gustavo's father was one of them."

"Laura!" called Doña Elvira.

"I'd better go to her," Laura said. "We can talk later."

"No," I said. "I want the truth now. What happened to my father? How do you know Miguela didn't kill him?"

"Alright," she said, sitting back down and drying her tears. "I'll tell you. You'd probably find out anyway. I know that Miguela didn't kill him because I did."

I felt as though a boulder had hit me in the chest. "What?" I stammered. "You?"

"Remember the song, Señora Mara? *'Se coló en sus aposentos / Lo encontró besando a otra.'* I was that other girl. He'd been cheating on her with me, but he was cheating on me with others. I saw Miguelita standing there, pregnant, and I knew my future. He would abandon me, just as he'd abandoned her. I flew into a rage, and I grabbed her dagger. Afterward, we— Miguelita and I—we made a pact. She couldn't stay at the Kehlmann hacienda because she was pregnant, so she would go back to the Morales estate, where her sister, Emilia, could hide her. Everyone would assume she was the murderess, but she didn't care, she said. She would leave as soon as she'd recovered from the delivery, she said. She knew how to disappear. I would stay put and go on as if nothing had happened. She promised to tell Emilia to contact me if anything went wrong. I washed up and went back to Doña Paulina's rooms. She was still sleeping while her favorite son lay dead in a far corner of the house in a pool of his own blood.

"Doña Paulina went berserk when she heard what had happened to Pedro. I felt miserable, not about him, but about her. I loved Doña Paulina. She'd pulled my mother, Gunnel, out of an Austrian orphanage, and then, when Don Gustavo got my mother pregnant, she'd given us a home. My mother went to work as a cook in Doña Paulina's kitchen. I grew up playing with the other children—the three boys, Gustavo, Mauricio, and Pedro—taking lessons with them, learning to read, learning to play chess and *Mühle.* I didn't know Pedro was my half brother, and neither did he. When I was around sixteen, he started to want to play a different kind of game.

By then, I'd become Doña Paulina's personal maid. I didn't want to hurt Doña Paulina, but… Pedro was just like his father…he couldn't keep his hands off the help. I wound up in his bed just like Miguela and all the other girls."

She was weeping quietly.

"So…" I whispered. "You're my father's sister…my aunt. Please go on. Did Emi ever contact you?" So… I wasn't the daughter of a murderess…

"It was my idea to move to the capital after Pedro died. I didn't want to see any of them ever again. I wanted to get away from the estate, and so did Doña Paulina. She'd lost interest in her husband years before, and Gustavo had gone away to study. Their second son, Mauricio, had married an uppity society girl and moved to her father's home. All three of us left Durango—Doña Paulina, my mother, and me. It wasn't until after we'd moved to the city that my mother told me Don Gustavo was my father. I started to hate him with a terrible hatred. After their eldest son died in the Revolution, Doña Paulina became ill. One minute she'd be fine, and then, for no reason at all, she'd swear that men wielding knives were hiding in corners, waiting to slit her throat. My mother and I swore to take care of her…until the end."

"You didn't answer my question," I said after a moment. I didn't mean to sound harsh, but I had to have an answer. "Did Emi ever contact you?"

"I contacted *her*. I told her that Doña Paulina and I were leaving Durango, and then later, I sent her my address in the capital. It wasn't easy to convey messages in those days. The mail service wasn't reliable and besides, it would have been suspicious, my writing to someone at the Morales estate. I had to wait until one of Doña Paulina's messengers left with a letter for Don Gustavo and bribe him to carry a note for me. Much later, when Emi was settled at Don Francisco Madero's house in the capital, she sent me her address. She told me you were with her, that you were safe and healthy, and that I should tell Miguela when I got a chance. Of course, neither of us knew when that would be. Miguela had said she would disappear, and she did. Where did she spend her nights and days? No one knew. In back alleys, maybe, or in some abandoned building."

"So did you ever get the chance to tell her that her daughter was okay?" I ask.

"Yes. Sometimes—maybe every six weeks or so—Miguela would sneak in late at night through the servants' entrance, and Obdulia and I would give her something to eat."

"Obdulia and you?"

"Obdulia... When they brought Gunnel to Mexico, they changed her name." She took a deep breath. "To Obdulia."

"Obdulia is your mother! And does she know about...what you did...to Pedro?"

"Of course she knows."

"And Tía Emi?"

"No, Miguela never told her. She wanted everyone to think she was the guilty one. She wanted to protect me, and she thought that if Emi knew the truth, she'd go to Don Gustavo. Miguela loved the notoriety, the legend that was growing up around her. She thought it was hilarious that everyone was looking for her. When the Revolution started, she became a soldadera—not just a camp follower, but a real woman soldier. She craved adventure. The war gave her the chance to take vengeance on men like Pedro Kehlmann. Afterward, she disappeared into the city's slums, but she remained in contact with me. Not with Emi, of course. There was still too much of a chance that Emi would go to the authorities. When Miguela became ill, she came here, and I cared for her until the end."

"She came *here*? Until the end? Who killed Miguela Ruiz?

If Don Gustavo died in 1932 and two of his sons died before him…was it Mauricio?"

"Nobody killed Miguela. She died of typhoid fever. Ordinarily, no one would notice when a woman like Miguela died, a slum rat who begged for food. But back in Durango, she was a legend. I sent an anonymous note to *La Verdad* that the notorious murderess Miguela Ruiz had died, and everybody who remembered the story of Pedro assumed she'd been murdered by someone in the Kehlmann clan. I also sent a telegram to your Tía Emi."

My head was spinning. I'd looked though the early copies of *La Verdad*, but never thought to examine the more recent ones. "One more thing," I murmured. "When did Doña Paulina die?"

Her eyes locked with mine. "I thought you were smarter than that." Her lips parted in a feeble smile. "I thought you would have figured it out by now. Doña Elvira is Doña Paulina. She wanted to obliterate the past. She wanted to be someone else, so Paulina Elvira became Elvira Paulina. This is the house we came to live in when we left Durango. We lived here with her aunt and uncle until they died. They had no children, so they left it to her. We've lived here together ever since—Elvira, Gunnel, and I."

I caught my breath. She got up and stood by the door.

"Are you going to inform the police?" she asked nervously.

"No, what for?"

"What for? I've just confessed to a murder."

I wrapped my arms around her. "You've relieved me of a terrible burden," I whispered. "Besides, this all happened so long ago. What would be the point of contacting the police?"

My embrace was not returned. She stood staring over my shoulder into space.

"Okay, then," she said. "Goodbye."

The following day, I left for Los Angeles.

"I've found out who your grandmother was," I told the girls during our next Sunday lunch. "She was a Revolutionary hero, a woman who stood up to abusive landowners and fought for justice." I didn't think the rest of the story was worth telling.

51

"Lew says there's a new movie offer!" announced Doña Antonia.

"I'd rather stay home and take care of you, Mami," said Lola. She was mixing up a batch of lemonade in the kitchen. It was Luz's day off, and Esperanza had gone to visit her niece.

"Don't you dare! I hate it when you fuss over me!"

"It's for the kind of film you love," piped in Lew from the hallway. "The kind that inspires. It's about the Revolution!"

I was back in Mexico for the summer—this time, just for a vacation.

"This film would give you another chance to work with the genius scenographer Gabriel Figueroa," interjected Lew. "And El Indio! But he's not directing. He'd be your leading man. The director is Ismael Rodríguez. And by the way," added Lew, "you'd have a costar."

Lola shrugged. "I don't mind sharing star billing with Emilio."

"No, not him. Someone else. A woman."

Lola frowned. She wasn't about to share the spotlight with another one of Emilio's teenage bed partners.

"María Félix!" said Lew calmly.

Doña Antonia burst into guffaws, then grabbed a handkerchief and began coughing violently. Lola poured her a glass of water and called for the nurse.

"See, Mami?" she said. "I need to be here with you!"

"You need to be on the set with María Félix, demonstrating how a real lady acts with a rival—gracious, friendly, diplomatic… This can't be easy for her either."

Lola agreed to read the script—the story of a passionate Revolutionary known as La Cucaracha who is madly in love with Colonel Antonio Zeta, played by El Indio. Zeta, however, is smitten with the widow Isabel, and naturally, the rivalry leads to an explosion.

"I will play La Cucaracha," announced Lola, putting down the batch of papers. She'd taken the script into her office and read the entire morning without pause. Lew slouched in a heavy armchair opposite her, pretending to read a book, but secretly observing her reactions.

"How can you think you'd play anyone but the cultured, elegant, Doña Isabel?" said Lew. "María will play the coarse, ragged Cucaracha. She could never play Doña Isabel."

As usual, Lola wanted me to go with her to her first meeting with María Félix. According to the press, María had a fiery personality and a colossal ego. Lola was sure she was going to insist on top billing. But Lola could be just as stubborn, and she had no intention of allowing her rival to grab the spotlight.

"If you're there," Lola said to me, "maybe she'll behave herself. She won't want you to witness a tantrum."

On the day of the appointment, I pulled a soft beige knit Chanel sheath with navy trim and a matching jacket out of Lola's closet. From her makeup box, I chose heavy eye shadow and Malaga-wine lipstick to highlight her high cheekbones and wide forehead. I combed her hair into a voluminous updo.

"You'll intimidate her with your sheer gorgeousness!" I quipped.

When we arrived at the studio for the contract negotiations, María was already there, also dressed to the hilt, in a short-waisted, powder blue Pierre Cardin jacket, and a matching skirt. I braced myself for a blowup.

"Don't give an inch," I whispered to Lola.

The two women stood staring at each other. Each was as breathtaking and resolute as the other. For a long while, no one said anything.

"Well," said María finally. "I read in the press that we hate each other."

"I've heard the same thing," responded Lola.

They stared at each other a minute more, tense and un-blinking.

Then, suddenly, both women burst out laughing.

"Gossip is like a snake waiting in the grass to bite the un-suspecting," murmured María.

Lola stepped back and ran her eyes from María's fedora all the way down to the tips of her Chanel shoes. "You're as stun-ning as they say you are," she said.

"So are you!"

I breathed a sigh of relief. In the end, they decided to share star billing. Their names would appear next to each other on the screen and on all publicity. It was the beginning of a long and satisfying friendship.

52

"Look!" she said, holding out her hand. "We did it!" She was downright giddy. The shiny gold wedding band and the diamond engagement ring glistened on her finger. "We finally got hitched. I wanted to do it before Mami…" Her voice cracked for a second. "I wanted her to see me married."

The sky was overcast, and the day was heavy, but Lola and I had driven to Santa Monica beach to spend the afternoon. It was too chilly to swim, so we sat on a bench on the boardwalk and licked ice cream cones like a couple of kids. "I'm sorry I couldn't be there," I said. What with work, the kids, and the grandkids… I just couldn't get away.

"It was a simple ceremony, but lovely, in a small chapel in Mexico City. It wasn't perfect, though. Some important people were missing. You, for example. Frida and Diego—as you know, he died three years after she did. Pedro Armendáriz. He couldn't travel. He suffers from severe hip pain."

"Doña Antonia must be thrilled!"

"Absolutely. She's convinced that this time it will be forever, and so am I. Lew is different from the other men I've known—mature, calm, steady, respectful of my career. I'm different, too. I'm more mature, less insecure about who I am as a woman and a professional. It took a long time, Mara, but I've finally grown up."

"Me, too. Finally, I know who I am. It's brought me a sense of closure."

"Maybe it's time for you to get married again, too, Mara. Dutch still asks about you."

"No," I said. "I'm too set in my ways, and too busy. Lolly has three kids and Gabi has two. Lupita is expecting, and Lexie just got married. And I'm still working at Marie's. I have no time for a husband, Lola! Anyway, once you've been married to a man like Gabe…"

Lola squeezed my hand. "We've been through so much together, Mara." She paused. "I'm worried about Mami," she went on. She swallowed hard and bit her lip. "The other day I went to her room. She was in bed, propped up on pillows, her hands scrunched up like dried fruit. Her knuckles were as swollen as walnuts. I looked down at my own hands and wondered if they would curl and knot like hers. I already feel pain in my fingers, and the doctor says that the joints of my toes are beginning to calcify. I'm old, Mara. I'm turning into her."

"Don't be silly, Lola. The press is always talking about your eternal beauty, your magnificent legs, your hands, your cheekbones, and your wrinkle-free chin. Marlene Dietrich said you were still the most beautiful woman in Hollywood!"

"That may be," said Lola, "but right now, I have to find a bathroom."

"Gosh, I think the public restrooms along the beach are closed in the winter."

"Well, it won't do for the world's ex-most-beautiful-woman to pee in her pants, so I have to find one that's open!"

We jumped into my car, and Lola sat with her legs crossed until we got to her hotel. I pulled up to the entrance, and she shot across the lobby like a bullet.

"Whew," she gasped, when she returned. "I almost didn't make it! I can see the headlines, 'Dolores del Río, Star of Stage and Screen, Soils Herself in the Lobby of the Beverly Hills Hotel!'" She burst out laughing. "Age," she sighed. "That's what happens when you're pushing sixty! Your kidneys go."

She was in Los Angeles to film *Flaming Star* with Elvis Presley.

"I play his mother!" she exclaimed, laughing.

She had expected Presley to be difficult, an arrogant pop singer trying to pass himself off as a real actor. But once rehearsals began, he won her over. He called her a great Hollywood legend and told her it was an honor to work with her. He even promised, since she was going to play his mother, to have contact lenses made so that his eyes would be exactly the color of hers. Lola loved that kind of adoration. She needed it, especially now that she was growing older. In a way, it was sad. It must be awful, I thought, to care so much about other people's opinions.

53

La Escondida, June 1962
Song of the Mourning Dove

The sky should have been gloomy. The trees should have been bare and the birds, silent, instead of chirping wildly in luxuriant trees under a clear clean blue sky. The nerve of those birds. Why weren't they in mourning? A leaden stillness filled the house.

I'd gone to Mexico to be with her. She'd begged me to come. She needed me, she said. At a time like this, even Lew wasn't enough. She needed her sister.

She was staring out the window. The gardener sang as he trimmed the hibiscus: *"Dicen que por las noches / nomás se le iba en puro llorar..."*

"Ah," whispered Lola, *"Cucurrucucú*, the 'Song of the Mourning Dove.'"

She rested her head on my shoulder and blinked back the tears. We all knew it was going to happen, so why had it taken her by surprise? But death is always a surprise—that instant when a living, breathing being is no longer. Everything seemed different. The rooms felt viscous, asphyxiating. The kitchen felt empty. Doña Antonia's chair rocked eerily in its corner, vacant. The dresser stood against the wall, strange and lonely, like an old piece of junk stuffed into a storage area

in someone else's house. Lola wandered from room to room
fingering objects. The doily that Mami had tatted years ago,
when her hands weren't gnarled with arthritis. The pillow
she'd brought from Los Angeles, because she couldn't sleep
on any other. Voices of people tittering and twittering floated
through the house. It had always been vibrant with people—
movie stars, writers, artists...people like Frida Kahlo and Pablo
Neruda, Dorothea Lange and Georgia O'Keeffe, Salvador
Novo and Emilio Fernández. Now it was empty, but sounds
still haunted the empty spaces.

Lola had held together during most of her mother's funeral
earlier that day, but when she witnessed the coffin being lowered into the ground, her body began to rack and tremble.

Afterward, the white page with the black marks was ter-
rifying in its starkness: Antonia López Negrete de Asúnsolo.
Under that, numbers. Under that, a cross. Lola signed the
death certificate with a shaky hand: María de los Dolores
Asúnsolo López-Negrete de Riley. June 22, 1962. It was over.
It was official. Her mother was dead. She was alone.

Well, not entirely alone. Lew was with her, of course, and
so was I. But the companion of her entire life, her friend and
confidante since birth, was gone.

Now, back at La Escondida, Lola stared out the window
dry-eyed. Doña Antonia's fragrance still wafted on the air.
Lola closed her eyes and breathed deeply. The rank odor of
blood and shit had vanished, and only the scent of vanilla and
gardenias remained.

The stillness of the rooms dizzied her. She buried her face
in her hands. What would she do without Mami? During
those heady days in Los Angeles, Mami was there. When
Jaime died, Mami was there. When Orson ran off to Brazil,
Mami was there. When El Indio Fernández pushed her into

the mud, Mami was there. A world without Doña Antonia didn't seem possible.

Outside, the gardener was still singing. His little boy was with him, and they were trimming back the morning glories. Lola watched them work, father and son, four perfectly coordinated hands. They clipped together in harmony, communicating without words, the way she and her mother once had. She would never have that bond with a child of her own. For decades, she'd told herself that she didn't care about having a family, that her career was enough. But observing the exquisitely synchronized movements of the gardener and his boy, she felt a throbbing emptiness. She didn't have to explain it to me. I could see it in her eyes.

Lola straightened the doily on the rocking chair. The gardener had stopped singing and was chatting softly with the child, explaining how to prune the roses without damaging them. He guided the boy's hands gently over the stems, careful to treat the thorns with respect.

We went into Doña Antonia's room. Lola sat on the bed and stared at the armoire. "What should I do now, Mami?" she asked the polished wood.

"Keep going, Gatita," I said. "That's what she would tell you. Listen to her voice in the sunrays bursting on the wall, in the tatted doily on the dresser, in the calla lilies. Listen to what she's telling you, 'Your life is your work, and besides, we *gatas* always land on our feet.'"

54

Los Angeles, Mexico City, 1964–1968
Two Conversations

Lucille Carver settled back in the chair, and I fastened a towel around her neck.

"Do you like the way I did it last time? I mean, the color... we went even lighter."

"I'm not sure. I'm not really convinced I want to go gray. Roy likes it light brown. What do you think?"

"Well, I've been making it lighter because you said you wanted to transition to your natural color, but if you've changed your mind, we can go darker today."

"Yes, let's go a smidgeon darker. Listen, did you see that new film with Sal Mineo?"

"Actually, I did see it. *Cheyenne Autumn*. The one about the Cheyenne Indians. Dolores del Río is in it. You always loved her films."

"No, she isn't."

"She plays a nameless character identified as 'the Spanish woman.'"

"Oh, I can't believe she'd take such a tiny role! I didn't even recognize her. Could you put in some highlights? It'll make the color look more natural."

"Of course, Mrs. Carver. She's still very beautiful, you know."

"I didn't even notice her."

So that's how it is, I thought. Bit parts. Anonymous characters that no one remembers. She hadn't had a good role since *Flaming Star*, about four years back.

"You know, Mrs. Carver," I ventured. "I actually know Dolores del Río. I've known her for years."

I expected her to say something like, *You! That's impossible! I don't believe it!* Instead, she said, "Really? How fascinating! I'm surprised you never mentioned it." She was silent for a while. "You know," she murmured, "you ought to write down your recollections. In a couple of years, no one will remember her."

Around the same time, Lola was having a different conversation with Lew—one she later described to me in detail.

They were driving through the city's sprawling slums toward the elegant Zona Rosa. A beggar woman on the corner stretched out her hand. "*Por favor, señorita. Para la niña.* Please, miss, for the child." She nodded toward a scrawny little girl clinging to her skirts.

"Stop the car, Lew."

"You can't give money to every beggar in Mexico, Lola. Forty percent of the population lives below the poverty line."

"Look at that child, Lew. She has beautiful features—wide brown eyes, such a pert little nose, but she's going to waste away if nobody helps. She should be in school."

"You think the ten pesos you're going to give her mother will make a difference?"

"*Para la niña,*" said Lola, handing some coins to the woman. She watched her own hand reach through the window and winced at the sight of her fingers—her mother's fingers—swollen and warped at the joints, but adorned with beautiful rings. The beggar stuffed the money into her apron pocket.

"*Dios la bendiga,* God bless you," she murmured, and then moved on to the next car.

Along the wall of a building, six or eight women were camped out on faded blankets that had once been blue or yellow or magenta. They'd come to the city from rural villages looking for work, only to wind up on the street begging for coins or selling chewing gum to motorists. Children dozed or played. One ragged woman pulled herself up, straightened her skirt, and dragged a half-sleeping child toward the curb. She stood there, holding a basket out toward passing cars. Toothless and twisted, she somehow exuded serenity. Someone flipped a coin into her basket. *"Dios le bendiga,"* she lisped. Some of the older children darted among the cars wiping windows, hoping for a "payment."

"I know it's not enough, Lew," said Lola, sighing. "When I left Hollywood, I thought, now I'm going to do something important. I'm going to make socially relevant films that will help shepherd in a new Mexico. And we do live in a new Mexico. I keep reading that Mexico has the most robust economy in Latin America. But look around you. The streets are full of emaciated beggars with gaunt children who are not learning how to read. Fifty years after the Revolution, life is better for a lot of people, but what about folks like that woman and her little daughter? I thought I could make a difference, but I haven't. I feel useless, Lew."

Lew took her hand. "You've made films that have inspired a nation, Lola."

"That's not what's needed now. Anyway, what do Mexican audiences want today? Horror films by El Santo or art films by Buñuel."

They drove through dark alleys, past dilapidated buildings with no running water, electricity, or heat. The tawdry areas my mother must have known. They drove to the outskirts of the city, where shantytowns lined the landscape. Children

MISS DEL RÍO   407

played soccer, using a can for a ball, in front of tents held together with cord and vulnerable to the rain and wind.

Lola had realized after *Flaming Star* that she was approaching the end of her career. I was growing old, too, but I had my girls, my grandchildren, and, since I'd identified my mother, a sense of my place in the world. But in spite of her fame and eternally smooth skin, Lola felt...ephemeral. Her health was deteriorating. Arthritis made it impossible for her to stand for long periods and bronchial problems were affecting her voice. She'd just played the allegory of Death in Alejandro Casona's play, *La dama del alba, The Lady of the Dawn*, and it made her acutely aware of her own mortality. And then, there was the suicide of her old friend and costar Pedro Armendáriz. He'd contracted cancer of the hips and smuggled a gun into UCLA Medical Center, where he was being treated. When the doctor told him his cancer was terminal, he used it.

"If I'm ever going to do something useful," said Lola, "I'd better do it now!"

"You're overreacting," scolded Lew. "Other people's misery is not your fault."

"Half the country is starving." She pointed to a fancy new hotel under construction. "Those men over there, the workers putting up that monument to opulence, they earn about a ten pesos a day, five dollars. How are they going to feed their families?"

She knew she couldn't solve all of Mexico's social dilemmas, but maybe she could find some way to offer a concrete solution to real problems that existed close to home. She was getting ready to star in *Casa de mujeres*, a new film by Julián Soler about prostitutes who adopt an abandoned baby. Maybe it would be her last major role, she thought, but even so, she was excited about the project because the foundling as an adult was going to be played by Enrique Álvarez Félix,

María's son. The script gave her an idea. "Maybe María will help me," she said.

Instead of relaxing during her off-screen moments, Lola roamed through the costume shop, the makeup supply, the stockroom, the prop room, the janitors' quarters. Everywhere women were working—exhausted-looking women with sad, pasty, lackluster foreheads and frail bodies, dowdy women with worried looks.

"Do you have children?" she asked each of them.

"*Sí, señorita, tres.*"

"*Sí, señorita, cinco.*"

"Who takes care of them while you work?"

She started visiting film studios, television studios, theaters. Everywhere, she saw women sewing, preparing food, nailing, building, painting, sweeping, mopping, and dusting. Most of them worked sixteen-hour shifts, almost always until late at night or even until the wee hours of the morning. Everywhere, she asked the same question: "Do you have children?"

"*Sí, señorita, un bebé de seis meses.*"

"Who takes care of her while you work?" The women's answers shocked her. Most had come from rural areas. In the metropolis, they found themselves alone, without the support systems they had grown up with—the mothers, aunts, and sisters who could help out in a pinch, the church communities that provided a meal and a cot, or at least, a pile of hay. Alone in the city and grateful to have work, they just made do.

"My oldest is nine, señorita. She takes care of the little ones."

"Doesn't she go to school?"

"She can't, señorita. She has to help at home."

Sometimes they left their babies and toddlers in *guarderías*, babysitting centers, or, literally, "keeping centers," where the children were simply "kept"—left alone for hours at a time with little supervision or stimulation. Sometimes one adult was responsible for twenty tots or more. At night, the children went to "sleeping centers," often on the studio or theater premises—rows or stacks of wooden boxes where the children had to sleep without making a sound lest they disrupt the show or awaken the others. Catacombs for live babies, thought Lola. Babies stacked up in boxes like shoes in a shoe store.

"Real day care centers are what we need for these women and children," Lola told me over the phone.

She met with the women of ANDA, the National Association of Actors, to plan a fundraiser for her project.

"A monster marathon on television," suggested María Félix.

"We'll call it the *planilla* Rosa Mexicano, 'the women's platform,' and put it to the entire membership," proposed Lola. "I'm sure they'll go along with María's idea."

Lola began reading books by Maria Montessori. She was getting excited.

"I wish I could help her," said Lolly when I told her about it. "I know about early childhood education."

"You can encourage her," I said. "You can suggest readings, give her ideas."

"I knew there was something God wanted me to do," Lola explained to me over the phone. "It was *this*! I'm finally using my knowledge of the movie business and my contacts to help people in a tangible way. You should see the look in those women's eyes when I tell them about my plans for their children. These new day care centers won't be called *guarderías*. We're not going to *guardar* anybody there. We're going to educate the children, give them opportunities for creative play, develop their minds and their souls. We're going to hire specially trained teachers. It's going to be beautiful!"

"I want to go to Mexico this summer and work with Aunt Lola," Lolly insisted. "I'll take the kids."

"And what about John?"

"I'd only go for three weeks, but at least I could help her get started…and I could show the children the country of my foremothers…my mother and my grandmother, the Aztec warrior queen!"

The girls were already constructing their own "legend of Miguela Ruiz," and that was fine with me!

Lolly didn't get to Mexico that year. She was expecting again and couldn't travel, but she sent Lola a couple of books by Jean Piaget and a list of children's books in Spanish that she thought might be useful.

On October 29, two days prior to All Hallows' Eve, and three before All Saints' Day, Lola was busy putting together baskets of sugar skulls and skeletons to take to the studio seamstresses for their children. She was also organizing a campaign to raise more money for day care centers. The monster marathon had been a success, but the grandiose project Lola envisioned would require more funds—for space, materials, teachers, and training. She was sure the money would be forthcoming, though. So many in the industry were supportive and promised to help. At last, she thought, she was making a real contribution. Everything was going so well. She was excited!

But then, as they say, every silver lining has a cloud. Things can't remain perfect forever or even for more than a day or two. It seems that while Lola was preparing her Halloween baskets for the seamstresses' children, her cousin Ramón was preparing a different kind of party.

I heard about it on the radio two days later and called Lola right away. I didn't want her to hear about it from some stranger, but she'd already spoken to Ramón's brother Eduardo. He'd told her that when Freddie Weber, Ramón's assistant, returned to work, he found the house in shambles and Ramón lying naked on the bed, a brown electric cord tied around his ankles. The letter *N*, or maybe *Z*, was carved on his neck. Freddie called the police right away. There were no suspects, but someone had written the word *Larry* four times on a notepad by the living room phone.

"Eduardo thinks it was a botched robbery attempt," said Lola, "although nothing was taken. Apparently, they were looking for cash."

We were both sobbing. "How could someone do this to another human being," she hiccuped, "let alone a gentle soul like Ramón?" She caught her breath. "The burial will be at St. Anne Melkite Cathedral."

"Of course I'll go," I said. I was devastated. I loved Ramón. Not the way I loved Gabe, of course, but Ramón had been my first crush. I'd become enamored of him decades ago, when I heard him play the guitar at Don Francisco's house. As an adult, I'd learned his secret, and I'd kept it. That had created a bond between us.

In the following days and weeks, the details unfolded in the newspapers and on the radio. It seems that the night before Halloween, Ramón invited two men, two male prostitutes, to his house. He did things like that sometimes. He actually told me about it. He was lonely and, well, it wasn't easy for a man like Ramón to find companionship.

They were brothers, Paul and Tom Ferguson. Paul was twenty-two, and Tom was seventeen. According to Paul's testimony, they called Ramón and told him that they'd gotten his number from a mutual friend, Larry Ortega, who had procured partners for him before. Ramón trusted Ortega, Paul said. Ortega knew his tastes and was cautious and discriminating. They were sure Ramón would invite them over if he thought Ortega had sent them.

They arrived around five o'clock. Ramón had set out a platter of sandwiches and a selection of drinks—Scotch, tequila, gin, vodka, and bourbon—on a silver tray on the bar. He'd obviously started imbibing before they arrived, according to Paul. They ate and drank and fooled around awhile. Ramón showed them pictures of himself as Ben-Hur and played the piano. Then they went into the bedroom, and were just getting started when Paul decided they had to be paid in advance.

Ramón was taken aback, but he went to his desk to write a check. Only Paul and Tom wanted cash. Paul said he was sure Ramón was hiding at least five hundred dollars in the house, and he threatened to tear the place apart to find it.

Ramón kept insisting that Larry Ortega knew how he did business. "Larry knows my checks are good," he kept saying. But Larry Ortega hadn't sent them at all. They'd gotten Ramón's name from some hustler they'd met at a party, a man who told them to say that Larry had sent them so that Ramón wouldn't be suspicious. Paul became furious. He and Tom started punching Ramón. Then Paul socked him in the gut so hard that he slumped over onto the ground.

When they realized that Ramón was dead, they decided to make the crime look like a robbery. They lifted his naked body onto the bed, stuck a condom between his fingers, and left signs around the house that would implicate Larry Ortega.

I don't remember where the police picked them up, but I do know that their case didn't go to trial until 1969, nearly nine months after the arrest. Tom bragged in prison about killing Ramón, and although he was only seventeen when the murder took place, he was tried as an adult. The jury gave both brothers life in prison, although the sentence was commuted. Both were later rearrested for violent crimes, including rape.

I never quite got over Ramón's death. Gabe's was devastating, of course, but those were the war years. We expected tragedy at every turn. And Tía Emi's? Well, Tía Emi was old, and she smoked like a chimney. But Ramón well, I'd seen how bullies sometimes tormented men like Ramón, but still, I never thought anything like this could ever happen, and neither did Lola.

After he died, she and I reminisced for hours over the phone. (It must have cost her a fortune, she was the one who placed the calls.) We remembered how he played the guitar while Lola danced at Don Francisco's, how he'd sneak off to the Jesuit retreat house when things got rough, how he'd make fun of the Hollywood snobs and flee from their boring parties, how he broke the rules and suffered the consequences. Most of all, I remembered how kind he'd been to me. He'd always treated me as a friend.

In a way, I think Ramón's passing affected me more than it did Lola, although, of course, I can't be sure. But she had Lew, her glamorous career, her day care centers, and her admirers. My life was simpler. I had my girls and my grandchildren but, aside from Lola and Ramón, few friends.

Ramón held a special place in my heart. He taught me about love—about the infinite varieties of love—and about friendship. I knew how torn he was between his faith and his desires. I knew how he suffered, and I'd kept his secret as I'd promised, never suspecting that a horrible tragedy would someday thrust it into the limelight.

I hope to God he has found peace. Every night I say a prayer for him.

El Señor todopoderoso tenga misericordia de nosotros, perdone nuestros pecados y nos lleve a la vida eterna. Amén.

55

Mexico City, 1975
Forever Lola

Even in the midst of tragedy, the show must go on. I settled
into my seat and took it all in. Chandeliers unfurled chrysanthemums of light over the packed auditorium. The Tiffany
glass curtain caught the reflection and sent flickers onto the
stage. A banner stretching above the proscenium read *Dolores
del Río, Fifty Years in Film.*

Women in embroidered silk peasant dresses and diamond-
studded hairpins sat in breathless anticipation. Sixties chic demanded affected hippiness—flowing skirts, artsy purples and
pinks—but show biz snobbery required expensive fabrics and
real gemstones. To appear counterculture in taffeta was the
ultimate triumph. The women eyed each other with curios-
ity. Who was just outrageous enough? Who was over-the-top?
The orchestra began a medley of themes from Lola's films—
Ramona, Bird of Paradise, La cucaracha. The last note faded and
the spectators cheered. Some cried, dabbing their eyes with
delicate handkerchiefs.

The master of ceremonies appeared. The spectators hushed.
"Ladies and gentlemen," he began. No one was interested in
his tedious introduction. The adoring public already knew all
the prizes that Dolores del Río had won—the Serape de Oro,

the Medalla de Oro, and on and on. Her fans didn't need a long, boring speech to tell them about her many accomplishments. All they wanted was Lola.

The fanfare began. The lights dimmed. A spotlight shone center stage. Dolores del Río, wearing a long white gown with a ruffled hem, floated onto the stage. She was seventy-one years old, yet the tiny lines that feathered outward from her eyes were hardly noticeable. When she took her position before the microphone, her smile blossomed, and the Dolores del Río of *Ramona* was standing before her public. Forever fresh. Forever beautiful. Forever Lola.

"Mis queridos amigos y amigas," she began. "I look back on a long career in motion pictures—one that began with a small part in a silent Hollywood film named *Joanna*—a film none of you saw and no one remembers, and it's just as well." Laughter.

"The talkies were a disaster for a lot of foreigners," she went on, "but my mother always taught me to be like a cat and land on my feet. That meant working hard to perfect my English and being willing to adapt to all kinds of roles. Hollywood brought me success and fame, yes, yet I never stopped being who I am—a daughter of Mexico." Cheers. Applause.

"I worked with wonderful directors in Hollywood, but I longed to act in Spanish, to do something more authentic. When, after the war, our studios began making truly Mexican films, ones that focused on Mexican history, Mexican society, Mexican culture, I yearned to be part of this new cinema. The gringos wanted pure entertainment, but in Mexico, the Golden Age of Cinema was beginning, so I packed my bags and moved back home."

Thunderous applause. Cries of *¡Viva México, ¡Viva Lola! ¡Viva el cine mexicano!*

"Working with virtuosos like Emilio, Gabriel, and Pedro, I was able to make a new kind of socially significant film, a

distinctly *Mexican* film, designed to educate the public about
our great nation and address the issues that confront us. For
me, acting in such films was a way of serving my country.
Now, after many years, I am working on a new film in English, *The Children of Sanchez*, with the legendary star Anthony
Quinn. I still love acting. It has been my life. Sometimes I take
small roles just for the joy of performing on a movie set! And
no, I am no longer able to play the adolescent seductress as I
once did. In *The Children of Sanchez*, I play the grandmother!"

Lola puckered her lips and made a face. Laughter.

"Aging is inevitable, even in Hollywood. However, age
does bring a more balanced sense of the world. Looking back
on the past fifty years, I think my greatest achievements took
place off-screen. First, I met the man of my dreams, my amazing husband, Lew Riley!" Cheers.

"But without a doubt, the project that has brought me the
most satisfaction in recent years is my work on behalf of children. With the support of ANDA, I have established day care
centers all over Mexico. These centers are open twenty-four
hours a day, at no cost to the parents, so that working mothers
in the entertainment industry, whether they're seamstresses or
actresses, will always have a clean, decent place to leave their
children. Children's Place receives children from six months to
six years old. Nurses, nannies, teachers and volunteers care for
them. This is the first day care center system of its kind in the
world. God never gave me children of my own, but the little
ones call me Mamá Lolita, and I love it!" Cheers and applause.

"When the newspapers write about me, what do they
say? *Even at her age she is still beautiful!* But what is beauty?
Real beauty does not come from creams or lotions, but from
thoughts and deeds. When we devote our lives to helping others, we become beautiful. When I die, I want them to write,
'She was a beautiful woman,' not because I still have high

cheekbones, but because I accomplished something worthwhile during my lifetime."

She paused. People were on their feet now, applauding, shouting, throwing flowers.

"Before I say good-night to you, there's one more person I want to mention. Someone who has been at my side since we were both children. She has been my hairdresser, my assistant, but most of all, my friend—a down-to-earth, practical, warm, and loyal soul mate. She stands by me when I need moral support and knocks sense into me when I get carried away with myself. I want to thank my true sister, María Amparo Estrada. Mara, please stand up."

The applause was so thunderous, I felt dizzy. I didn't quite understand what was happening. I stood up only for an instant. I had no place in this world of glitz and glamour, and all those eyes staring at me made me reel. I sank back into my seat.

Up on the stage, Lola was beaming, even as tears trickled down her cheeks. She blew me a kiss, then bowed and blew kisses to her fans. Once again, the chandeliers unfurled chrysanthemums of light. Emilio and Gabriel were at her side with enormous bouquets. They'd remained friends all these years, despite everything. The orchestra played "Ramona."

EPILOGUE

On April 13, 1983, the newspaper published this article.

DOLORES DEL RÍO, 78, IS DEAD; FILM STAR IN US AND MEXICO.

Dolores del Río, an actress of extraordinary beauty who became a film star in Hollywood and in her native Mexico, died Monday at her home in Newport Beach, California, of liver failure. She was seventy-eight years old and had been in failing health. During the days of silent films, Miss del Río's face, elegant and expressive, made her one of Hollywood's most sought-after actresses and one of its first Latin stars.

Vigils formed all over Mexico. Across the United States, fans held memorials. Carla Myer wrote a long and eloquent obituary, in which she called Dolores del Río "a great actress and a great lady." A few days later, Myer announced her own retirement.

When Lola became seriously ill, I visited her in the hospital, of course, but when the end finally came, I found out from the newspaper Mrs. Carver brought in to the shop. Nobody called me, not even Lew. It wasn't surprising really. I'd never been close with Lew, and almost no one else knew that Lola had been my friend. Mrs. Carver had cried buckets, she said. The career of Dolores del Río had spanned her lifetime, and now the star was gone. She felt as though she'd lost a personal friend.

"You said you knew her," she reminded me. "Write her story. No one else can."

I called my daughters, who came over. We reminisced about Lola, and we wept together. Afterward, we all went into the kitchen, made dinner, and sat down to eat.

That evening, after they had gone, I sat back down at the kitchen table and thought about what Mrs. Carver had said. I thought back over the long years I'd spent by Lola's side. Then I picked up my pen.

★ ★ ★ ★ ★

AUTHOR'S NOTE

I have been fascinated by Mexican cinema for as long as I can remember. Growing up in Los Angeles, I would often take the bus downtown with my girlfriends to the Mexican movie theaters. By then, Dolores del Río was no longer a box office draw. My favorite stars were Rosita Quintana, Lola Beltrán, and Amalia Mendoza. I must have seen *¿Dónde estás, corazón?* at least twenty times.

My interest in Dolores del Río, known as Lola to her intimates, didn't blossom until decades later, when I wrote the novel *Frida*. As a friend of Frida Kahlo and Diego Rivera, del Río came up repeatedly in my research, and she figured in my book as an elegant foil to Kahlo, a foul-mouthed, irreverent rebel. I began to watch the films del Río had made during her heyday in Mexico—those exquisite avatars of the Golden Age of Mexican Cinema directed by Emilio Fernández—and mentioning her in courses I taught at Georgetown University on Kahlo and the art of the Mexican Revolution.

I was impressed with del Río's talent, her enduring beauty, and the way she flirted with the camera, positioning herself just so to highlight her colossal brown eyes and sculpted cheekbones. But after I began reading about her, I realized that Dolores del Río was more than just a pretty face. She was an extraordinarily resilient woman who learned early in life to cope with adversity. In spite of her professional success, she was painfully aware of the vapidity of Hollywood life and yearned to make socially relevant films. Although she was born into a wealthy family, she never lost sight of those less fortunate than herself. Once she returned to Mexico, she was able to star in films that exalted Mexico's rich cultural heritage and Indigenous peoples. Over the years, she became a symbol of Mexican womanhood, an icon of female Mexican beauty. Her project to establish day care centers for working women illustrates her commitment to serve the needs of her people. Once I had learned about her fascinating life, I realized that I had to novelize her story.

Naturally, a biofictional novel combines fact and fiction. The historical situations depicted in *Miss del Río* are true: the escape from Durango, Jaime's failure as a scriptwriter, the miscegenation laws, the Hays Code, Lola's return to Mexico, etc. Yet, although biographical fiction draws on fact, the bio-novelist must sift through the verifiable data to determine what is relevant to the portrayal of the subject's deeper dramatic truth. Bio-novelists do not seek merely to recount their subjects' lives, but to convey the essence of their subjects' personalities. To do so, they may have to modify history, imagining intimate moments or even inventing new characters. Merely to describe the life of Dolores del Río would have produced a biography (not a novel) devoid of the personal perspective—the reactions, judgments, and intimate interactions—necessary to make the character come alive. Therefore, I invented an unabashedly opinionated narrative voice for *Miss del Río*.

Lola's best friend, the fictional hairdresser Mara, is based on my own mother, Frieda, who, like Miss Marie, studied cosmetology at the prestigious Marinello School of Beauty, moved to California, and worked in beauty shops similar to Mr. Edmond's. I grew up hearing about the beauty business, although I was never very good at doing my own hair. My mother was a champion Marcelizer, and, although Marcel curls went out of style long before I was born, I knew what a Marcel iron was by the time I was seven. Mrs. Carver, Miss Marie's loyal customer, is based on one of my mother's steady customers. Mr. Edmond and Miss Kathy are fictional characters based on my mother's first employers. Other fictional characters include Tía Emi and Carla Myer, reporter for the fictional *Star World*.

Even when characters are real, sometimes uncertain or conflicting information exists about them. In those cases, the novelist must make a choice. For example, some sources give Cedric Gibbons's birth date as 1890 and others as 1893. I chose 1893 to make his age closer to Lola's. Some sources give his birth place as New York City, others as Dublin. I chose Dublin because an important theme of the book is the immigrant experience.

A project of the scope and size of *Miss del Río* requires more than one person to bring to fruition. I wish to thank my husband, Mauro, for his encouragement and abiding faith in my work. I am also indebted to my fabulous agent, Leticia Gómez, and my editors, Melanie Fried and Gina Macedo.

RESOURCES

Miss del Río required ample research, but fortunately, several useful biographies of Dolores del Río and her friends exist. David Ramón's Dolores del Río trilogy—*Un cuento de hadas, Volver al origen,* and *Consagración de una diva* provided important details about del Río's upbringing, marriages, and career, as did Linda B. Hall's *Dolores del Río: Beauty in Light and Shade. Dolores del Río,* by Jesse Russell and Ronald Cohn, gave me an overview of del Río's life. Joanne Hershfield's *The Invention of Dolores del Río,* which analyzes del Río's rise to stardom through the lens of race and gender, was a valuable resource for the descriptions of discrimination in early Hollywood. In *More Fabulous Faces,* Larry Carr shows how del Río evolved as a beauty and fashion icon, essential information for my development of the protagonist.

Two biographies of Marlene Dietrich—*Marlene,* by Charlotte Chandler, and *Marlene Dietrich: The Life,* by Maria Riva—afforded me with information about one of del Río's close friends, while *Beyond Paradise: The Life of Ramon Novarro,* by André Soares, contributed specifics about the life and struggles of her cousin.

Other invaluable sources for my re-creation of early Hollywood were *American Silent Film*, by William K. Everson; *After the Silents*, by Michael Slowik; *Latino/a Stars in U.S. Eyes,* by Mary Beltrán; and several books from the Images of America Series: *Early Hollywood*, by Marc Wanamaker and Robert W. Nudelman; *Hollywoodland*, by Mary Mallory and Hollywood Heritage, Inc.; and *Beverly Hills 1930-2005*, by Marc Wanamaker. I also consulted several studies of the Golden Age of Mexican Cinema and of filmmaking in Latin America, notably *The Classical Mexican Cinema: The Poetics of the Exceptional Golden Age Films*, by Charles Ramírez Berg, and *Latin American Cinema: A Comparative History*, by Paul A. Schroeder Rodríguez.

MISS DEL RÍO

BÁRBARA MUJICA

Reader's Guide

GRAYDON
HOUSE

1. Compare Lola's upbringing with Mara's. What do their upbringings tell us about the social structure of pre-Revolutionary Mexico. How does the Mexican Revolution influence the trajectory of each woman's life?

2. How does Lola and Mara's friendship blossom and sustain them throughout their lives, despite the obstacles they encounter? Have you had a similar lifelong friendship?

3. Discuss Lola's romantic relationships in the novel. Why do you think she often makes poor choices when it comes to men? Did you understand her decision to marry Jaime del Río? Is Mara right to judge Lola harshly for her relationship with Carewe? How is Lew Riley ultimately different from the other men who came before him?

4. What does Mara expect from marriage? How are these expectations similar or different from Lola's?

5. What do Lola's early experiences in Hollywood tell us about the exploitation of women in the movie industry? How have things changed or not changed today?

6. What is the role of the press (as represented in the novel by Carla Myer and *Star World*) in the creation of a celebrity?

7. How do attitudes and laws concerning race affect Lola's career?

8. What is the role of education in the lives of Lola and Mara?

9. Is Tía Emi a positive or a negative influence in Mara's life? Did your perception of her change over the course of the story?

10. Discuss Ramón and Mara's friendship. Why do you think they have such a strong connection?

11. Doña Antonia and Lola are both described as cats with strong survival instincts who are able to adapt to different circumstances. Where do we see them act this way in the novel?

12. How does World War II radically alter the lives of both Lola and Mara?

13. Discuss Lola's relationship with Frida Kahlo.

14. Why does Lola decide to return to Mexico? How does she rebuild her life there?

15. How do Lola's efforts to establish day care centers in Mexico alter our perception of her?

16. Would you have liked to live in the Hollywood of the twenties and thirties? In the Mexico of the thirties and forties? Why or why not?